Praise for

#1 National Regency Romance Bestseller
Romance Writers of America Golden Heart® Finalist

"Her Husband's Harlot is a pleasing, out of the ordinary read." -*Dear Author*

"Wow! I loved this book so much! Very sexy, very emotional read. If you like erotic romance, historical romance, erotic historical romance or just a good damn book.... BUY IT!!!" -Jess Michaels, *USA Today* Bestselling Author

"Erotic historical romance isn't as plentiful as many would think, but here you have a very well-written example of this genre. It's entertaining and fun and a darn good read." -*The Book Binge*

"I liked that Helena was shy and sweet, but knew she loved him and knew what she had to do to please him, and in the process ended up finding passion herself. As for Nicholas, hubba-hubba, what more can you say about a man trying to better himself, yet still have that fire and intensity, especially for his wife." -Eva, *Amazon*

"I loved these down to earth, humanlike characters who crept into my heart with all their antics and kept me glued to the pages." -Zena, *Amazon*

"I devoured this book in a couple of hours!.... If you love a story with a heroine who is a wallflower with a backbone of steel or a damaged hero then you will love this one too." *-Love Romance Passion*

"Loved the tortured hero and the unsure heroine!" -LM, *BookBub*

"This book was definitely on the top of romance novels I have read. I loved this. It had an actual plot instead of just sex with some plot....I love how hard they worked at their marriage. I really admire their relationship. This book was surprisingly emotional. There were several scenes that rip out your heart a bit. In the end it was all worth it." - Michelle, *Goodreads*

"Everything you could want in a historical erotic romance." -Gamer31, *Apple Books*

"I adore this super sensual and unique story of sexual awakening, passion, acceptance, and love and the bumpy path the H and h are on to get there. Excellent introduction to characters to come (literally) in rest of series. I love how Nicholas and Helena grew together as a couple; sexy, playful, hopeful." -Dagmar, *Goodreads*

"HOT, HOT, HOT! This story starts off with a bang and doesn't let go. This story features a couple already married. I loved the development of their characters, and how they grew to know and love one another better. There are some dark secrets in their path, and the secondary characters make the story even more delightful." -Laura, *BookBub*

"Grace Callaway writes the way Loretta Chase would if she got kind of dark and VERY naughty." -Nicole, *Goodreads*

Also by Grace Callaway

MAYHEM IN MAYFAIR

Her Husband's Harlot

Her Wanton Wager

Her Protector's Pleasure

Her Prodigal Passion

HEART OF ENQUIRY (The Kents)

The Widow Vanishes (Prequel Novella)

The Duke Who Knew Too Much

M is for Marquess

The Lady Who Came in from the Cold

The Viscount Always Knocks Twice

Never Say Never to an Earl

The Gentleman Who Loved Me

GAME OF DUKES

The Duke Identity

Enter the Duke

Regarding the Duke

The Duke Redemption

The Return of the Duke

Steamy Winter Wishes (A Holiday Short Story)

LADY CHARLOTTE'S SOCIETY OF ANGELS

Olivia and the Masked Duke

Pippa and the Prince of Secrets

Fiona and the Enigmatic Earl

Mrs. Peabody and the Unexpected Duke (A Holiday Novelette)

Glory and the Master of Shadows

Charlotte and the Seductive Spymaster (January 2024)

HER *Husband's* HARLOT

BOOK ONE

USA TODAY BESTSELLING AUTHOR

Print ISBN: 978-1-939537-26-3

Cover Art: EDH Designs

Cover Image: Period Image

Cover Typography: KM Designs

Formatting: Colchester & Page

For my husband

Chapter One

1817, LONDON, ENGLAND

The lush burgundy carpeting deadened all noise, bestowing an eerie silence upon the corridor. Lady Helena Harteford shivered as a draft stirred the satin water-lilies pinned to her white tunic and brushed her bare shoulders in a ghostly caress. Given the capricious clime of London in the spring, her water nymph costume had perhaps not proven the wisest choice, but the impetuous nature of her plan had allowed little in the way of preparation. She stifled a sudden nervous laugh. Even if she had had more time for deliberation, would she have found the appropriate attire?

What, after all, was the proper garment for hunting down one's husband at a high-priced bawdy house?

An answer, she reflected, unlikely to be found in her well-worn copy of Lady Epplethistle's *Compleat Guide to the Comportment of Ladies.*

In the distance, a grandfather clock tolled the hour, the twelve sonorous rings underscoring the urgency of her mission. Helena studied the dimly lit stretch ahead of her. Along both sides of the hallway, life-sized statues stood watch over a series of doors. Cautiously, she approached the first door and pressed her ear against the cool wood. No sound escaped. Indeed, the walls appeared thick and solid, designed to ensure the privacy of the activities conducted within. The very thought of her husband engaging in such activities bolstered her courage and hastened her footsteps along the corridor.

Earlier, from a second-floor balcony, she had witnessed Nicholas' arrival to the rowdy masquerade below. Under her feathered mask, jealousy had flamed her cheeks as she watched him dance with two of the "Nuns"—courtesans wearing rouge and not much else. The way the women had rubbed themselves against her husband, like hungry cats ... Startled by the loud *snap*, Helena had looked down to see the sticks of her fan broken in half. She'd begun breathing again only when he had departed the dance floor (thankfully, *alone*) and strode up the staircase. He had to be in one of the current rooms on the second floor; she meant to search him out.

It would be easy to spot her husband, despite the black silk mask that he wore. For one, Nicholas stood a head taller than most men. With his swarthy skin and powerful build, he resembled a pirate more than a lord of the realm. His short, coal-black hair topped a face more rugged than handsome, and yet she found his bold nose and broadly-planed cheekbones utterly arresting. And there were his eyes. Orbs of ever-changing grey, they were at times dark and fathomless as a well and at others the silver of fog above water.

Even deprived of sight, Helena would have known her husband. His presence affected her in a disturbingly profound, disturbingly primal, manner. When he was near, her breath heightened, her skin quivered with almost unbearable sensitivity, and her blood pumped languid heat into unmentionable parts of her person. Just the thought of her husband stirred her secret imagination and infused her with most unladylike longing ...

Helena swayed a little and grasped the protruding edge of a marble statue for balance. Perhaps she ought not to have partaken of the lemonade. It had tasted odd, unlike any lemonade she had imbibed before. Not only had it been lukewarm, but it had seemed to heat her mouth and insides as she drank it. But when the proprietress had offered the beverage, it had seemed ungracious not to accept. Besides, she had been thirsty, and there had been naught else to do while she waited for Nicholas to arrive.

Steadying herself, Helena squinted in the gloom at the statue. The stone face had a beard and ... horns? Recognition dawned as she registered the lascivious expression. A satyr, she thought wonderingly, half-man, half-goat, like the drawings she had once glimpsed in a book pilfered from her father's collection.

She looked down at the thick, long jut of stone beneath her fingers and gasped, her fingers flying free as if singed by flame.

Merciful heavens! Her cheeks pulsed hotly against the silk-lined interior of her mask. *Surely 'tis not an accurate representation. Why, it could span both my hands ...*

She swallowed, remembering the invading hardness, the sensation of unbearable stretching between her legs on her wedding night. Was *that* what Nicholas had tried to ... to push inside her? She had been far too afraid to look, but seeing the marble phallus now, the way it thrust resolutely forward, she released a horrified moan.

Of course it had not worked! Why, 'twas against the very laws of nature. Despite her plump curves, her frame was quite petite, with her eye level reaching in the low vicinities of her husband's chest. It was one of the things that delighted her, feeling small and utterly feminine next to his bold, virile physique. But mayhap their difference in size contributed to a certain mismatch in other areas. Rather like trying to thread a rope through a needle.

Eyes darting side to side, she leaned forward to take a closer peek at the statue. She knew her curiosity to be most indecent yet her hand stretched forward, seemingly of its own accord. Her index finger hesitated against the base of the phallus; she noted with surprise the fruit that hung beneath. The rounded sac looked just like a summer peach, juice-swollen and dangling from a thick branch. She grew bolder, continuing her exploration upward. The marble felt cool and hard beneath her fingertip. Slowly, she traced the raised veins twisting along the shaft until she arrived at the end, which flared unexpectedly into a plump mushroom. Her fingertip paused in the peculiar indentation at the tip.

"Right this way, milord," a female voice purred. "We are not far from the room."

At the sound, Helena snapped to her senses, snatching her hand away. Her mind blanked in panic as footsteps approached. The glow of a candle licked the walls, dissolving the spell of the satyr. All would be ruined if she was recognized. Her instincts finally took hold and propelled her down the corridor. Her hands shaking, she grasped the brass knob of the nearest door. *Locked.* She raced forward, trying door after door to no avail. Her breath caught in her chest as she came to the end of the hallway. The last room. Relief shot through her as she saw that the door rested slightly ajar. She slipped inside, easing the door closed behind her.

For a moment, Helena found herself enveloped in pure darkness. In the next moment, she heard a man's rumbled words— Goodness gracious, the room was *occupied*. Her hand shot to the door knob. To her astonishment, the smooth brass was already turning, twisting in her hand. A lusty laugh sounded from the other side of the door. Helena gasped, dropping to the ground. With stealth born of pure fear, she scrambled backward from the widening shaft of light. Blindly, she turned onto her knees and crawled, seeking the safety of darkness. She plunged forward, feeling her way past the spindly legs of a pianoforte and the velvet back of a settee.

"Well, what have we here?"

At the drawling tones, her mind emptied to a void. She could find no words to speak. Shaking, praying that her costume disguised her, she slowly twisted her neck around. But there was no one behind her, only the outlines of furniture which resembled ghostly beasts under the faint dusting of candlelight. It took a minute for her thoughts to flow again. Whoever it was, he was not addressing her. Relief stabbed her chest.

"I found a friend, St. John. Her name is Lucy." This was another man's voice, the accents high-pitched and well-born. "And she's *very* friendly, aren't you, wench?"

Lucy giggled as if to prove it.

"The more the merrier, I always say," St. John said.

Once it sank in that there were *two* gentlemen with the lady, Helena exhaled softly. Grossly scandalous as her current situation might be, at least she had not intruded upon a sexual assignation. Likely she had intruded upon a friendly supper, or perhaps a card game suited to three players. Lowering her cheek to the floor, Helena peered through the legs of the settee. Her face burned suddenly and not from the rough bristle of carpet beneath her cheek. Framed by men's boots on both sides, a pair of stocking-clad legs rose from a glimmering pool of fabric. As she watched, one curvy leg kicked aside the discarded gown and wound sensuously around the boot in front of it. At the same time, the other leg nestled into the Hessians behind.

"Ooo, milords, it appears I am caught 'twixt a rock and a hard spot," Lucy cooed. "Why don't we sit us down and get to know one another better?"

Helena's eyes widened as the boots and silk-covered feet advanced in her direction. Tugging desperately at her skirts, she clambered away from the settee. Her knees chafed against the coarse carpet as she pitched to the right, searching for a place to hide. Behind her, there was the soft thud of bodies falling onto cushions, followed by guttural, animal sounds. Helena moved faster, her breath a harsh wheezing in her ear.

Surely they will hear me! Sweet heavens, what shall I do if …?

Then she saw it, a dark wall rising in front of her. She raised a trembling hand to touch it. The surface slid smooth and solid beneath her fingertips. *A desk*. She followed its perimeter and scurried into the cove beneath. Hugging her knees to her chest, Helena waited for the pounding in her ears to subside.

"Do you like what you see, milords?" Lucy's throaty laughter seemed to reverberate within the wooden cave and sent an odd shiver over Helena's skin.

"Yes, that's it, show your wares," the man called St. John drawled. "Lift those tits a bit higher, won't you? Yes, that's it, press them together, frig those nipples for us. Make them wet, love. Brookeston here prefers his fruit juicy."

The other man—Brookeston, presumably—groaned in agreement.

Then came the sound of rustling, the whispered fall of something onto the carpet. Silence followed, broken by a very low sound. Helena strained to hear as her imagination raced. Lucy's mewling groan tore the quiet asunder. The voices of the men joined her, urging her on. As embers of tension heated the room, Helena felt the air in her lungs grow heavy and humid. She bit down upon her fist.

"Now spread that sweet little cunt of yours. Hmm, very nice. Brookeston, what do you think? Would you care to examine the merchandise?"

After a pause, Lucy moaned out a lusty, "Oh, *yes*," and Brookeston made a strangled sound. "God, St. John. She's wetter than the streets after a rain. I want to fuck her now."

"Perhaps, my impatient friend, we might start off with an *amuse bouche*, so to speak." St. John laughed softly. "There's a love, go suck on Brookeston's cock, the monster is fairly twitching for you."

A charged stillness followed. Helena waited with held breath. Suddenly, a loud slurping pierced the air. Then more noises, redolent of decadent feasting, of sucking succulent meat off the bone. Even to her inexperienced ears, the animal sounds conveyed a frenzied enjoyment. The lapping of wet flesh against wet flesh pulled eager cries from Brookeston. An odd tingling spread over Helena's skin. Feeling a wave of dizziness, she lowered her head to her knees.

"You taste delicious, milord." Lucy's voice purred over the words. "How enormous you are, I can hardly get my mouth around your rod ..."

"Like being stuffed full of cock, do you now?" Brookeston crowed. "Like having me thrust into your naughty little mouth. Take some more of it then, take it deep!"

Lucy's obliging gurgles, issued from a mouth clearly preoccupied, made Helena's heart race even faster. Her face flamed as images flooded her mind. Was it *possible*, what she envisioned? Her mind flashed to the statue of the satyr. This time, however, a woman knelt in front of it, her lips parted in salacious anticipation ... Was *this* what men desired? Was this why Nicolas avoided her bed, because he wanted *this*? For in all her wildest imaginings, she had never even conceived of such a notion ...

Feverishly, she recalled the one time she had seen her husband unclothed. Over a month ago, on their wedding night. He had doused the candles, and it had been darker than a tomb. At the time, she had been grateful for the cover of darkness; it hid her altogether too plump figure and her nervousness. Trembling beneath the sheets and not knowing what else to do, she had clung to her mother's precise instructions:

"Close your eyes, my darling, and pretend yourself elsewhere. Or better still, engaging in a pleasant activity of your choosing. I, myself, have always been partial to visiting the milliner. I imagine a lovely pink silk hat, embroidered with peonies and topped with an ostrich feather. Sometimes it is a rather rakish poke bonnet of green straw accented with a sprig of apple blossoms, but ..."—her mother had patted her awkwardly on the hand—"the important thing is to lie still as can be and practice forbearance with a ladylike demeanor. Remember, you are first and foremost a *lady*. With any luck, before your bonnet shopping is complete, you will have done your duty, and the dreadful business will be over."

So Helena had lain in her voluminous frilled night rail, still as death, eyes closed, waiting for Nicholas to do his duty. She had peeped once, enough to see that he wore a white nightshirt with laces that had become untied at his throat. She had just glimpsed a rather intriguing patch of dark, curling hair when his bleak voice made her shut her eyes again.

Be a lady, she had repeated to herself. *Practice ladylike forbearance.*

"I'm sorry, Helena. I will—I will be as gentle as I can."

For a moment, she had wondered at the starkness of his voice. Then she had felt something hard, massive, pushing between her legs. With rising panic, she had realized that he meant to pierce her there, a space too small for so large ... and then the pain, the sudden, intense hot edge of it that cut off her breath. She had not remembered to shop for bonnets or pick wildflowers for a bouquet. With shame, Helena remembered that she had shrieked aloud without any resemblance to ladylike comportment.

Nicholas had sprung off her, a look of horror on his face.

He had avoided her ever since.

Oh, he remained polite, exquisitely so, the brief moments they encountered one another in the breakfast parlor or at a soiree. Inevitably, he would be leaving just as she arrived. As Helena recalled their last exchange at Lady Wetherly's ball five nights ago, a tear leaked out of one eye and trickled slowly below her mask. Her husband had bowed over her hand, his eyes impenetrable as smoked glass. He might have been a stranger and that their first introduction. He had been so different during their whirlwind courtship. Though their embraces had been few and chaste then, she could still remember the exotic male spice of his scent, the gentle brush of his lips against her hand.

What had she done to lose his affection?

"Has your mouth had enough of my cock? Perhaps you'd like to beg for it elsewhere, another wet, juicy hole waiting to be had."

The man's stunning words jarred Helena back to the room. Perhaps, she thought dizzily, it had been what she *hadn't* done. Could her mother have been wrong? Could the conjugal act be about something other than visits to the milliner or passive acceptance of one's wifely duty?

"Yes, *yes*! That's it, milord, harder, oooh, like that, how my cunny craves to be fed ..."

Surely Nicholas could not want a similar sort of behavior from me ... Could he?

'Twas almost unthinkable, but he *was* a man. Yesterday, in one of her secret, wistful meanderings through her husband's rooms, she had discovered the admission ticket to the bawdy house. Protruding from an envelope, the gleam of silver had caught her eye. Though she had chastised herself for intruding upon her husband's privacy, curiosity had nevertheless compelled her to extract the thinly pressed metal billet. The size of a playing card, the entry ticket had appeared innocuous enough at first. Embossed on the surface were the words "Get Thee to the Nunnery."

Turning the ticket over, her jaw had dropped. The crude image depicted an unclothed woman with enormous breasts genuflecting in a mockery of prayer. A date of admission had been inscribed beneath the figure. A sudden ringing had exploded in her ears as she had realized Nicholas was planning on attending this den of iniquity the very next night.

Sheltered though she was, Helena had heard whispers about the infamous club. The Nunnery was rumored to be an expensive gaming and bawdy house where the classes mingled. During the weekly masquerade, peers of the realm hob-nobbed with merchants and solicitors and whoever else possessed sufficient coin to drink, gamble, and enjoy the company of the exquisite demimonde. Even more shocking, according to her friend Lady Marianne Draven, certain married ladies of the *ton* frequented the masquerade as well.

"When one is disguised, one's true nature is unleashed," Marianne had said, with an indifferent wave of her fan. "After all, the need for amorous diversion is not the sole province of men. What is sauce for the gander and all that."

Helena knew she had risked all—her pride, her very reputation—to come tonight. She had thought in her love-addled mind to beg Nicholas to reconsider consorting with a whore; for her, the pain of a shattered heart would far surpass the physical pain she had experienced during their wedding consummation. She would do whatever he wanted to lift the fog from his eyes, to feel again the warmth of his affection. Fierce longing surged through her to be the kind of wife Nicholas would want. She would do anything to have him love her again. *Anything*.

And, she reasoned now with renewed determination, learning to please her husband in the bedchamber could not differ much from learning any other skill, could it? If she felt confident in anything, it rested in her aptitude as a pupil. She prided herself on being a student with good sense. Had not her tutors always commented on her quickness in acquiring proficiency in various subjects, from French to watercolors? Why, much to the amazement of her piano instructor it had taken her only a fortnight's practice to competently render a tricky passage of Master Bach's fugue in C-minor.

So, too, could she learn to be a wife.

All she required was instruction. Or, at the very least, the benefit of careful observation.

Emboldened by hope and desperation, Helena edged out of her hiding space and peered around the desk. With her eyes adjusted to the dimness, she could make out the lines of the furniture and—*Heavens!*—the soles of the woman's feet waving madly above the back of the settee. The figures themselves hovered below her line of vision. How could she observe and remain hidden at the same time? As she pondered the dilemma, she noticed the heavy velvet drapes to the left of the seating area. The curtains hung from ceiling to floor, and there looked to be voluminous layers of drapery behind them. Deep enough to conceal even several persons.

Perfect.

Only one task remained: to reach the curtains undetected. Helena ran her palms against the loose material of her tunic and felt the rustle of her petticoats. Her stays, too, restricted her movement. They would have to go. After several minutes of struggle, she managed to release the strings that bound the layers of undergarments to her and eased out of them like a butterfly shedding its fragile skin. Hoarse cries provided the perfect cover.

'Tis now or never.

She took a deep breath and crawled toward the curtains, her skirt barely a whisper against the carpet. With each movement forward, the distance seemed to lengthen. She expected discovery at any moment, an angry voice or a hand to halt her progress. Still, she crept onward with blind determination. By the time she slipped into the safety of the velvety folds, her palms were clammy, and her body shook with nervous excitement.

Then she bumped into a hard, warm object.

Her breath froze in her throat. As she thought to scream, a large hand clamped over her mouth while another trapped her at the waist. She was rendered immobile. Shock warred with a horrifying realization.

She was not alone.

"Be still or we risk discovery," a familiar voice whispered in her ear.

If possible, her heart thudded even faster.

"Do you understand?" His voice was so low she could barely hear it, but she would know those deep masculine tones anywhere. The mixture of dread and relief made her giddy. Slowly, she turned her head and looked up into orbs of fathomless darkness. *Nicholas.*

In the silvery moonlight from the windows behind them, she could see that he had removed his mask. Shadows obscured the details of his face, but she could make out the granite set of his jaw, the tight line of his lips.

She held her breath, waiting for her husband's reaction. What would he say to encountering his wife at such a time, in such a fashion?

"Do you understand?" he repeated as quietly as the last.

Numb with shock, she nodded.

Merciful heavens, he does not recognize me!

He released her, and belatedly she reached up to touch her cheek. She felt the feathery shell of the mask securely in place. Her fingers wandered to the profusion of curls—brassy red, she'd chosen, to disguise her own straight brown locks. Likely the paints, too, retained their concealing power. At the start of the evening, she'd dipped her brush into the tiny copper pots with a liberal hand to complete the disguise. She'd felt a thrill of excitement peering into the looking glass. No one would recognize the demure Lady Helena in the scarlet lips, smoky eyelids, and darkened lashes. No one would look at the water nymph with brazenly red hair and scandalously low décolletage and see the Marchioness of Harteford.

Apparently not even the Marquess of Harteford himself.

Chapter Two

Nicholas Morgan, the sixth Marquess of Harteford, slowly released the luscious baggage in front of him. He forced himself to count to ten in his head to cool the fire in his blood. To forget the softness of the skin beneath his palm but a moment ago, the delicate un-corseted waist he had circled with an arm, and the plush rounded bottom that had wriggled enticingly against his groin.

Unbelievable. He'd never accounted himself a prurient man, but now, for a second time in a month, he found himself reduced to a morass of raging animal desires. The first instance had been his wedding night; his loins had been fired by his beautiful, virginal wife—who, as it turned out, wanted nothing to do with him. Now, he felt his frustrated passions channel toward a ladybird, who might be beautiful—it was difficult to ascertain in the darkness—but who certainly had little to do with virginity.

Agony twisted in his chest, not for the first time since his marriage. He had always told himself that being raised in the stews did not necessitate acting like an undisciplined beast. Not that a blue-blooded upbringing was any guarantee of gentlemanly conduct: the sire he had never met, the former marquess, had been a famed debaucher. Nicholas himself was living proof of that. For most of his life, he'd believed himself the cast-off bastard of a whore. The truth concerning the legitimacy of his birth, when it had been delivered by a somber-looking solicitor a year ago, had turned his world on its end. It still hadn't righted itself.

His marriage only threw him further off balance.

I'm not good enough for Helena. I should never have married her.

Yet from the first moment he had laid eyes on her, he'd been held in her thrall. He'd first spotted her four months ago, at a ball as tedious as all the rest. Having made the obligatory rounds, he'd been intent upon escape when he noticed her. She had occupied a chair at the back of the room. At first glance, he might have missed her altogether, for her loose, putty-colored gown bore an unfortunate resemblance to the drapery beside which she sat. Moreover, she slumped in her chair, her shoulders curving inward like folded wings. It appeared that she wished to withdraw into herself so fully that she might disappear altogether.

Yes, he might have overlooked her completely, had she not turned her head at that very moment. His breath had caught when her gaze collided with his. Her wide tilted eyes, the color of sunlight reflected on a garden pond, had held an expression of infinite sadness. An expression which, for some unfathomable reason, wrought a twin ache in his own heart. He had waited for her expression to change, that infinitesimal shifting of muscles that always occurred when he was recognized. The curl to the lip, the slightly raised brow that bespoke volumes.

Son of a whore. Dirtied by trade. The Makeshift Marquess.

To his astonishment, Helena's gaze had remained open and guileless, and a shy smile surfaced on her lips. When her eyes had shifted downward, it had been with dainty acquiescence rather than haughty dismissal. All at once, he had been struck by a great many details about her: the fullness of her mouth, the Madonna-like curve of her cheeks, the delicately shaped foot that swung invitingly from beneath the heavy fortress of her dress. Then he had become intrigued by the manner in which she sat apart from the other young ladies, not a prodigious hothouse bloom nor yet a desperate wallflower. Rather, she was some furled, exotic breed, a mysterious bud poised to yield its passionate secrets. For the first time in his life, he had been gripped by a longing so intense that it dwarfed his reasoning.

Despite knowing better, he had sought an introduction and courted her, the only daughter of the Earl of Northgate. His path had been cleared by way of his fortune. Northgate, for all his venerable titles, lived in dun territory; the profligate gamester could not afford to turn down the generous settlement accompanying Nicholas' suit. With determined propriety, Nicholas had wooed his betrothed, to persuade himself as much as anyone else that he could be worthy of so fine a lady. He had taken Helena on chaperoned strolls in the park. They'd danced no more than twice at any ball. He'd made polite conversation with her family over afternoon tea, forcing down tiny watercress sandwiches drier than sand.

After every proper encounter during their courtship, Nicholas had returned to his chambers, rigid with want of her—in every way that was *not* decent. The carnal desires he kept carefully hidden in her presence shattered through the dam of his control. Lying in his bath, he would palm his rampant cock as he pictured her. Steamy images of her on her stomach, her luscious hips draped over pillows so that her pussy canted upwards, spread and waiting for him. She would be looking back at him, her big eyes soft and glowing with lust and adoration.

Please Nicholas, she would beg. *Please take me.*

In his fantasy, he would take his time teasing his impatient girl. He'd finger her silky cunny until she purred with pleasure. Then, kneeling between her thighs, he would do what he had never done before, what he had never *wanted* to do until he met her. Aye, from the first he'd wanted to put his mouth on her forbidden flesh, to taste this part of her that must be as sweet as all the rest.

He would eat her until she cried out her first release. Only then would he move over her, entering her with such slow precision they could both feel inch by burning inch his possession of her. There would be no doubt that he belonged there, buried all the way into her womanly core. With her eager, sweet entreaties in his ear, he would make love to her, teasing her with slow playful nudges, appeasing her with deep silken thrusts.

As the water rippled with his desperate strokes, his fantasies grew baser, more intense. Sometimes, he would stop, plunged to the bollocks in her trembling heat. He would moisten his fingers with her juices and explore the lovely crevice of her buttocks until he found the secret pucker. He would slick that delicate rim until it flared with excitement. Gently, he would ease his finger into her nether passage even as his cock throbbed in the sheath beneath.

At that moment, he would feel her entire body receiving him: his cock, his finger, his very soul. There would be no escaping his possession of her or her of him. For surely, as she pleaded to be thoroughly fucked by her ill-bred husband, loving it, loving *him*, he would fall only deeper under her spell.

Truly, he was the worst kind of bastard. He had no right to touch his wife with hands dirtied in the gutter and capable of unspeakable sins. Moreover, newly joined to the *ton* as he was, even he understood that true gentlemen did not slake desires of the flesh in their wives' well-appointed bedchambers. No, they preserved their wives' delicate sensibilities and found the sort of woman who would embrace this baser side of life. For if Helena ever knew, ever *suspected* this animal side of him ...

Nicholas shuddered, recalling the revulsion and pain he'd seen on her face on their wedding night. He had never made love to a lady before. In the past, his sexual exchanges had functioned with one purpose in mind: to slake his physical needs. But that night, it had been his wife trembling in innocence in his bed. She had lain as rigid as a board, as still as death itself. He had fumbled to make things as quick and least distressing as possible for her, but it had not been enough.

To this day, her screams of pain tortured him. How could he have hurt her so? Were ladies so very different from the sort of females he'd known in his past? In those brief moments, she had seen through the fragile skin of nobility to the depraved beast that he was. The shame of it made his bones ache. Surely, she despised him. She would never want him to touch her again.

To spare her, he had to find a way to ease his torturous longing. The daily—nay, *thrice* a day—sessions of frigging himself were, unfortunately, not the answer. Stroking his own cock somehow frustrated him more and served to inflame the already assiduous desire for his wife. When he spewed his seed, he felt only a fleeting physical release—and no relief at all from the aching, bone-deep loneliness.

Thus, he'd come to terms with another solution. No longer able to deny the needs of his flesh, Nicholas had sought out an appropriate venue. The Nunnery, known equally for its depravity and its discretion, had seemed as good a place as any to indulge his sinful appetites. But tonight, as he'd scanned the opulent masquerade, he'd seen naught of interest. He'd danced with several doxies nevertheless, telling himself that he simply needed to fuck a woman—any woman—to relieve his lust. But the rubbing of their breasts against his chest, the coy undulation of their hips against his thigh had brought no fire to his loins. A particularly bold brunette had gone so far as to whisper her skills with a certain flogging technique in his ear. He had felt nothing.

Despair had slowly taken over, and he had roamed to an empty room above stairs. Alone in a winged armchair, he'd thought of the only woman who mattered: how pink her nipples must be, how he would tease them with his fingers until she begged for him to suckle her tits ... and instantly his sex sprang to attention. With a sigh, he'd given in to the richness of his fantasy, undoing his trousers with hands that became soft and white and tipped with perfect oval fingernails. He'd sought solace in the way those hands gripped his cock, urging the blood to rush to the stretched dome already slickening with seeped seed.

Except solace was not to be his, not even in this. Because moments later, the door had opened and instinctively he'd leapt from the chair to the nearest shelter. Bad enough that he'd already been branded the Makeshift Marquess by the vicious sticklers of the *ton*—he could only imagine the repercussions of being caught in this particular solecism. So that was how he, Lord Nicholas Harteford, found himself behind curtains, trousers undone, hiding from an amorous *ménage à trois* intent upon fucking until dawn or one of them expired from overexertion.

Having an aversion to closed spaces, Nicholas had felt cold sweat prickle his brow as time ticked away behind the smothering thick velvet. He had resisted, but his mind began the inexorable slide down the dark tunnels of his past. The choke of soot filled his throat, and he felt the urge to gasp for breath as an airless passage closed around him. A sudden scuffling sound had him tensing against the wall. He expected to see the terror of his dreams, the bearded face, the menacing grin—

Instead, he found himself discovered. Not by the screwing threesome, but by a light skirt. A doxy who appeared out of nowhere, whose scent of orange blossoms and spring leaves banished the dank odors of his memories. Whose plump arse and creamy breasts tempted his hands beyond comprehension. Lust shot through him like a geyser, instantly dislodging the panic.

Verily, his life was fast becoming a farce.

Unable to avoid the reality of his situation any longer, Nicholas studied his partner in hiding. After her initial shock at finding company behind the drapery, the nymph scrupulously avoided making eye contact with him. She appeared absorbed by the scene beyond the velvet; only her profile was revealed to him. Her feathered mask concealed much of her face, but he would guess delicate cheekbones accompanied the piquant point of her chin. In the faint moonlight, he could not make out the color of her eyes, but they appeared huge and luminous, seductively framed by dark, sweeping lashes and smoky eyelids.

And her mouth ... he could see its generous bottom curve, how it jutted out in saucy welcome. Even in the dimness, he could tell that it had been painted red. A siren's red. Luscious and ripe, a cherry for the tasting. The fruit of her lips trembled, and he realized she was engrossed by the activities visible through the slit of drapery. *The naughty little minx.* Reluctant amusement mingled with burgeoning arousal as he angled his head forward, so that he, too, could catch the sex play.

Illuminated by candlelight, a slim brunette writhed on her back as one of the men, a stocky, sandy-haired fellow, drove eagerly between her legs. She appeared to be participating with great enthusiasm from the way her slender legs encircled the man's hips and drew him in deeper with each thrust. Beside her on the carpet, a blonde man lay naked on his side. His erection flared crimson within the ardent clasp of her hand. He bent his head to sample her apple-sized breasts.

"Lovely Lucy, do you like what Brookeston is doing to your cunt?" The blonde man inquired after a moment. His fingers plucked playfully at her small dark nipples.

"Oh, yes," Lucy panted, arching her spine. "Lord Brookeston ... ram your rod into my cunt ... my hungry cunt needs your fucking ... feel how wet it is, how it salivates for your mighty sword ... oh please ... yes, like that, pierce me harder ... !"

Lucy's words seemed to stir Brookeston into a frenzy. His hips slapped against her thighs with greater urgency. His words emerged in gasps. "God, St. John, the wench is so hot, I am going to ..."

"Control yourself, man." With an idle shove, St. John unbalanced Brookeston. The latter landed on his rear with a grunt of surprise. His sex vibrated like a flagpole in the air.

"What did you do that for?" Brookeston demanded angrily.

"My turn," St. John replied blithely as he took his friend's place between the woman's legs. "You never could hold your liquor or your stamina."

At Brookeston's indignant sputter, Lucy intervened with a saucy smile. "Gentlemen, may I suggest that there is room enough for all? Lord Brookeston, if you would be so kind as to come to the head of the table?" So saying, she rolled over languidly so that she was on her hands and knees. She cast a come-hither look over the shoulder.

Brookeston complied with ungainly haste. He groaned aloud as Lucy took his erection between her lips. At the same time, St. John began to pump into her from behind. With each grunt of pleasure, he drove Lucy forward, impaling her mouth upon his friend's cock. Lucy's eyes rolled back in her head, her face wild as she moved to the erotic rhythm of two lovers.

Moonlight shifted behind the curtain. Nicholas looked at his masked conspirator, whose face now played with shadows. She was, he noticed, of similar build to Helena. Curvy, with a nipped-in middle and a sinfully rounded backside. The firm, rounded tops of her breasts seemed to quiver, and in his mind he saw those tits bobbing rhythmically with each ferocious thrust of his cock. He felt his control slipping as he imagined the fiery nymph under him, pleading for his rod with words as hot as the ones that echoed through the room. Inflamed beyond bearing, Nicholas closed his hands around the woman's waist and turned her to face him.

The nymph's eyes widened and, for a brief moment, Nicholas had the humiliating thought that she, too, would reject his advances. But, no, with a silent sigh her eyes closed, and her lips parted in acquiescence. Slowly, carefully so as to not disturb the curtain, Nicholas pulled her closer. With a feeling of elation, he tested the lushness of that bottom lip with his finger, caressing that soft, plump ledge. He traced the outline of her mouth, his cock throbbing at the thought of tasting those lips, of plundering her sweetness with his tongue.

But he would not. He had vowed this to himself, to keep that one act sacred to his marriage. He would pour his love, the light of his soul, into his chaste kisses with Helena and pray that she might keep them in safety. Even as guilt and self-loathing burned in his gut, he knew this night there was no turning back. His demons had been roused; they clamored for satisfaction, for the satiation of their voracious appetites.

Ah, my love. Forgive me.

Nicholas stroked the woman's lower lip, requesting entrance. His nostrils flared as the tip of her tongue appeared and flicked against the pad of his finger. Licking him slowly, delicately, as if he were a sweet. He pushed his finger in deeper. Again, her eyes widened. Lord, but that act of innocence inflamed him. He thrust the full length of his finger into her mouth, stifling a groan as her cheeks hollowed on instinct, sucking him into her moist depths. His erection strained painfully against the placket of his trousers. Would the damned threesome never stop fucking?

As if in answer, guttural male groans spilled into the room, followed by high keening female cries. Moments later, he heard a few giggles, the clink of guineas exchanging hands, and then—about bloody time—the opening and closing of the door. Nicholas' eyes roamed over the masked vixen in his arms. She appeared wantonly oblivious to anything at the moment, her eyes half-closed, her generous breasts rising and falling in rapid rhythm. Some of the paint had smeared around the edge of her lips; he found that imperfection strangely erotic.

Lust bolted through him. With a swift movement, he jerked her into his arms and yanked aside the curtain. Before she had time to make a sound, he laid her on the nearest available surface, the desk. She was spread like a feast, and he felt like a survivor of an endless famine. She made a movement as if to protest. He merely ran his hands over the tiny sleeves of her loose white tunic, pulling them down, imprisoning her shapely arms. Her bodice had no choice but to follow the sleeves, the edge of satin rubbing over creamy mounds before exposing plump nipples. Ripe as berries they were, puckered sweetly atop full flawless tits. He filled his hands with the abundance, and the blood roared in his head when she moaned.

His fingers found her nipples, thrummed the buds until her moans became breathy, desperate. God, but she was an inferno. He had a mind to taste her fire before he went up in flames himself. He yanked up her skirt. Arousal blasted through him to find no impeding undergarments save a thin chemise. He slid the hem of the chemise up farther, past her luscious stocking-clad legs, past the frilled garters, all the way up. At the top of all that delight, he found even more of heaven—downy soft curls, a shy pussy. He ran his finger reverently down her slit, found it plump and moist and slippery with wanting.

She gave a muffled shriek.

He placed his hand over her mouth, noticing how bronzed his hand appeared against her lily white softness. For a doxy, she had the skin of a lady. "Shh, sweet, unless you wish to invite others to our party. You would not want that, would you?"

Her eyes grew huge. She shook her head.

"Good." Satisfaction humming in his veins, Nicholas slid his hand lower, holding her gently at the throat. "I am not a man to share."

With his other hand, he unbuttoned his pantaloons. His turgid flesh sprang free, curving upward in triumphant freedom. He brought the bulging tip to the mouth of her sex, tormenting them both by rubbing the sensitive head against her damp curls. Up and down he stroked, nudging her hidden peak with the head of his cock. She gasped, her eyes closing.

"Look at me." Gently, he pressed down on her throat. "Tell me you want me."

Her eyes flew open. He nearly spilled his seed at her expression, the oh-so seemingly innocent sweep of long eyelashes, the surely feigned shock widening her eyes. One would almost believe that beneath that exotic feathered mask one would find the blushing fresh cheeks of a debutante.

Yes, he had found himself a veritable actress. The perfect harlot, one who could not only satisfy his rod, but also fulfill his darkest innermost desire: to transform innocence into wanton passion. To turn a lady—his lady—into a sweet, uninhibited slut.

"Tell me then, my sweet, what is it that you want?"

His vixen moaned, arching her hips against his erection, instinctively seeking hardness to rub against her softness. Her desire left the head of his shaft slippery, quivering for entry into the moist paradise. Nicholas withdrew, his expression stern. "A well-bred miss such as yourself surely knows to answer a question when asked. Answer me, or we shall cease."

She looked at him, eyes huge. When she spoke, her words were soft, husky, and wholly unexpected. "*Monsieur, s'il vous plaît. Je ne comprends pas* ..."

She was French then, likely newly arrived in England. He found her accent entrancing and oddly familiar ... which did not make any sense. Then she shifted against him again, pleading with his cock, coating it in intoxicating wetness. Though he knew only rudimentary French, the language of lust was universal. He responded with a deliberate thrust forward, allowing the distended tip to nudge past her lush lips.

"*Mademoiselle*, is this what you want?" He moved in a little deeper, feeling her passage clench before slowly giving way to him. She was surprisingly tight. He could feel the rim of her stretching to accommodate his erection. He would not be able to continue with this game much longer.

To his relief, she nodded, as if in understanding.

"'Tis my cock you're wanting then. My cock in your sweet pussy." He spoke the words as a tutor would to an apt pupil. He thrust in deeper, slowly stretching her, feeling his chest swell with her cries of pleasure. He sank farther into her molten depths. "Ask for it, sweeting. More of my cock."

"Cock," she echoed in breathy accents, her head moving side to side as he rewarded her with another inch of his rod. "*S'il vous plaît, monsieur* ... more ... cock!"

With a hoarse groan, he filled his hands with the full curves of her ass, luxuriating in its womanly softness. He lifted her hips and slammed his length all the way into her. She was instant fire, pure flame wrapping along his shaft as he moved within her. She moaned, arching off the table to receive his thrusts. Seeking leverage, he gripped the edge of the desk as he worked himself deeper and deeper, fucking to the heart of her pussy. Crazed with lust, he pounded into her as she chanted wantonly, "*J'adore le* cock, *monsieur*, ohhhh ... more ..."

The overwhelming desire blurred the edges of his vision and tore deep growls from his throat. Even as he ground into her tight passage, her entire body arched to receive him, wanting more. Her lips released words in French that he did not understand, yet the pleading tone of the silky syllables had him thrusting harder, deeper. As he'd imagined, her full tits swayed gorgeously with each thrust, her nipples engorged and begging for attention. He leaned down and captured a tip in his mouth. He suckled in rhythm with his pistoning cock.

That was all it took. She shrieked—there was no other word for it—a high, almost startled sound that poured like a balm over his chafed soul. She came like the beautiful wanton she was: her pussy gripped him with brazen insistence, milking him with a cadence of sharp contractions. His eyes closed as the pressure expanded in his bollocks, intensifying, and finally bubbling upward along his shaft. Delving into her folds, he found the center of her pleasure.

Her scream sizzled in his ears even as his vision turned to black. With his last ounce of control, he wrenched himself out. A harsh shout escaped his lips, disguising a beloved's name, as his pleasure shot in glistening trails across the desk.

Chapter Three

Seated in the blue and white drawing room, Helena sipped her tea and avoided Lady Marianne Draven's eyes. She feared those intelligent emerald eyes held an all too knowing expression. She had not stopped blushing since last evening, a state of pinkness that her astute friend had likely already observed. Truth be told, she was fairly bursting to talk about the extraordinary events that had transpired a few hours ago, but how did one discuss delirious fornication with one's husband in polite company?

Her cup rattled as she settled it into the saucer, the steam from the tea curling upward into the slants of morning light. From the mantel, the ormolu clock chimed eight times. Despite the lack of sleep, Helena's insides frothed with energy. She eyed the plate of tarts on the rosewood coffee table. Bejeweled with dollops of Cook's delicious blackberry jam, the pastries seemed to wink at her. With a resolute sigh, Helena turned her gaze back to her cup. If she wanted to win Nicholas back, she needed to stick with her slimming plan.

"My dear, that tea, fine Ceylon though it may be, can hardly bear such studious observation," Marianne remarked. Seated on the adjacent Sheraton sofa, she removed her butter-colored gloves in a graceful motion. "Wouldn't you care to discuss what truly holds your attention?"

Helena's eyes darted to her friend's face. Gifted with silver-blonde hair and classically sculpted features, Marianne's beauty had the effect of staring directly into the sun. She had known Marianne since the schoolroom and still she could not help but blink at her friend's physical perfection. Despite the early hour, no shadows detracted from the vividness of Marianne's gaze, and her skin glowed with the health of the well-rested. Not that Marianne could have gotten much sleep—she had been the one to deposit Helena at the Nunnery last night, en route to her other entertainments. Dubbed *The Merry Widow*, Marianne never stepped foot inside her townhouse before dawn.

"Tea is easier than candid conversation," Helena admitted. "I hardly know where to begin."

"Is Lord Harteford at home this morning?" Marianne inquired.

"No. He ... he did not return last evening." Helena took a gulp of tea. "I suppose he stayed at his club."

"Excellent. My calling at this ungodly hour will not be a wasted effort. I suggest, then, that you start where my driver left you off—at the bawdy house," Marianne said.

Helena bit back a smile. Some things did not change. Nee Miss Marianne Blunt, Lady Draven continued to well suit her maiden name.

Truth be told, she had missed Marianne dreadfully these five years past. At the age of nineteen, Marianne had wed the wealthy and reclusive Lord Draven. She had been promptly whisked off to the wilds of Yorkshire, a place apparently unreachable by Helena's many posts. When Helena had perchance encountered the newly widowed Marianne at an assembly last month, she had felt like an awkward dowd next to her once bosom companion. Always beautiful, Marianne had exuded a new sensual confidence and a brittle wit which distinguished her even amongst the fast crowd she ran with.

To Helena, who favored intellectual salons populated by bluestockings and spinsters, Marianne's glamorous self-possession had seemed slightly terrifying. But once the two had started talking, the intimacy of their childhood days had sprouted and re-sown itself. And while it was true that Marianne had changed in some ways, in other ways she had changed not a whit. Marianne had always been clever, the friend to turn to in a time of need. The day before, in a fit of desperation Helena had found herself confessing about the state of her marriage and the admission ticket she had found in Nicholas' rooms. Marianne's strategic plan had been worthy of the great Wellington himself.

Helena eyed her friend. "Are you always this tactful?"

"I arranged your visit to the Nunnery last evening, did I not? What would one call that, if not tact?" Curiosity gleamed in Marianne's clear green eyes. "Did all go as planned?"

"Yes, after your driver deposited me at the back entrance, the ... Abbess let me in."

How strange a name for a bawd, and stranger yet that Marianne should count the proprietor of a bawdy house among her acquaintances. Helena knew better than to ask, however. 'Twas not Marianne's style to offer much in the way of explanation. "She was quite pleasant, and not at all what I imagined. Do you know she actually offered me lemonade?"

Marianne laughed, arranging her tangerine-colored skirts with an elegant flick of the wrist. "The Abbess can be charming when it pleases her. When I told her of your plight, she quite enjoyed the tale of your wifely devotion. That, and the extra guineas I supplied for her discretion. Did she make good on her promise of a private room?"

Helena felt heat creep up her neck. She took another swallow of tea.

"She did not? I shall have to have a word with her." A tinge of peach appeared on Marianne's high cheekbones. "I specifically instructed her to—"

"Oh no, it was not the Abbess' fault," Helena protested, setting down the saucer. "She did have a room. It is just that I—I did not make it quite that far. To the room, I mean."

"Oh, Helena, tell me you did not play the part of the wilting orchid. Really, after all my efforts! Did you even find your husband?"

Helena's chin rose a little at Marianne's mocking tone. "I found Harteford."

"And what transpired? Did you confront him with your demands for fidelity?"

"Well, in truth, our conversation did not progress that far."

"He was angry, then, that you followed him to the Nunnery. How very hypocritical of him. And how typically male." Rolling her eyes, Marianne crossed her arms beneath her bosom. The movement elevated her bodice *à la Grecque* to eye-popping effect. Helena glanced down at her own neckline and shrugged experimentally. Nothing. The starched surface of her chemisette obscured any interesting movement.

"He was not angry, exactly. At least, he did not appear so." Shifting against the cushions, Helena felt the blush suffuse her cheeks. "He seemed quite ... pleased, actually."

"Pleased? If you did not talk with him, why in Heaven's name would he ..." Grasping the implication of Helena's words, Marianne gave a wicked peal of laughter. "Dearest, did you seduce your own husband?"

Helena nodded, a *frisson* of pleasure sweeping through her body. Her breasts suddenly ached with their own weight, and her nipples tightened at the memory of his long fingers, the way he had cupped and stroked and kneaded her there. He'd called them her *tits*, chanted his praise of them in a voice so dark and thick it raised goose bumps on her flesh even now.

"Dare I ask ... the event, was it enjoyable?"

Helena looked at Marianne's laughing, candid eyes and felt something loosen in her chest. All her life, she had been taught that certain topics were never to be thought of or, heaven forbid, *alluded* to in polite company. But thinking about her mother's inadequate wedding night advice, she felt another rebellious tug and then suddenly something flew open within her. "Oh, Marianne, it was quite so!"

There, she'd said it. Exhilarated, she almost snatched a jam tart from the plate. She caught herself in time and clasped her hands together instead. She waited for her friend's reaction. Surely, she had managed to shock Marianne.

"And well it should be," Marianne said. "I have often wondered why the *beau monde* considers love matches to be unfashionable. In my experience, loveless marriages become quite tedious in a short space of time."

"I am not certain ours is a love match. At least, not on his part." The reality of her night's activities deflated some of her elation.

"Did you not say your reunion was quite satisfactory?"

Helena's skin tingled as she recalled the hunger in Nicholas' expression. When she had touched his chest, his whole body had vibrated like the string of a finely-tuned violin. Then came that glittering moment, when she'd felt heat swoosh between her legs and explode like firecrackers throughout her body ... and *his* hoarse cries had mingled with hers. In that instant, feeling the gallop of his heart beat next to hers, inhaling the musky scent of their shared pleasure, she had experienced a shattering joy. A bewildering pain.

"He did not know it was me," Helena said through stiff lips.

"I beg your pardon?"

"Last night, Harteford did not know it was me. It was dark, and I did not remove my mask or wig."

"But surely when you spoke ..."

"I spoke in French to disguise my voice."

"To disguise your voice ... but why?" Marianne asked.

"Because ... because ..." Helena strove to explain the fever that had overcome her. Behind the mask, she had been a different sort of woman than her ordinary self. The sort of woman who might entice a man, who might respond to his desires with brazen wants of her own. Wants that she had not known existed until Nicholas unleashed them with his bold hands and his wicked mouth.

A shiver ran up her legs remembering the way he had kissed her breasts at the same time that his turgid flesh invaded her. Overcome by a desperate hunger, she had pleaded for more of him, as if she'd been starved for his touch, on her, *inside* her ... Disguised by flaming red hair and paint, she had truly transformed into a harlot! The sense of freedom had been as exhilarating as it had been foreign.

Only afterward, when Nicholas had extricated himself from her embrace and began to dress with cool efficiency, had reality returned. What had come over her? How could she have responded with such enthusiasm, such unbridled *wantonness*, to his caresses? Sweet heavens, what would Nicholas do if she were to expose herself to him then and there, as a doxy who had but moments ago begged him for more and more? A tide of shame and horror had crashed over her as the words of his marriage proposal suddenly echoed in her mind.

I ask the greatest privilege of your hand in marriage. While I am undeserving of your pure and virtuous nature, I do prize it above all. I will strive to be a worthy husband, if you will have me.

Pure and virtuous? No indeed—she was positively shameless.

Blanching, Helena said, "I was afraid to reveal my true identity. You see, after it was over, he got up and dressed like nothing had happened. He ... he did not even look at me."

"Well, if he thought you were a whore," Marianne said reasonably, "how else was he to treat you?"

And there was the crux of the problem. She, Helena Morgan, the Marchioness of Harteford, had played the part of a strumpet so convincingly that she had fooled her own husband. But what if her actions had not been playacting at all? What if ... what if it was her *virtue* that was false? Recalling Nicholas' indifferent manner after their coupling last night, Helena shivered. Could he love her, knowing her true nature? Or would he think himself deceived? Duped, by his harlot of a wife.

"Did he say anything to you at all?"

"Pardon?" Helena whispered.

"Any words conveyed. To your person," Marianne repeated impatiently.

Squirming with humiliation, Helena admitted, "Yes. Before he left, he said, *Thank you.* And he ... he left a fifty pound note on the desk."

"A fifty pound note! You shall certainly not run short of pin money this month."

"That is not amusing, Marianne," Helena said, feeling hot pressure behind her eyelids.

Marianne's eyes gleamed. "Oh, but I think it is. Imagine, the Marquess of Harteford paying for favors that he has already purchased through marriage. Surely you see the humor in that."

"I most certainly do *not*! My husband will be most ... *vexed* if he were to find out." With an agitated hand, Helena dashed away the tears that had spilled over. "He will never forgive me for deceiving him in such a fashion."

"From that perspective ..." Marianne shrugged. "Things would have been rather simpler if you had confessed your true identity then and there. Why did you not?"

Helena lowered her head. "I was afraid."

"Afraid? After such an enjoyable coupling? I confess, my dear, you have got me quite, quite confused."

"Marianne, when you were married, did you ever ... ever ..."

"Yes, my dear?"

"Respond somewhat ... with rather a great deal of enthusiasm for ..."

"Do speak plainly, Helena. You know I do not appreciate inane niceties."

"Did you ever beg for your husband's lovemaking?" Helena asked in a rush.

Marianne gave a startled laugh. "Beg? Of course not!"

"'Tis true, then. I am a whore." Helena spoke the words with dull acceptance, though her bottom lip quivered. "Harteford will never love me now."

"I am sure there is no need for such dramatics." Marianne reached for her tea. Grimacing after a sip, she set the cup and saucer back on the table. "If you were simply to explain ..."

"Last night, Marianne, I ... I acted like a wanton! I begged my husband to—"

"Yes, well, as I have said that is rather common in happy marriages."

"You said *you* never begged for your husband's attentions," Helena pointed out.

"That is because I have not had the privilege of a happy marriage," her friend responded tartly.

"Oh. I—I am sorry."

"It is of no consequence. After all, I gained a great deal from the match, including the freedoms I now enjoy." Marianne raised a delicately arched eyebrow. "Freedoms that would allow me to comment that the enjoyment of *affaires* is a commonplace thing."

"But you do not understand. I *truly* enjoyed it. So much so that I begged Harteford to ..." Helena felt a panicked sob rise in her throat.

"To what, Helena? You will have to tell me if I am to help."

Helena shut her eyes. "To fuck me. I begged him to fuck me. With his ... his *cock*."

"My, that is rather forward." Marianne cleared her throat. "Where exactly did you learn such words?"

"Well, from Harteford, of course. He told me to say them last night." Helena blinked. "Where else would I learn them?"

"And how did your lord respond when you uttered those words to him?"

Helena paused, coloring. "He grew rather ... frantic in his movements."

"My, my." Marianne fanned herself with her gloves. "And you found his passion enjoyable, yes?"

"It was the most wonderful thing I have ever experienced," Helena said fervently.

"Then why should he feel any differently about you?"

Helena tilted her head. "I beg your pardon?"

"Why should your husband not likewise enjoy passion from you?"

She had not thought of it that way before. "It's just that ... before we were married, when he seemed quite fond of me, he often commented about my proper nature. In point of fact, he once praised me as a paragon of virtue. Like Caesar's wife—beyond reproach."

Marianne rolled her eyes. "My dear, no man wishes to bed a paragon, no matter what he says. May I be frank with you?"

"Yes, of course." Struck by the enormity of her confessions, Helena suddenly giggled. She had never talked so honestly in all her life. "After all I have confided, need you ask?"

"Your husband married you for a reason. Despite his unfortunate origins, Harteford's fortune still caused many a matchmaking matron to fall into paroxysms of excitement. But he chose you. Why did he, do you think?"

"Because of my family's connections?" Helena ventured.

"Marrying into the peerage was a boon," Marianne conceded. "But then again, there were several ladies on the market with titles and dowries that surpassed your own. If it was simply blue blood that Harteford was after, why did he not pursue a greater matrimonial prize?"

"I do not know." Without thinking, Helena reached for one of the pastries. She stopped, her fingers trembling a hair's-breadth away from the fluted buttery edge. Swallowing, she said, "But you are correct in one regard. Financially speaking, I was no prize. You know that after ... after Thomas passed, our fortunes changed."

The clock grew louder in the silence that followed, as did the hustle and bustle of the servants as they carried on their duties beyond the drawing room doors. Helena wondered if a time would ever come when she could talk of her older brother's death without feeling the ache of emptiness. To compound the darkness of that time, Marianne had married and left for Yorkshire a month after Thomas' funeral.

"Thomas was well loved by all who knew him," Marianne said quietly.

"Yes, well, who wouldn't love him? He was perfect." Helena paused, studying her hands. "They never got over it. My parents, I mean. My father took to gaming and my mother to her bedchamber. Before long, the debts mounted. There was only one solution."

"A daughter's duty." Marianne's voice was as hard as ice.

"As my mother always pointed out, I had so little else to recommend me that I needed to make my behavior as amenable as possible in order to attract suitors. Do you know I memorized Lady Epplethistle's *Compleat Guide* line by line?" Helena shrugged. "But it was for naught. I am nothing special. Not a beauty, and too plump for the current fashion. Before Harteford's proposal, my mother feared that I would end up on the shelf. It was nearing the end of my Season. My father could not afford a second."

"You are not too plump. Men adore women with a voluptuous figure. And you are certainly not dull," Marianne said. "Modesty may be becoming, but it will not help you understand your husband."

"But I really do not know why Hartford chose me." Helena threw her hands up in defeat. "Other than my virtue, which we have now allowed does not exist, I am not sure what he finds appealing. I am accomplished but not extraordinarily so in the realms of art, music, and languages."

"Oh, for God's sake. As pretty as your performance is at the piano, that is not why your husband married you," Marianne snapped.

"I know it." Helena gave her friend a hurt look. "Why are you angry at me?"

"Because you are blind to the fortune in front of you."

"What fortune? Truly, Marianne, could you not be more specific?"

Marianne pinned her with a blunt green gaze. "Have you not noticed the way your husband looks at you? I have seen the hunger in his eyes, try as he might to mask it. Dearest, he looks at you the way you have been looking at that blessed tart—like he is longing to eat you up, every last bite."

Helena's jaw dropped.

"Why are you shocked, Helena? Have you forgotten the night of passion you spent in your husband's arms?"

"He thought I was another." The pain of betrayal was confusing, given that it was *she* who had deceived *him*. Yet he had broken his marriage vows; why had he seen fit to share with a stranger intimacies that he kept from his own wife? With a hitch to her voice, she said, "He lay with me believing I was a doxy at the ball."

"Perhaps he would not be seeking a doxy if he found a warmer welcome in his home."

Helena's cheeks flamed. "I had thought of that. I should never have listened to my mother's advice about bonnet shopping."

At Marianne's inquisitive look, Helena explained what she had been told about conjugal duties.

"Oh, Lord." For once, Marianne appeared at a loss for words. Her mouth opened and closed several times before she said, "Can I safely assume that last evening no bonnets were bought or sold?"

"None whatsoever," Helena responded fervently.

"Excellent." Marianne patted Helena's hand. "You love your husband?"

"You know that I do!"

"And you are certain you cannot tell him that you were the harlot?"

"I can't," Helena whispered. "He'll despise me ... for lying to him."

For acting like a harlot. Sweet heavens, for ... being *one.*

Marianne sighed. "Very well, then, here's my advice. Find a way to seduce him, this time as his wife. Show him he has no need to return to the bawdy house."

"Do you think I can?" Uncertainty and hope wavered in Helena's voice.

"Of course. Men are simple creatures, my dear, and, above all, lazy. Convenience is your greatest ally. If Harteford finds everything he desires in his own home, he will not bother to stray. But remember: you are competing with a harlot, so you must use whatever means necessary."

"Means? What means have I?"

Marianne scrutinized her person with such intensity that Helena felt astonishingly naked despite her chemise, stays, and petticoats. She reassured herself that she specifically had her morning dress designed, like all the garments in her wardrobe, to hide her embarrassing abundance of flesh. It was one thing to mention one's plumpness and quite another for one's friend to actually *see* it.

"It appears your means are quite generous, yet you somehow manage to depress them with the poor cut of your gown, enough petticoats to clothe a village, and, Oh Lord, is that a corset you are wearing?" Marianne finished in mock horror.

"I know it is not currently *de rigueur*," Helena said with dignity, "but my dressmaker assures me that many ladies of the *ton* still rely upon them to convey a more fashionable figure."

"I was not aware that the shape of a trussed-up chicken was the rage this season." Leaning forward, Marianne poked her in the ribs. "How, may I ask, do you manage to breathe in that monstrosity?"

"Do stop." Helena slapped her friend's hand away. "We cannot all possess naturally svelte figures like you."

Marianne patted her skirts complacently. "Well, that is true. But why must you hide your own particular gifts?"

"I am hiding nothing." Helena spoke through clenched teeth. "I am merely attempting to minimize my flaws."

"In doing so, you have minimized any approximate shape to your body. Your dress has enough material to cover the both of us. And," her friend added ruthlessly, "enough lace and flounces to decorate the nation of France."

Humiliation swelled hot and prickly in Helena's chest. Marianne was probably right. After all, Marianne always looked as if she had stepped off the pages of *La Belle Assemblée*.

"It just so happens I have an appointment tomorrow afternoon with Madame Rousseau. You shall accompany me."

"Madame Rousseau would see me and on such short notice?" Helena asked doubtfully. "It is said she clothes only the *crème de la crème* of Society."

Grinning, Marianne helped herself to a tart. "She will take one look at you and declare you her greatest challenge."

Chapter Four

Nicholas woke to the sounds of muffled shouting, followed by a thunderous crash that shook the floor and reverberated through his body. Lively curses issued from the warehouse floor below stairs. Minutes later, a sweet, pungent smell drifted into the room. Recalling that a new shipment of rum had arrived yesterday from the West Indies, Nicholas groaned. He rolled over on the lumpy couch and pulled the rough woolen blanket more securely around him. At the moment, he did not want to face another day at the office.

What he wanted to do was to fall back asleep and into the arms of the dream vixen who had been torturing him with impudent kisses. Kisses that had brought him to a throbbing morning cockstand. With a sigh and eyes still closed, Nicholas unbuttoned his smalls. He concentrated on the dream girl's mouth, cherry ripe beneath her feathered mask. The full, luscious mouth that was planting soft kisses along his jaw and down his neck. His breath came faster as she ran her hands down the rigid muscles of his chest, and her tongue followed, licking fire against his nipples.

She moved like a water nymph, her chestnut hair a cool silken wave over his skin. She sank naturally between his legs, as if she belonged there. Her small hands played with his stones. The gentle circular strokes made his blood roar. Then she set her mouth on him. Nicholas bit back a growl as she lapped at his balls like waves to a shore. Each tide pulled him deeper and deeper into an ocean of pleasure. Twining his hands in her hair, he guided her mouth upward and crammed himself inside. Hot, fast thrusts that blurred her words of love and lust. As he neared his climax, he reached for her mask and tore it off.

Golden hazel eyes met his.

"I love you," Helena whispered.

He came in violent surges.

Panting, Nicholas lay flat on his back on the sofa. Gradually, he became aware of the world again—the loud brass of cockney voices, the lulling splash of the tides, the marine-and-refuse perfume of the river. The physical release did nothing for his guilt, so he breathed in deeply, taking comfort in the elixir of damp salt air, tar, and coal smoke from the metal works downstream. The tang of the Thames might make others cover up their noses, but to him the complex odors spoke of new beginnings, of possibilities open to any man with the determination and drive to improve his station in life.

Nicholas rose, and, looking down, winced at the wet stain. He went to the cupboard to withdraw clean garments. As he changed, he looked out the large window behind his desk. At this time of morning, the Thames resembled a sunburned forest, with red ochre sails fluttering from hundreds of masts. Lighters jostled irritably against one another, vying for space within the walls of the West India Dock. Vessels fortunate enough to be moored wharfside were being unloaded by teams of porters who moved as tirelessly as ants between dock and warehouse.

Nicholas felt as always the pull of the river's energy. For sixteen years, he'd routinely arrived at the warehouse on the Isle of Dogs before the break of dawn and left in similar darkness. In his early years with the company, he'd heard the snickered comments of the other clerks. *Toad-eater*, they'd called him, disparaging his work ethic as a ploy to get in the good graces of the owner, Jeremiah Fines.

Nicholas had ignored the jibes and worked harder. It was true that he sought to re-pay Jeremiah for giving him the opportunity to work at the company. But soon the need to please his mentor was eclipsed by something else, a deeper desire. Working became his lifeblood, success his sustaining breath. The snickers faded into the distance as he rose through the company ranks.

But lately work had lost some of its powerful appeal. The money he made, the successes he accumulated—nothing seemed to satisfy him. As he stood looking out over the dockside world that had defined him, Nicholas did something he rarely permitted himself to do. He stopped and reflected. As he did so, a sense of emptiness began to gnaw at his gut. The feeling grew and intensified. Fragments of the past began creeping in, insidious images that pounded against his temples and dampened his palms.

Looking down, he saw the hands of a man who'd clawed his way up from the gutter. His knuckles bore the scars of countless brawls, his fingers and palms the calluses of crude labor. And that was only the surface. Beneath the thickened skin lay deeper disfigurement: the secret cuts and burn marks sustained by a boy who'd cleaned chimneys to survive. Who'd welcomed the days in soot-choked stacks because they were a bloody sight better than the nights spent cowering in fear.

Fear of the squealing hinges that heralded the opening of the master's door. Fear of the black-bearded man who emerged and blocked out all the light. Fear that Ben Grimes' small, dark eyes might land on him that night. And the trembling, paralyzing terror of that crooking finger, the whizzing of the crop, that squalid room with flea-eaten sheets, he would not go there again, he could *not*—

With a harsh breath, Nicholas slammed the door on the swirling darkness. His hands gripped the edge of the desk as his heart continued to thump like a trapped rabbit. *It's over. Grimes is dead.* He repeated the words until he could breathe again. Until he could remember who he was and what he was now. No longer a helpless boy, but a man. A tide of anguished rage broke over him. Aye, he was a man—but what kind of a man?

One who harbored a despicable secret. One whose blood was tainted, whose bestial nature dictated his destiny. His eyes shut. Bloody hell, last night he'd fornicated with a whore—and compounded his sin by pretending she was his wife. He pictured the real Helena with her shy smile and innocent eyes, and his stomach churned with self-disgust.

"Forgive me," he whispered.

"For what?"

Nicholas jerked around. It took his frozen brain a moment to recognize Paul Fines. The younger man removed his fashionable tall hat as he entered the room, his golden hair gleaming like a new guinea. As usual, Paul wore impeccably tailored clothes, with not a wrinkle to be found on his dove-grey coat and trousers. A complicated cravat grazed his chin. His waistcoat was yellow, and a bloom of that same shade bobbed cheerfully in his buttonhole.

"I thought I would find you here, Morgan," Paul said. "Working too hard as usual. Can't be a good sign that you're conversing with yourself."

Nicholas gathered his wits behind a mocking expression. "I'm surprised to see you, Fines. It is not yet noon. I thought you fashionable fellows refused to rise during the light of day."

"Oh, I haven't risen yet," Paul responded, "for I haven't yet to bed."

Nicholas grunted. He loved Paul like a brother (albeit a younger, spoiled sibling), but he would never understand how the man could live the way he did, sleeping all day, carousing all night. He and Paul could not be more different. As Jeremiah's only son, Paul had been doted upon since birth. He lived the life of rich, middle class leisure—that is to say, he lived idly and with considerable indulgence.

Paul flicked a glance over the utilitarian room. "I see not much has changed since my last visit. More's the pity." Picking a stack of ledgers up off a chair, he deposited the papers unceremoniously upon the threadbare carpet. He shuddered when a puff of dust rose in reply. "Good God, man, now that you're the Marquess of such and such, shouldn't your office befit your title? Where are the velvet pillows with the embroidered crests? The gilded cherubs? The droves of footmen bearing champagne?"

"It is the footmen's year off." Nicholas went to the washstand. The icy splash of water felt good, purifying, and returned him fully to the present. Feeling the rough growth of his morning beard, he reached for shaving implements. "Unlike you, I have obligations in life and greater concerns than the decoration of my office."

Paul's expression turned knowing. "Ah, the obligations of a newlywed."

The iniquities he'd performed with the harlot assailed Nicholas, spilled acid over his insides. *All you've done is prove that you're not good enough for Helena—that you never were.* Looking into the cracked mirror above the washstand, he forced himself to continue shaving.

"That is not what I meant." He cut through the soap in quick, economic strokes. "I have simply been busy. We had a large shipment in yesterday."

Paul withdrew a large handkerchief and placed it carefully upon the chair before seating himself. "Shouldn't you have your valet doing that for you? You might cut a vein, and you know how I abhor the sight of blood."

"If you're afraid of bloodshed, I take it you wouldn't care to join me in the ring?" Nicholas raised a brow in challenge. To his mind, there was no better way to blow off steam than with his fists. He'd had a boxing ring custom built in the adjoining antechamber

—the one luxury he'd allowed himself since taking the reins of Fines and Co. "How about going a round or two, eh?"

"Good God, Morgan, at this uncivilized hour?" Paul rolled his eyes. "I have a better idea. I am headed to Long Meg's, and you shall join me."

Sighing, Nicholas wiped off his jaw. He finished dressing with the efficiency of a man who'd seen to his own needs for most his life. As he was already behind schedule, it was on his tongue to refuse Paul's invitation, but his stomach growled. "A cup of coffee wouldn't hurt, I suppose."

"Excellent. No one brews the stuff like Long Meg." Paul eyed Nicholas' completed ensemble with something akin to horror. "Do tell me you are not prepared to leave the room dressed like that."

"We do not all aspire to be dandies," Nicholas said, scowling. "Some of us have more pressing matters to attend to than the style of our cravat. Like the running of a business, for example."

Since this was a running source of banter between them, Paul merely shrugged at Nicholas' pointed words. "My father, bless his soul, understood that his only son and heir never had a head for business. Which is why, after his death, he entrusted the daily operations of Fines and Company to you, his ever industrious partner."

Nicholas shook his head. "I told Jeremiah it should be you running the company, not me."

"What difference does it make when I receive half the profits? You know I've never held a grudge against you for all your canny mercantile ways," Paul said. "If it hadn't been for your timely appearance in our lives, Father might have forced me to put in a hard day's work. Then where would I be?"

Nicholas shot Paul a look of exasperated affection. "Doing something useful, one would hope."

"Please." Paul shuddered visibly as he rose. "Do not mix the word *useful* and I in the same sentence. We have a constitutional aversion to one another. Rather like water and oil."

They descended two flights to the main floor. Nicholas did a quick survey of the cavernous warehouse. Stacks of wooden crates and barrels stood neat as hedgerows, while a mountain of sugar sacks leaned against one wall. All appeared as usual, save for the group of men huddled by the spice containers. When they saw him, the men stopped talking, their expressions mulish. He was about to issue a sharp reprimand to return to work when Jibotts, his trusted office steward, hurried over.

"Good morning, Mr. Fines. Lord Harteford, I did not see you come in this morning." Behind his spectacles, Jibotts' faded blue eyes had a pinched, tense look. "I was here by six o' clock. When did you arrive?"

Aware of Paul's interested gaze, Nicholas cleared his throat. "Slightly before that. I heard the commotion. Apprise me of the situation."

"It was one of the rum barrels, my lord," Jibotts said. "Jim Buckley, he slipped on account of his bad back, and the weight became too much for the other two. I've had the spillage cleared."

"How is Jim?"

"I sent him home to bed rest. He wished to convey his apologies to you personally." Jibotts paused. "He was quite concerned that his wages would be garnished."

"For having a bad back?" Nicholas asked.

It was a rhetorical question as he knew intimately what the life of the laboring class was like. He had begun his career on the docks just as Jim Buckley had. If Jeremiah hadn't taken a chance on him, he might be there still, hefting the immeasurable weight of poverty upon his shoulders. At least this explained the mutiny before him. Nicholas could feel the daggered looks of the workers as they listened to every word.

A stocky, bearded man, clearly the leader of the group, spoke up. "Jim 'as 'im a wife and eight young 'uns countin' on 'im. A man breaks 'is back but 'tisn't enough fer your *lordship*—now you want to rip the bread out o' the mouths o' women an' children.

Pox on this place, I says!" He spat, the action inciting angry murmurs from the others.

Nicholas turned to face him. "Your name?"

"Isaac Bragg," the man said. His barrel chest puffed like a peacock's, and his small dark eyes gleamed with insolence.

"Mr. Bragg, what position do you occupy in this company?" Nicholas asked sharply.

"I'm a porter," Bragg said, with a swagger true to his name. "An' you can fire me. Always work fer the likes of me—Milligan's 'iring a block away wif wages that a man can live on. Isn't that right, boys?"

Muttered assent rose from behind him.

Nicholas silenced the group with a look. "As an owner of Fines and Company, let me make myself very clear. We have not in the past, nor shall we in the future, punish workers for sustaining injuries in the line of work. Any man who says differently will answer to me."

"'Tis exactly as his lordship says," Jibotts said in brisk tones. The steward scanned the small group of workers, his eyes settling on a thin, red-haired man in the back. "You there, James Gordon. What happened when you broke your arm several months back?"

Gordon shifted on his feet, leaning heavily on a wooden crutch. His words could barely be heard as they were aimed at the ground. "The Master gave me my wages while I recovered."

"What else?" Jibotts asked.

"Dr. Farraday came to see me," Gordon admitted, with a cautious look at Bragg. "He weren't no quack either. He helped me, tied my arm up real good. Gave me a new crutch, too, on account o' the old one not fittin' me proper no more."

There were shrugs, uncomfortable looks among the men.

"Get back to work, then," Nicholas said. He leveled a glance at Bragg, who glared but said nothing. "I expect any man with a problem to speak directly to me."

The workers scattered like marbles. Once they were out of

earshot, Nicholas turned to Jibotts with a frown. "Tell me about Bragg. I don't recognize him."

"He's a new porter, sir. Joined a few months back. Has a mouth and a temper, but he follows his time and does his work."

"Keep an eye on him." Something about Bragg's belligerent stance did not sit right in Nicholas' gut. "And have Farraday attend to Jim Buckley."

"Yes, of course, my lord," Jibotts said, mopping his brow with a yellowed handkerchief.

"In the meantime, his lordship and I are heading out for breakfast," Paul intervened. "He shall not be back until after eleven."

"I will be back by ten, Jibotts," Nicholas corrected, "and I will expect to review the shipping reports with you at that time."

They walked the short distance to the coffee house, making their way down a street crammed with taverns, street vendors, and the swearing, jostling men of the docks. Eschewing the outdoor tables where the prostitutes tended to ply their trade, the two entered the indoor premises of Long Meg's. The savory aromas of browning butter and grilled meat greeted them as they claimed the remaining table. The small room was packed with customers—merchants and dockmen, mostly—conversing in earnest tones over generous platters of food. The interior was drab, but clean, like the apron-clad woman approaching the table.

"Nicholas Morgan, I han't seen you in a dog's age," Meg said. True to her name, her frizzled grey hair nearly touched the low ceiling. Her face resembled an apple left too long in the sun. "Thought maybe you forgot ol' Meg now that you's 'is 'ighness."

"Morgan's not royalty, yet." Paul gave her a wink. Nicholas scowled and turned his attention to the menu on the wall. "Just a mere marquess."

"Ooo, a marquess is it?" Meg cackled. "When are you going to sweep me off my feet then an' carry me out o' this 'ere dump?"

"Eh, you can leave 'ere anytime you want!" Bumpy Tim, Meg's husband, poked his pock-marked face out from the kitchen. His comment elicited boisterous laughter from the customers.

"'Oo asked you, ya gotch-gutted bastard?" Meg shouted back. "Mind the eggs afore I come an' mind you!"

When Bumpy Tim's head retreated like a turtle's, Meg leveled a gap-toothed grin at Paul and Nicholas. "What will it be then, boys?"

"Two ploughman's," Nicholas said. "And coffee, please."

As Meg strode away, Paul aimed an amused look at Nicholas. "I believe your title discomforts you, my lord."

"Bloody right it does." Nicholas ran a hand through his rumpled hair. "You try being a lowly merchant in the *ton* and a blasted marquess in the stews. See how you like it."

"I don't have to try it. I know I shouldn't like it at all." Paul waited for Meg to deposit the cups of steaming brew. "How tiresome it must be to straddle two worlds when one would suffice."

"What do you mean by that?"

"Tell me, why do you persist in mercantile labors when there's no longer a need?"

"No need?" Nicholas felt a surge of irritation as he watched Paul stir liberal amounts of sugar and cream into his coffee, as if the other man had not a care in the world. "Easy enough for you to say, when you haven't put in a day's work—"

"Well, this is not about me, is it?" Paul replied. "This is about you. When your father saw fit to declare your legitimacy in his will, you inherited a fortune along with the title. You hardly need the income from Fines and Co.—which, by the way, we both know Jibotts would take to running like a pig to mud. There is no need for you to oversee the daily operations, yet you find every excuse to bury yourself down at the docks. Why is that?"

"You have no idea what it takes to run Fines and Co.,"

Nicholas snapped. "Your father put his life's blood into that company. He made something out of nothing. I will not fail him."

"You may paint my father a saint, but the man spent his life chained to the company, to the detriment of everything else in his life. You do not have to make the same choice."

"Jeremiah worked so that you might have the luxuries you take for granted," Nicholas said acidly.

"Father worked because he did not know what else to do." Though he said the words lightly, Paul's characteristically jovial blue eyes were shadowed over the rim of his cup. "Because he could not stop himself, even when he knew my mother waited until the candles gutted out for him to come home."

As Meg returned and plunked down plates heaped high with eggs, bacon, and thick buttered toast, Nicholas mulled over Paul's words. He had not viewed his mentor in this light before. To him, Jeremiah had defined purpose and determination. A man who worked hard to make his life amount to something. A man who could escape his past by the grace of his own sweat. Yet, remembering his own moments of restlessness, Nicholas experienced a spark of unease. Was he following in the footsteps of folly?

He shook his head. "Anna and Jeremiah had a fine marriage."

"My parents loved each other, yes, each in their own fashion. When my father was home, my mother lit up like a candle." Paul's smile was edged with melancholy as he cut into a rasher of bacon. "It was the other times she'd be weeping, alone in her bedchamber where she thought no one could hear."

The image made Nicholas' chest constrict. Anna Fines was the closest to a mother that he'd known. She'd always made a point of inviting him to supper, knowing he had no place else to go. He felt a twinge of guilt now; he'd been so tied up in his own affairs that he had not called upon her since his wedding. "How is Anna faring?"

"She's not been the same since Father passed a year ago, as you know. But she is carrying on. My sister Percy is a great comfort to her, of course. Unlike her one and only son." Paul chewed thoughtfully. "Mother tells me I am in danger of becoming a wastrel."

"In *danger* of becoming one?" Nicholas asked, quirking a brow.

"Amusing, is it not? She says I should talk to you. So you can beat some sense into me, I suppose. In truth, I think she would like a call from you and your lady ..." Paul stopped, a tinge of red appearing along his cheekbones. "Scratch that last part."

"Worried I'm going to pummel you into a responsible sort?"

"No, not that part." Under his breath, Paul added, "As *if* you could pummel me."

"Which then?"

"The bit about you and your lady calling. Forget I mentioned it, or Mother will have my head."

"Why would Anna fault you for inviting us over?" When Paul did not immediately respond, Nicholas jested, "Is she afraid your table manners will scare away the fine company?"

His smile faded at Paul's silence.

"She's not afraid of having *you*, of course," Paul said with obvious discomfort. "You may be a marquess now, but you'll always be a nodcock to us."

Nicholas ignored the attempt at light-heartedness. "It's Helena, then. Anna objects to her presence."

"Yes, but not in the way you mean," Paul protested. "From her brief meeting with Lady Helena, Mother liked your wife very much."

Nicholas relaxed a fraction. "What is it, then?"

"Mother has never entertained a member of the upper class before." Paul shrugged. "She finds the prospect somewhat intimidating."

Nicholas ate his eggs and brooded on his friend's admission. It pained him that Anna would think such a thing. Yet, if he was honest, did he not harbor similar concerns about how well Helena would get along in his world? She was no aristocratic snob, to be sure, but her blood lines stretched long and blue. She had been gently reared, her innocence sheltered. Her sphere was that of the finest drawing rooms. It was where she belonged.

"Tell Anna I will call soon," Nicholas said. "She need not concern herself about rarefied company."

"I did not mean …" Paul winced. "That is to say, I am sure your wife is most welcome."

"I will come alone."

"Dammit, Nicholas, that is the problem. You are too much alone. Everyone thinks so: Mother, Percy, and myself included. Ever since you came into the title and married—"

"No one can be faulted for that decision but me. I sleep in a bed of my own making," Nicholas said.

"And a pleasant bed it should be." Paul cleared his throat. "Which begs the question of why you would choose to sleep in a warehouse rather than in the sumptuous splendor of your marital bower."

Damn Fines' nosy nature.

"That is none of your business," Nicholas said in a warning tone.

"I have never aspired to much, but I do pride myself an expert on the fairer sex. If you are experiencing any, er, difficulties, I daresay I can help," Paul said, with no pretensions to modesty.

Which he didn't need, because everyone knew of Paul's reputation with the ladies, the term however loosely applied. The man could charm the scales off a snake—and the skirts off many a female, from the greengrocer's daughter to the bored solicitor's wife. Paul's affairs never lasted long, but he did seem to possess, through experience, an intimate knowledge of the female psyche.

"I lend you my ears, in all their tainted glory," Paul offered.

For an instant, Nicholas considered sharing his marital woes. But the shame of his actions last evening and on his wedding night kept him imprisoned in silence. He was a beast, a bastard through and through, and there wasn't a thing anyone could do about it.

He took one last gulp of coffee, grimly relishing its bitterness. Standing, he deposited a handful of coins on the table. "I have to get back to work," he said.

Nicholas strode into his office. He'd had enough of the soul-searching and belly-aching; he intended to bury himself in work. Seeing the new stack of paper on his desk, he headed over with eager steps. Excellent, the shipping report. As he reached for the top page, he felt the blood suddenly drain from his head. An icy hand clamped around his heart. With shaking fingers, he lifted the scrap of parchment lying atop the report.

There was no salutation, no signature, nothing but six words written in neat, black ink:

I know your dirty little secret.

Chapter Five

The following afternoon, Helena followed Marianne into a dress shop situated on fashionable Bond Street. A tiny silver bell tinkled overhead as they entered, and an assistant dressed all in black came to greet them. As Helena looked around the front salon, she noted that all the furnishings were done in tones of white and gold, and the plush carpet was of the palest blue. A bow window filtered afternoon sunlight into the shop, bathing everything in a mellow glow. It gave one the impression of stepping into a chamber above the clouds.

The assistant seated them in delicate gilt chairs and brought tea in paper-thin porcelain cups. With an eye on the spotless upholstery, Helena gingerly sipped her beverage. Moments later, Madame Rousseau emerged. The modiste looked as Helena feared she would; small, dark-haired, and relentlessly thin, the Frenchwoman had snapping black eyes which missed nothing.

"Lady Draven, what a pleasure it is, as always," Madame Rousseau said in softly-accented English. "And today you bring a friend. I am honored to welcome you to my humble salon."

"Lady Helena Harteford, may I introduce Amelie Rousseau?

Madame Rousseau is the *artiste* behind my fine feathers," Marianne said.

"Beauty such as Lady Draven's requires little art," Madame Rousseau murmured. "Merely the wisdom to allow Nature to shine through. As expected, the daffodil silk most becomes you, my lady."

Marianne inclined her head gracefully at the compliment, her fingers brushing lovingly over the intricate gold-thread embroidery on her skirts.

"May I suggest, however, a very small adjustment to your ensemble?"

So saying, Madame Rousseau spoke in rapid French to her assistant. The latter scurried out of the room and returned shortly to press something into her employer's hand.

The modiste motioned Marianne toward a cheval glass. "If I may?"

Reaching for Marianne's nape, the modiste unclasped the chandelier necklace of amber and gold. In its stead, she tied a simple ribbon of aquamarine satin.

"*Maintenant, c'est parfait,*" Madame Rousseau said.

Helena's breath caught at the change. Earlier, she had admired Marianne's necklace, remarking upon how perfectly the dripping mass of golden jewels matched the yellow silk. Madame Rousseau's action, however, aimed for an entirely opposite effect. Helena could see now that harmony had dulled rather than elevated her friend's charms. The new contrast of blue to yellow, of plain to intricate, suggested a mystery—a hidden vulnerability, perhaps, beneath all the glittering sophistication. Marianne appeared more enticing than ever.

Watching her friend preen in front of the mirror, Helena felt twin stabs of desperation and hope.

"Madame Rousseau, do you think you can help me?" she blurted.

The other two women turned to look at her.

Helena flushed. "I am no beauty like Marianne. But I would be most appreciative of anything you could do to help me."

"What she means to say is that she needs a wardrobe to seduce a man," Marianne said *sotto voce*.

"Ah, no need to say more. *Je comprends tout.*" Madame Rousseau's eyes gleamed. "For this, we must retire to a private salon. Follow me, please."

The modiste led them into one of the dressing rooms at the back of the shop.

"Please." Madame Rousseau gestured for Helena to step onto a small wooden platform surrounded by mirrors on three sides.

Helena took a deep breath and did as the dressmaker asked. Once upon the little stand, she kept her gaze trained on her slippers.

"*Oui*, I see the problem," Madame said, after several long minutes.

Helena felt her heart thudding. "Yes, Madame Rousseau?"

"You hide too much of yourself."

At that, Helena raised her eyes to the mirror and met the modiste's penetrating black gaze.

"I said the same thing," Marianne chimed in.

"To lure a lover into an intrigue, one must, as the English put it, *set the bait*." Madame Rousseau circled Helena as she spoke, her eyes darting like curious fish. With clever hands, she took measure of assets and weaknesses, muttering to herself all the while. Helena blushed when Madame Rousseau's touch smoothed over her breasts and hips and dipped lower to cup her bottom.

"'Tis not a lover she hopes to seduce, but her husband," Marianne said.

"Your husband!" Madame Rousseau stopped circling. "Lady Harteford, I see that you are a woman of many surprises. *Alors*, you must tell me all as I work my magic."

Sometime later, Helena found herself sitting opposite Marianne in the latter's smart barouche. With a contented sigh, she sank back against the lavender velvet squabs. Madame Rousseau had lived up to her reputation as the finest modiste in all of London. If these gowns did not entice Nicholas, nothing would. Madame had even agreed to rush the order so that Helena could have the first of her new dresses within the week.

"Do you think Harteford will like my new gowns, Marianne?"

"I should hope so, given the exorbitant sum he paid for them," Marianne said.

Helena's brow furrowed. "Do you think I was too extravagant? I have never opened an account before, but Madame Rousseau said that is how all the ladies handle their transactions. Perhaps I ought to have adhered to the allowance I have on hand."

"Do stop fretting. If Harteford can afford fifty pounds for a whore, he can certainly provide his wife *carte blanche*."

Helena grimaced. Marianne was never one to mince words.

The barouche turned onto Upper Brook Street and rolled to a stop in front of the townhouse. On impulse, Helena threw her arms around her friend. "Oh, Marianne, however am I to thank you?"

"Dearest, your happiness is thanks enough," the other said in amused tones, even as she extricated herself from the hug. "Besides, I am not finished with you yet."

"What do you mean?"

"Today was mere window dressing. Surely you do not think a few dresses will be enough to win your husband's interest."

Helena bit her lip. She had hoped ... she chided herself for being naive. "What else do you suggest, Marianne?"

"You will have to learn the secrets of flirtation, of course. And I think you could brush up on your knowledge of the sexual arts,"

Marianne said matter-of-factly. "I know just the place for you to learn both. The proprietress throws parties of such depravity that even *I* blush—"

"Oh, no! I c-couldn't," Helena stammered. "I mean, I could never go back to such a place."

Her friend gave her a long look. "Why ever not?"

Because I am not a harlot, I'm not. The thought of engaging in further wicked escapades made her heart race. With a nervous little laugh, she said, "I am done with that, Marianne. That night at the Nunnery was an exception. I was not my usual self—I did it only out of desperation. From here on in, I shall try to win my husband's affections with more, er, conventional means."

"You are certain of that?"

Helena gave an emphatic nod.

"Have it your way, then." Marianne sounded indifferent. "Good luck with Harteford. And send me a note if you have need of anything."

Before Helena could say anything more, Marianne summoned the footman with a rap on the door. The servant appeared instantly, and Helena found herself being helped to the ground. She turned around to reiterate her thanks, but the door was already closed. Within seconds, the silver barouche glided away.

Sighing, she entered the townhouse. She returned Crikstaff's greeting and inquired if Lord Harteford was at home. She did not let disappointment weigh her down when the butler replied that the master was not, nor had he left a message about his plans or whereabouts. Truly, she was not prepared to see Nicholas; how would she react to him, knowing what had transpired between them?

More to the point, how was she to go about seducing an unwitting, perhaps even *unwilling* bridegroom? As Helena ascended the staircase to her dressing room, worry began to fray the edge of hope. The beautiful clothes would help, of course. But that still left a great deal unaccounted for. Perhaps she should not have rejected Marianne's suggestion out of hand ... she shivered. She could not risk exposing herself to such licentiousness again. Look at what had happened the last time. How immodestly she'd acted. No, the way to win her husband's heart was to entice him ... with her *wifely* skills.

Gnawing on her lip, Helena entered her chambers. Bessie, her lady's maid, stopped in the task of tying a ribbon on a straw bonnet to bob a curtsy. Helena nodded absent-mindedly and settled down at the secretaire by the window. Pushing aside the stack of Shakespeare's plays she'd recently purchased, she placed a sheet of parchment on the polished walnut burl and picked up her quill.

Nibbling on the tip of the feather, she considered the task at hand. Really, planning a seduction was little different than planning anything else, was it not? And she was an excellent planner. After the death of her brother, her mother had entertained very little; by default, Helena had been left in charge of organizing any occasions that merited celebration. Thinking of her preparations for her father's fiftieth birthday festivities, Helena scribbled a list.

Feeling better already, she contemplated the categories one by one. The first was the guest list. Well, that was obvious enough, wasn't it? She jotted in *Nicholas and Helena*. The sight of her name linked with her husband's drew a wistful smile. The next item on the list: locale. Given that Nicholas was hardly likely to barge into her bedchamber (or her, his), the site of the seduction would have to begin elsewhere, in a more public arena. Well, why not combine refreshments with location, and start with an intimate dinner for two?

Inspired, Helena hurried past a startled-looking Bessie and down the staircase. She headed to the drawing room first, deciding that a pre-prandial drink might prove an elegant touch. She knew her husband preferred whiskey over sherry; she would be sure to have the finest single malt served in a crystal glass. As she surveyed the well-appointed space, imagining the addition of candles and pink-hued flowers to flare the romantic spirit, she could not help but feel a touch of satisfaction. She may have disappointed Nicholas in the way of marital relations, but in other ways she had assumed her wifely duties in a most proficient manner.

Before their marriage, Nicholas had paid little mind to the running of his household—he had simply continued with the archaic system instituted by the former marquess. When Helena had crossed the proverbial threshold of her new home for the first time, she had been secretly horrified at the dusty rooms and aged furnishings. Bits of the plaster moldings had routinely crumbled onto the stained carpets (and, if one was not careful, onto one's coiffure). The servants had slouched around in uniforms tattered at the edges; more significantly, she'd later learned, the wages of the house staff had not been increased for several years.

Helena had spent much of her time as a new bride attending to the domestic chaos. She was rather proud of the results. As she looked about the clean and airy room, she noted with satisfaction that the surfaces shone with polish and the Aubusson rug had been restored to a silky luster. With the substantial increase in their earnings, the staff had showed a renewed vigor and commitment to their duties. They beamed as brightly as the golden buttons on their new livery.

Smiling wistfully, Helena pictured Nicholas and her sitting by the fire on the new maize damask loveseat. After a day of work, he would appreciate the fine whiskey and witty conversation she would supply him with. Perhaps she would arrange for some hors d'oeuvres as well. She recalled that Nicholas had seemed partial to the watercress sandwiches her mother served at tea and decided to add those to the list of preparations. She was about to ring for the housekeeper to discuss the dinner menu when she heard the front door open and close. Crikstaff's somber tones could be heard, followed by a deeper, commanding voice.

Every fiber of her being sparked with recognition. And, truth be told, a panicky sort of anticipation.

Nicholas was home.

Helena heard the footsteps approaching the drawing room. She flung herself onto the loveseat and frantically arranged her skirts, striving for a casual yet attractive pose. Dash it all, how would Marianne sit? She tried crossing her ankles. No, too prim. She uncrossed them and propped her elbow against the armrest instead, thrusting her bosom forward. The steps grew closer and closer. Her lips froze in a welcoming smile as the breath raced in and out of her lungs. The steps were pausing now, outside the door ... and then they continued past. It took a moment for her numbed mind to recognize what was happening.

Nicholas was walking away. He was leaving. Again.

Instinct took over. Somehow, she was at the door, flinging it open, her voice shaping his name. She cringed at the shrill, desperate tone that escaped her. She sounded less like a siren bent on seduction on more like a Billingsgate fishwife.

"Harteford," she managed more calmly over the thudding in her ears. "Y-you are home."

Nicholas turned on the stairwell landing. Lord, but the sight of him made her knees weak. He wore unembellished black, and the austerity of his clothes emphasized the brawny musculature beneath. Her breath quickened at the memory of that hard, sinewy body moving against her own. His hooded eyes had flared with passion as he pushed himself deep inside her. Trembling, she noticed that a tuft of black hair stood out a little above his ear, the after-effects of removing his hat no doubt. How she longed to smooth it straight, to ease the crease between his brows with her fingers, to draw him closer ...

Her hands clenched against her skirts.

Nicholas' dark inscrutable eyes traveled slowly over her. There was no lover-like glow in his gaze. His mouth formed a tight line. Flushing, Helena realized that she had not yet changed her clothes since her outing with Marianne. There were dirt stains on her hem, and her hair ... her eyes widened. Good heavens, *her hair*. She had not even glanced at her coiffure since removing her bonnet, so enthralled had she been by her clever plan to seduce her husband. Now, she could almost feel the wayward wisps frizzing about her face as Nicholas took impassive stock of her—his frumpy wife, with the hair of a banshee.

She retreated a step as Nicholas descended the stairs. He stopped in front of her and bowed. Politely, as if to a stranger. There was a stiff quality to his posture and his expression, as if he was not pleased that she had detained him. Well, who would want to be hindered by an unattractive shrew of a wife, Helena thought, fighting back mortified tears. Here was her opportunity—and she was ruining everything. Numbly, she led him into the drawing room.

"Good afternoon," Nicholas said. "I trust everything is well?"

"Quite well," Helena said.

Except that I feel like throwing myself down the nearest well.

She realized then that Nicholas was still standing because she had forgotten to sit down. Hastily, she plopped down on the nearest chair. So much for a winsome pose. The flush on her cheek began to burn. "H-how have you been? I have not seen much of you these days past." The moment she said the words, she wished she could retract them. 'Twas as if she'd lost control over her voice—she'd not intended the words to sound accusatory.

A look of distaste crossed Nicholas' features as he folded his large frame into an adjacent chair. "I have been occupied of late."

"Of course," she said quickly.

If there is not a well nearby, a ditch will do.

"Is there something I can assist you with?" Nicholas was studying the fireplace, not quite meeting her eyes. Who could blame him? Her mind raced to find an acceptable excuse for having solicited his attention.

"Th-the Dewitt musicale," she stammered. "It is on Saturday. I wanted to remind you that we are promised to attend."

Nicholas knitted his brows. "I do not recall accepting the invitation."

"Lady Dewitt is my mother's cousin, if you'll recall."

"Actually, I do not recall," he said.

There was something about his tone that had her chin lifting. "She sat to the right of my mother at our wedding breakfast. She invited us at that time to her annual musicale, and I promised her we would both come."

At the time, it had seemed a trifling matter to do so. But, of course, that had been *before* their wedding night—and before the polite amicability that had settled over them like a pall.

"I wish you had consulted me first," Nicholas said, frowning.

Before her lord had decided to avoid her bed and her company.

"I may have a prior commitment," he continued.

Before he had decided to bed a whore.

A wave of emotions crashed over Helena. Everything she had experienced in the past two days swelled in her chest. She could hardly catch her breath, and her limbs were shaking.

With ... anger.

"I believe I reminded you of it last week," she said sharply. "Or at least, I left a message with Crikstaff to do so since you have so often been out."

"You have already remarked upon my absence." Nicholas' tone matched hers. "Though it surprises me that you would notice, given your busy social schedule."

Helena's teeth clicked together. "I have been *busy* refurbishing your home, my lord. Or perhaps that has escaped your attention?"

Nicholas flicked a glance around him.

"It looks fine," he said.

Fine. Helena felt like flinging one of the Chinese vases she had carefully arranged on the mantelpiece.

"I am glad you think so," she replied acidly.

"Hmm," Nicholas said, drumming his fingers on the armrest.

Better yet, she could smash the priceless porcelain over his head.

"Is there anything else you require?" her husband was asking.

"You will attend the musicale, then?" It was unlike her to be so persistent. She did not know why she was pressing the issue, other than his obvious reluctance to oblige her. "My parents will be in attendance as well. I am sure they would like to see you."

Nicholas looked disgruntled and not particularly happy at the prospect of seeing his in-laws. "I suppose I can fit it in."

"You are too kind, my lord," she said in cool tones.

Nicholas cleared his throat in the silence that followed.

"Well, if there is nothing else ..." he began.

"No, there is not."

"I will take my leave, then."

"Of course. I will detain you no further," she said, rising.

He bowed again. In a few powerful strides, he exited the drawing room. A few moments later, she heard the door to his bedchamber opening and closing on the floor above. With a stiff gait, she walked back to the loveseat, sat, and stared into the space recently vacated by her husband. What in heaven's name had transpired just now? She had planned to seduce him, and instead she had managed to make matters worse.

Not that Nicholas had helped. In fact, she thought in a daze of bewilderment and anger, he had not helped one bit.

How dare he belittle her decorating skills?

How dare he refuse her infinitesimally small request to attend the Dewitts' party?

How *dare* he look at her so dispassionately, when but two nights ago he had growled with ecstasy in her arms?

After a while, she wiped her eyes on her sleeve and noticed her list lying on the ground. She picked it up and smoothed out the wrinkles. Well, she had certainly bungled the first three categories of seduction. Guests? After this, Nicholas would prove a reluctant participant at best. Location? Obviously, he was not overly impressed by her attempts to create a domestic paradise. And refreshments? She sniffled. She was willing to wager he had lost all appetite after their encounter. As had she.

The last item wavered in front of her eyes.

Entertainments.

She closed her eyes wearily. And prayed Marianne would have some advice for that.

Chapter Six

The next morning, Nicholas instructed the driver to drop him off several blocks away from the warehouse. He wanted a walk to clear his head. Cloaked in a gloomy yellow fog, the docklands at daybreak perfectly suited his mood. He made his way along the narrow street lined by cramped buildings, absorbing the ungoverned energy of those who pushed by him. The sounds of fog horns and sea gulls echoed through the mist. Nicholas inhaled, the salt and tar-tinged air loosening and expanding his chest. Leaving Mayfair was like shedding a confining jacket. Here by the river, he was back where he belonged.

He stopped at a cart to purchase a bun from a gap-toothed woman and turned left toward the quay. Once there, he leaned against a wooden post and looked over the mist-covered water. The fog blanketed the lighters, but he could feel the looming presence of the ships. Ghost-like, the wooden hulls bumped hollowly against the wharf. It was a forlorn sound. If it were not for the shouts of the river men—the colliers and sailors—one might suspect some sort of other-worldly enterprise, rather than one that was purely human.

Nicholas took a bite of the pastry and winced. It had the

density of a boulder. Indeed, the bun may have rivaled prehistoric rock in the length of its existence. Chewing moodily, he reflected on the sumptuous breakfast that would have greeted him at home. Since Helena's arrival, the quality of the fare served on his table had improved dramatically. Nowadays, coddled eggs, grilled kidney, and well-seasoned potatoes greeted him in the morning. On some days, there were cornmeal cakes, tender rounds brushed with a buttered rum sauce and dotted with currants. A feast fit for a king—but apparently not for the likes of him.

Because *he* had chosen to skulk like a thief from his own house at the break of dawn. Without waking his valet. Without eating a majestic breakfast.

Without running into his wife.

Nicholas tossed the bun aside. It bounced along the wooden planks, attracting a swarm of squawking gulls. He felt like a bloody jackanapes for avoiding his own wife. But for Helena's sake, he had to stay away. To spare her from his bestial needs ... and God knew what else was lying in wait for him.

I know your dirty little secret.

As he had so many times since finding the note, he told himself that in all likelihood it was merely a prank: an act of spite by some disgruntled worker. That fellow Bragg came readily enough to mind. The note's message was vague, after all, so that any recipient with a guilty conscience would feel spooked and brought down a notch or two. That was likely the full intent of it. A deed of harmless malice—one with no teeth.

But what if it was not just a hoax?

What if someone actually knew who he'd been ... and what he'd done?

Panic rippled over his heart as he contemplated the water with bleak eyes. He couldn't risk the taint of his past touching Helena. For now, it was best to distance himself from her. He'd done a fair job of that, until yesterday. Having run out of clean shirts, he'd had to return to the townhouse. He'd thought to make a discreet entry and exit, only his wife had stepped out of the drawing room at precisely the wrong moment.

Her voice had called to him, the sweetest of snares. He'd been caught, red-handed as a poacher, with no choice but to face her. To gaze upon her innocent, smiling face, her eyes warm as a golden wheat field and her hair wild and loose as if she'd recently tumbled in one. Instantly, he'd been gripped by competing torrents of desire and guilt. Aye, it had nigh suffocated him, robbed him of mind and breath to even converse with her.

So he'd stood there like a bloody fool.

Wanting her.

Hating himself.

What had transpired next bewildered him even further.

They had actually *quarreled*. Or something perilously close to that. Though there had been no harsh words or raised voices, the tension in the room had been as thick as the fog that presently surrounded him. And over what? A bloody party, for Christ's sake. Helena had never cared before whether or not he accompanied her on the torturous rounds of the Season—why did she care now, and so vehemently? At the mention of the musicale, his heretofore gentle, sweet-tempered wife had suddenly vanished, to be replaced by a goddess whose ire blazed brighter than the sun.

Did she like musicales so much then?

The spark in her eyes as she'd done battle with him—he'd never seen such spirit in her before. In fact, she had seemed like another person altogether. In all the time he had known Helena, she had never asked anything of him. Always, she had been accommodating, acquiescent, the epitome of womanly virtue.

What the hell had happened to his demure wife?

It was bloody confusing.

And more than a little arousing.

Nicholas rubbed his forehead, damp from the misty air. Damn his lustful appetites to hell and back. The truth was a good fight always stirred his juices. It had been a fortunate thing that he'd made his exit quickly, graceless as it was. A minute more and he might have done something to truly regret. It was just another reminder of the differences between the two of them: his wife had engaged him in a genteel disagreement, while he'd had the urge to solve the problem in a much more primitive manner. By quelling her words with his mouth. And other parts of his anatomy.

Apparently even bedding the whore had not assuaged his desire to fuck his wife. Seeing the fire in Helena's eyes and knowing he was the cause of it, he'd been seized by a primal urge to toss her onto the floor and cram himself inside her. All the way inside, so deep that there would be no separating her flesh from his. So deep that she would be marked forever his. So deep that she would scream with pleasure, even if she remained royally pissed at him.

All this he'd wanted, tortured himself over—and his wife had just sat there, looking as fresh and ripe as a summer orchard. God, he almost resented her for it. As a result, he'd acted like a complete and utter ass. He'd deliberately belittled the considerable improvements she had brought to his home. The irony of it, he realized, was that his boorish behavior might prove the best thing for the both of them. It might serve to drive his wife away. The farther the better, for her sake.

Shoving his hands in his pockets, Nicholas trudged toward the warehouse. He had to stop ruminating or else he'd go mad. About a block away from Fines and Co., he chanced to look down one of the alleys between the buildings. He saw two figures standing there in the shadows. Their backs were turned to him and their heads huddled as they spoke. He was too far away to hear their whispered words, but there was something furtive about their postures, the way the lapels of their coats were pulled up high about their faces.

Nicholas stopped and squinted, trying to discern the identity of the figures. As if alerted to his presence, one of the men jerked his head up. Nicholas had a glimpse of small malicious eyes and black-bristled jowls before the figure turned and walked rapidly toward the opposite end of the alley. The other man followed close behind. Within seconds, they turned the corner and vanished from sight.

Nicholas continued on his way to the warehouse. On the main floor, he nodded to the greetings from the workers, his thoughts churning. What the hell was Isaac Bragg up to? For he was certain the man he had seen was the surly porter. Why was Bragg lurking like a cutthroat in the shadows, and who was the second man in the alley, the one Bragg had been conspiring with? Did any of this have to do with the note?

Nicholas had a mind to let Bragg go and be done with the business, but there was the morale of the other porters to consider. Bragg, damn his stinking hide, had a way of stirring the pot. Besides, what if the blackguard actually knew Nicholas' secret? What would he plan to do with such information—blackmail or some other such infamy? And if he knew, why hadn't he done anything yet? Frustrated, Nicholas had to admit the cleverness of the note's ambiguity: he could not question Bragg directly without giving away the fact that he had something to hide.

So lost was Nicholas in his thoughts that he all but collided with James Gordon as the younger man rounded the corner. Gordon fell backwards, his crutch clattering against the wall behind him. The sack he was carrying exploded as it landed. Coffee beans rained upon the floor. The porter rushed to gather the scattered pods but slipped again in his haste. With a sigh, Nicholas heaved up the stammering Gordon and handed him his crutch.

"Have a care, lad," Nicholas said. "You don't want to go breaking anything else now."

"S-sorry, sir," Gordon said, his face red as his hair. His blue eyes were huge with fear. "I'll clean it up right aways. I swear, I'll get every bean back in the sack and sew it up myself—"

"I'm not talking about the coffee," Nicholas said in exasperation, "but your bloody bones. I'd like to leave Dr. Farraday time occasionally to see patients other than you."

"Y-yes, sir. Th-thank you, sir."

With an impatient jerk of his chin, Nicholas sent the porter on his way. Nicholas headed up to the office and planted himself at the desk. Opening a ledger, he proceeded to study the accounts of the past week. After all of five minutes, he slammed the book shut with an oath. The single-minded focus he prided himself on was nowhere in evidence. Instead, a morass of images swirled in his head: Helena's smiling eyes turning to golden fire, the ripe bounce of the whore's breasts, ghosts of fog rising all around ...

The knock on the door nearly sent him out of his skin.

Jibotts peered in. "My lord? I was wondering if you had a moment. If not, I can come back ..."

Recovering his senses, Nicholas noticed the stiffness of the other man's wiry posture. Old Jibotts had a stick up his arse to begin with—his eye for detail, in fact, made him an exceptional office steward. Whatever the cause, the stick appeared especially large today. The thought cheered Nicholas. He could use the distraction.

"A problem?" Nicholas asked.

Frowning, Jibotts took a seat opposite the desk. The steward's back was ramrod straight, and he immediately opened the black leather notebook that accompanied him wherever he went. "I have just now been reviewing inventory. It appears we are short this week—by a negligible amount, but short nonetheless."

"By how much?"

"Two crates of tobacco, three sacks of coffee, and a barrel of rum, sir."

Nicholas snorted. This was indeed negligible. Most traders suffered hundreds of pounds a month on losses without turning a hair. As a member of the West India Merchants Association, he'd headed a task force to address the thievery that ran rampant on the river. His team's efforts had led to the funding of a private security force. Since the inception of the Thames River Police, losses had decreased to a significant degree.

Privately, Nicholas knew that theft could never fully be eradicated. Along the docks, stealing was seen as taking what was rightfully owed. No more immoral than netting a trout from a stream full of fish or taking a breath from an endless supply of air. As a lad, he'd lived by a simple philosophy of survival—*finder's keepers, loser's weepers.* There had been a time when he'd filled his belly with anything he could lay his hands on: basically, anything not locked up or nailed down. He'd prowled the market days at Covent Garden, helping himself to fruit, cheese, a meat pasty or two if it was a good day. And if a silk handkerchief or piece of silver made its way into his pockets, who was he to complain?

Never once had he concerned himself with the merchants he "borrowed" from. Why should he? They were fat pigs, the lot of them, lolling about in piles of gold.

The irony did not escape him that he now occupied the part of the swine.

"It is not the amount that concerns me but the pattern," Jibotts was saying.

Nicholas pulled himself back to the present. "What pattern?"

"In the past two months, I have noticed similar discrepancies. On three separate occasions, small items have gone missing—minor enough that it would be overlooked by most."

Nicholas felt his lips twitch. "By most, but not by you, eh Jibotts?"

The steward calmly wiped his spectacles with a handkerchief. "I do believe in keeping the house in precise order, my lord."

"You are to be commended on your precision, of course," Nicholas said. He meant it. Rare indeed was the steward who could keep track of a missing sack or two in a busy warehouse—and rarer still the one who wasn't filching the said sack himself. Jibotts was as honest as he was particular.

"Thank you, my lord. How would you like me to proceed?"

"An inside job, I presume?"

"Yes. This isn't the work of mud larks or petty thieves. The goods go missing after they arrive. There are no signs of entry, forced or otherwise."

"A porter with sticky fingers, then." Nicholas drummed his fingers on the desk. "We cannot allow that to continue. We will have to ferret him out."

"Yes, sir. Shall I contact Mr. Ambrose Kent?"

Nicholas frowned. A well-regarded member of the Thames River Police, Ambrose Kent was a man to be trusted in situations such as these. Kent had proven helpful once before, when goods had mysteriously gone missing from a guarded vessel. Kent had run surveillance on the ship and within three days captured the gang of villains involved. Unbeknownst to the guards, their coffee had been laced with a sleeping draught—they had dreamed away blissfully while the thieves made off with the cargo.

Despite Kent's considerable skills, Nicholas hesitated. Because of his history, he had no liking for Charleys, thief takers, or others who sought to enforce the law for profit. There was something about Kent that made him uneasy; likely it was the zealous, single-minded determination to see justice through. Those pale eyes seemed to miss nothing, seemed to pierce into the recesses of one's soul ...

He shuddered. God help him if Kent was to discover the crimes in his past.

"Lord Harteford?"

Nicholas shook off his fanciful imaginings. Kent had no other-worldly powers; he was just a man who did his job well. In this circumstance, competence was something to be respected, not feared. "Yes, get in touch with Kent and set up a meeting. I would like to speak with him personally. In the meantime, keep an eye on Isaac Bragg."

"My lord?"

"I saw him earlier on the docks. I haven't any proof, but my gut tells me the man is up to mischief. See that he is carefully monitored."

"Of course. I will see to it personally." Jibotts scratched into his notebook. He adjusted his spectacles and looked expectantly at Nicholas. "Is there anything else, my lord?"

Nicholas paused, picking up the paperweight on his desk. It had become a habit, hefting the smooth dome between his palms. Inside the clear glass, brightly twisted ropes of colored glass had been cut cross-wise, the effect resembling a field of tiny wildflowers frozen in time. *Millefiori*, Helena had called it, some sort of glass-making technique. He remembered her shy smile as she'd presented the weight to him at their wedding breakfast.

He heard himself saying, "There is one thing."

"Yes?" Quill poised above the notebook, Jibotts cocked his head.

"I would like your opinion on a matter."

"Of course, my lord."

"You have been married for some time, have you not?"

The steward's quill quivered. "I beg your pardon?"

"I take it there has been a Mrs. Jibotts for many years," Nicholas said impatiently.

Jibotts gave an uncertain nod.

"So you must, therefore, have some experience with the workings of the female mind."

"Oh, sir, I wouldn't say that," Jibotts protested.

"In your experience, why does a woman change her mind?"

Nicholas had never seen Jibotts flummoxed before. The man was as straight as a stick pin, always direct to the point. But now the steward was looking at him, his mouth hanging slightly open, but no words emerging.

"You have been married for some time," Nicholas repeated. "Surely there have been occasions when Mrs. Jibotts experiences a sudden change of heart, with no logical explanation whatsoever?"

It took a moment for Jibotts to recover himself. He carefully closed his notebook and put away the pen. "You are asking about my personal experience, sir? Within the matrimonial realm."

"Precisely," Nicholas said, feeling the reddening of his cheekbones. Thank God the man finally caught on. He did not know how much longer he could continue with this line of discussion. It was damned uncomfortable.

"In my twenty years of marriage, I have come to the conclusion that a woman's mind does not work like a man's," Jibotts said.

"You are hardly blowing the gaff on that one," Nicholas muttered.

"However," Jibotts continued, holding up a finger, "it is a mind to be reckoned with nonetheless. Take Mrs. Jibotts, for example. A mild-mannered lady who never raises her voice. In fact, her genteel disposition was one of the reasons why I married her."

"How fortunate for you," Nicholas said.

Jibotts shook his head, clearly warming to his subject. "Alas, one can never predict a woman's fancy. Gentle as Mrs. Jibotts may seem, when she decides upon a thing, it will be done. Last year, she took it to her head that the parlor needed redecorating. It was a perfectly fine parlor, mind you. But there was no peace to be had until she had spent twenty pounds—*twenty pounds*, by God—changing this thing and that. Now I dine amidst chartreuse brocade and oriental birds."

"Chartreuse?"

"A shade of green," Jibotts clarified glumly. "The color of a seaman's face before he casts up his accounts."

Nicholas could not think of what to say for a moment. This is what he had to look forward to—furniture the color of nausea? "Surely there must be a way to dissuade one's wife from, ah, irrational behavior."

"None whatsoever. And in matters of a domestic nature, I caution you not to try."

"There must be some remedy," Nicholas insisted, "some strategy that you have gainfully employed."

A strange expression passed over the steward's face, which suddenly turned pink. Perspiration beaded on his forehead.

"So there is something to be done," Nicholas said with some relief. "Well, spit it out, man."

Jibotts hesitated, his flush deepening. "It is not so much something to *do*, sir ..."

"Yes?"

"But more *when* not to do it. A Fabian tactic, if you will."

"What the hell is that?"

"A delaying maneuver." Jibotts' spectacles were beginning to fog. For once the steward lost his perfect posture—he was slouching low in the chair, as if he wished he could find a way to slip out of the conversation altogether. "I have found it best in my interactions with Mrs. Jibotts to avoid certain times when the *irrationality*, as you so delicately put it, is particularly evident."

"You are not making an ounce of sense," Nicholas said.

"It is prudent, shall we say, to avoid discussion altogether during certain, ahem, times?"

Nicholas furrowed his brow. "I don't understand. To what times do you refer?"

"Blimey." Jibotts expelled a sigh. "Certain times, of the ... *month*?"

All at once, the steward's meaning became clear. Nicholas felt his neck burn beneath his collar.

"I see," he said. An awkward silence followed. "Well, er, thank you for your input, Jibotts."

The other man mopped his brow. "You are welcome, my lord. If there's nothing else, I will attend to my duties."

Nicholas watched the steward's rapid retreat with some relief. At least some of Helena's behavior now made sense. Helena's momentary insanity was due to her ... womanly constitution. Why didn't he think of it himself? He frowned, realizing there was a perfectly good reason why: he had never had to deal so intimately with a female before. While he had visited women in the past—at his convenience and theirs—he had never kept a regular mistress. He preferred his affairs simple. Rarely did he stay the night, and never did he have to manage conversation over breakfast the next morning.

But now he was *living* with a woman, for Christ's sake. Though he planned to minimize his interactions with his wife, he knew he couldn't avoid her entirely. At least, not without the risk of hurting her feelings, and that was the last thing he wanted. It struck him that if he wished to have any semblance of peace in his life, he would have to establish the kind of marriage valued amongst the *ton*. One that was civil yet cool. Sophisticated and bloodless.

One that was the very opposite of what he yearned for.

It was, however, the logical solution for the time being. Logic further dictated that if Helena's volatile behavior was due to her monthly flux, then *after* the blasted time had passed, surely she would return to the demure lady he had married. His brow eased. Of course. It was but a temporary madness. Likely, she was even now feeling sorry for what she had put him through over the silly party. Poor little thing probably felt mortified over the way she had taken him to task.

Feeling somewhat better, Nicholas decided he could take the high road in this instance. He would attend the musicale at the end of week and play the dutiful husband. Perhaps if his wife wasn't feeling too indisposed because of her condition, he might solicit a dance. He had never enjoyed dancing, but he knew she did. He would make it a priority to restore their relationship to its previous state of courteous equilibrium.

He heaved a sigh. Given his shortcomings, it was the least he could do.

Chapter Seven

"Cecily has quite outdone herself this year, don't you agree Helena? She tells me the champagne fountain is quite *en vogue* in Paris this year, which is why her chef —French, you know—insisted upon it. He added crushed strawberries to color the champagne pink. Is that not the cleverest thing you have ever heard?"

Seated on a settee next to her mother, Helena nodded absent-mindedly. Guests eddied around them, chatting and laughing, enjoying the intermission between dinner and the impending musical entertainments. Her attention was on the receiving line. The butler had announced a flurry of names, not one of them Nicholas'. Where was he? Had he decided to stay away from the musicale after all? He had promised to come, but perhaps he had said so only to placate her. Perhaps he was angry at her for insisting on his presence.

She felt the tremor of a headache at her temples.

"I have always admired the design of Cecily's house. So very convenient for entertaining," her mama enthused. "Why, with all the doors folded back and the rooms flowing into one another, it is as large as one of the fields at Vauxhall!"

Helena forced a smile.

Why, oh why, had she railed at Nicholas like a termagant? Ever since the confrontation in the drawing room, she had berated herself over her most indecorous behavior. No man liked to be taken to task by his wife. Novice to marriage that she was, even she understood that. If her goal was to win her husband's heart, why had she acted in so foolish a manner?

Her fingers twisted in the fringes of her cashmere shawl. Because she had been angry, that was why. Furious as she had never been in her entire existence. As if all the failures of her life had hit her at once, and she had been *tired* of waiting for dreams that never materialized. Anger and desperation had made her reckless. Now, thanks to her rash behavior, she had made a mull of her marriage in more ways than one. Bad enough that she had seduced her husband masquerading as a harlot—now she had managed to enrage him acting as a wife.

Good heavens, could matters get any worse?

"Whatever is the matter with you tonight, Helena?"

Helena blinked. It was not her mother's habit to take notice of her state of mind. Growing up, she had daydreamed for hours while her parent chattered on (ironically, usually about the importance of etiquette). She really must compose herself if Mama perceived that something was amiss.

"Nothing is the matter," Helena said, summoning a bright smile. "I was just, er, thinking about household concerns."

"Now that you are a married lady, I hasten to remind you that *keen attention* lies at the heart of a happy marriage. However will you learn to please your husband, if your head remains forever in the clouds?"

Helena's smile deflated a little.

"Of course, Mama," she said.

The Countess of Northgate nodded, her grey velvet turban slipping over her faded brown curls. Her small hands fluttered to push the headpiece back in place as she spoke in soft, rapid tones.

"One must work very hard to please one's husband, Helena. At times, it may seem a monumental task. I, myself, have benefitted from consulting Lady Epplethistle's *Compleat Guide* from time to time. Have you reviewed it lately? There are specific guidelines summarized, I believe, beginning on page one hundred and three ..."

Helena tried to appear attentive. Once Mama started on a topic, attempts to stop her proved futile. Especially in social situations such as these, which tended to stimulate her delicate nerves. The countess had always possessed a finely balanced constitution, but since Thomas' death it seemed the smallest provocation could agitate her sensibilities.

"... keeping up with the vinegar ablutions I suggested? If not, I would fear the return of those dreaded freckles, my dear. Gracious me, I can almost imagine those pesky spots growing right there on the very tip of your nose! You mustn't allow that to happen, really you mustn't. Why, what would Harteford say ..."

Since her husband did not notice anything about her, the presence of a mere freckle was unlikely to disturb his equilibrium. But she could not tell her mother that. Not when Mama was already showing the telltale signs of aggravated nerves, from the accelerating speech to the nervous head movements. She resembled a curious sparrow, craning her neck this way and that.

With growing worry, Helena realized she had to do something before Mama succumbed to an attack. The sequence always followed the same pattern—an excess of excitement culminating in collapse and weeks in bed. As a young girl, she'd dreaded visiting her mother when the shades were drawn and the air burned with camphor. Seeing her mother pale and wane in the curtained bed had filled her with nameless panic. It had taken years for her to realize that her mother would not expire from what the physician termed a disorder of the nerves.

Still, the countess' condition had worsened in the years since Thomas' passing. The episodes came more frequently and often lasted for weeks. Once an attack took place, nothing seemed to help but bed rest and a minimum of stimulation. Mama led a reclusive life as it was, drifting from room to room on the country estate. But even amidst the rural solitude, Helena knew her mother had started adding laudanum to the milk at bedtime.

Helena felt a stab of guilt. Though she corresponded daily with her mother, she had been too caught up in her new life to return to Hampshire for a visit. How amiss she had been in her daughterly duties. And her wifely ones as well.

Dash it all, could she do *nothing* right these days?

"I shall be happy to lend you some of my whitening powder. I have it specifically concocted by the Apothecary on Piccadilly and always make a point of refreshing my supplies on my visits to London," her mother said with a trilling laugh. "Oh look, Helena, at the clever satin appliqués on Lady Marlough's gown. They are like leaves cascading to her hem! Are they not delicious?"

"Yes, Mama," Helena murmured. "Perhaps we should ..."

"I do so love London during the Season! And this is my most *favorite* event of all. I do hope dear, *dear* Caroline will give a performance. I declare, she outshines all the professional musicians Cecily hires for this occasion!"

Helena rather thought that was the point of the whole evening: to highlight her cousin Caroline's superiority. Immediately, she chastised herself for the petty thought. It was small of her to harbor childhood resentments. For reasons not entirely clear, she and Caroline had never quite rubbed along. Likely it had something to do with the fact that whenever Caroline was present Helena felt like a court jester entertaining the queen.

At any rate, Helena reminded herself, she had larger concerns to contend with—like the hurricane of air being generated by the countess' fan.

Helena placed a hand on her mother's arm. The frail muscles vibrated beneath her touch. "Mama, shall we take a stroll? Aunt Cecily has a lovely garden out in the back."

"A wonderful idea!" The countess sprang up, her slight frame emanating an agitated energy. "I shall lead the way. It has been too long since I have circulated among the *beau monde*, so many people to see, la!"

"Mama," Helena protested.

But it was too late. Her mother had taken flight into the throng. Helena had no choice but to follow as her mother darted out of the drawing room. The countess headed through the open doors into the music room, where rows of chairs had been placed facing a gleaming pianoforte. An arch of peach-colored camellias framed the stage.

"Lady Yardley! Dearest Baroness de Gagney! So delighted to see you!"

Helena flushed with embarrassment as the Countess continued to call out greetings to the occupants of the room. Despite the polite murmured replies, she saw the raised brows and secret smirks behind the champagne flutes. She could practically hear what they were thinking. *The Countess of Northgate, fit for Bedlam*. She managed to secure her mother's arm.

"Mama, we were to visit the garden," she said.

"Oh, yes, let's," the countess enthused, her brown eyes wide and child-like.

Helena began to steer the way, but was stopped by a silky voice.

"Is that you, Aunt Amelia? And Cousin Helena?"

Resplendent in peacock-blue satin, Caroline was standing but a few feet away, surrounded by a ring of suitors. The gentlemen parted as Caroline glided forward.

"My dear Caroline, but you do look stunning this evening!" Countess Northgate exclaimed.

Helena had to agree. Cut in the latest classical fashion, Caroline's gown gathered under the bosom and fell in a soft, graceful column. The delicate puff sleeves bared most of her shoulders, and the neckline was trimmed with tiny golden tassels which shimmered with each movement. Indeed, Caroline looked like a princess, with her hair in a coronet and a strand of diamonds woven into her auburn locks.

"Wh-what a lovely gown," Helena stammered, as her cousin kissed the air near her cheek. "I have never seen anything so beautiful."

"This old thing?" Caroline laughed, showing her perfectly white, even teeth. "I thought I would give it a final whirl before bestowing it upon my maid. If you admire it so, I would be happy to give it to you instead, dearest cousin."

Helena felt her ears burn. Had her compliment been too gauche? Awkwardly she added, "Oh, that is not what I meant—"

"But, then again, you do not need *my* advice when it comes to fashion. You do set a style all your own. How very original to wear velvet this Season," Caroline said, with another light laugh.

Helena felt the heat spread to her face. How she wished her new wardrobe from Madame Rousseau's had arrived in time for this evening. But it had not, so she had resigned herself to wearing one of her old dresses. The rose-colored velvet *was* heavy and rather shapeless. She had chosen it only because she thought it showed her bosom to an advantage. Compared to the other ladies in the room, however, she could see that her neckline appeared practically prudish.

The countess plunged into the awkward silence. "Are those sapphires in your necklace, Caroline? How very brilliantly they shine!"

"Why, thank you, Aunt." Caroline's gloved fingers lovingly caressed the large, sparkling stones at her bosom. "A gift from Papa. It is a lucky daughter to have so generous a father, don't you agree, Helena?"

"Yes." Her own father, as Caroline must know, had been sunk in debt these past years.

"Where is Uncle tonight? I do so long to say hello," Caroline continued.

"Northgate is here somewhere. The card room, likely," the countess responded cheerfully. "The man loves his whist."

Helena looked at her mother with incredulous eyes. Was she *mad*? Father was at the cards again, and she was smiling about it? Did her mother not realize the danger he was in? That they were all in? Something had to be done. *Immediately*.

"Excuse me," Helena said quickly, "but I have been reminded of something I need to speak with Father about."

"Of course." Caroline's smile edged into a smirk. "Such a pleasure to see you, Helena. We really should visit more often now that you are in Town, and we are moving in similar circles."

Similar, but not the same circles. Helena registered the barb, but at this point she had more pressing concerns. Like preventing her father from gambling away the family estate.

"Helena, I think I will stay and chat with Caroline," her mother was saying.

"I will take excellent care of her," Caroline said, still smirking.

Oh no. She could *not* leave her mother in the den of wolves. But what was she to do?

"Good evening, ladies," a deep voice said from behind her.

Helena turned to see Nicholas, breathtakingly masculine in his formal clothes. The cut of his dinner jacket emphasized the width of his shoulders, whilst his trousers skimmed down his narrow hips and muscular legs before tucking into gleaming Hessians. He was bowing to them. When he raised his head, she caught his eye. With an inward sigh of relief, she saw that he had evidently recovered from their row. He did not appear angry. He was not smiling, of course, for it was not his habit to do so. Yet his grey eyes were warm, his lips relaxed.

"Hello, my lord," Helena said, a tad breathlessly.

Countess Northgate beamed at her son-in-law. "Harteford, you remember Lady Caroline Dewitt, my sister's daughter, do you not?"

"Lord Harteford and I met at the wedding breakfast," Caroline said. Curtsying gracefully, she offered her hand. "But perhaps he does not remember me."

Helena frowned at the silky, purring undertone of her cousin's voice.

Nicholas bowed over Caroline's hand. "Of course I do, my lady."

Helena felt a clutching sensation in her chest. *Calm yourself. He is just being polite.* But her teeth clenched as Caroline proceeded to engage Nicholas in witty repartee, artfully batting eyelashes all the while. Caroline gave a silvery laugh, one that conveyed to the listener how interesting he was, how manly and how intelligent. And Nicholas just stood there, like a great big ... *oaf*. Likely he was as besotted by Caroline's charms as all the other men in the room.

By the time Caroline gave Nicholas a playful tap with her fan, Helena had had quite enough.

"Harteford, where were you at supper?" The question came out more bluntly than she intended, for all three heads turned to her. *Oh, well done.* Compared to Caroline's tinkling, musical laughter, she sounded more like a shrew than ever.

"Wh-What I mean to say is we missed your presence earlier," Helena said. "The turtle supper was most delicious. I am sorry you missed it."

"Thank you for your concern," Nicholas said in the silence that followed. "I am afraid I got caught up."

"Our Helena is such a mother hen, is she not?" Caroline gave that floaty laugh again, her light jade eyes gleaming. "She is forever looking after others. When we were girls, I recall Helena counting the tea cakes to make sure there were enough to go around. Remember how you kept those cakes under a watchful eye, Cousin?"

Helena's cheeks flamed.

"Helena was always partial to cream cakes," the countess agreed dreamily. "We had to tell Cook to stop preparing them for fear of Helena growing too—"

"Mama," Helena blurted, "you were interested in the garden, were you not? Perhaps Harteford would enjoy accompanying us on a stroll. I am sure Caroline must ready herself for the performance."

"Yes, we must see Cecily's famous ranunculus before the evening is done!" her mother exclaimed. "There are none others like it in all of London."

Caroline's smile was feline. "Please do enjoy yourselves. I will see you after the performance, I hope?"

The last part seemed directed at Nicholas. He bowed.

After Caroline departed, the three made their way through the milling guests to the ballroom. They exited through the open French doors into the garden. Scores of lanterns lit the spacious, well-groomed green. A large stone fountain splashed in the middle, and a gazebo rested in the furthest corner. They followed the stepping stones, stopping here and there for the countess to admire the flower specimens. As her mother raced forward to sniff a cluster of sweet peas, Helena turned to her husband.

"I take it you are enjoying yourself this evening, my lord." She bit her lip at the accusatory tone of her words. What was wrong with her this evening? Hopefully Nicholas would not notice.

"You were the one who requested my presence, as I recall," her husband replied. His eyes were fathomless in the moonlight. "Was my enjoyment of it not part of your plan?"

"Of course I want you to have a pleasurable evening." *But with me, not Caroline.* She felt flustered, desperately jealous as a matter of fact, but she could not tell her husband that. She studied a camellia hedge, the top of which had been pruned into the undulating shape of a wave. If only she knew how to flirt as Caroline did.

"Is something amiss?" Nicholas inquired.

Everything was amiss, Helena thought miserably. Her husband was flirting with Caroline. Her mother was nearing a fit of vapors.

And her father ... Sweet heavens, *her father*. Her stomach dropped to her toes. How could she have forgotten?

"Harteford, I must go," she said.

"Go? Where?"

She hesitated. She did not want to tell Nicholas the truth. In all honesty, it felt shameful—as if she was somehow betraying her father's trust. For all Papa's feckless ways, she loved him. Before Thomas' death, the Earl of Northgate had been a different man, his *joie de vivre* expressed through his affection for his family and friends rather than at the card table. She remembered the Christmases and birthdays of her childhood overflowing with Papa's generous, larger-than-life spirit. But Nicholas had not known her father then, and she feared he would only see the earl as he was now. A man who needed his own daughter to rein him in.

As she debated what to say, Nicholas' brow eased as if in sudden understanding. "Ah. Well. I trust you are feeling ... well enough? I will summon the carriage if you like."

Now it was her turn to be perplexed. "The carriage? Whatever for?"

Nicholas looked distinctly ill-at-ease. Even in the darkness, a tinge of ruddy color could be seen on his rugged features. "For the condition which, ah, ails you."

"To what condition do you refer?" Helena asked, truly puzzled now. "I have no problems with my health, sir."

"However you wish to call it, I am nonetheless happy to assist you. Shall I have a servant bring you anything? Perhaps you could rest unobtrusively in the gazebo ..."

"Whatever are you talking about?" Helena asked. "Why would I need to rest?"

A pained expression crossed over Nicholas' face. "I am sure there is no need to entertain the specifics."

"I am finding this conversation most baffling," Helena said.

"That is one way to put it," her husband muttered, rubbing the back of his neck.

"Look at the ranunculus!" the countess exclaimed.

As her mother darted toward the prized collection, Helena took a deep breath and said, "I need to fetch my father. That is what *I* am talking about."

"Your father. I see." Nicholas cleared his throat.

"And what topic were *you* addressing, my lord?"

Her husband appeared discomfited. "Nothing of import. In fact, it has quite escaped me now."

Helena eyed him doubtfully. "But a minute ago you were—"

"Why must you fetch him?" Nicholas asked. "Your father, that is."

Helena traced the stepping stone with the tip of her slipper. Could she trust him not to judge her father too harshly? Meeting Nicholas' intent gaze, she said, "He is in the card room at present."

The heat rose in her face, and she prayed she would have to say no more. How appalling it would be to have to explain that one's father could not control his gambling habits and that one had to intercede on his behalf. At the same time, she felt guilty for exposing her father's weakness—even if it was to her own husband, who in reality must know something of the problem.

Helena was aware that Nicholas had assisted with the Northgate debts as part of the marriage settlement. From her mother's recent letters, brimming with descriptions of new millinery and furnishings, Helena had gleaned that all had returned to normal on the estate. Papa had even purchased a new carriage and a pair of chestnuts to lead it with. But now, to admit that her father had not changed his ways, even after so narrow an escape from ruin ...

"I wished to ask him about a specific matter," she said in as bright a tone as she could muster, "and had forgotten about it until this moment. Would you mind escorting my mother until I return?"

She made to leave, but was stopped by Nicholas' hand on her arm.

"I have not yet spoken to your father this evening," he said. "Allow me the honor of paying my respects."

Helena shook her head in misery. "But I must find him. You see, he is—"

"I shall find him and bring him to you and Lady Northgate directly." Nicholas dropped his hand, but he looked steadily into her eyes.

Helena felt her knees weaken. From his brief touch, yes, but more so from the relief that threatened to bring tears to her eyes. It had been so long since she'd had a shoulder to lean on—not since Thomas in fact.

"D-do you think you could persuade him ...?" she asked shakily.

"Give me ten minutes," her husband said, "before rejoining you in the music room."

Chapter Eight

Nicholas strode off in the direction of the card room. *Damn and blast Northgate.* The man could no more resist a hand of whist than a drunkard could a bottle of blue ruin. At this rate, Northgate would soon be back flailing in a bog of arrears. Nicholas did not particularly care if his father-in-law ended up in the Fleet—it would probably do the earl good to see what happened to a man, even a peer of the realm, who failed to honor his debts. That was justice, pure and simple.

What did infuriate him was the worry darkening Helena's countenance, the slump of her shoulders as she bore the brunt of her father's reckless behavior. Northgate was oblivious to the shame and ruin he was about to bring down on his own head; Helena was not. Despite her demure appearance, she was a loyal little thing. His lips curved grimly. Brave or foolhardy as well, depending on how one looked at it. How exactly was she planning to extricate her sire from the gaming tables? She was too slight to do it by force, too innocent to resort to other means.

Since he was neither slight nor innocent, he did not anticipate any trouble whatsoever.

Nicholas entered the gaming parlor, where the guests milled

around the half-dozen occupied card tables. He spotted Northgate immediately. Seated with cards in hand, the earl wore a burgundy velvet jacket, and his face was a matching florid shade under his whiskers. His typically jovial expression was replaced by a feral look. His eyes moved furiously around in their sockets, like a beast that had been cornered. Nicholas heaved an irritated breath. No wonder the man ruined himself at cards. He was an easy mark if there ever was one.

Ignoring the looks aimed in his direction, Nicholas made his way to the table. He returned the stiff nods of two gentlemen who did not quite meet his gaze. His mouth thinned. Two weeks ago in his office, Yardley and Caverstock had been much friendlier when they received news that their investments in a Fines and Company venture had tripled in value. To his recollection, they had all but tripped over themselves in their eagerness to shake his hand. But now, under the watchful eyes of the *ton*, they could afford little more than a fractional inclination of the head. Nicholas understood the unspoken rules.

One did not socialize, after all, with the help.

He circled the table once, stopping at Northgate's side. He kept his expression neutral even as he gave another inward sigh. He hoped Northgate had not wagered a vast sum on this particular hand.

But, of course, the bloody fool had.

Nicholas waited until the table had been cleared and the earl scribbled his vowels. Nicholas almost snorted. The promissory note was worth less than the paper it was written on. He should know, as he oversaw Northgate's accounts. It had been a stipulation on his part (and a damned prudent one) that if he was to resolve the earl's debts, the earl would have to answer to him in all matters financial. He did not wish to make a habit of bailing his father-in-law out of trouble. It would be like sailing a hole-filled dinghy with nothing but a bucket in hand.

"Good evening, Northgate." Nicholas clamped a hand on the

earl's shoulder. The old man jumped in his seat, so focused had he been on the deck of cards about to be dealt.

"Harteford," Northgate sputtered. "What the blazes are you doing here?"

"I could ask you the same thing," Nicholas said, keeping his voice low. "Be that as it may, this is a musicale, and I am here escorting my wife and yours. I've come to invite you to join our group as the ladies desire your presence."

Northgate turned even ruddier. "Good God, man. I cannot abandon my partner in the middle of a game. Besides, this next hand is to be my lucky one, I can feel it in my bones. Tell the ladies I'll be there shortly." He turned back to the table.

"You are wanted immediately." Ignoring the tittering of the other players, Nicholas spoke in a tone that brooked no refusal. "I am sure your presence here will be excused."

"I do not want to leave," Northgate said stubbornly.

"I say, it is most ungentlemanly to stand between a man and his cards," the middle-aged man across the table drawled. "You should know better, Harteford."

There was a twitter of laughter.

Nicholas felt his fist bunch at his side, but he ignored the jibe. He had better things to do than waste time on the likes of Sir Danvers Jacoby, heir to an ancient baronetcy and known profligate. He focused his attention instead on Northgate. The earl's velvet-clad shoulders were hunched over the table, as if he planned to stay there awhile. As if he had every right to wager money that was not his. As if he could do as he chose and damn the consequences to others. Cold rage spread through Nicholas' veins. He leaned over and spoke tersely near the earl's ear.

Northgate's eyes widened.

"Northgate, are you in?" Jacoby asked, deck in manicured hand.

"No, I'm afraid not," the earl said. He shot a nasty look at Nicholas. "Harteford here reminds me of other duties."

"Duties at a time like this? Harteford, do stop being such a killjoy. In fact, why don't you take Northgate's place and lighten your purse a little." Jacoby adjusted the diamond studs on his cuff, smirking as he added, "How dreary it must be to carry all those bags of coin around. A hazard of the merchant profession, I suppose."

Remain calm, Nicholas told himself as mocking laughter surrounded him. How he would love to plant a facer on Jacoby's arrogant, grinning face. His palms actually tingled with longing. At this moment, he could imagine no greater joy than knocking the bugger off his high horse.

But he would not. He had learned early on in the *ton* that responding to the subtle taunts and underhanded cracks only made matters worse. That was why they bear-baited him in the first place—they hoped for some uncivilized response they could further ridicule. So they could poke at him with their pointed insults and barbed wit. At heart, Mayfair was no different from the stews he'd grown up in. The fine lords and ladies were just as savage, thirsting for blood at every turn. Well, he'd be damned if he gave them that pleasure.

"I am afraid I haven't the time." Nicholas bowed mockingly and raised a brow at Northgate. With a petulant turn to his mouth, the earl got up. Nicholas could hear the excited whispering behind them as they made their way out of the card room.

"That was deuced embarrassing," Northgate hissed, as soon as they reached the hallway. "I will never again be able to hold my head high in front of those people."

"And you would be able to do so, living on Fleet Street?" Nicholas inquired in tones of granite. "You think your friends will be visiting you there, in the debtors' slums?"

Northgate's face approached an apoplectic purple. "That is preposterous! I am the Earl of Northgate. I would never find myself in such a position. How dare you suggest—"

"That is exactly the point. I do dare." Nicholas inclined his head politely as a couple walked past.

Northgate's expression froze into a grin that bordered on frightening. Once the couple was out of earshot, he said furiously, "Show some respect, sirrah. You are my son-in-law and therefore obliged to respect—"

"Respect this, my lord." Nicholas' voice was dangerously soft. "Everything you currently own, from the bricks of your manor house to the stitches on your back, belongs to *me*. Every rent you collect goes towards repaying your debt to *me*. Every pound, every bloody guinea you blow on the cards, comes from *my* pocket. You are living on my good graces, Northgate, and I swear to you that at the moment they are wearing thin."

Northgate paled.

"I do not wish to repeat this conversation, so let me make myself very clear," Nicholas continued. His eyes bored into his father-in-law's rapidly blinking orbs. "You will not receive so much as another farthing from me if you continue to game. I will cut you off. Completely."

"Y-you would not dare," Northgate whispered. "Helena would never allow—"

"Helena will know nothing of it," Nicholas said, "unless you wish to inform your daughter that you have gambled away the earldom's assets. That the only thing standing between you and ruin is the coin of a merchant."

Northgate swallowed. "You heartless bastard."

Nicholas smiled without humor. "That I am."

A bell could be heard ringing once, twice, three times.

"The programme is about to begin," Nicholas said, with a mocking lift of the brow. "Now that the matter is settled, we would not want to be late, would we?"

Rage blazed in Northgate's eyes. "God as my witness, I will see you pay for this! May you rot in hell, you bastard." Turning on his heel, he stormed away.

Nicholas consulted his watch fob and followed at a more leisurely pace. Sixteen minutes. It had taken six minutes more than he had promised Helena, but not bad, considering the task he had accomplished. He might have felt pleased with himself, too, had it not been for the throbbing at his left temple. He was reminded of the reason he avoided Society's playground in the first place: the *ton* gave him a pounding headache.

Nonetheless, he took his place in the line of guests waiting to enter the music room. Several ladies studied him discreetly above their waving fans—gathering fuel, no doubt, for drawing room gossip. He was certain they could content themselves for days doling out the details of the Makeshift Marquess and how his lowly origins betrayed him.

He did not bother to avert his gaze when a particularly bold lady ogled him as she might an exotic artifact at the British Museum. Like he was some of sort of grotesque Sphinx, offensive to the sensibilities yet all the more titillating because of it. When her eyes met his, he returned her look for look, his mouth curling derisively. She gasped and turned her head. Moments later, she was squawking in the ear of her companion, whose feathers quivered with excitement.

They could go to hell, every bloody last one of them.

By the time he reached the door, the music had begun. He noted with growing irritation that the Dewitts had not planned for the size of the crowd for there were more guests than chairs. He found a space at the back of the room and tried to ignore the giant pulsing vein that had taken residence in his head. Scanning the seated audience, he located Helena sitting between her parents in one of the middle rows. She was turned to her right, her profile exposed to him. Northgate was whispering in her ear. From the emphatic gestures and contorted expression, Northgate was clearly furious.

Nicholas felt a rush of blood to the head, bringing the pounding to a near unbearable intensity. *Goddamn* Northgate.

Likely he was spinning some Cheltenham tragedy about mistreatment at the hands of his son-in-law. The innocent, noble lord being lambasted by the ill-bred, penny-pinching merchant. It was material rich enough for Drury Lane. Watching the movement of Northgate's lips, Nicholas could almost hear the words.

Bastard ... good-for-nothing ... laughingstock ...

The muscle twitched along Nicholas' jaw. While he didn't care about Northgate's lies, he did care about Helena's reaction. How would she take to the slandering of her husband? Suddenly, the question seemed of great importance to him, as if his future was somehow hinging upon her response.

He studied his wife's face, willing her to ... what?

Yell at her father?

Slap the old man in the face?

Surely, he did not expect her to do any of those things.

Yet neither did he expect her eyes to well with tears, nor her hands to clasp the earl's in a comforting gesture. Or perhaps, he thought with blinding fury, he *did* expect it. Had expected all along that she would soothe her father's injuries and leave her husband to bleed in the gutter. After all, had she not tried to protect her father earlier on in the evening? She had attempted to hide Northgate's activities from him—*her own husband*—until he had convinced her he could help her father.

He rubbed a hand over his eyes.

"Lord Harteford?"

He turned his head at the low whisper. A footman was holding the door open, his head cocked in question. Nicholas went over. Once outside the room, he said, "Yes. What is it?"

"This came for you, my lord." The footman bowed and handed him a note.

Brow furrowing, Nicholas broke the seal and unfolded the heavy stationary. At that moment, the orchestra reached a crescendo, a fusillade of sound exploding in his head. His vision wavered.

"My lord? Is everything alright?"

Fighting down a surge of nausea, Nicholas re-folded the note and managed, "Who gave you this?"

"I'm not sure, my lord." The servant looked uneasy. "It just appeared on the missive salver, and the butler instructed me to deliver it. If there is a problem—"

"There is not. That will be all."

Nicholas tossed a coin to the footman. He managed to hold onto his composure until the servant disappeared down the empty hall. Then his knees gave out. He caught himself, bracing his forearm against the wall. Some distant part of his brain registered that the orchestra was still playing, that the air was scented with camellias, champagne, and candle-wax. A musicale in Mayfair, he thought numbly. The last place he'd thought to be ambushed, hunted down at last by the past. He didn't have to look at the note again; the lines glowed red-hot in his head.

You didn't think you could bury Ben Grimes forever, did you? The price for keeping your crime secret is upon you. Await my instruction.

Darkness closed over him. His lungs burned, suffocating with soot and terror as he felt himself being pinned by a wall of hairy muscle and fat, the stench of onions and sweat scalding his nostrils. His pleas were drowned by a fist and the bright, rusty welling in his mouth. He flailed out, mindless as an animal. A trickle of sweat cleaved his palm as it bumped against something smooth, something jutting from Grimes' back pocket. A knife—

"Harteford?"

He jumped. It took him an instant to recognize Helena. She was standing there, looking at him with wide eyes. "Harteford, what is the matter? I saw you leave during the performance. Are you unwell—"

She raised a hand toward him.

"*Do not touch me.*" The words left him in a hiss. He stumbled back.

For a second, her hand remained arrested mid-air. Then it dropped slowly to her side. "I b-beg your pardon. I only came to apologize."

"For what?" he bit out.

"Please, you must forgive Papa," she said. "He cannot help himself. He was born to a gentleman's life, you see, and I think ... it is sometimes difficult for him to imagine there could be consequences to his actions." She flushed, her lashes sweeping downward. "All his friends play at the cards, after all."

God's blood, he could hardly think. He needed to get away, to get *air*. Like a caged beast, he swiped out blindly. "Damn your father to hell. Because he is a *gentleman* his every behavior is to be excused. That is how the *ton* treats liars and cheats—by overlooking, nay, exalting such behavior."

"Papa isn't a liar—"

"Your father is a liar of the *worst* kind. Masquerading as a noble, virtuous lord," Nicholas snarled, "when, in truth, he's nothing more than a bloody, degenerate gambler. He is digging his own grave, and I forbid you to assist him in that endeavor."

Helena lifted a hand to her mouth. Her eyes shimmered as she said in a suffocated voice, "He is my father. I have always h-helped where I could. 'Tis my duty."

"Choosing your duty as a daughter over a wife," he sneered. "Hardly surprising."

"Harteford," she whispered, "what are you saying?"

End it. End it now, and get the hell out.

"Nothing but the truth," he said. "This marriage was a mistake, and we both know it."

She looked as if he'd struck her. "You can't mean that—"

He felt himself coming apart inside. Her beauty and innocence heightened the sense of filth crawling over his skin, the self-disgust roiling in his stomach. He'd never been good enough for her and never would; that he'd thought otherwise made him the dumbest bugger who'd ever lived.

"I do mean it, Helena." Each word burned like acid on his tongue. "Marrying you was the worst thing I have done in my life."

Before she could reply, he turned and walked away.

From his wife. From the life that would never be his.

Chapter Nine

"You are quiet this evening," Marianne remarked from the other side of the carriage. "Are you certain you wish to do this?"

Helena gave a determined nod. Through the window, she saw they had turned onto a secluded, one-ended street close to Piccadilly. She had never visited this neighborhood at night. Under the street lamps, the row of unadorned, Palladian-style buildings possessed a ghostly aura. Shades were drawn over the windows, concealing any sign of the activities within. A tremor crossed over her nape, but she stiffened her shoulders.

"My marriage is at stake," she said. "I have to win Harteford back."

"And you are certain, dearest, that you cannot just tell him you were the harlot he tupped?"

Three days had passed since the musicale, yet the memory of her last interaction with Nicholas retained a frozen sort of clarity. *This marriage was a mistake.* She blinked back tears. Surely he hadn't meant that. Surely it had been his frustration talking, and she couldn't blame him for that, not when Papa had treated him so badly. But the loathing in Nicholas' eyes as he'd spoken of liars—

those who *masqueraded* as virtuous ... she swallowed painfully. "That is not an option, Marianne. He cannot know that I deceived him."

"If you say so." The other smoothed the fingers of her sapphire satin gloves. "Well, then, here we are."

The footman let down the steps and helped them to descend. With increasing curiosity Helena trailed her friend to a plain-fronted shop. The weathered sign above contained an advertisement for ladies' conveniences. Helena frowned. 'Twas not a wardrobe she was in need of but more direct reinforcements. Perhaps Marianne had misunderstood her request.

"I have already purchased the necessaries from Madame Rousseau and do not need more clothing. Rather, I had hoped that you might show me ..." Helena began.

But Marianne had already disappeared into the shadowed entrance. With a sigh, Helena followed.

This store was much different from Madame Rousseau's. The interior was dark, for one, and the merchandise exhibited in haphazard fashion. A handful of glass-topped cases crowded the small front room, showing gloves of dubious quality alongside bits of hosiery and other frippery. Growing ever more intrigued, Helena was examining a rather risqué pair of black stockings trimmed in fuchsia ribbon when a robust, middle-aged woman appeared from behind a blue curtain. She wore a low-cut gown and a spangle of glittering jewels upon her generous bosom. Her fleshy fingers sparkled with rings.

"Lady Draven, how nice to see you," she said, her simpering tone at odds with her imposing person.

Marianne inclined her head. "Good day, Mrs. Bell. I have brought a friend with me. I hope that will not be a problem."

"Of course not, dearie," Mrs. Bell replied. "Guests are included in your subscription. And lucky for her, we have a nice selection today. Fresh from market." She laughed. "Follow me, then."

Before Helena could ask, "A selection of what?," she was

ushered through the curtain. She found herself in a dim passageway lit by wall sconces.

"Right this way," Mrs. Bell said, taking the lead. Helena looked at Marianne, who merely smiled and gestured for her to follow. Helena found herself taking quick steps to keep up.

"What is it exactly that you sell, Mrs. Bell?" Helena asked, a trifle breathlessly.

"Why, didn't Lady Draven tell you?" Mrs. Bell asked in astonishment. "My merchandise is the finest in all of London—in all of England, I daresay."

"Yes, but what *is* it?"

They stopped at a heavy oak door guarded by a cloaked footman.

"Give the lady a look then, Jim," Mrs. Bell said.

The footman slid open the viewing hole.

Helena peered inside and gasped.

"*Amour*, dearie, the most premium lot of it you ever saw. Just like I said." Mrs. Bell looked at Marianne, her thinly plucked eyebrows raised. "What is your flavor today?"

"Crimson for me," Marianne said. "White for my friend."

"Here you go, then." From a basket, Mrs. Bell withdrew fabric masks of the specified colors and handed them to Marianne and Helena, who took hers with uncertain fingers. Seeing Helena's hesitation, Mrs. Bell laughed. "Go on, luvie. It won't bite you."

"What is it for?" Helena asked, as she tied the gold laces behind her ears.

"To let the others know what kind of *amour* you're looking for. Keeps the guessing out of the game. Let me take your coats, and enjoy yourselves a time, miladies."

The footman opened the door, releasing a swell of voices and music.

On the threshold of decadent debauchery, Helena felt her determination teeter. She gripped Marianne's arm. "I do not know if I can do this."

"Fustian," Marianne whispered. "You said you wanted to win your husband back. There is no better place in London to learn the art of seduction."

Desperation warred with a lifetime's upbringing. On one side of the battlefield, Helena could imagine her mother and Lady Epplethistle. They both wore horrified looks and were emphatically shaking their heads. On the other, there was Nicholas—dangerous and irresistible, he stood alone, his eyes smoldering with sensual promise. His mouth took on a wicked curve, and he crooked his finger toward her.

Oh, Nicholas ...

Helena stepped inside, and the door closed behind her.

"You have acquainted yourself with the Nunnery. The only difference here is that only the best *ton* is permitted entrance," Marianne said. "Mrs. Bell is more of a stickler than the patronesses at Almack's combined. Believe me, I had to submit to several inquisitions before my subscription was accepted."

Helena's gaze flitted over the opulently dressed masked women circulating about the room. "You mean those women are not courtesans?"

"They are duchesses and countesses, perhaps even a princess or two thrown in," Marianne said. "All here with one purpose in mind: to seduce a lover for the evening. That is why we are here. There is no better place to learn how to seduce a man."

Helena swallowed. "And the masks? What do the colors signify?"

Marianne's lips curved. "Not to worry, dear. White means you are here to observe only."

"And red?"

Marianne's smile took on a feral quality. "Perhaps there is more than one purpose for our visit."

Marianne led Helena in a slow promenade around the room which, by Helena's reckoning, was similar in size to Almack's. But that was where the similarity ended. Mrs. Bell's establishment was the furthest thing imaginable from a genteel assembly. Decorated in a vivid red and orange Oriental motif, the room catered to exotic fantasy. The strings of paper lanterns overhead shed a muted, seductive glow. Along the perimeter of the room, alcoves sheltered by painted bamboo screens and curtains of raw silk provided customers with the privacy to indulge in their heart's desire. Spicy sweet notes of sandalwood and cinnamon mingled with the musky scent of pleasure.

Helena felt her senses whirl.

"Marianne, may we sit down?" she asked unsteadily.

"Over there." Marianne gestured to a chaise longue situated next to an enormous potted palm.

Helena sank gratefully onto the maroon and gold brocade. Her relief was short-lived, however, when she saw that Marianne remained standing.

"I will return in an hour's time," her friend was saying. "Observe and learn, Helena, if you wish to win your husband."

"Marianne, don't leave—"

But Marianne had already melted into the melee.

With a huff, Helena leaned back against the cushions. After a minute, she slid a furtive glance around her. Once one got past the impropriety of it all, the scene was really quite ... fascinating. Caroline's batting of eyelashes was child's play compared to the flirtation happening here. Eyes widening, Helena observed a woman dressed head to toe in scarlet. Every movement the woman made—from the parting of the lips to the caress of the necklace at her bosom—seemed imbued with secret meaning. *Sexual* meaning that held her partner in a thrall, bound to her as if by invisible strings.

With a renewed sense of purpose, Helena sought to learn all she could. She attempted to decipher the meaning of the masks. On a nearby settee, a woman wearing a pink mask sat next to her companion. He was feeding her berries from a glass dish. When the fruit's juice dribbled down the woman's chin, the man leaned over and leisurely licked up each sweet trail. The woman sighed. The man reached for another berry. The game continued, with no touch between them save soft, nibbling kisses.

Other lovers had bolder diversions in mind. On the dance floor, a pair in red masks moved in a shockingly sensual rendition of the waltz. As Helena watched, the male cupped his partner's bottom and lifted her against him. He allowed her to slide slowly downward, her flesh pressed against his. This clearly aroused them both: their mouths tangled fiercely before they departed the dance floor. In their haste to reach the privacy of an alcove, they nearly collided with two purple-masked women holding hands.

Not all the secrets of the masks revealed themselves so easily. Helena puzzled over a couple standing by the refreshment table. The man sported no jacket, only a linen shirt worn open at the neck. His black waistcoat matched his tightly fitted black leather breeches, which, to Helena's mind, made for a rather odd choice of evening wear. Even stranger, he held a black leather strap, the end of which was attached to the collar worn by the woman beside him. His mask was black, hers yellow. As Helena watched, the man held up a glass of champagne. When he tugged on the strap, the woman's lips parted obediently to receive the sparkling liquid.

"Might I share this seat with you?"

The male voice jolted Helena into awareness. She shifted her gaze upward to see a man smiling at her. His hair stood in ginger-colored tufts above his white mask.

"I apologize if I startled you. It is only that my legs grow weary from all the standing. As you can see, the other seats are occupied."

A swift glance around the room confirmed his words. Helena had no choice but to nod. When the man sat down next to her, she inched closer to the opposite end.

"Fine evening, what," he said in a cultured voice.

"Yes," she replied stiffly.

She did not want to make polite conversation. She did not want to be sitting next to a stranger. Her brain searched feverishly for the correct etiquette in such a situation. As usual, Lady Epplethistle's advice came up short.

"Do you come often, then?"

"No." *Please go away.*

"I do," he said. After a silence, "I've often wondered what the ladies' entrance is like."

"I beg your pardon?"

"Where you ladies enter this fine establishment. We gentlemen employ the walking stick shop on the street behind. Devilishly clever, isn't it?" At Helena's blank look, the man laughed. "A place to purchase a hard rod, what."

Helena felt her cheeks flame.

"Personally, I come to watch all the fucking." Suddenly, his breath burned against her ear. "Have you seen what happens in the alcoves?"

Helena shot to her feet and walked away as quickly as she could without running. Palm fronds whipped her face as she stumbled forward. Pulse hammering, she wove through the throng of laughing people. She pressed desperately on, her head turning back now and again, fearful of any flashes of orange hair. She came upon a row of alcoves and, spotting an unoccupied space, darted in. She yanked the silk coverings closed behind her, her heart galloping in her chest.

Several minutes passed before her pulse steadied. She regained enough of her senses to realize that she ought to look for Marianne. It was then that she heard the sounds. Low and throaty, the very music of seduction. On legs that trembled, Helena walked toward the wooden screen that separated her alcove from the one beside it. The panel was painted with knots to resemble a row of bamboo and affixed with exotic images of birds and flowers. Amongst the white plumage of a crane, Helena noticed a slight gap in the wood. She pressed her cheek against the cool slats.

She glimpsed the profiles of a dark-haired pair sitting upon on a divan. Both the man and the woman had their upper faces hidden behind scarlet masks. At first glance, the two appeared to be conversing, but there was an intimacy about their postures which gave Helena pause. She saw that the woman held a long-stemmed rose between her white satin-covered fingers. With a husky laugh, the lady caressed the flower over her décolletage; the crimson head fluttered and dipped over the generous mounds. When one petal detached and drifted into the bodice, she sent her companion a coy look.

The man obliged immediately. Encased in fine dark leather, his hands came to cup her breasts, squeezing, kneading in such a way that had her sighing. Then he touched inside the bodice, and his actions there made the woman gasp and bite her lip. She dropped the flower, her hands going around her partner's neck. Their mouths collided in a hungry, open-mouthed kiss that went on and on. When the man finally broke away, he nuzzled the woman's ear. Whatever he whispered sent a flush up the slender column of her neck. With a throaty giggle, she gave a nod. His eyes gleamed behind the mask as she rose ... then sank to her knees between his legs.

Shameful arousal flooded Helena. She knew she shouldn't be watching, and yet she couldn't detach her gaze from the unfolding action. The woman parted her lover's trousers, a hum leaving her as she removed his engorged flesh. With an elegant movement, she encircled the girth with her fingers. Helena's breath caught at the sensual play of snowy satin against the darkly-veined phallus. The contrast was strangely, wholly erotic. And the way the lovers were looking at one another ...

How she longed to see that same desire smoldering in Nicholas' dark eyes. To make him want her, to *burn* for her ... Desperate, determined, she pressed closer against the screen.

The woman had bent her head. She was carefully tonguing her lover's cock. Heat trickled through Helena's veins as she followed the languid path of that small, pink organ over and around the flared head, below the crest, up and down the shaft. The woman was clearly savoring the task—much to her partner's appreciation. Groaning, the man slid his gloved hands into her chestnut curls, scattering plumes and pins. His hoarse commands escalated in volume.

Deeper. Suck me, love. Ah, yes, let me fuck your lovely mouth.

His hips were arching in a steady, smooth rhythm that drove him deeper and deeper into his lady's kiss. She made eager little sounds around his cock, seeming to have no difficulty taking him in this manner. Her forehead glazed with perspiration, Helena took note of the woman's hands, how one circled and pumped the base of the shaft, while the other played with his heavy stones. 'Twas a concerto of hands and lips moving in sensual unison. The man growled a sudden warning, pulling his lover's head away from his groin.

God's teeth, I'm close ...

The woman looked up at him with adoration and lust in her gaze as she continued to handle him with firm strokes. *Spend for me, my darling. Shower me. Your seed feels so exquisite upon my breasts.*

The man groaned. He worked his hips harder and faster, shoving his rampant manhood into the woman's grasp. The scene was so debauched, so wildly titillating that Helena felt her intimate muscles clench in response. Her pussy gripped on to the memory of Nicholas' cock, the stretched, almost too full feeling of his flesh driving into her. Her entire body throbbed with heat. The hardened tips of her breasts strained against her bodice, and moisture flushed from her center.

I'm coming, love. Take it, feel me—

With a shout, the man erupted, his seed spraying upon his lover's bosom. When he finished, he sagged against the cushions, his chest still surging. The woman touched her finger to her jaw and caught a stray drop. She brought her satin-covered finger to her lips, licked the tip, and smiled.

Exquisite, my lord, she told him.

He gave a husky laugh. *Have a care, wife, or you'll stain your gloves.* Taking her hand, he peeled off the pristine material. A wedding band gleamed on the delicate fingers he brought to his lips. *On second thought, devil take the damn gloves—I'll buy you a drawer full if it comes to that.*

His lady giggled as he bent and kissed her on the nose.

Shaking all over, Helena turned away from the viewing hole. She slumped onto a bench. She ought to be shocked by what she had just witnessed. By the fact that she had shamelessly spied upon what appeared to be torrid, *marital* lovemaking. Instead, a flare of recognition heated her insides as she understood, finally, what was possible in a marriage. What she had always longed for with Nicholas. She wanted his love, yes, but she also yearned for the decadent pleasure he'd shown her at the Nunnery.

For the hot, male taste of him filling her senses.

For his devastating touch on her breasts and the aching place between her thighs.

For the intensity of his possession, his cock thrusting against the very limits of her restraint, making her beg for more and more.

Sweetness above, she *was* a harlot.

Sitting there upon the bench, a strange calm settled over her. As she studied the string of paper lanterns overhead, it occurred to her that the frail shells, pretty as they were, obscured a rather vital glow. A tear trickled from beneath her mask.

After a few moments, she wiped away the dampness.

And began to plan.

Chapter Ten

Later that week, Nicholas handed his coat and hat to the butler, relieved to find the foyer empty.

"Is Lady Harteford out, Crikstaff?" he asked, running a hand through his disheveled hair.

"Yes, my lord," Crikstaff intoned.

Nicholas felt relieved even as he mentally cursed his own cowardice. Lord, he was becoming a spineless fool. He had avoided Helena all week. He had no desire for a repeat performance of their interaction at the musicale, and he didn't know what he would say if he did see her. Not the truth, that was for certain.

I'm sorry, but you've married a murderer wasn't something one confessed to a gently bred lady. Or to anyone, for that matter.

His lips tightened.

The butler was not finished jabbering. "Lady Harteford did leave word that she would be dining in this evening. She specifically requested your presence should your lordship be at home. She has asked Chef to prepare a most special repast."

At the thought of Helena asking for him, Nicholas' pulse leaped. Seeing her would be courting danger—how much longer could he hide his desire for her and keep her at arm's length? Yet how could he refuse without obviously disregarding his wife's wishes in front of the staff?

He gave a curt nod.

The normally somber Crikstaff looked ready to skip down the halls. "I am sure you will find the menu this evening most delightful—"

"I will be down at seven o'clock. Be sure that the meal is ready, as I will be leaving for an engagement at eight." Nicholas stalked away, turning to add, "And I wish to be undisturbed until we dine."

He tried to ignore the fallen look on the butler's face. Was he so much of a disappointment that even his servants found him lacking? A year ago, he'd inherited the house staff along with the property; frankly, he'd had no idea what to do with the lot of them. Before his marriage, he'd kept the arrangement simple, the way he liked: he paid their wages, and they stayed out of his way.

His method had worked fine until Helena came along. She seemed to inspire in the servants (and old stick-in-the-mud Crikstaff especially) some sort of domestic fervor. They became full of questions: *Is the soup to your liking, my lord? Would you prefer your cravat à la Brutus or in a Waterfall, this evening?*

How the hell was he to know what the French soup was supposed to taste like, or how his bloody neck cloth should be tied?

He had problems—*real* ones—that were a sight more pressing.

Striding into his study, he shut the door behind him. He regarded the polished mahogany and dark green tones of his private sanctuary with relief. At least here no one dared to seek him out. He poured himself a whiskey and slouched into the chair behind his desk. As he sipped, savoring the burn, he grimly contemplated his situation.

Someone had somehow discovered his secret. Whoever had

sent those notes knew that seventeen years ago he'd killed that bastard Ben Grimes. That he'd stuck that black-hearted bugger in the chest and run. For weeks after the murder, he'd huddled with the mud-larks beneath the docks, numb with shock and the certainty of retribution. Yet justice had not come for him. Instead, a rumor had finally pierced his petrified brain: Grimes' flash house had gone down in flames. Grimes' body had been recovered, charred and unrecognizable, and the fire had been blamed for his death. Nicholas alone had known the truth. He'd kept running, never feeling safe, always fearing his secret would be revealed.

The price for keeping your crime secret is upon you. Nicholas' throat clenched. Who was this faceless enemy? How had this would-be blackmailer come by the information about his past? And why hadn't any demands been made as of yet? Questions crowded against his temples, making them pulse. As much as Nicholas disliked Isaac Bragg, the man didn't seem to have the brains to concoct such a scheme. Looting, yes, but blackmail ... Bragg couldn't keep such a juicy secret to himself.

He'd have Bragg followed, Nicholas decided, but by whom? He didn't trust the Bow Street Runners or any investigators for hire, for that matter. As far as he was concerned, that lot had far too much in common with the criminals they hunted—and the last thing he needed was for some unscrupulous detective to ferret out his past. The option left, then, was Ambrose Kent. His instincts told him Kent was honest. He'd have to think of some way to ask for Kent's assistance, without alerting the policeman to his wrongdoing. Perhaps he could ask the detective to follow Bragg as a potential suspect in the warehouse losses.

A knock on the door startled Nicholas from his brooding. Before he could respond, the door swung slowly open. Recovering himself, he snapped, "What the devil is it? I said I was not to be ..."

He stopped mid-sentence when he saw Helena's head peer around the doorway. The sight of her heart-shaped countenance made him instantly ache all over. Then his brow creased. She *never* entered his study. In fact, she never entered any part of the house considered his domain. Not his bedchamber and certainly not this room. What the hell was she doing here now?

"How can I help you?" Incredulity made his words sharper than he had intended.

Helena responded with a shy smile. "I know you are busy, my lord, but I was wondering if I might have a few minutes of your time."

Nicholas blinked. She had never asked for his time before either. Then his jaw tautened. Of course. Presumably, she wanted to take him to task over his behavior at the musicale. He couldn't blame her—he *had* acted boorishly. He couldn't very well tell her the reason for it, that he needed to drive her away for her own good. But he wasn't about to apologize for whatever lies her father had poured into her ear, either. He'd be damned if he let her rake him over the coals over Northgate's alleged mistreatment.

Nicholas rose stiffly from the desk as Helena came toward him. He noted that she must have returned from a recent excursion as she still wore her pelisse. Trimmed in ermine and spun in cornflower blue, the cloak set off the purity of her features. The rounded curve of her cheeks reminded him of a blushing peach. She wore her hair simply today, the silky rich mass of it secured by a blue ribbon at her nape. The smell of spring trailed in her wake.

In spite of his frustration, he could not help but drink in the sight of her, and this increased his irritability further. Did she *have* to possess such pleasing curves, such softness about her? Did she have to smell like fruit and flowers, the very essence of femininity? Out of nowhere, brazen red hair and a body made for sinning assailed his mind's eye. Skin smooth as silk beneath his fingers, and a hot, voracious mouth ...

He caught himself, nearly shook his head in disgust. Why would he think of the doxy at such a time? He must be depraved indeed to allow such libidinous thoughts to sully the presence of his lady wife. Bloody hell. Now he had to contend with the nasty prickles of his conscience on top of everything else. He might as well get the business over with.

"What is it that you want to discuss?" he asked curtly, knowing full well the answer.

Helena walked up to his desk. She held a leather box in each hand. "I am having the most difficult time trying to decide which necklace to wear with my gown this evening. Since you have the most exquisite taste, I am depending on your kind assistance, my lord."

Her request distracted him from the counter-arguments he had been formulating about her ass of a father. Nicholas' eyes narrowed. Had he missed something? So this was not about her father, then? Nor about their quarrel at the musicale? This was about ... jewelry?

"I beg your pardon?" he asked.

"I should like the loan of your exquisite sense of style," his wife said.

His exquisite style? He hardly knew what his valet dressed him in each morning. Prior to inheriting his title, he'd had his man dress him in simple garb befitting his office at the warehouse. Prior to that, there had been a time when he'd committed the ultimate offense to gentility by dressing himself. No care needed getting ready for a day working the docks.

Though he had managed to obscure that charming part of his history with fancy lessons in elocution and etiquette, the truth was he had earned his success the hard way, without power or privilege. Bad enough that the *ton* scorned him for being a merchant—what would they, or his lady wife, daughter of an earl, say if they'd known he'd once been nothing but a common laborer, hefting ten stone sacks with the rest of the riffraff struggling about the wharves?

"My lord, would you help me, please?"

Though he tried to resist, he found himself once more a powerless captive to her sweet, inquisitive eyes. Hazel, they were, with flecks of green and gold swirled into rich brandy pools. Her eyes did not lie, and they were not angry. They were ... smiling. At him. Despite everything, a knot began to loosen in his chest. Her mouth imitated her eyes, so now her whole face was smiling at him. Beaming goodwill and wifeliness as she held the jewelry box toward him.

Reluctantly, Nicholas removed the necklace from its white satin lining. The rubies caught fire in the sinking light of the sun, sending fiery prisms onto the walls and carpet. He had never seen the necklace out of its box. After their disastrous wedding night, he had left it for Helena at the breakfast table. A shameful apology, a silent penance. Since then his wrongdoings had only multiplied: no amount of baubles could atone for the harm he'd done her by tying her to a murderer. A brute and a coward.

The jewels weighed heavily in his palm.

"Oh wait. I have forgotten to remove my pelisse." Helena untied the silken cords and tossed the cloak onto his chair.

Nicholas felt the air escape his lungs. The sudden gust left him light-headed, unable to hold onto a thought save one. *Who was the creature in front of him?* The Helena he knew wore primly proper dresses, with pieces of starchy-looking fabric tucked neatly in the neckline. An abundance of ribbons and flounces and other embellishments for which he had no name typically covered her from head to toe. Thankfully for him, those decorations tended to hide the lushness of her figure and provided some minor respite from temptation.

This Helena, however, wore a gown that draped her figure like a swath of moonlight. The airy white fabric glimmered with silver and was nearly as transparent as a moonbeam. The square bodice bared her plump, white breasts almost to the nipple. In fact, he surely *could* see her nipples, the faint outline of puckered buds visible under the gossamer breath of silk. The thin silver ribbon tied beneath her breasts emphasized the ripeness of the fruit above, larger than apples, more delicious than summer-sweet melons. He felt his mouth water. A man could gorge himself all day on those luscious tits. Plump pink nipples, he decided. Full buds shaped to tempt a man's tongue.

"Harteford?"

His wife was looking at him, her eyebrows raised and a small smile playing on her lush lips. He realized he had the necklace still clutched in his fist. Shaking himself from his erotic reverie, he felt a surge of anger. What was his wife playing at, dressing in such an immodest fashion? Why was she flaunting herself in such a manner that any hot-blooded male would be sniffing at her skirts like a hound scenting its prey? A simultaneous throbbing began at his temples and at his groin.

"Perhaps there is a fabric shortage I am unaware of?" he asked.

"Whatever do you mean, my lord?" His wife's expression appeared as pure as freshly fallen snow.

"Surely that would be the only acceptable explanation for constructing the garment you are wearing," Nicholas answered through clenched teeth. "For example, an entire bolt of cloth seems to be missing from your chest."

"You have the most exquisite sense of humor, my lord," Helena replied with a little laugh.

There she was with that word *exquisite* again. His Helena did not use flowery words. Nor did her laugh resemble the floating, flirtatious sound that tickled his ear like a caress, sending a bolt of lust straight to his loins. His balls tightened. His cock twitched with interest.

"I cannot approve of your attire," Nicholas persevered in a tight voice. "That gown is scandalous."

"Nonsense, this gown is the height of fashion. Madame

Rousseau designed it, and she has dressed everyone from Lady Jersey to Harriette Wilson," Helena answered serenely.

At the mention of the notorious courtesan, Nicholas felt heat rise along his neck. What the bloody hell was Helena doing, modeling herself after a member of the Fashionable Impure?

"What's good for the likes of Harriette Wilson is not fit for you," he growled.

Helena said nothing, merely smiled and turned her back to him. She lifted her hair, the silken mass of it dripping through her fingers. "Don't be silly, Harteford. Help me with the necklace, will you please?"

Nicholas stared at the sight proffered to him. All thoughts of further argument flew from his mind. The skin of her nape gleamed, so translucent and flawless that it reminded him of porcelain shipped from the Orient. His gaze roamed lower, narrowed as it took in how the dress clung to his wife's plush backside, emphasizing generous hips and a full, voluptuous ass, the kind a man could hold onto as he fucked a woman senseless ...

With a snarl, he slung the necklace around Helena's neck. From his vantage point, he could see the rubies sliding into the shadowed crevice between her tits, and Jesus, he *could* see her nipples now. They *were* a deep rosy pink, they *were* shaped like the kind of summer berries that burst with sweetness on the tongue ... His hands were shaking as he struggled with the delicate gold clasp. A few strands of her hair escaped and lashed his hands with gentle fire, tormenting him with their softness and fresh, blossomy scent. He ached to spear his fingers into her luxuriant mane, to pull her head back so he could taste her, drink in the honey of her lips as his hands filled themselves with tit flesh ...

A rush of violent want gripped him in its fist, tugging on his cock, easing down its length and drawing his balls upward. If he leaned but an inch forward, he could grab her by the hips. He could hold her luscious backside against him as he slid his burning prick along the secret valley of her ass. He would hold her tightly against him as he rocked up and down. He'd move his hand in front and delve into her cream-soaked cunny. He'd find her beautiful, glistening little pearl and stroke her over and again ...

So vivid was his fantasy that his hand slackened. The glistening strand of rubies slowly escaped his fingers. With lust and horror, Nicholas watched as the necklace slid down the slopes of his wife's beautiful breasts, landing in her cleavage before slithering further down into the flimsy bodice.

"Oh dear," Helena said with a gurgling laugh. She dropped her hair and felt along the outside of her bodice. Nicholas swallowed thickly as his wife ran searching hands over her breasts. Did the Lord have no mercy? Apparently not, as she went from touching her breasts on the outside of her dress to fishing diligently *inside* her bodice. He closed his eyes, unable to bear the sight of her tiny fingers prodding her tits, mayhap encountering those cheerful pink nipples, mayhap brushing them with an accidental caress ...

"I believe I have retrieved it," his wife announced triumphantly. She held the necklace out to him. He had no choice but to take the jewelry in his hand and feel its agonizing warmth, knowing from whence that heat came. Surely, his hand would bear the brand of his wife's infernal necklace, the way it burned against his skin.

"There it is," he said, his voice cracking a little. Damn if that blasted clasp hadn't given him more trouble than the team of thieves he'd once caught ransacking one of the warehouses. As a matter of fact, at this moment he would prefer an army of armed cutthroats to the sweet torture of Helena's closeness. He gritted his teeth as she continued to debate the merits of the ruby versus the sapphire necklace. The thought of having to assist her with another piece of jewelry jolted him into action.

"The ruby definitely is the better choice," he blurted. "It brings out the ... the ..."*—the juicy redness of your lips,* his mind whispered wickedly, *the delectable blush of your nipples—*"the color of your eyes."

"My eyes, sir? Are you implying my eyes are *red*?"

"No, of course not," he answered crossly. A stroke of inspiration saved him. "They merely shine like the brightest jewels."

"Oh, Harteford, what a perfectly wonderful thing to say!"

Before he could blink, his wife threw herself at him. Literally, wrapped her arms around his neck and looked up at him with glowing eyes. He went instantly rigid as the rest of her melted sensuously against him. He could feel the warmth of her seeping through his jacket, his waistcoat, through the thin linen of his shirt. His very skin felt scorched by her closeness. Was it possible to feel the points of her nipples through all that material? Because he swore he *could* feel them, hardened buds rocking tantalizingly against the taut muscles of his chest.

"It has been so long since you have given me a compliment," she breathed.

Do not lose control, he warned himself. *Remember you must protect her. Until you can figure out a permanent solution, keep your bloody paws off her.*

His good sense had no effect, however, on his erection, which grew with every breath his wife took. Each subtle movement of respiration shifted her body against his, and every fiber of his body —most notably his rampant cock—responded by growing harder, hotter, until he was fairly certain he might explode from her inadvertently teasing touch.

"I thought ... I thought perhaps you were disappointed. In my looks," she confessed. Her eyelashes fluttered like dark butterflies against her creamy skin.

Her words finally caught his attention.

What in God's name was she talking about now?

Perplexed, he gently removed her arms from around his neck and willed the thickened ridge in his trousers to subside. "Why would I be disappointed?"

"I know I am not a Diamond of the First Water. But I have a

plan, you see, to improve my looks. I have consulted Doctor Smythe on a promising slimming diet that—"

"Why on earth would you need a slimming diet?" Nicholas interrupted.

"Because ... well, is it not obvious?" Helena appeared to study the folds of his cravat. Her next words emerged as mere whispers. "I am overly plump."

"Overly *plump*?" Nicholas echoed incredulously. "*You*?"

"There is no need to emphasize the issue. I am aware of the problem," she responded a bit crossly.

Nicholas stared at his wife. Then he couldn't help himself. He threw back his head and laughed.

"What, pray tell, do you find so amusing?"

His wife's icy tones cut through his chuckling. Her cheeks were stained with crimson, and her mouth wobbled ever so slightly. Tenderness flooded his chest even as another chuckle escaped his lips.

"For God's sake, Helena, I am not laughing at you." Unable to resist, Nicholas caught a tear that rolled down her cheek. "I am laughing because you are the most beautiful creature in the world, and for you to think otherwise is absurd."

"Truly? Truly you think I am ... beautiful? But my figure is abundantly ..."

"Beautiful beyond words," Nicholas stated solemnly. "Perfect exactly as you are."

"Oh." His wife looked at him with shining eyes, the expression in them so wondrous that he had difficulty regaining his breath. Her head seemed to tilt slightly backward, a shy invitation that he could not accept if he wished to refrain from spreading his wife on his desk and having at her like a footman might a housemaid in the linen closet.

Christ, had he no scruples?

He realized his wife was looking at him now in her distinctly perceptive manner. "If what you say is true, that my appearance has not disappointed you …"

He had no choice but to nod, dreading where her all too logical mind was headed.

"Then I wish to know why you think our marriage was a mistake," she whispered.

Of course she would ask.

And of course, he could not tell her.

Taking her arms from his neck, he returned them firmly to her sides. "It has nothing to do with you," he said. That much was true at least. "Truth be told, the fault is mine. I was too impetuous in offering for you. We did not have sufficient time to … understand our differences. Differences that I have come to see will make marriage difficult."

Her cheeks flushed, her lashes lowering. In a small voice, she said, "Are you referring to what … happened, on our wedding night? Because, you see, I think with practice I could learn to be a … a better wife."

God Almighty, he could not bear the sweet sincerity of her plea. One more minute of this, and she'd find herself being fucked within an inch of her life. By a man who was not fit to shine her boots, let alone share her bed.

"That is not it," he said, swallowing.

"Then what is it?" his wife persisted.

Jaw clenched, Nicholas retreated behind his desk. He shuffled some papers. "I—I simply cannot be the husband you deserve."

"But you are! You are everything I've ever wanted in—"

"*For God's sake woman, that is enough. You do not know me, and you never will.*" His roar seemed to shock both of them equally. Helena stood there, white-faced, staring at him. Exhaling, he said more calmly, "Do not press me further on this. Suffice it to say, I assume the blame for the situation we find ourselves in. I will, therefore, find a solution. Until that time, I think it best that we keep a cordial distance."

A pause. In a quiet voice, Helena asked, "What sort of *solution* do you mean, Harteford?"

The nerve at his temple twitched. Despite the endless hours mulling over that question, he had no answer. The chances of being granted a divorce were slim to none. An annulment? His solicitor had told him the odds were no better. Apparently there were only three acceptable grounds for annulment: fraud, incompetence, or impotence. Though he hadn't been honest with her about his past, he couldn't claim fraud in a legal sense. Nor could he prove he'd been insane at the time of their marriage, though certainly he had been. Which left the third option.

God's blood. It was not one a hot-blooded man could contemplate. Besides, if he was put to test, he'd fail for certain: he walked around in a constant state of rut these days.

Still, if an annulment was somehow possible, then Helena could get on with her life. She could put this mistake of a marriage behind her. Claim her place in Society as she was meant to. In time, she'd find a suitable man to marry, to give her children ... Everything in him tensed in denial. He wanted to punch something. To roar savagely at anyone who'd take her from him.

He had to wait for the red haze to fade before saying, "I don't know as yet. But for the time being, I am certain we will manage as others in your class do. By having separate lives and not interfering with one another."

A pause. "*Our* class, my lord."

"I beg your pardon?"

His wife was watching him, her eyes narrowed. "You said *your* class. Last I looked, both of our families were listed in Debrett's."

"Of course that is what I meant," he muttered, furious at his slip. "At any rate, I have work to finish before supper. We have an understanding, do we not?"

For once, her hazel eyes were enigmatic. Veiled. "We are not to live in each other's pockets. We are to have a distant but civil relationship. Am I missing anything?" she asked tartly.

"That about covers it."

She went to the door, her hand pausing on the handle. When she turned to look back at him, he jerked his gaze hastily from where it had latched onto her bottom. Damn his soul.

"For the record, since we hardly see one another as it is, I don't see how this changes anything. As for what you said earlier, about *knowing* you." Her chin lifted. "How could I, when you make it impossible?"

The door slammed behind her.

Chapter Eleven

Helena did not see Nicholas the next morning in the breakfast parlor. In gloomy tones, Crikstaff informed her that the master had received a missive before sunrise and had departed in haste.

"Without even trying Cook's gooseberry crumpets," the butler added.

To ward off one of Cook's temperamental displays, Helena took two of the fine pastries. She fiddled with the buttered rounds and pushed the eggs around her plate. Her thoughts were a million miles away. All last night she'd tossed in her bed as her head whirled in confusion, her emotions running a wild gamut from hope to anger. Nicholas' words replayed, over and over.

Perfect just as you are.

No one had ever said such a thing to her before. At least, not since Thomas, and he, being an older brother, had never been so eloquent. Mostly, Thomas had sought to comfort her after her countless scrapes as a child. Whether it was getting thistle weed tangled in her hair or shattering her mother's favorite vase, she could count on Thomas to provide an antidote to her tears. *You'll do*, he'd say in his gruff way. Helena had treasured those rare tokens of affection.

But no one had ever called her *perfect* before. Not too plump, too tomboyish, or too shy—just perfect as she was. It recalled to her mind the first time she'd met Nicholas. Even then, he had seemed to see through her dowdy dress and wallflower demeanor to the person beneath. His shadowed gaze had seemed to penetrate her very essence; she had seen her secret passionate longings reflected in the dark well of his eyes. Yesterday, when he'd helped her with the necklace, she'd thought she glimpsed that look again. Desire and loneliness, melded together.

But then, when she had dared to embrace him, his demeanor had undergone a complete turnaround. She felt her cheeks burn, recalling how he'd cut off her attempt to discuss their marital relations. If he professed to find her attractive, why did he not wish to ... make love with her? Was he merely lying about her looks to make her feel better? Or was there something else, something deeper, hidden ...

You do not know me and never will.

With a frustrated sigh, she departed the table with breakfast half-finished and mounted the steps to her sitting room. How was she to understand the blasted man if he closed her off at every opportunity? Her attempts to initiate an honest conversation about their relationship had led nowhere, and she was not a mind-reader, after all. At times, his actions suggested that he might desire her ... and at others, he seemed intent upon pushing her away. On erecting a wall between them—for what reason, she could not begin to guess.

'Twas enough to drive a rational woman mad.

Feeling a spark of temper, Helena seated herself at her desk. She was not going to be the only one to work on this marriage. If Nicholas was determined to freeze her out, so be it. She was *not* going to try to thaw her way to his heart with nothing but a match in hand. She was tired of all the worrying, of trying to please him.

She was not going to waste another minute on that futile task. She would stop thinking about him and attend to her routines.

This strategy worked well for the rest of the morning. With reading spectacles perched upon her nose, Helena busied herself reviewing the household accounts and attending to matters of a domestic nature. She planned the next week's menu and met with both the housekeeper and Crikstaff to discuss their concerns. New linens were ordered, an extra scullery maid was hired, and the second footman was given permission to visit his ailing mother in the country.

At half past eleven, Helena removed her spectacles and rubbed her eyes. She had addressed all pressing matters and, truth be told, thoughts of Nicholas had begun to fray the edges of her concentration. She felt too restless for the pianoforte, but perhaps fresh air would do her some good. She was debating between going for a ride in Hyde Park or calling upon one of the young matrons she had met at the Misses Berry's weekly salon when she was interrupted by a soft rapping. At her bidding, the maid entered and presented her with a lavender calling card.

"Lady Draven to see you, my lady," she said.

Perfect. A distraction.

Helena went downstairs and affixed a bright smile on her face. The smile slipped a notch, however, when Marianne walked in. She had never seen the other in such a state. Normally, her friend's toilette was immaculate—not a hair out of place, every stitch and seam in perfect accordance with high fashion.

Today, however, Marianne wore a nondescript blue walking dress, the kind that eschewed any particular style and that a countrified lady might wear. Helena herself had a closetful of such plain gowns. Rather than its usual elaborate curled coiffure, Marianne's hair hung in a simple braid. Silver-blonde wisps haloed her face.

"Marianne, how are you?" Helena asked cautiously.

"I am well, thank you." Marianne seated herself and removed her gloves. Her foot tapped against the carpet. She ran her gaze listlessly around the room. "I am simply dying of boredom and thought you might care to join me for a ride."

"Where?" Helena asked, after a moment's hesitation.

The old Marianne flashed her wry smile. "Do not concern yourself, dear. I had nothing more exciting in mind than Hyde Park. We will have to find a quiet corner, mind you, to avoid the parade of Cits on a Saturday."

"Well, yes, then," Helena said. "That sounds agreeable."

Soon thereafter, Marianne's barouche deposited them on a relatively quiet stretch of the park along the edge of the Serpentine. On the verdant lawn, a trio of ladies picnicked under the shade of parasols while, under the watchful eye of the nannies, their progeny tossed crumbs to the ducks. Marianne and Helena started along the pebbled path that wound alongside the river.

"Lovely day, is it not?" Marianne said from beneath the brim of her rather large hat. A breeze ruffled the translucent veil that shielded her face.

Helena frowned. The Marianne she knew never bothered with niceties. And she could not help but notice that her friend seemed a trifle energetic, looking about as if she expected to see someone. "What *is* the matter, Marianne? You do not seem yourself."

"Do I not?" Marianne's laugh sounded forced. "'Tis merely malaise. Who would guess that depravity could become tiresome? You must cheer me up, my dear, with news of your *imbroglio*. How goes it with Harteford?"

Helena hesitated, but in the end her frustration with her husband won out. A certain relief came from describing Nicholas' incomprehensible behavior to Marianne. Perhaps her wise friend could unravel the mysteries of the male mind.

When she finished, Marianne said, "It sounds to me that Harteford thinks he is undeserving of you. Makes sense, I suppose."

Though she was annoyed at Nicholas, Helena found herself

jumping to his defense. "Why do you say that? Harteford is a catch in every way. He is handsome, successful, titled—"

"Come, Helena, you cannot be as naive as all that. Everyone knows your lord is the product of a brief fling between the former marquess and an opera singer. The fact that the marquess was married for a short time to said singer, long enough to make Harteford legitimate, does not change how the *ton* views your husband. And the fact that he has a profession ..." Marianne shrugged, as if no further explanation was required. "It would hardly be a surprise if he harbors insecurities about his position in Society."

Nicholas, *insecure*? 'Twas a bewildering notion, given that she'd always seen him as so utterly self-possessed. So masculine and powerful.

"Harteford has mentioned nothing of this," Helena said in disbelief. "Of course I know about his parentage, but what does it matter? Why, I should think people would admire him as I do for all he has accomplished on his own merit. And I cannot recall any snubs or untoward behavior directed at him."

"Love really is blind, then." Marianne gave her a faint smile. "Given your lord's status and influence, it's true that the slights are subtle. But they are there. I have also noticed that your husband tends to avoid the affairs of the *ton*."

"Harteford is busy. He does not care overly much for social gatherings."

Even as she spoke, Helena was feverishly reviewing the evidence. If only she had paid more attention to how others reacted to Nicholas—but she hadn't, because she'd been too intent on pleasing him. On not letting *him* down in Society's eyes. Had her own insecurities, those of a perennial wallflower, blinded her to Nicholas' ostracism?

Thinking back, on the rare occasion that Nicholas had accompanied her to a society event, he *had* seemed tense. And perhaps there *had* been a few subtle smirks and whispering behind fluttering fans. She had thought herself the outcast, but could it be that Nicholas—strong, magnificent *Nicholas*—was an object of ridicule?

"Harteford may be admitted into the finest drawing rooms because of his title and his connection to your family, but that is not the same as true acceptance," Marianne said.

With prickling remorse, Helena wondered if he had run into those prejudices at the musicale. The musicale that *she* had insisted he attend when he obviously had not wished to go. Was that why he had been so angry? And, to top it off, the scene that Papa had caused ... and she had defended her father's actions as being those of a gentleman. Her lashes fluttered. Could it truly be that Nicholas thought he was not good enough for her?

"Oh, Nicholas, could you be such a fool?" she whispered.

"He is, after all, a man," Marianne said.

"I must speak to him at once." Helena stopped abruptly in the middle of the path. "I must tell him that it is not true, that I care not about his origins or his past—"

"Since you are considering the business of honesty, might I suggest you confess your secrets as well?"

Helena swallowed. The fear that she kept suppressed, that had been omnipresent since that night at the Nunnery, bubbled to the surface. What if Nicholas found her lack of virtue disappointing—or worse yet, an insurmountable barrier to his affection? Could he love her if she was not the lady he believed her to be? And could he forgive her for deceiving him?

"I will tell him eventually," she said in a small voice. "When things are more settled between the two of us."

"The longer you put it off, the harder it will be." When Helena gave her a pleading look, Marianne sighed. "For what it's worth, take my advice. Whenever and however you choose to reveal the truth, seduce him first. It will improve his disposition."

Chapter Twelve

"Welcome home, my lord."

Well aware of the disapproval lacing Crikstaff's words, Nicholas tossed the butler his hat and greatcoat and strode into the house. With the furor at the warehouse, he hadn't been home in three days. He badly needed a bath and a meal. Perhaps then he might be able to catch a few hours of sleep before heading back to attend to the crisis. He glanced at the clock in the hallway. Nearly half past two. He sighed. Ambrose Kent of the Thames River Police was due to call at three. The man kept time more precisely than a damned Charley. So much for sleep.

He'd decided to settle for a quick bath when he heard the music. Soft and mournful, the melody wrapped itself around his senses and pulled him toward the drawing room. The door rested partially ajar, and he could not help himself from peering inside. Helena sat at the pianoforte, her fingers gliding over the keys. He could see her profile, the sensuous tilt of her chin as her head moved with the music. The flawless ivory of her skin was like a cameo juxtaposed against the blue wall behind her. Her eyes were closed. A dreamy smile shaped her lips as she lost herself in the beauty she was creating.

He backed away.

A floor board creaked.

The music halted. The next instant, his wife was in the doorway. Based on their last meeting, he didn't know what to expect from her—anger or coldness, both of which he fully deserved. Yet her full lips formed a hesitant smile. Her luminous brown eyes, shot with green and gold, were searching his, and he felt as if he was drowning in the warmth of a summer pond.

"My lord, you are home," she said.

It took him a moment to recover his wits. "Please, do not let me disturb your practice," he said. "I was on my way upstairs—"

"I was nearly finished and about to take tea. Won't you join me?"

He was about to refuse, but his stomach growled.

A dimple peeped out from his wife's cheek. "I'll take that as a yes."

When still he hesitated, she gave him an exasperated look. "For heaven's sake, Harteford, I know we are to live separate lives, but surely we can have tea from time to time. I don't bite, you know. We can converse on nothing beyond the weather, if it suits you."

Feeling like an idiot, he nodded. He followed his wife to the sitting area and watched with hooded eyes as she served him. She poured his tea the way he preferred it, with plenty of cream and no sugar; despite himself, it charmed him that she remembered. With silver tongs, she filled a plate with sandwiches and bits of pastry and fruit. Her movements were as graceful as the music she played and wove a similar enchantment around his senses.

"Thank you," he said, taking the plate she offered.

He bit into a sandwich. The bread was soft with butter and layered with thin slices of savory ham. Suddenly ravenous, he took another bite. It seemed he had consumed an ocean of coffee today, yet he could not recall when he had last eaten. His plate was clean before he knew it. He eyed the service, only to realize that Helena was observing him, an amused glint in her eye.

"Not had time to eat today, my lord?" she asked, as she refilled his plate.

"Not much," he admitted. He drank his tea. It was hot and fortifying. "I have been otherwise occupied. The warehouse has been in an uproar."

Helena handed him the replenished plate. "Really? Over what?"

He hesitated. He swallowed a mouthful of lemon pudding before answering, "Theft."

"At the warehouse?" his wife asked in incredulous tones.

He nodded. "The place was ransacked three days ago. The thieves got away with rum and tobacco. We're still counting up the spice inventory to see what is missing. The pepper bins—" He stopped abruptly, remembering who he was talking to.

His wife, a lady who should not be hearing about the vulgar details of trade.

His wife, whom he vowed to distance himself from.

Yet the concern in her eyes quite undid him. "That is quite a lot of cargo, is it not? Will it hurt the profits badly?" she asked.

"It won't help, that's for certain, but it would take a much larger hit to hurt Fines and Company." Nicholas gulped down more tea. "The River Police has been alerted. The other merchants on the dock have been informed as well, for the thieves may try to sell off their bounty. A concerted effort may help recover some of the goods."

"The other merchants, they will help?" Helena asked, a little wrinkle between her brows. "After all, I imagine the lure of quality goods at a cheap price must be great."

At his wife's perceptive comment, Nicholas felt the corner of his mouth edge upward. It would serve him well to remember that despite her fragile appearance and inexperience in worldly matters, his lady possessed an unusually agile mind.

"Under ordinary circumstances, you would be correct," he

said. "However, it has long been the understanding of us merchants that our interests are best served when we band together in the face of those who threaten our well-being—be it pilferage or detrimental political agendas. Our association met this morning to determine the best plan of action."

His wife slanted him a glance from beneath her lashes. "So this is why you have been away from home the last three days?"

"Yes." Feeling the stress and lack of sleep advancing upon him, Nicholas deposited his plate on the coffee table. He leaned his elbows on his thighs and rubbed his hands over his face. "And, I am sorry to say, it is not yet over."

He stiffened when he felt the cushion depress beside him. Hands, soft and supple, moved over the shoulders of his jacket. He jerked upright.

"What are you doing?" His voice was raspy, incredulous.

Next to him on the couch, Helena smiled in what could only be termed a wifely manner. "Helping you to relax, my lord. Such fatigue cannot be healthful."

Her hands rolled over his tense muscles again. No doubt she intended her touch to be gentle, soothing. Instead, the pressure of her fingers sent fire raging through his veins.

"Such ministrations are not necessary," he managed, trying to shift away.

"Nonsense. Hold still. This shan't help if you are moving all about."

"Helena, you mustn't—"

His words were lost in a groan as she found the knots at the junction of neck and shoulder. With unerring strokes, she worked at loosening the balled sinew. Shocks of pleasure-pain jolted through his system. His scalp tingled. Dimly, he knew he should stop this madness immediately, but *Christ Almighty* her hands felt good.

Her voice brushed his ear from behind. "You work too hard,

Harteford. Though I admire your industriousness more than I can say, you must take better care of yourself. See how stiff you are?"

He was *beyond* stiff, Nicholas thought with an inward groan. His belly twitched, his groin burgeoning with heat. He should pull away, go ... but her wifely solicitude was too much to resist. He shuddered as her fingers slipped beneath his cravat and sent the noose drifting to the floor. With a nimble touch, she sought and released the points of tension along his neck, rubbing deeply, caressing softly. No one had ever done this for him before. His mind went fuzzy with bliss. His neck arched into her hands.

"How does that feel, my lord?" Helena's voice feathered against his ear.

"Bloody good." He groaned a little as her fingers pushed deeper into his tensed flesh. He was acutely aware of her sitting behind him, the puff of her breath. Tension crackled in the space between their bodies. When her fingers massaged upward, over his neck and onto his jaw, he gave into temptation. He captured her hand in his own and pressed a kiss in her palm.

"My lord, do you want me to stop?"

Her breathy tones came from the depths of his darkest fantasies. For an instant, he teetered between desire and sense.

"Don't ever stop," he growled.

In the next breath, he was upon her. His lips took hers in a kiss of burning possession as he pressed her back into the cushions. By God, she was soft. Sweet. Through the haze of lust, a faint notion appeared, telling him to slow down, to be careful lest he frighten her again, but she opened to him, welcoming him into her warmth. The shy brush of her tongue annihilated his rationality, his restraint. His sordid past became a blur, his numerous faults incidental as he plundered what she offered. The beast within him roared to life—he had to have her. Nothing else mattered but the primal recognition that she was *his*.

He thrust himself deeper into her silky cavern. She tasted of tea and honey, of everything good. His tongue found hers, and the slick twining made them both moan. His fingers tightened in her soft locks, holding her still as he drank and drank of her. The little sounds she made drove him insane. As did the plush softness of her curves as she wiggled against him. She was so innocent, so damned arousing ...

Unable to resist, he broke from her lips to nuzzle a soft spot behind her ear. The scent of orange blossoms filled his head, luring him down the column of her neck. The skin there was just as fragrant, just as delectable. He flicked his tongue against the pulse throbbing at the hollowed junction. She gasped, her neck arching upward. He obliged her, his mouth traveling to the quivering tops of her tits. He kissed the firm flesh and licked into the crevice between.

"Oh, yes," she panted. "Please."

His nostrils flared at the pleading in her voice. A knot deep in his chest relaxed. By some miracle, even after their wedding night, she wasn't afraid of him, disgusted by him. Could it be that his demure lady *wanted* his touch?

"Again, darling," he rasped against her breasts. "Ask me for it again."

"Please." Her voice hitched as he brought his hands to join his mouth. "More, Nicholas. *Please*."

Arousal rushed to his head at the sound of his name. His thumbs found the hardened nipples beneath the soft fabric of her bodice. Tenderly, he worked them, rolling, squeezing until she whimpered in pleasure. Her fingers dug into his shoulders, a silent plea for more. He groaned. How ready he was to give it to her. His turgid cock throbbed against his smalls. His head dipped for a kiss, the silky slide of her tongue enticing him into imagining how hot and wet another entrance must be ...

There was a knock at the door.

He froze, refusing to believe the Gods would be so cruel.

More knocking.

Perhaps if he ignored whoever it was, the bastard would go away.

"Harteford," his wife gasped. "We must—"

"Shh," he whispered. "If we remain silent—"

The rapping came again, this time more insistently.

Helena began to struggle in earnest beneath him. Her wriggles spread wildfire over his loins, already taut as a mast in full wind.

"*Bloody hell.*" He issued several more choice words before extricating himself from the tangle of his wife's skirts. He helped Helena to sit up; her hands fluttered immediately to her hair. Wincing, he attempted to find a comfortable sitting position, one that did not strain his erection any further. In the end, he blew out a breath and settled his jacket over his lap.

"Yes, come in." He all but snarled the words.

Crikstaff edged through the door. He looked ready to bolt at any minute. Good. The man had some sense of self-preservation at least.

Flushed and flustered, Helena nonetheless smiled at the butler. "Yes, Crikstaff?"

Crikstaff warmed immediately and bowed low. "My lady. There is a gentleman to see Lord Harteford." The butler sniffed to emphasize that the word *gentleman* was applied generously in this case. "His name is Mr. Ambrose Kent, and he identifies himself as a member of the River Police. He claims he is expected."

As exact as the damned night watchman.

"Send him in," Nicholas said.

After Crikstaff retreated, Nicholas turned to Helena. Even as reality splashed over his brain like a bucket of icy water, he felt his lips twitch. She was madly pushing pins into her gloriously wild locks. With her kiss-swollen lips pursed in concentration, she attempted to smooth her skirts this way and that. He might have told her it was no use—the crumpled material looked as if it had been trampled on by a herd of elephants. But she was adorable, muttering to herself, in complete and utter disarray.

The door swung open.

Ambrose Kent entered. He moved with determined energy despite his considerable height. His well-worn garments hung from thin limbs, giving him the appearance of a ragged scarecrow. He had a long ascetic face, like that of a monk. His eyes were an odd shade, like the pale amber of ale, and they immediately took stock of the room. From his past interactions with Kent, Nicholas suspected the man missed very little. It was the reason he both trusted and remained wary of Kent. The policeman's eyes sharpened on Helena.

"Lady Harteford, may I introduce Mr. Ambrose Kent, of the Thames River Police," Nicholas said as he stood, carefully keeping his jacket in front.

"Lady Harteford," Kent said, sweeping an unexpectedly elegant bow. "My felicitations on your recent nuptials."

"Thank you, Mr. Kent. Won't you sit and have some tea?"

Kent looked nonplussed at her invitation. On the social ladder, a policeman fell several rungs below even a merchant, hovering just above the criminals he apprehended. Nicholas supposed it was an unusual day when Kent was offered tea by a marchioness.

Not that Kent was complaining. He was too busy polishing off a slice of cream cake and enjoying the attention Helena lavished him with.

"Is it true that children are oft found to be perpetrators of crime?" Helena asked.

"Aye. The prisons are full of them." Kent took a gulp of his tea. "Newgate, for instance, is rife with thieves as young as five or six."

"Five or six?" Helena echoed, clearly appalled. "I should think a child is not capable of knowing his own mind at so tender an age. How can he possibly be aware of the consequences of his actions?"

"You speak like a reformist, my lady," Kent said.

Helena blushed. "Such political energies I cannot claim, Mr. Kent. However, at the weekly salon I attend there is often talk of the works of Mrs. Fry and others like her. I find their approach more humane than the gallows or deportation. Education, the relief of poverty—these seem more effective strategies for managing the ills of our society, don't you agree?"

Kent grunted. "I have no idea, my lady. My job is to apprehend criminals, not nurse them."

"But wouldn't you say that all people, given food in their bellies and schooling for their minds, might be strengthened against vice?"

Taking pity on Kent, Nicholas said lightly, "One might say that point of view smacks of democratic fervor, my lady."

"I do not strive to be political," Helena insisted. "My only point is that children ought to be protected from, not punished for, their unfortunate circumstances of birth."

To that, Nicholas could think of no response. His wife was full of surprises today. He stared at her, wondering if she knew just how close she had come to describing her own husband's origins.

Silence weighed heavily for a moment. Helena got to her feet. Both Nicholas and Kent rose immediately.

"I am afraid I have taken too much of your time," she said. "As I am sure you gentlemen have important matters to discuss, I will excuse myself."

At the door, she stopped and turned. "My lord?"

"Yes?" Nicholas asked warily.

She blushed prettily, her lashes lowering. "I wanted to thank you for having tea with me today. I most enjoyed it."

With a swish of skirts, she was gone. A trace of her perfume lingered in the air.

Nicholas felt himself getting hard again.

"If you do not mind my saying, my lord, your wife is a fascinating woman."

"Yes, she is," Nicholas muttered.

Running his hands through his hair, he sat and tried to clear his head. He couldn't believe what he had let happen just now. How he had lost control with his own wife. But he couldn't bring himself to regret it either, not with the taste and feel of her still sparkling over his senses.

"Thank you for agreeing to meet with me at your residence, my lord." Kent took the adjacent chair and stretched his legs in front. "Given the state of the warehouse, this seemed a more private and safer place to discuss my recent findings."

That succeeded in securing Nicholas' attention. He focused on the other man and saw smug lines fanning from the investigator's pale eyes. "What news do you bring?"

"I have finished questioning the porters on guard duty the night of the theft—one of the two, at least. It seems Patrick Riley had drunk enough blue ruin to sink a ship and was three sheets to the wind while the thieves emptied the place." Kent shook his head in disgust. "The man could barely recall his mother's name, let alone any details of what happened."

"And the second porter?"

"James Gordon has disappeared and is nowhere to be found."

The picture of a timid, red-haired man came to Nicholas' mind. Crippled, with the manner of a mouse, Gordon seemed incapable of walking without tripping over his own two feet, let alone plotting a crime. "Do you think the villains got to him that night?" Nicholas asked tersely.

"I detected no signs of foul play at the warehouse," Kent replied, "so if they did Gordon in, they did it elsewhere. And there were no new floaters in the Thames matching his description. So either the fish got to him or he's rotting someplace else ... or he was somehow involved."

Nicholas frowned. "I take it you have conducted a search."

"Gordon's home, the taverns and brothels he frequented. His wife and friends say they haven't seen hide nor hair of him since the night of the robbery."

"It is a bloody hell of a coincidence that the man's gone missing," Nicholas admitted.

"I do not believe in coincidences," Kent replied. "Which is why I spent the earlier half of this afternoon at one of the brothels."

Nicholas refrained from making a joking rejoinder. In his past dealings with Kent, the man had shown himself to be singularly lacking in humor. "What did you discover?"

"I am always amazed at how much better informed the molls are than the wives. Or perhaps their selling price is simply cheaper. Gordon thought himself in love with a pretty piece named Sally Loverling. Convenient name for a whore, is it not? For the price of a shilling, Ms. Loverling rattled off an entire list of Gordon's known associates."

"Any names ring a bell?"

"Only one," Kent said. "It seems our friend Gordon has come up a ways from his origins. He grew up in the stews of St. Giles. His father died when Gordon was ten, and the family had a rough time of it. The mother remarried. A tough bastard by the name of Gerald Bragg. Bragg already had a son, ten years Gordon's senior—"

"Named Isaac." Nicholas felt the hairs rise on the back of his neck. "Goddamn it. Isaac Bragg is Gordon's *step-brother*?"

"I spoke to your steward. Jibotts did not know anything of it, but he did recall hiring Bragg partly on Gordon's recommendation. He also mentioned that Bragg has caused some trouble among the workers?"

"Bragg has been up to no good since the day he arrived." The blackmail notes flashed in Nicholas' head, and he told himself to tread carefully. After a brief hesitation, he added, "Perhaps a fortnight ago, I saw him lurking with another fellow in an alley by the warehouse. They looked suspicious—like they were doing something that couldn't see the light of day. They scurried off when I approached."

"Well, Bragg certainly was brazen as anything at work today, wasn't he? Raised quite a fuss about having to participate in the clean up." Kent's eyes grew crafty. "My men are monitoring his whereabouts as we speak. If he is our fiend, we will trail him to his lair and ambush him there tonight."

"I am coming," Nicholas said.

Kent's brows reached his hairline. "You, my lord? I do not think that wise. St. Giles is no place for a gentleman."

"Trust me, I can take care of myself," Nicholas said with grim certainty. "It is Bragg who has something to worry about."

Chapter Thirteen

St. Giles was just as Nicholas remembered, and the familiarity of it chilled him to the marrow. It seemed he had never left this place, this nightmarish maze of crooked streets and dark alleyways, where the air was thick with urine, vomit, and other remnants of human misery. He stood in the shadows, watching the drunks stumble out of the gin houses positioned at every corner of the square. They were met by a parade of whores, brightly painted to obscure the signs of disease. After bargaining for their pleasure, they headed in pairs or larger groups to the narrow gaps of alleys, where the fucking was cheap and quick, with no bed but the rough stone wall against your back.

Nicholas shook his head to clear it. He was here for a reason, and he had to stay focused. Beside him, Kent watched and waited with the patience of a saint. He seemed undisturbed by the surroundings, his policeman's eyes taking in all with cool detachment. His attention was focused on the flash house across the street, the den of vice that supported all manner of criminal activity. Nicholas knew inside the fire was warm, the gin even warmer; inside, thieves, murderers, and whores played after a long day's work.

He did not have to enter the premises to see the interior. All flash houses were the same. The scarred tables would offer cards, tin platters of hot, greasy food and tankards of soul-obliterating drink. Underneath the boisterous roar of the crowd, the rhythm of depravity continued: thieves haggled with their fences, pick pockets plied their trade, and gin-bloated cutthroats started brawls that ended bloody. If you had the coin to escape upstairs, you might have a moment of peace between the well-traveled thighs of a wench, at fifteen or sixteen already past her prime. She might tell you she loved you, and you might believe it, if you were desperate enough.

Kent was saying something to him, and the words brought him back to the task at hand. He nodded at Kent's instructions to stay put and watched as the other man slipped away into the shadows. Likely Kent was checking on the other entrances—a flash house always had multiple escape routes. Nicholas felt grudging admiration for the man's thoroughness. For a member of the police force, Kent seemed decent enough, not like the thief takers who would bend the law for a shilling or two. Or for other forms of payment, performed in fear and darkness.

Nicholas shook away the memories. There were too many of them tonight, crowding in on him like hungry ghosts. Maybe he should not have come. He dispelled that thought immediately. He was not a man to rest on his laurels while some bastard stole from him. While some coward toyed with him and penned threatening notes about the past.

At that moment, he saw a lone figure emerge from the front entrance of the flash house. He had his collar pulled high and his hat pulled low. Nothing unusual about that in the stews. But there was something about the man's swagger that made Nicholas look closer. Sure enough, when the man stopped to light his tobacco, the spark of the flint revealed beady eyes and a bearded face.

Bragg.

Nicholas felt his fists curl in their gloves.

Bragg finished his smoke and started off into the night. There was no sign of Kent or any of Kent's three men. Bragg must have slipped beneath their noses. Nicholas briefly considered alerting them, but he would alert Bragg as well, and he could not risk that. At large in the rookery, Bragg would be harder to find than a fish let loose in the Thames. Besides, it might be better to go this alone; if Bragg turned out to be the blackmailer, Nicholas wanted to settle the business far from the eyes of the law.

Nicholas moved stealthily, keeping to the shadows. Some habits never died, and he knew well enough how to stay out of sight. He kept to Bragg's blind spot, stopping now and again to fake interest in the barrows of fenced goods. The fog had turned to drizzle now, and the slickened streets began to empty of the hawkers and whores. Bragg continued to strut along as if he owned the streets, a bottle of gin fueling his journey.

They were heading east, into the heart of the slums. Nicholas knew these parts as surely as he knew his own face. After all, he had grown up in his aunt's house in Bottom's End, a row aptly named for the place its inhabitants occupied in the world. *Aunt Amy*. Her image ambushed him: the puffed face and greasy lank hair, the satisfied gleam in her small eyes as she'd counted the bag of coins—shillings, she'd sold him for. Shillings for a life of indentured hell. But he had escaped that life and would never have seen her again, had it not been at the insistence of Jeremiah Fines.

"You must make peace with your past, if there is to be a future, my boy," Jeremiah had said.

Accompanied by his new mentor, he had returned to that house, found it as rotted and foul as ever. Nothing had changed. Rats had played with the screaming babes as Aunt Amy looked Jeremiah up and down. She'd made a pretense of listening to Jeremiah's praise of him, of his potential to become a worthy merchant; all along, Nicholas had seen her sizing up his mentor's fine clothes, the gold watch fob dangling from the waistcoat. When she had finally spoken, her accusation had been so abhorrent that Jeremiah had actually paled. But it was with her next words that his aunt revealed her true character.

"I don't care 'ow you want to use the boy, guv'nor. So long as I get me fair share for putting up wif 'im all 'em years."

Jeremiah had hauled him out of the house, Aunt Amy's curses ringing behind them.

Those curses echoed now as two drunks brawled in the street. The houses grew more decrepit, the road more narrow, at some parts barely wide enough for two men to pass without bumping shoulders. Nicholas stayed a safe distance behind, aware that there would be no place to hide should he be spotted. He kept his hand in his pocket, next to the solid handle of the pistol he carried. There was the knife, too, concealed in his boot. Habit, again. He had lived in the stews long enough to know that a man foolhardy enough to wander the streets unarmed was inviting trouble.

Bragg turned a corner, and Nicholas counted to ten before following. Several steps along, a ruckus erupted from one of the houses. A body propelled out of a doorway, slamming into him. Nicholas held onto his balance, stumbling backward as another body followed the first. He stepped out of harm's way as the fists began to fly. There was shouting and the crack of glass against stone. The men circled each other, broken bottles in hand. A crowd gathered round to cheer on the violence.

Nicholas craned his neck to look past the growing mob. His eyes collided with small ones which widened like those of a cornered rat. Bragg dropped his bottle and broke into a run. Swearing, Nicholas made after him, slowed by the bodies jostling against one another for the best view of the bloodshed. When he finally made it past the throng, he glimpsed Bragg rounding a corner up ahead. He raced after him, his boots slippery in the mud.

He turned left and saw immediately that it was a dead end. There were a handful of buildings on both sides, all of them nothing but rotted frames and gutted-out insides, waiting to be felled by a strong gust. Nevertheless, a faint glow emanated from some of the broken windows; the desperate could not afford to be choosy. Taking a few cautious steps forward, Nicholas took measure of the darkness. There were many places for a man to hide. A sudden shuffle to his left had the hairs rising on his neck. Even as he turned toward the house, his hand tightening on the pistol, he knew it was too late.

He sensed rather than saw the movement from the shadowed interior.

A blast tore through the night.

He fell to the ground, a pain like wildfire spreading across his head. Footsteps neared, and he curled instinctively against the voice that rasped over him. Blood trickled into his eyes, obscuring the shape looming over him in the darkness.

"We could have done this easy, but your lordship had to interfere," came the low, silky tones. "That's the problem with the peerage—they just can't follow instructions."

Nicholas struggled to hold onto consciousness. "B-bugger your instructions. Who are you? What ... what do you want?"

The laughter shivered down Nicholas' spine. "I'm a ghost from your past, of course. Come to exact the ultimate price ... unless you do exactly as I say."

"Do what you will." Pain robbed his voice of emphasis, made his mind weak, but Nicholas clung on, breathing hard. "I'll not be blackmailed by the likes of you."

"Won't you now?" Another soft, menacing laugh. "Not even for your wife? To guarantee the delectable Lady Helena's continued good health?"

"*Keep her out of this.*" In a blind rage, Nicholas lunged upward. A boot connected with his wound, and he gasped in agony, the world spinning into pitch.

"Await my instructions," the voice said.

Dimly, Nicholas heard a shout in the distance. Another shot fired. Footsteps approaching. As the darkness closed around him, he felt a fear more suffocating than death. *Please God, don't let anything happen to her.* His past bore down upon him, the slick of blood upon his hands again, the sickening coppery smell of it filling his nostrils. Somehow, he had always known it would end this way for him: alone, surrounded by the stench and filth of the stews. He had never escaped, not really. The rookery always claimed its own.

His other life had been but a mirage, a beautiful dream.

Helena, my love.

Then he felt nothing at all.

Chapter Fourteen

"My lady, you do look a treat," Bessie said, running the brush a final time through Helena's loose tresses.

Helena studied her reflection in the dressing table mirror. She thought she did look rather well, with her hair tumbling free over her shoulders and down her back. Her cheeks were pink and her eyes sparkling with anticipation. It was nearing midnight; Nicholas would be home at any moment. He and Mr. Kent had departed on business together this afternoon, and he had left word with Crikstaff that he would return later tonight.

That would be her opportunity. It was now or never to try to seduce her hard-headed husband. She would invite him into her sitting room for refreshment, conversation ... and wherever else that led. She smiled to herself. Given what had transpired earlier in the drawing room, she thought her chances of success rather good.

"The French do have a way with fashions," Bessie continued, leaning down to fuss with the tie on Helena's peignoir. "Who would have thought to make a dressing gown out of chiffon?"

"No tailor residing in London, that is for sure," Helena agreed, rubbing her arms.

"Goodness me, are you chilled my lady?" Bessie asked. "I had thought the fire warm enough, but here I am in my woolens. I will call Mary to build up the fire—"

"I am fine," Helena reassured her. "But perhaps you can check with Crikstaff to make sure the supper is ready."

"Of course," Bessie said. "And where would you like it served?"

"Here in the sitting room will do nicely," Helena said. "Have the footmen set up a small table by the fire. And do not let Crikstaff forget the champagne."

"Yes, my lady," the maid said with a twinkle in her eye. She hurried off.

Helena got up from the dressing table and walked over to the full-length looking glass. Turning this way and that, she experienced a giddy sense of satisfaction. The sensual creature in the mirror could not be her—and yet it was. Garbed in a sheer peignoir that drifted to the floor in hazy bronze swirls, the woman looked the very picture of seduction. She threw back her shoulders, and the chiffon slid down her arms, baring the thin straps of a glimmering bronze negligee.

Madame Rousseau had assured her that the negligee was all the rage in Paris and worn by all the fashionable ladies. Clearly, it was a garment designed for the purposes of *amour*: the neckline plunged daringly between the breasts and halfway to the navel. Honey lace filled the deep crevice, creating intriguing peek-a-boo views of her bosom. The body-skimming satin fell to her ankles, and movement was made possible by the twin slits that began mid-hip. In her whole life, Helena had never worn anything so scandalous. It was almost like being naked. More so, in fact, as the satin and chiffon seemed to draw attention to select parts of her nakedness.

It felt most daring, most wanton.

She hoped Nicholas would like it.

Readjusting her peignoir, she looked at the clock on the mantel. Ten minutes to midnight. Nicholas would surely be home soon. She needed to occupy herself until his return, or she would burst out of her skin. Settling into one of the wingback chairs by the fireplace, she draped a blanket over herself and examined the small stack of books on the side table. She picked up a heavy, well-worn volume. The book was on loan from Miss Lavinia Haversham, a friendly spinster she had met through the Misses Berry's weekly salon. The topic at one meeting had been female philosophers; Miss Lavinia had been quite shocked that Helena had never heard of Mary Wollstonecraft.

"Goodness gracious, where *have* you been hiding?" Miss Lavinia had asked.

Helena had explained that before her marriage she had been allowed to read only the most genteel of literatures intended to improve the mind of young ladies. Lady Epplethistle's *Compleat Guide*, for instance. While she had managed to pilfer a few volumes of Shakespeare's plays from her father's library, that had been the extent of it. The good Miss Lavinia had snorted and, at the following meeting, handed Helena a book. Opening the burgundy leather cover now, Helena studied the title page.

A Vindication of the Rights of Women.

It sounded promising enough. Within moments, she lost herself in the passionate, rambling, and altogether mind-altering prose.

When Helena finally looked up, she blinked fuzzily at the clock. It could not be—*two hours* had passed? It was nearing two in the morning, and Nicholas had not yet returned. With a frown, she put down the book and went to the table the servants had brought in. Thank goodness she had chosen to serve a simple collation which could be enjoyed at room temperature. The champagne, the only item that needed to be chilled, rested in a silver bucket filled with melting ice. She plucked a grape from the artfully arranged platter and bit into the purple globe.

Nicholas should have been home by now. What could have detained him?

Pacing in front of the fire, she tried to calm herself. There must be some good explanation. Most likely he and Mr. Kent had got caught up in details surrounding the theft. Or perhaps Nicholas had stopped by his club for a drink. He'd gotten held up in a game of cards or something of the like.

But Nicholas did not gaming—he thought it a waste of time. And would he be still consulting with Mr. Kent at *two in the morning*?

Helena gnawed on the tip of her thumbnail. Perhaps it was the influence of Miss Wollstonecraft's writings, but at this moment her capacity to reason seemed dwarfed by the tides of sensibility washing over her. This behavior was most unlike her and more like ... *her mother's*.

With a groan, Helena pushed away that thought. She had enough to worry about without upending that particular pin drawer. Despite her best efforts to rationally analyze the situation, she felt a rising panic. Nicholas could be lying injured somewhere. Beset by footpads. Or, sweet heavens, could he have gone back to the Nunnery? That possibility shocked her system like icy water. What if even now he was searching for the mystery nymph? Prowling the bawdy house, ready to select a substitute if he did not find her ...?

Attempting to breathe deeply, she pulled on the bell.

Several minutes later, a sleepy-eyed Bessie came into the room. The maid slanted a look at the untouched supper service, and her eyes grew large.

"Is everything alright, my lady?" Bessie asked.

Helena forced herself to speak calmly. "Lord Harteford has not yet returned. If you would be so kind as to see if he sent word?"

"Of course," Bessie said.

But of course he had not. Crikstaff would have informed her immediately if the master had sent a note. Helena took up the pacing again. Just as she was contemplating summoning the carriage and heading to the Nunnery herself, she heard a sound from below stairs. She went still, her breathing loud in her ears. Yes, there it was again, the unmistakable sound of a key rattling in the front door. She hurried toward the bedchamber door, remembering just in time to throw on a woolen dressing gown. She cracked open the door and peered out. The hallway was empty save for flickering shadows.

She could hear murmurs now, coming from below stairs. There was Crikstaff and ... yes, Nicholas. She let out the breath she had not realized she'd been holding. Then her brows puckered. Yes, that was Nicholas' distinctively deep voice, but his tones were rumbling in a most unusual manner. Good heavens, was he ... *singing*? And there were other male voices now, quiet and low, voices she could not quite place.

What on earth was going on?

She tied the sash of the robe tightly at the waist and headed to the stairs. Halfway down, she was met by Bessie coming up.

"Oh, my lady, I was just coming to fetch you." The maid's lips trembled, and some of her brown curls had escaped from beneath her mob cap. "Mr. Crikstaff said to—"

"Whatever is the matter, Bessie?"

"It's Lord Harteford," Bessie whispered. "He's been shot."

It took a moment for the words to register.

Nicholas. *Shot.*

Helena flew past Bessie and down the stairs. She hurtled toward the voices coming from the drawing room. She stopped short in the doorway. Nicholas was slumped on the settee, Mr. Kent standing to one side of him. Another man she did not recognize was checking on the bandage wrapped around Nicholas' head.

"H-how badly is he injured?" she asked in a choked voice.

At her words, Mr. Kent and the other man turned. Nicholas blinked owlishly.

"Lady Harteford." Mr. Kent bowed, speaking quickly. "Pray do not concern yourself. Lord Harteford is fine. He has encountered a mere flesh wound and has been recovering rapidly under Dr. Farraday's care."

"Quite so." Tall and distinguished-looking, Dr. Farraday

appeared to be in his fifties and spoke with a thick Scottish accent. "'Tis quite fortunate I arrived when I did. Mr. Morg—, I mean to say Lord Harteford, suffered no great blood loss. The bullet only grazed the temple. It took but a few stitches to patch him up. He's right as rain now, aren't you, lad?"

Recovering her senses, Helena stumbled over to the settee. Kneeling, she looked up at her husband's ragged face. Beneath the snowy bandage, his forehead was pale. His jaw was stubbly with a night beard, and lines bracketed his mouth. His hazy grey eyes appeared blood-shot and slightly unfocused.

To her, he was the most precious sight in the whole world.

"Thank God," she whispered, rubbing her cheek against his hand before looking up. "Does it hurt very much, my darling?"

"Better bloody believe it," Nicholas agreed cheerfully. "Like 'avin' a flamin' poker shoved 'tween the ears. Or up the—"

"Dr. Farraday," Helena said with a frown, "your patient is in *pain*. Is there nothing you can do?"

Dr. Farraday smiled wryly. "Your husband already finished a bottle of whiskey. I would not advise more pain relief than that. After a good night's sleep, he should be fit as a fiddle."

"Harteford's got a hard skull," Mr. Kent agreed.

The two men apparently found that remark humorous as they both stood there with smirks upon their faces.

Helena continued to frown at the good doctor as Nicholas picked up her hand and began to kiss it playfully. "Surely you have instructions for his care, Doctor. Is there anything specific I am to do?"

"I 'ave some ideas fer you," Nicholas said, with a good-natured leer.

"In a minute, my love," Helena said soothingly as she extricated her hand. She stood to face the doctor and Mr. Kent. Her eyes narrowed at the ill-concealed looks of amusement on the men's faces. "Do you not think you are taking my husband's injury a bit too lightly, Dr. Farraday?"

Dr. Farraday stopped smiling. "Lady Harteford, I am an experienced physician. I have seen hundreds of such cases and far worse, I might add."

"In your *experience* then, Dr. Farraday," Helena said, "is there not some intervention for a patient who at this very moment professes to be in agonizing pain?"

"Yer a 'eartless bastard, Farraday," Nicholas agreed and yawned hugely.

"Furthermore," Helena continued, crossing her arms, "what is your advice on monitoring the state of my husband's injury? What are the signs of infection that I should be aware of? How oft need his dressing be changed? What is the expected healing time for such a wound?"

Dr. Farraday turned a dull shade of red.

Ambrose Kent spoke up. "Lady Harteford," he said in the placating tones that one might use with a high-strung horse or a slow-witted child, "I understand your concern. But, you see, Farraday here is one of the finest physicians in London. He has attended countless such injuries before—"

Helena cut him off with a hand. "Yes, speaking of injuries, I confess I am most curious as to how my husband sustained his. How is it, Mr. Kent, that the Marquess of Harteford came to arrive home with a bullet wound to the head?"

Mr. Kent shoved his hands in his pockets. He exchanged looks with Dr. Farraday, who shrugged as if to say, *You're on your own with that one, lad*.

"It was but a small matter, my lady," Mr. Kent began.

"A *small* matter?" Helena's hands braced her hips. "You return my husband to me, bloody and bandaged, and you call that a *small* matter?"

For a moment, Kent looked almost shamefaced. Then he jerked his head toward the couch.

"It was his lordship's own idea," he muttered. "I told him St. Giles was no place—"

Helena whitened at the mention of the notorious slum. "You took Harteford to *St. Giles*? No one in their right mind ventures forth there! Why, it is said that there are gin houses on every block and places called rookeries where crime flourishes among men, women, even children ..."

"You are remarkably well informed, my lady," Kent said, a touch of admiration in his voice. "The literary society again, I presume?"

"What in *heaven's name* were you doing there with my husband?"

Kent shrank back a little at the fierce look in Helena's eyes.

"We were following a man suspected to be involved in the warehouse theft." Kent spoke with his shoulders hunched. "I told your husband to stay in position while I checked in with my men. But he must have seen the villain and took off after him like some bloody hero. He was lucky I had one of my men posted farther up along the street. He followed your husband and the suspect for most of the way and intervened when he saw Lord Harteford getting ... ahem, injured."

"Obviously, the timing of your man's intervention leaves something to be desired," Helena snapped.

"Caster is one of my best men," Kent said stiffly. "He did all he could. If it hadn't been for him, Harteford might have sustained a more serious injury."

"I must be sure to convey my gratitude, then."

"It was his lordship's own idea to follow the suspect," Kent grumbled. "I told him to stay put. For God's sake, back me on this, Harteford—"

A soft snoring emerged from the couch. Nicholas had fallen asleep sitting up.

For a moment, Helena observed her sleeping lord. Then she sighed. If he was to be passed out drunk as a wheelbarrow, he might as well do so comfortably. She bent over and lifted her husband's legs one by one onto the seat cushions. Her breath puffed with the effort it required to move his muscular limbs. Once Nicholas was sprawled fully on the couch, she arranged a tasseled cushion under his head. He continued to snore blissfully, undisturbed even as she began to pull off his left boot.

A dangerous-looking blade tumbled out.

She turned accusing eyes at Mr. Kent. The policeman kept his gaze glued to a landscape on the wall, his concentration worthy of an art critic at the Royal Academy. With an unladylike snort, Helena finished tending to Nicholas, tucking his discarded jacket securely around him and brushing her fingers over his bristly jaw. In his sleep, his mouth hung open a little, like a child's after a particularly exhausting afternoon of play.

Only Nicholas had not been playing—he had been busy getting shot at. Why had he acted so recklessly? Why, she thought with helpless frustration, did she understand so little about this husband of hers?

Straightening, she faced the other two men in the room. Both looked like they wished to be elsewhere. Dr. Farraday, she noticed, had inched closer toward the door.

"Perhaps we should take our leave," Mr. Kent said in a low, hopeful voice. "It has been a long night, and we would not want to intrude upon your hospitality."

"Allow me to offer some refreshment," Helena said evenly, "and afterward you will tell me everything. And I do mean *everything*."

Chapter Fifteen

Nicholas opened his eyes.

For a blessed moment, he thought it all a dream. He was in his bedchamber, lying in his own bed. He had no idea what time of day it was. When he tried to sit up, sudden bright pain lanced through his head. He fell back on the pillow and had to wait to regain his breath. Grimacing, he brought his hand to his temple and encountered a swaddled barrier. Not a dream, then. He shut his eyes as it came back to him, all of it.

The night in the rookery, the specters of the past rising all around him. The sickening, humiliating fear that would never leave him—that wrenched his gut even now as he realized the consequences of his selfishness. It was his fault that Helena was now in jeopardy; by marrying her, he'd all but thrust her in harm's way. For the villain, whoever he was, knew about her. Had threatened to harm her if Nicholas refused to obey whatever nefarious demands were sure to follow.

Bile rose in Nicholas' throat. Moaning, he tried to turn onto his side, to reach the edge of the bed in time. Miracle of miracles, a chamber pot stood there waiting. His insides emptied in sour wave. The door opened. He looked up with bleary, stinging eyes to see Helena rushing toward him.

"Nicholas. Oh, my poor darling. Here, let me help you."

For an instant, he fancied he'd died, for she appeared as heavenly as any angel. His own guardian angel, with hair as bright as a halo and eyes so loving that they momentarily stopped his mortal breath. Her soft hands brushed his forehead, guided his head back to the pillow. As she hovered over him, he allowed her grace to distract him from the horror of the night, like an oasis in a world of endless desolation. But even as he drank in her beauty, shame began to crawl over his skin.

He could smell his own stench. He could imagine how he looked, bandaged and bloodied. And the danger he had placed her in ...

Wrinkling her nose, his wife picked up the chamber pot. "Let me dispose of this, and I shall be right back. Do try not to move too much—your wound is not healed, my love."

His throat clenched at the endearment. Paralyzed with misery, he could only stare after her shapely, robe-clad form as she left with the offending object. She returned minutes later, with two maids in tow. They deposited a steaming basin and a tray by the bedside. The homey smell of beef tea wafted to his nostrils.

"Thank you, Bessie, Mary," Helena said. "That will be all."

Behind her, the maids peered at him, wide-eyed, before scampering off.

Helena dipped the towel into the water, wringing it out before leaning over him. "We'll clean you up a bit first, I think."

He caught her wrist. His voice emerged as a croak. "I can do it myself."

"Nonsense," she chided. "You can barely sit up."

To his surprise, he found she was right: he could not get up without her assistance. So he had to allow her to prop him up on feather pillows, humiliation and desire twisting his insides as he submitted to her gentle ministrations. She wiped his face and neck, behind his ears. The warm, clean linen felt blessedly good against his clammy skin.

"Now, that is better, isn't it?" Turning, she arranged something, and then the mattress dipped as she perched on the edge of the bed, glass and spoon in hand. "Do you think you can take some of this? They're ice chips—Dr. Farraday said it might be better for keeping the liquid down."

Come to think of it, his throat did feel like fire. He gave a reluctant nod.

She carefully scooped up the ice and fed him a spoonful. The cold liquid pooled in his mouth, and he swallowed, wincing at the initial pleasure-pain of water trickling down his parched insides.

"More?"

"Yes," he said, and she continued to feed him spoonful by spoonful. Perhaps as a mother might a babe, although he could not claim that knowledge for himself. He was certain his own mother, what little memory he had of her, had never bothered. He did not blame her; maternal instincts were a luxury a whore could ill afford.

He allowed himself to bask in his wife's tender attention even as he despised his own weakness. After last night, there was no question of being with Helena. That he had not been killed last evening was a miracle, but he knew the clock of justice was ticking. With each silent, inexorable beat he felt the urgency of borrowed time. An eye for an eye, a tooth for a tooth.

A life for a life.

As it was, his life had already been extended by sixteen years. But fate was coming for him now. He could feel the hounds of hell breathing at his neck.

But he could not—*would* not—allow his presence to put Helena in danger.

"I suppose you are wondering how you got up to bed," his wife said as she gave him the last of the ice. "Or do you recall the events that transpired after your return home last night?"

His memories of the night were of demons, of darkness and filth permeating his very soul. "No," he said tautly, "my memory fades after Farraday practicing his particular form of torture."

Helena frowned. "Dr. Farraday put half a dozen stitches along your left temple. We are to leave the bandage in place for several days to keep the wound clean, but he assured me you will heal nicely. Although I am not at all sure I trust Dr. Farraday—he seemed overly cavalier about the whole business. I told him so last night, as a matter of fact."

Despite his bleak mood, Nicholas' lips twitched. He'd wager all the horses in his stable Farraday had bristled at having his authority questioned. "Farraday served in the 33rd Regiment. He was at Quatre Bras and Waterloo and tended to the great Wellington himself."

"Well, I hope he knows what he is doing where you are concerned," Helena said primly. She stood and fussed with the coverlet, not looking at him. "I had two of the footmen carry you upstairs after the doctor and Mr. Kent left. I thought you would be more comfortable."

"That was kind of you." He did not know what else to say. That he did not deserve such tender consideration from her? That her wifely care was wasted on a marriage not destined to be? That the best thing for her would be for him to leave and never come back? "I am sorry for the inconvenience I have caused."

"Inconvenience?" Helena's head snapped up. His chest squeezed at the heightened brightness of her eyes. "You could have died last night, and you apologize for the *inconvenience*?"

Grimly, Nicholas met her wounded, bewildered gaze. "What else do you wish me to say?"

What was there *to* say, after all? She would not understand, because he could not explain his past to her. It suddenly occurred to him that it would be easier this way, letting her hurt and anger build a wall of separation. Lord knew his own self-control had proved perilously thin where she was concerned. It would be for her own good to stay far away from him—even if it took her hate to accomplish it.

He could live with that, at least temporarily, until he could figure out a more permanent solution for keeping her safe. His mind raced. An annulment would have to be procured; as soon as he could get himself out of bed, he'd light the fire beneath his solicitor's arse to make it happen. To remove himself from her well-ordered existence was the only fool-proof solution.

But he needed time to make that happen.

Fueling her hatred would buy him that time.

"I wish to know," Helena said, her voice quivering, "what you were doing in the dashed slums in the first place. I wish to know why you never tell me, your own wife, *anything*. Oh, Nicholas, why must you strive to keep the doors closed between us?"

Because the closer you get, the more I endanger you. Because I won't be the cause of you coming to harm. Because I'd die before I let anything happen to you.

Heart thudding, he forced himself to shrug. Carelessly. Deliberately. "'Tis as I told you at the Dewitt's. I made an error in offering for you. I married you because I thought I needed a wife with connections. You married me to settle your family's debts. It all sounded advantageous—but I fear I've grown weary of matrimony."

"Y-you cannot mean that," Helena stammered.

"Why not?" He lifted a brow, his words measured. "It is the truth."

Helena bit her lip. Then, she said in a rush, "Are you saying this because you think ... there are differences between us? Because I swear to you, I care not about your origins. Or what the *ton* says about your ... your ..."

"Legitimacy? Or the fact that I am in trade? Can you not even speak the words?"

"Of course I can. I was just trying to be delicate," she said, her lower lip wobbling. "This isn't like you, Nicholas—why are you acting this way?"

Nicholas let his own lip curl and his polished accents drop. "I'm not *actin'* in any way, milady. I'm jus' callin' the cards as I see 'em. The fact is, I thought I could do this, but it's been a li'l o'er a month, han't it, an' I'm bored to tears with wedlock. Seems I need more variety, so to speak."

"But what of our courtship, the w-way you have held me ..." Tears were leaking unheeded down her face as she stared at him in horror. "You told me I was *beautiful.*"

"An' you took those words to 'eart, did you, luv?"

"Yes," she whispered.

"Then I told you what you wanted to 'ear. For the sake o' havin' some peace." Nicholas lifted his shoulders. "Sorry, but that's the honest to God truth."

Helena was biting her bottom lip as if she could somehow clamp down on the emotions so clearly trembling within her. "I cannot believe the affection between us is a lie. You cannot deny that you care something for me, as I for you."

"Time passes, as do flights o' fancy," he heard himself say. "What can I say, but our weddin' night squashed that bit o' folly. But what's done is done, eh? We must look to the future, an' I reckon there's a way to salvage the situation."

The color drained from his wife's face. For an instant, he feared she would swoon. That he had pushed her delicate sensibilities beyond the limit.

"Wh-what are you saying?" she said faintly.

He forced himself to continue in a brash, cheerful manner that twisted his insides with self-loathing. "I'm talkin' about an annulment, o' course. I'm rich as Croesus these days an' can afford to 'ire a team o' law men if need be. Wha'ever it takes, I'll see this union between us dissolved. By the by, don't worry your 'ead about a thing—you'll 'ave as much o' the ready as you need for the rest o' your life, I promise you that."

Helena was staring at him as if she'd never seen him before. "I don't want your money," she said in a low voice.

"Suit yourself. I warrant you'll be singin' a different tune when *Papa* comes for 'elp. At any rate, I've promised to look after you, an' I will. I 'ave only one condition."

"What is it?"

"I want you to leave. Get out o' London an' go stay with your folks in the country," he said bluntly. "It'll 'elp build the case for the annulment if we ain't livin' beneath the same roof."

Helena was looking at him in a way that made him distinctly uneasy. She took a step backward from the bed, and his first thought was that she meant to leave, that he had finally driven her away. But she did not move any further. Instead, her hands went to the tie of her woolen wrapper. She seemed to hesitate. Then, in a quick movement, she jerked loose the knot. She shed the heavy layer, letting it pool at her feet.

Christ. Bloody fucking Christ.

It took every ounce of willpower he possessed not to react to the sight of Helena in what had to be the poorest excuse for a nightgown known to mankind. The bronze material barely covered her breasts and drew the eye to her perfectly rounded curves. Flushed as Aphrodite rising from the sea, she embodied everything he wanted in a woman. She trembled, but kept her head courageously high and her hands at her sides. His dream goddess, both innocent and sensual. Nay, she was beyond every fantasy he'd ever had of her. Yearning bordering on pain clawed at his gut.

"I'll go if you can tell me you don't want me," she said, her voice tremulous, "that you don't care for me, even a little."

If only she knew how much he wanted, how much he cared. So much so that he would do whatever was required to protect her.

"Put your clothes on before you embarrass yourself further," he snapped. "You disgust me. You're acting no better than a sixpenny whore."

Helena looked stricken. Her cheeks grew red and blotchy as if he had physically slapped her. She scrambled for her heavy robe. "I —I didn't mean to—"

"If I wanted a cheap tumble, I know enough where to get one," he said with crude precision. "A man wants a lady for a wife, not a bleeding strumpet."

Her hands fumbled with the ties. She was looking down at the belt, mumbling as if to herself. "W-we should not be having this conversation. Your senses have not recovered from the shock. The blood loss has addled your senses."

"This conversation will not change. Truthfully, we should have had this discussion long ago. To prevent any future misunderstanding, let me make myself very clear: I want you out of here, out of my life. Do you understand?"

Veiled by downcast lashes, her eyes remained hidden from him.

"When I ask a question, you will answer," he said curtly.

She did raise her eyes then, and they were bright with humiliation and fury. It took every shred of self-control to resist from pulling her into his arms. To resist from holding her, comforting her, begging for her forgiveness. Which he could not do, if he loved her.

Which, of course, he did.

"Go to hell," she choked out and fled to the door.

Too late for that, he thought with weary resignation. He was already there. Had never left, and that was the bleeding truth.

Chapter Sixteen

"Lady Harteford, do come join us!"

Helena looked in the direction of the voices. When she spied the trio of familiar faces, she pasted a smile on her face. She had met Lady Tillycott and the Misses Haversham at a literary salon when she first arrived in London and counted the ladies in her small circle of friends. She found their company an enjoyable distraction—and she was badly in need of distraction this evening.

Tonight was her first time out of the townhouse in days. After Nicholas had torn up at her, she'd holed herself up in her bedchamber. The numbness had slowly faded; her emotional state now teetered precariously between self-pity and rage. What was wrong with her that Nicholas would treat her so? Remembering his reaction to her *negligee*, she felt humiliation creep upon her nape. What had she done, other than try to please him at every turn? She had disguised herself as a whore, for heaven's sake, and for what? He'd used her and tossed her aside when she was the doxy; as a wife, she'd received no better treatment.

You disgust me. You're acting no better than a sixpenny whore.

She swallowed the swell of resentment and sailed toward her seated friends, her head held high. Well, no more. She was done. She had wasted enough energy and tears on her scoundrel of a husband.

"How do you do, ladies?" she said, taking the seat they had saved for her. Though truth be told there was really no need—hardly anyone desired the rickety little chairs at the back of the ballroom. Wallflowers and spinsters had the pick of the lot.

"Not nearly as well as you, Lady Harteford," Miss Lavinia Haversham said.

Unmarried and at an unmentionable age, Miss Haversham was considered firmly on the shelf. She possessed a gaunt, spare figure and large, rather protruding eyes. Unfortunately, the bug-like quality of her gaze was not helped by the lorgnette she wielded. Her faded blue eye blinked, grotesquely magnified as she took in Helena's appearance. "I do declare you shine like the brightest star this evening! Is that a new gown?"

Beside her, her twin sister, Miss Matilda Haversham, bobbed her head in agreement.

"Thank you," Helena replied with a grateful smile. She had taken special care with her toilette this evening, wearing a scandalously low-cut dress of indigo satin. So Nicholas did not find her desirable—well, she would show him. No longer would she play the role of the shrinking violet; in her remaining days in London, she would be the merriest, most dashing matron the *ton* had ever seen.

For she'd written her parents, and, as it turned out, they had begged off on her visit for another fortnight; apparently, Papa had a hunting party ensconced in all the rooms. Not wanting to alert them to the state of her marriage, Helena had responded simply that she would come at their convenience. She'd penned Nicholas a note as well—a chilly one informing him that he would have to bear her presence for a few more weeks. She hadn't received a response. In fact, she'd seen neither hide nor hair of him since their estrangement.

Helena became aware that Miss Lavinia was asking her about the source of her improved wardrobe. "Oh, Madame Rousseau designed it," she said.

"Madame Rousseau! She is very expensive, is she not?" This came from Lady Tillycot, the last lady to make up the trio. Wearing a fussy pink gown that clashed magnificently with her hennaed hair, she was as fleshy as Miss Lavinia was thin. "I'm told she caters to only the most elite of clientele."

Helena ignored the jibe. "Lady Marianne Draven secured an appointment for me."

"Perhaps she could get one for me," Miss Lavinia said. Miss Matilda nodded eagerly as well.

"I shall ask her," Helena promised.

Lady Tillycot sniffed. "I would watch who I indebt myself to, Miss Lavinia." She turned to Helena. "I have been meaning to say something about your friendship with Lady Draven. You came with her tonight, did you not?"

Helena nodded. Marianne had shown up on her doorstep earlier, insisting that wallowing helped nothing and Helena would be better off accompanying her to the Fraser's ball instead. As usual, Marianne had had the right of it.

"Yes, I did," Helena said. "Lady Draven is an old and dear friend of mine."

"Then I tell you this for your own good. I should not want your consequence tainted by this association."

"Now, Lady Tillycot ..." Miss Lavinia began.

"Tainted?" Helena asked, puzzled. "Whatever do you mean, Lady Tillycot?"

Lady Tillycot leaned closer, the long plume in her turban nearly poking Helena in the eye. Her tone was low and smug. "Marianne Draven runs with a fast crowd, Lady Harteford. I will not soil your ears with what I have heard, but suffice it to say, she is a lady of loose morals and questionable character."

Reticule strings pulled tight between Helena's fingers. "I should question the character of anyone who passes along gossip as truth, Lady Tillycot."

"'Tis not gossip but fact that Marianne Draven did not spend so much as a day in mourning for her late husband before she began carousing about Town," Lady Tillycot said. "And I am not the only one to observe that nary a stitch of widow's weeds has ever graced her person."

"'*My grief lies within, and these external manners of lament are merely shadows to the unseen grief*,'" Helena retorted.

"Mr. William Shakespeare, *King Richard II, Act IV*, if I am not mistaken," Miss Lavinia said, clapping her hands together. "Bravo, Lady Harteford!"

Lady Tillycot's eyes slit with malice. "The tale of Clytemnestra and Agamemnon is the more apt analogy, I believe—or haven't you heard the rumors concerning Draven's rather sudden passing?"

"You go too far," Helena said, her voice shaking with anger.

Lady Tillycot rose, a casual movement that nevertheless resulted in a cataclysmic shifting of flesh. "Suit yourself, Lady Harteford. I cannot be faulted for my attempt to salvage your reputation, little that it may be."

She walked off with a satisfied swagger which made Helena's blood boil.

"Never mind Lady Tillycot," Miss Lavinia said. "She is having an attack of the doldrums today and relieves herself by making everyone around her miserable as well."

"What does she have to be miserable about?"

"Lord Tillycot, of course," Miss Lavinia said matter-of-factly. "He lost ten thousand pounds on a hand of hazard they say. The creditors are leaving their calling cards."

Despite her annoyance, Helena felt a stir of pity. She knew

only too well the effects of gaming. Had it not been for Nicholas, her father might be living in France, seeking refuge from debtor's prison. Her brow puckered at the thought of Nicholas again. The dashed man had a mercurial temperament, that was for certain. One minute he was all that was kind and generous, and the next ...

He had humiliated her, cut her to the bone with his rejection.

She was *not* going to waste one more thought on him.

She cleared her throat. "Will the Tillycots recover, do you think?"

"Who is to know?" Miss Lavinia shrugged at the same time as Miss Matilda did. "'*Cards and dice—the ultimate vice*,' as they say. By the by, have you heard about the recent debates in Parliament concerning the penalties for debtors? There are efforts to reform the current laws, met with fierce opposition, of course, by the Tories ..."

Helena spent the next hour engrossed in discussion. The Havershams deserved their reputations as having the most well-informed minds in the *ton*. The self-proclaimed bluestockings conversed with facility on all manner of topics, ranging from penal law reforms to Wollstonecraft's masterpiece. They had just begun to debate the merits of sensibility versus reason when Helena felt a light tap on her shoulder. She turned around in her seat.

Marianne, resplendent in a silver gauze gown striped with blue, gave her an amused look. "So this is where you have been hiding, Lady Harteford."

Helena introduced the tongue-tied Havershams to Marianne, who smiled and complimented them on their matching gowns. The sisters flushed with pleasure.

"Of course, our dresses are humble compared to yours," Miss Lavinia said diffidently.

"Do you like it? I would be happy to introduce you to my modiste."

"You would?" Miss Lavinia's pale lips trembled.

"Of course. I will let Madame Rousseau know to expect you

both. Now, come, Lady Harteford, won't you join me for a promenade?"

"I would like that," Helena said. "Miss Lavinia? Miss Matilda?"

"Oh no, we'll stay here," Miss Lavinia said, her eyes bright with excitement.

As Helena departed with Marianne, she heard the Havershams exclaim at once, "Madame Rousseau!"

"That was kind of you," Helena said, smiling. "I do believe you have made the Havershams' evening."

"It was little enough." Marianne yawned delicately behind her fan, a confection of silver silk iridescent with sequins. "Lord, the Frasers throw a crashing bore of a party."

"Do you think so?" Helena looked around the ballroom. The theme appeared to be a Grecian Garden, with plaster pillars and statues placed to resemble ancient ruins. Garlands of pink and white flowers hung from the high ceiling and draped over the tables. "I thought it rather charming."

Marianne fluttered her fan. "If you say so."

They strolled along the perimeter of the ballroom, stopping to chat with acquaintances. Helena cast surreptitious glances at her friend. Marianne appeared recovered from the malaise of several days ago. Once again her stunning self, she sparkled as she conversed, her wit drawing admiring laughs from those around her. But Helena thought she noticed a certain feverishness beneath her friend's gaiety and strain underlying her light repartee. Notes of music began to play, and Marianne became besieged by eager dance partners. To Helena's surprise and gratification, a number of gentlemen approached her as well.

"Our dance cards are full," Marianne informed the suitors in a laughing voice, and taking Helena's arm, she led her away from the disappointed faces and toward the terrace.

Once outside, Helena could not hide her astonishment. "I have never before had so many invitations to dance!"

Marianne smiled. "Well, you are quite transformed, my dear. 'Twas a stroke of genius for Madame Rousseau to layer matching tulle over that indigo satin. And to pair the gold necklace and eardrops—an inspired choice. You look positively pagan tonight."

"Thank you." Helena paused. "I have been meaning to ask you ... is everything quite alright, Marianne?"

"Whatever do you mean, dearest?"

"Is there something troubling you?" Helena blurted. "Something that caused your recent malaise? Because I should like to help, if I can."

Marianne's lips parted, but she said nothing.

Seeing the ripple of uncertainty that passed over her friend's exquisite features, Helen forged on. "You've rarely spoken about your ... your marriage. I know you are much wiser than I, but if there is anything at all I can do, Marianne—if there is any pain or grief that I might help ease ..." Helena gave her a rueful smile. "Lord knows you've heard enough about *my* troubles."

"Pain or grief?" Marianne echoed. She laughed, then, a sound like glass breaking. "Oh, dearest, I think not. At least, not in the way you mean."

"In any way, then," Helena said earnestly. "You can confide in me. Please know that you can."

Marianne's smile seemed a little sad. "I do know it. And I treasure our friendship all the more. Perhaps one day, Helena."

"Because you do not think me ready and able to help?"

"No," Marianne said, her voice hollow. "Because I do not think myself ready."

Hearing both an admission and a warning in those words, Helena let the matter drop. She could only hope that Marianne would one day choose to unload the burdens of her heart. When that time came, she would be there for her friend. They walked to the edge of the terrace, looking out into the shadowy gardens. The chirping of night crickets filled the silence.

At length, Marianne said, "What are you going to do next?" She didn't need to clarify what she meant.

"What is there *to* do?" Helena gave her friend a bitter smile. "When Papa gives me leave, I will return to Hampshire. There I shall rusticate for the rest of my life."

"Come now, that is doing it a bit brown, is it not? Though I know things are at sixes and sevens with Harteford, I cannot help but think your husband's behavior is out of character. He's not acting at all like I expected." Marianne frowned. "Are you certain the two of you have discussed matters thoroughly?"

"I tried, Marianne! I told him I didn't care about his past, I tried to be a loving wife, I even tried to ..." Unable to disclose Nicholas' humiliating rejection of her person, even to her best friend, Helena clamped her lips. "I did everything in my power to seduce him, and it all came to naught."

"Did you tell him about that night at the Nunnery?"

Helena huffed out a breath. "I couldn't. He more or less implied that he had no interest in ... in a passionate marriage. He said a man doesn't want a strumpet for a wife, so I was not about to humiliate myself further by confessing what I had done."

"Fustian." Marianne snorted. "There must be something else Harteford is not telling you."

"Well, I cannot read his mind, can I?" Helena said acidly. "And frankly I'm tired of trying. *Sick* and tired, as point of fact."

"'Tis understandable, of course."

"I don't know what he wants—I don't think *he* knows what he wants."

"An unfortunate male characteristic," Marianne agreed.

"Furthermore," Helena fumed, her hands fisting upon the stone balustrade, "even if I wished to speak to him again—which I empathically do *not*—it would be easier to get an audience with Prinny than with my dashed husband. Do you know I have not seen him *once* since he ordered me out of his life?"

"I wonder what he is up to," Marianne mused.

For some reason, that comment fed Helena's ire further. "Well, it's none of my business, is it? If he wants to get shot in St. Giles, that is up to him. If he wants to work himself to an early grave at that blasted warehouse of his, it has nothing to do with me. He thinks to rid himself of me like a ... an old shoe—"

"There must be a reason, dear—"

"To hell with his reasons!" Helena burst out. "Nicholas is like everyone in my life. Mama, Papa ... no matter what I do, how hard I try, I cannot please them. I thought it would be different with Nicholas, but I was just a fool, wasn't I? Deceiving myself, thinking I could win his affection. And this is how he responds—by slapping an annulment in my face." Anger bubbled over, scalding her insides. "If I was a man, I'd call him out!"

A measured silence. Marianne raised one delicate blonde eyebrow. "Would you?"

Helena felt the weight of her ear-bobs as she nodded vehemently. "Pistols at dawn."

"How I adore that passionate streak in you! Even as a girl, you were always a hoyden beneath those starchy pinafores your mama made you wear." When Helena grimaced, Marianne gave a throaty chuckle. "You do realize, don't you, dear, that battles need not be waged with pesky things like pistols? There are ways far cleverer—and neater—to exact revenge."

"What do you mean?"

Emerald eyes narrowed in a considering manner. "Tell me, do you wish to teach your lord a lesson? Have him admit he was wrong about not wanting you?"

The notion definitely had its appeal. Her head tilting, Helena said doubtfully, "In what manner could I do so? There's no talking to the man: he's as stubborn as a mule and as like as one to apologize. Besides, he won't even see me—"

"Oh, I wouldn't worry too much about those details. All I need to know is this: are you prepared to show Harteford the error of his ways? Make him regret the abysmal fashion in which he has treated you?"

An image of Nicholas materialized before Helena's eyes. Her lord, upon bended knee. Begging her forgiveness, pleading with her to take him back. She'd send him packing ... wouldn't she?

She gulped. "Yes."

"Then, my dearest, leave the rest to me."

Chapter Seventeen

Nicholas eyed Kent, wondering how much he could hide from the other man. Across the desk, Kent sat with his shoulders in a habitual hunch as he relayed the progress on the warehouse looting and attempted murder. The policeman's eyes stood out in his gaunt face; like twin lamps, those eyes seemed capable of piercing into the darkest recesses of human nature. Nicholas felt a cold stirring at his nape. He would not like to be a criminal skewered on the opposite end of that gaze. As it was, he felt uneasy, wondering at the details Kent might be picking up on.

For one, Nicholas knew he must look rumpled. He had slept in the office for an entire week now, and his appearance showed the effects. His hair had grown shaggy and his eyes shadowed from the sleepless nights upon the couch. Wrinkled and mismatched, his clothes obviously lacked the caring touch of a valet. And he had cut himself shaving twice this week, so there were nicks on his jaw to complement the healing red scar upon his temple.

All in all, he was certain he looked as he felt: weary, frustrated, hunted.

During the days, the constant hub-bub of the warehouse

provided a temporary distraction. He had been almost thankful for the skirmish with the excise officers over duties for the imported rum and the usual wrangling with merchants over their insolvent accounts. Still, his temper had become downright nasty this week. The porters took one look at his scowling demeanor and scurried out of his path. Yesterday, he had nearly bit Jibotts' head off for interrupting him at his desk. He supposed he owed the steward a raise for putting up with his fiendish moods.

Worst of all were the nights. Alone on the knobby couch, he relived the scene in the drawing room, the moment of delirious joy when he'd almost let himself seduce his wife. The feel of her, soft and yielding beneath him, her luscious lips parted beneath his, her breathy pleas—and his cock burgeoned with helpless yearning. His entire being craved to surge into her, to take her so deeply he'd shoot himself inside her womb. In the loneliest hours of twilight, he was tortured with images of little girls with hair of burnished oak and a dark-haired boy or two with their mother's hazel eyes and hopefully her temperament as well. A house full of rollicking children. A real home.

Aye, there was a dream. Only it was destined to remain just that: a dream, not reality, because at this moment a team of well-paid barristers was strategizing on how to secure him an annulment. And because, as of now, Helena hated him. He had made certain of that.

Bloody hell, how has it come to this?

His eyes closed briefly.

"Is the wound still bothering you, my lord?"

From across the desk, Kent scrutinized him.

Nicholas forced himself to focus. "It is nothing. So, from what I gather thus far, the bottom line is you believe that Bragg is responsible for the shooting. Your man Caster scared him off before he could finish the deed, and now Bragg is in hiding, likely somewhere in St. Giles."

Kent nodded. "We are closing in on his trail. Yesterday, one of my men discovered his sleeping place in the bowels of a flash house. We have reason to believe that he will return this evening. When he does, we will have him."

"I commend you on your persistence," Nicholas said, "but there is one problem."

"A problem?"

Exhaling, Nicholas hoped the gamble he was about to take was worth the risk. "After I was shot, I heard a voice. I am not certain it was Bragg's."

"You heard a voice that night? Why did you not mention this earlier?" Kent frowned.

"Er, the wound must have addled my memory until now." He had omitted any mention of the blackmailer's threats because he did not want Kent nosing around his past. Yet he could not allow Kent to follow a false trail, not when the true villain might pounce at any moment. It was a tricky business to alert the investigator to the possibility of another shooter, whilst at the same time keeping secrets hidden. He felt like one of the acrobatic acts at Vauxhall, balancing three tea cups on his nose whilst juggling apples and riding on horseback simultaneously.

"Can you be certain that the voice you heard was not Bragg's, my lord?" Skepticism lined Kent's brow. "After all, you had been injured, and there was loss of blood. And a man can disguise his voice, if he chooses it."

"Why would Bragg alter his voice? If anything, the man is a braggart and would happily announce his victory to me and all the world."

"What were the exact words you heard, my lord?" Kent had taken out a small notebook and had a quill poised above.

"Er, I cannot recall precisely," Nicholas hedged, "just that the voice was higher, thinner than Bragg's."

Kent snapped the notebook shut. "So allow me to repeat what you have just said. You had forgotten that you heard a voice until just now. But now that you recall it, you do not remember what it was saying. Just that it sounded different from Isaac Bragg's."

Put that way, it sounded quite idiotic. Nicholas nodded curtly.

"If not Bragg, then who?" Kent's clear gold eyes bored into his. "My lord, you will forgive my impertinence, but I must ask: do you have any enemies? Anyone who might wish to do you harm?"

"No." Nicholas willed his voice to remain steady and calm. "That is, yes, I am sure I have enemies as any man of trade does—disgruntled workers, angry clients, and the like. But no, there is no man I specifically know of who would wish me dead."

"Hmm."

Nicholas did not like the other man's speculative tone.

"And you are absolutely certain there is nothing else that you have neglected to tell me?" Kent asked. "Nothing that might have, ahem, slipped your mind due to blood loss?"

Nicholas gave him a withering stare worthy of any marquess. "Of course not. But my gut tells me there is more involved in this than petty theft."

"What do you mean?"

"At a meeting with the West India merchants this week, I mentioned that prior to the warehouse being ransacked, my steward had reported small amounts of goods being stolen. Paltry stuff. A few crates of tobacco, several barrels of rum, that sort of thing."

"Yes?"

"That triggered other merchants to review their ledgers with a fine tooth comb. As it turns out, similar amounts of goods have gone missing from their warehouses as well."

"Interesting," Kent said, "but hardly surprising. The building of the walled docks has helped, but not stymied completely the acts of theft. I doubt stealing can ever be fully suppressed."

"I agree, but it is the timing of it all that concerns me," Nicholas said. "Jibotts reports that goods began to go missing in noticeable quantities only in the past four months. The other merchants are now reporting losses during the same time period."

"An intriguing coincidence," Kent admitted. His expression sharpened like a hawk's. "A new criminal mastermind, then, at work on the docks."

"He is no ordinary criminal," Nicholas agreed, "for he eschews instant gratification for slow and subtle skimming. It would take patience, control, and considerable skill to organize such an endeavor. Furthermore, how is he smuggling the goods past the guards at the dock gates?"

"Who would be capable of such a deed?" Kent mused.

There was a knock, and Jibotts poked his head in. "Mr. Fines is here to see you, sir. I told him you were in a meeting."

"Send him up," Nicholas said.

"As I was saying, I can imagine only a select few with skills of this caliber." The policeman's eyes were narrowed, and his fingers drummed rhythmically against the arm of the chair. "Hodgkins? No, he was recaptured after his last escape from Newgate. Richardson, perhaps, or Gerrins, though last I heard the latter had been shipped to the Australian colonies."

"I find it difficult picturing Bragg among the list of possible suspects," Nicholas said.

"He has more brawn than brains," Kent said grudgingly, "and I checked with Bow Street. The magistrate's records showed petty crimes. Nothing more organized than the drunken looting of a pub during which he made off with a barrel of ale and a serving wench."

"Exactly." Nicholas raised a brow. "You see why I suspect someone else was the shooter?"

"It could still be Bragg doing the shooting, but someone else behind these robberies. It could be the two are not at all connected." At the thump of approaching footsteps, Kent got to his feet. "I will investigate further. In the meantime, my lord, if I may be so bold as to offer a few words of advice?"

Nicholas gave a curt nod.

"Trust no one, not your enemies, nor your closest friends. And I would urge you once again to consider traveling under protection. My men are fully trained and equipped to—"

He would have Kent's men tagging his heels when hell froze over. While he might risk his own safety, however, he'd not compromise Helena's. At the very moment, the pair of Runners he'd hired was shadowing her every movement. "I've attended to the matter already, thank you."

"As you wish."

With a bow, the investigator headed to the door. It opened before he could reach for the knob.

"Well, hello there," Paul Fines said. "I'm not interrupting anything, am I?"

"Not at all. Mr. Kent was just leaving," Nicholas said.

Paul shook the policeman's hand. "I do admire you fellows over at the Thames River Police."

"Have we met before?" Kent inquired, his eyes sharp.

"Wouldn't think so." Paul tossed his hat between his hands. "Any leads on the nefarious persons responsible for looting the warehouse and putting a dent in Morgan's hard skull?"

"This gentleman, so obviously concerned about my welfare, is Mr. Paul Fines," Nicholas inserted dryly. "He is the son of the company's founder and my partner in the business."

"We are working on a list of suspects, Mr. Fines," Kent said. His gaze roved over Paul's ensemble of impeccable beige superfine. "I was just cautioning his lordship to watch his back in the meantime."

"How exciting," Paul said. "But don't worry about Morgan here. He can take care of himself. As a matter of fact, I am here to help him practice. Ready for a few rounds in the ring, old boy?"

Kent took his leave, and Nicholas unlocked the door to the sparring room. Without another word, he and Paul Fines readied themselves for a bout, removing their jackets and donning scarred leather gloves. He felt charged with restlessness, like a stallion before the storm. He had spent the week physically cooped up in his office, but more so there was the sense of pent-up emotion. Avoiding Helena—not just her presence, but his thoughts and relentless desire for her—required more energy than he had imagined possible.

It was a relief to focus on his opponent as he circled, arms held in defensive position. It felt good to shake the stinging sweat from his eyes. He barely dodged a right hook, his feet slipping on the mats as he sought to regain his balance. Swearing, he steadied himself against the ropes and felt the burn of air in his lungs. There was no time to rest, however, as Paul swooped in. He threw a left jab at the other man's midriff and felt the frustrating sensation of his glove contacting empty air.

"Is that the best you've got, my lord?" Bouncing lightly back and forth on his feet, Paul looked as fresh as a damned spring daisy. "All that time with the nobs has made you soft. Or perhaps the shot to the noggin has brought you down a notch."

Nicholas' eyes narrowed. "Even if I were half the man I was, I could still pummel you."

Paul laughed, low and taunting. With his glove, he beckoned Nicholas toward him. "Let's see what you've got then."

The match continued with an exchange of punches and parries that elevated Nicholas' heart beat and his mood. Having sparred regularly with Paul in the past, Nicholas knew better than to allow this particular opponent to take control of the match. Though Paul was shorter than he and possessed a slimmer physique, Nicholas knew from past experience the bruising power of the younger man's blows. The trick with Paul was not to be distracted by his cheerfully disparaging comments and to focus instead on his one weakness: a tendency to favor his right side.

For the next three rounds, they remained evenly matched, trading blow for blow. In the fifth round, Nicholas advanced, keeping watch on Paul's footwork. A side to side movement usually preceded a lunge forward, and sure enough Nicholas found himself parrying a swift series of jabs to his upper body. He feinted left, and when Paul responded with a right-sided uppercut, Nicholas swayed to the right and answered with a cross-cut. Adrenaline surged when his glove connected resoundingly with flesh and bone.

Paul stumbled back a few steps, steadying himself against the rough hemp ropes. He shook his head as if to clear it.

"Haven't lost your touch then, eh?" Stripping off his gloves, Paul lowered himself to the ground. He rubbed a manicured hand tentatively against his jaw. "I do believe that is going to leave a mark."

Nicholas shot him an unrepentant grin. "Care to go a few more rounds?"

"Thank you, no," Paul said, scowling. "I will be in the suds with my valet as it is. Trust you to land a facer when a jab to the stomach would have sufficed. And, might I add, the latter would have been a great deal more civilized."

"Civility is not my strong point." Picking up a towel, Nicholas mopped it over his face and chest. His muscles vibrated pleasantly from the exercise, and he felt more limber and relaxed than he had in days. "Join me for a drink?"

Eyes brightening, Paul got to his feet. "Mayhap your finest whiskey will ease the pain. I have a few minutes to spare before my next appointment."

Nicholas led the way back into his office. He poured two glasses of whiskey before joining Paul in the chairs by the fire. Drink in hand, he sank against the cushions.

"You were sparring like the devil himself was after you." Paul swallowed the amber beverage and smacked his lips in pleasure. "Bashing out the demons, eh?"

Nicholas slanted a look beneath his lashes. "In a manner of speaking."

"So, still no leads on the theft or the man who shot at you?"

"Kent is pursuing the matter. He believes the main suspect to be Isaac Bragg."

"The rather hostile fellow, red face, currants for eyes?"

Nicholas smiled dryly at the description. "That's the man. I have my own doubts, of course. Why would Bragg want to see me killed?"

Slouched comfortably in the chair, Paul imbibed his whiskey in contemplative sips. "Why would anyone want to see you dead? Have you any enemies, Morgan, who might wish you harm?"

Nicholas stared into the fire and said nothing.

"It has crossed my mind," Paul said with uncharacteristic hesitation, "that the shooting took place in St. Giles. You were living there before you came to work for Father, were you not? Could there possibly be a connection?"

Nicholas closed his eyes briefly. Despite all that the Fines family had done for him, he had never found the courage to expose his past in its sordid entirety. Jeremiah had seen the place that birthed him, met the woman who called herself his aunt; it would have been no great stretch for Jeremiah to ascertain how a boy of fourteen years with no skills and little schooling had made a living upon the streets. Yet Jeremiah had never held it against him. He had merely looked him in the eye and said, "Are you ready for a new life, lad? One that will put the past behind?"

He had not believed such a thing was possible.

But with Jeremiah's guidance it had been. For sixteen blessed years, it had.

"I did not mean to pry," Paul said quietly. "I know you have always valued your privacy."

"Paul, do you believe it possible that a man can leave his past behind?" Nicholas' voice felt thick in his throat. "That if he works hard enough, changes his ways, changes *himself*—he might escape the sins he once committed?"

"It would depend on the man and the sins, I suppose." Paul was looking at him closely, his blue eyes steady. "And if the man repented and his actions showed he had chosen a new path. I am no clergyman, Morgan, but I believe redemption is possible."

"Is it?" Nicholas looked into his empty glass. "Or is that, too, a dream?"

Paul sat up in his chair, his face earnest. "Morgan, whatever your past holds, if it poses a danger to you currently, you must face it. If you cannot tell me, tell Kent. Have him take precautionary measures for your safety."

"I cannot tell Kent." When Paul made to speak, Nicholas met his eyes very deliberately. "There are reasons for it. I would not launch myself out of the pot and into the flames."

"Ah. Because he is a member of the policing force," Paul said slowly, "and you wish to avoid detection of certain aspects of your past."

Nicholas gave a terse nod.

"Hmm. That *is* a dilemma." Paul scratched his chin. "Hire someone else for protection, then, someone who has no interest in you beyond the coin you provide."

"I'll look into it," Nicholas muttered into his glass.

"In the meantime, it would be best to keep a low profile. Which reminds me, my sister's birthday party is next week. I'll let Percy know that something has come up for you—"

"Damn it, I refuse to scurry for cover like a bloody mouse." Nicholas rose and refilled his drink. "I accepted Percy's invitation so I will be there."

"Ah, yes. I was going to ask you about that," Paul said.

"About what?"

"Well, it's just that Mama, Percy, and I noticed that your response omitted a certain lovely lady. I hoped it wasn't because of anything I said that time at Long Meg's—"

Nicholas gulped his whiskey. "The matter has nothing to do with you."

"Why isn't your wife coming, then?"

He could have lied. Made some excuse that Helena had

another commitment. But for some reason, he heard himself saying, "I did not inform her of the invitation."

"You did not invite your own wife? I say, Morgan, that's doing it a bit Siberian." Paul cocked his head. "Has the calf-love worn off, then?"

Going to the fire, Nicholas braced his arm against the mantel. He stared down into the flames. "I'm hardly the mooning sort, Fines. The problem is not with her but me. I ... I made a mistake in marrying her. She deserves someone better. A real gentleman, born and bred. Not an imposter like me."

"You're no imposter. You're a gentleman in every way that counts," Paul said quietly. "Do not let the reactions of society color your marriage, Nicholas. My father always said that a man is not born but made."

"Your father was a singular man, Paul, with views not commonly shared."

"All the same, your achievements surely convey that you have never been one to be held back by his origins. Why begin to be such a man now? If you want my advice, forget all this nonsense and concentrate on making your lady happy."

"I am not sure I can."

Paul glanced heavenward. "At your wedding, the chit had stars in her eyes. I'd never seen a more glowing bride. Which only proves the adage that love *is* blind. For reasons unfathomable, one surly, half-baked smile from you and the poor deluded thing will surely melt into a puddle." Downing the last of his whiskey, he set down the glass and reached for his greatcoat. "Regretfully, my friend, that is all the marital advice I can stomach for now. I hear the siren's call of whist at Boodle's, and I must oblige."

"Boodle's?" Nicholas frowned. "It is not yet three in the afternoon."

"Who am I to resist a siren's call at any hour?" Paul drawled.

Nicholas kept silent as Paul re-arranged his ensemble with the care of Brummell himself. He saw Paul out and when they reached the street, he hesitated before saying, "The play can get deep in the clubs. You're being careful, I take?"

Paul snorted, his hair golden in the sun. "Yes, Papa. And I'll be sure to say my prayers like a good lad. Any other pearls of wisdom?"

"It seems the wisdom today has been yours." Nicholas held out his hand. "Thank you, Fines."

After Paul's carriage drove off, Nicholas turned to re-enter the warehouse. He found himself almost colliding with a street urchin.

"Careful there, lad," he said, steadying the boy by the shoulders.

From beneath a ragged, putty-colored cap, a pair of eyes narrowed up at him. "You Lord 'Arteford?"

A chill chased up Nicholas's spine. "Yes."

His dread grew as the boy held out a slip of paper with grimy hands. "Then I got's a message fer you."

Chapter Eighteen

The last time she was here, she'd been a newlywed, frightened and unsure, desperate for her husband's love. How things had changed in the last two months. This time around, Helena walked past the lewd sculptures and bawdy goings-on without blinking an eye. She followed the footman up to the first floor and into a scarlet-and-gilt chamber in which the most prominent feature was a wide, curtained bed.

Seeing the Abbess seated at a small table, Helena greeted her. She declined the offer of lemonade. Instead, she asked in a rush, "Would you be so kind as to have your men ascertain that there are no untoward persons lurking about outside?"

The Abbess' thin mouth bent with humor. "Milady, this is a brothel. There are always untoward persons lurking about. Anyone in particular you want us to keep an eye out for?"

Too restless to sit, Helena wandered to the nearby looking glass. A familiar, smoky-eyed nymph peered back at her. Shivering, she adjusted her demi-mask and said, "This afternoon when I was shopping on Bond Street I happened to notice two men in dark coats. They seemed to be everywhere I went. I thought it might be a coincidence, but then later on tonight, I saw the same two villains from the window of Lady Draven's townhouse."

"Cutthroats, do you think?" the Abbess inquired. "Ever since the attack on Lady de Lacey last month, they've been out in droves. This new breed—they've no qualms about holding a lady at knifepoint to score her jewels ... and other personal effects."

Cringing at the Abbess' matter-of-fact description of mayhem, Helena said, "I am not certain. But if I see them again, I will contact the magistrate." Her hands were not quite steady as she smoothed the brassy curls of her wig. "Lady Draven arranged for her carriage to meet me at the back of her townhouse, so at least I left undetected tonight." Dryly she added, "I suppose it was just as well that I happened to be in disguise."

"And a fine one it is, milady—or should I say *mademoiselle*?" The Abbess gave a knowing chuckle. "Don't worry a thing about the blackguards. I'll have my boys clear the area of any filth."

"Thank you," Helena said with relief.

The Abbess grinned. "Likewise. Thought I'd seen the last of you, hadn't I? But when Lady Draven asked me to send your lord that note on behalf of *Mademoiselle Nymph*, I was tickled. For a bashful thing, you've got pluck, eh? I haven't enjoyed myself so much for a long time."

"I hope he comes."

"Oh, I'm quite sure he will. Come, that is." The other woman chortled. "What hot-blooded man could resist such an invitation?"

Humiliated anger flared in Helena's chest. Why was it that her husband would choose a whore over her? Why would he come at a whore's bidding, yet avoid his own wife at every turn? "When I was a demure wife, he sought a harlot. When I tried to seduce him, he called me a *strumpet*," she said, jaw tight. "I have no idea what my husband can or cannot resist, but tonight I mean to show him the error of his ways."

"Pluck, as I said," the Abbess said with a chuckle.

Taking a breath, Helena continued more calmly, "My husband

will discover that a wife cannot be so easily put aside. I am going to seduce him—and then I'm going to show him who I really am." She felt a grim sort of satisfaction. "He'll have no choice but to admit he wants me, after all."

"*Hell hath no fury*," the Abbess said, still looking amused. "But what is it that you're after, milady, revenge or something ... sweeter?"

Helena's heart gave a traitorous lurch. Before she could respond, however, there was a rap on the door. A footman entered with the announcement that his lordship arrived.

"Give us ten minutes, Jim," the Abbess said, "then bring him in."

After the servant departed, the madam gave Helena a discerning once-over. "Let's get you set up a bit, luvie. Set the stage, so to speak, for the show to follow."

So saying, she instructed Helena to lie on her side on the bed. Helena shivered as the Abbess tugged the sleeves of the tunic lower, baring her bosom almost to the nipples. The madam arranged a long, red curl to lie atop the bobbing mounds and then fussed with Helena's skirt, draping the white folds to leave one leg bare to the thigh. Declaring herself satisfied, the Abbess brought the chamber to shadowy dimness, with a single candle left burning on the table.

"Good luck then, milady." Coming from the darkness, the Abbess' voice had a sudden feral quality. "May you teach your husband a lesson he'll never forget." With a final cackle, she was gone.

Palms damp, Helena waited as the shadows danced around her. She heard footfalls approaching and experienced the sudden urge to run. To abandon this bold and brazen and altogether mad stratagem ... and do what? Go rusticate in the country? Run back to parents who did not want her? Hide with her tail between her legs from the husband who also did not want her?

Marianne's parting words rang in Helena's head. *My plan will bring Harteford to you, but the rest is up to you. If you want him to admit his folly, you'll have to prove to him just how wrong he is. How much he wants you—which, despite his mercurial behavior, I do not doubt he does.*

The door opened. The sudden shaft of light and the large, familiar silhouette jammed Helena's heart into her throat. Yet she steeled her spine. *You can do this. Show him you won't be discarded like ... like an old toy. A worthless plaything.*

The door closed, returning the room to darkness. In a few long strides, he was there, looming at the side of the bed. Despite everything, Helena felt a tumult of longing at the sight of her husband's haggard features. He had dark shadows beneath his eyes, as if he hadn't slept since she'd last seen him. Bristle covered his jaw, and his overgrown hair brushed his collar. Upon his temple, the scar gleamed, puckered and tender-looking.

"*Monsieur,*" she remembered to say in her breathy harlot's voice. "*Merci d'être venu. Je voudrais—*"

To her shock, a large finger pressed against her lips, stilling her words.

"*Mademoiselle,*" he said in a low, rough voice, "I have come at your invitation, but tonight I have a request."

"*Qu'est-ce que vous voulez, monsieur?*"

He met her gaze squarely. "I wish for you not to speak tonight. To remain silent. Do you think you could do this for me?"

Belly aflutter, Helena recalled her supposed lack of fluency in English. She furrowed her brow. "*Je ne comprends pas.*"

"'Tis just as well you don't," Nicholas muttered.

Before she could wonder what he meant, he pinched her lips lightly together, as if to seal them. "No talking," he said. "No words tonight, whatever I say or do. If you please."

She nodded, her heart thumping madly. "*Ah. Bien. Maintenant, je comprends.*"

"Good." The dark satisfaction in his voice curled over her

senses. Before she could think how to respond, he had one knee upon the bed. She trembled as his hand captured her jaw, his thumb rubbing against her lips, an imitation of kissing. Like the last time, he made no move to touch his lips to hers. Instead, his gaze traveled lower to her breasts, and she could see the banked fire leap to life in his eyes.

When he ran a long finger over the trembling hills of white flesh, she had to bite her lip to keep from moaning. Her skin prickled with awareness. *Stay focused,* she told herself. *You almost have him. Wait until he is driven wild with desire and then ... then ...*

She couldn't help the gasp that escaped for he'd yanked the tunic below her bosom. Her breasts were now fully exposed, her arms trapped by the small sleeves. He pushed her onto her back. She caught the silver gleam of hunger before he bent his head. The hot, wet swipe of his tongue made her squirm against the satin sheets. Lord in heaven, it felt so *good*. Low sounds escaped from his throat as he suckled her more roughly, drawing her hard bud into his mouth. All the while, he played with the other breast, titillating the tip with his callused fingertips. When his teeth grazed her, she moaned aloud.

"Please, *monsieur*," she heard herself beg in another's voice. "More."

Though his finger pressed against her lips, a reminder of silence, he sucked harder, and she was panting by the time his hand landed on her bare hip. She wore no unmentionables beneath her nymph's costume. Her spine arched off the bed as he found and penetrated her most vulnerable place. His finger slid all the way in, as if he belonged there. When he began to drive into her, his palm smacking lightly against her soaked sex, her eyes closed, and she forgot herself again.

"*Mon dieu*," she cried out. "*Oh, monsieur, s'il vous plaît—*"

His hand muffled the rest of her sentence. Despite the desire fogging her brain, she noted the feverish glaze to his eyes. He was breathing hard, staring down at her. Looking at her—through her? Suddenly, she realized that his focus was somewhere else, somewhere deeper ... and her pulse began to hammer as her plan came back to her. *Does he recognize me? Is now the time to confront him ...?*

Yet there was no sign that he'd discovered her true identity. After a few heartbeats, he lifted his hand from her mouth and unwound his cravat. Her eyes widened when she realized what he intended.

"I won't hurt you. I give you my word, *mademoiselle*." The shadows limned the foreboding austerity of his countenance. "I'll pay you extra for the favor, but I need you to stay quiet. To allow me to do as I wish. Please."

She could hardly breathe. Why was her silence so important to him? What was he after? In a flash, it occurred to her Nicholas had never asked anything of her before. What were his needs ... his desires? If only the blasted man had tried talking to her instead of running away time after time. Yet, she thought with growing unease and anticipation, was it her he was running from ... or something else? What secrets did her husband hide?

What would she do to discover them?

"May I?" he asked quietly.

She looked at the length of linen between his hands and to his hard face again. All of a sudden, her anger and hurt gave way to burning curiosity. Intuitively, she knew she might never again have a chance to know what lay within her husband's soul. To know *him*, just once, as she'd always wished to. Swallowing, she nodded.

He helped her to sitting and, after a moment's hesitation, slipped the cravat over her mouth. The spicy, masculine scent of the material filled her nostrils, and her nerves tingled with shocking excitement.

"Is that too tight?" he asked hoarsely.

She shook her head.

His gaze returned to her breasts. Instead of touching her there, however, he turned her onto her hands and knees. A deep flush spread beneath the surface of her skin as he peeled away her flimsy costume, leaving her utterly bare and in a most lascivious pose. She heard the sound of clothing being shed and then he was on the bed next to her, in naked, sinewy glory. Her blood thickened to honey at the sight of his powerfully broad chest with its dusting of dark hair, the lean rippling of his abdomen, and lower ... ah, yes.

He was every bit as magnificent as she remembered.

Desire pooled in her belly, and she discovered she retained the capacity for embarrassment after all when moisture seeped onto her thigh. On instinct, she shifted on her knees, trying to close her legs together to hide the mortifying trickle.

"No, my love," he whispered, moving behind her. "Don't try to hide your desire from me. It pleases me that you want me. I have wanted to have you this way for so long."

He had been fantasizing about the whore, then? Helena felt her heart clench with pain even as confusing pleasure jolted through her system. For he was touching her, praising her as he did so.

"You've a pretty pussy," he husked. "Soft and wet and sweet, just as I knew it would be. Just as I imagined, from the first time I saw you, sitting alone at that ball."

Helena's eyes widened as his words sunk in. She turned her head back to look at him, only to have her spine melt as his fingers found her knot. Her head collapsed onto the mattress, her breath puffing against the cravat as he thumbed her in delirious circles.

"Beautiful," he growled. "I like you with your arse up for me. Wanton and sweet, all at once. That's it, my love, work your beautiful cunt against me—"

Head spinning, she could do nothing but obey. She shamelessly rode his hand. He was fingering her pearl and delving into her channel at the same time. His desire for her emerged in half-utterances, snippets of tortured fantasy.

"Don't care that I'm not good enough ... I want to fuck you ... in the carriage ... on that new bloody couch in the drawing room ... hell, on your goddamn piano ... you'd like that wouldn't you?"

Her cheek pressed against the mattress. She felt as if she was drowning in waves of wondrous confusion. Sensations crashed over her, too many, too intense to take in. A wild sob caught in her throat. The crisis hit her, a barrage of pleasure-sparks that lit her from inside out. Tremors shook her body, and before they had subsided, she felt the thick, hard heat of him pushing inside her. His cock stretched her utterly; he lunged, pushing her breath out against the cloth binding.

"Tonight you're mine." She felt the vise of his fingers holding her hips in place as he withdrew and slammed inside again. The bliss of impact drew a whimper from her lips. "I won't let him stand between us ... not him, not the past, nothing ..." He groaned as if in anguish. "God, you're so tight. So perfect ..."

Dimly, she realized that questions should be forming in her mind, yet her husband's cock was drilling away the capacity for thought. He was pounding into her, harder, deeper, her breasts swaying from the power of each thrust. Suddenly, he nudged a deep and exquisite place. Her vision blurred; a dam burst open within her. She heard her own muffled scream as she spent again, her pussy clenching on his shaft, the pleasure almost too much to bear.

"*Helena, my love.*"

His guttural cry rang in her ears, and she felt him wrench out, felt the molten splatter against the curve of her spine. For several moments, she lay still, listening to his harsh breaths, absorbing the heat of his body lying collapsed atop her. There was a tugging against her cheek; the cravat loosened, fell away. Large hands turned her gently onto her back and pulled a sheet to cover her trembling nakedness.

"I didn't hurt you, did I?" Nicholas asked gruffly.

In the flickering dimness, she saw with shock the raw sheen in his eyes and the tell-tale moisture that glittered on his dark lashes. In all the times she had imagined this scenario—of her triumph, his defeat—she had never pictured him thus. Had never known this side of Nicholas existed. In this moment, he was not arrogant or omnipotent or indifferent.

He was hurting ... exposed.

Vulnerable.

As if catching wind of her thoughts, he sat up and turned away to sit at the edge of the bed. She had to bite back a gasp. His *back* ... it was marred with old scars. Even in the quasi-darkness she could discern the raised and jagged lines that flexed as he scrubbed his hands over his face. Tension hung in the air, so thick and palpable that she could feel it clogging her own lungs. She was choked by horror, by helpless fury. What had happened to him? Who had hurt him so?

Still not facing her, he said, "Ironic, isn't it? Pretending a whore is my wife." He gave a harsh laugh, and even in her shocked state, she could hear the guilt and self-loathing in his voice. "But better than the alternative. I'd rather be skinned alive than let her know what I'm capable of. The bastard I truly am."

Pulse thrumming, she saw that he had his forearms resting upon his thighs. He was staring at his hands in disgust. What was he seeing? What had he done?

She released a shaky breath. "*Monsieur?*"

"It's for her own good," he said, his voice eerie and distant. "I can't explain it to her, but I'm doing what is best. So help me God, what I must do now that he's found me."

Who was *he*? The bounder who had given Nicholas the scars?

She wet her lips and tried to summon the courage to tell Nicholas who she was. To demand to know what was going on. Yet as she watched, his hands curled to fists, and she knew he was battling whatever demons lived inside him. His chest rose and fell in uneven surges. The raw weight of the moment pressed upon her: she was filled with stunning, bewildering remorse.

What had she been thinking, to trick him this way? To deceive him into exposing the tattered skin of his secrets? How would he react now, if she was to reveal her true identity?

Forgive me, Nicholas. I didn't know. Yet how could I, when you never told me?

He aimed a glance back at her. His mouth twisted when he caught her looking at his back. "Ugly, aren't they? That's what happens when a boy lets himself be whipped like a mongrel. And worse." The humiliation in his eyes made her want to weep. "Yet another thing I'll take to my grave rather than let my wife see." He halted, his voice sharpening with sudden apprehension. "You don't understand a word I'm saying, do you?"

Head reeling, she did not know how to respond. How could she admit who she was now? So she blurted instead, "*Monsieur?*"

Relief eased the lines around his mouth. "As I said, 'tis just as well."

Rising, he went to collect his discarded clothes and began to dress with the single-minded purpose of a man who could not get out of there soon enough. When he was finished, he was once more his impassive self, with not a trace of emotion in his dark eyes. He'd closed himself off the way a valet packed a traveling case. Snap and shut.

If nothing else, this convinced her she had made the right choice for now. For if she was to confront him, he would only block her out, as he'd been doing all along. Given her duplicity, she wouldn't blame him, either. Her earlier frustration, her righteous anger gave way to more poignant emotion.

"Thank you, *mademoiselle*." He deposited a bank note on the table. Bowing, he said in gruff tones, "This will be our last meeting. Do not contact me again."

When his broad shoulders disappeared through the door, she let the hot push of tears spill over. She'd been going about things all wrong, she realized. She'd thought he didn't want her, didn't find her desirable enough. But now she was beginning to understand that what separated them was not lack of desire ... but trust.

'Twas not a problem to be solved by a harlot.

Trust in a marriage had to be earned.

By husband ... and by wife.

Chapter Nineteen

Three days later, Helena found herself before a row of tidy terraced houses in Bloomsbury. Though it lacked the grandeur of Mayfair, the neighborhood was nevertheless well maintained, with freshly painted buildings and small cheerful gardens. The sound of children playing could be heard on the street. The smell of laundry being washed and freshly baked bread wafted on the cool breeze. Home to the increasingly prosperous middling sort, the area possessed an air of comfortable charm.

As she climbed the front steps of the large corner house, a carriage pulled up.

Just in time, she thought with a nervous flutter.

Her husband ascended the steps, looking none too pleased.

"What the hell do you think you're doing?" he said.

"Good afternoon, Harteford," she said pleasantly. "I see you got my note. How lovely that you could join me in paying a call on Mrs. Fines."

"I'm not joining you in anything. We are leaving this instant—"

Smiling sweetly, she rang the bell.

The door was opened almost immediately by a wizened maid-servant in a mobcap. To Helena's astonishment, the tiny woman took one look at Nicholas and began to scold him.

"Well, it's high time you showed your face in these parts, young man." The maid crossed her arms over her non-existent bosom. "And where have you been all this time?"

Clearly trying to rein in his temper, Nicholas said shortly, "I've been busy, Lisbett. My apologies. But unfortunately there's been a change in plans, and my wife and I won't be staying after—"

"Hello, Lisbett. I am Lady Harteford." Peering around her husband, Helena gave the maid a bright smile. "'Tis very nice to meet you, and of course we will be staying. I have been looking forward to this visit for some time."

Lisbett bobbed at the knees. "Pleased to meet you, your ladyship." To Nicholas, she admonished, "Well, don't keep your lady on the doorstep, you scoundrel. You don't need another lesson from Lisbett in manners, do you? For I'll be glad to teach you—marquess or no, you're still a young whippersnapper to me."

A muscle ticked in Nicholas' jaw. An ominous sign. But to Helena's relief, he stepped aside, and she wasted no time in slipping past him and into the house. Inside, the foyer was spacious, marked by a polished walnut table topped with a vase of roses.

"I'll let Mrs. Fines know you've arrived," Lisbett said. "Then I'm off to fetch the rolls from the oven—you still remember my buns, don't you, my boy? I made your favorites especially."

Nicholas' expression softened as he regarded the old woman. "Apricot, of course. Thank you, Lisbett." To Helena's surprise, he bent to kiss her cheek.

"Oh, off with you, you charmer," Lisbett said, blushing.

A soft voice drifted into the room. "Nicholas, is that you?"

Anna Fines appeared from the hallway, her eyes eager behind her small rounded spectacles. She was a lady of comfortable years, with a maternal quality about her, from her rosy rounded cheeks to the downy faded curls peeping from under a lace cap. She stopped short at the sight of Helena and made an awkward curtsy. "M-my lady."

"Mrs. Fines, how nice to see you again," Helena said warmly. "Please, call me Helena."

A flicker of uncertainty passed behind Mrs. Fines' spectacles. "Thank you for gracing us with your presence. I was delighted to receive your note." She looked over at Nicholas, her gaze warming. "We have not seen Nic—I mean, Lord Harteford for quite some time."

Nicholas took Anna's hand; the affection in the gesture was unmistakable. "In this house, I will always be Nicholas Morgan," he murmured. "I am sorry I have been away so long. How are you, Anna?"

"As well as a woman of my advanced years can be," their hostess replied with a tremulous smile. Her hands clasped Nicholas'. "Doing my best to attend to home and hearth and the children, of course."

"Your home is lovely. Thank you for having us," Helena said. "And I do look forward to seeing Miss Percy and Mr. Fines again."

Anna looked at Helena, then back to Nicholas. Her smile broadened. "You are most welcome, my dear. The children will be back shortly from an errand. In the meanwhile, do come in and refresh yourselves."

They retired to a homey front parlor, where Lisbett had laid out a cold collation of pickled meats, cheeses, and her famous apricot buns. Holding a surly-looking pug in her lap, Anna expounded upon her plans for the small garden in the back. Helena nodded and nibbled at one of the golden rolls. She noticed that beady canine eyes followed her every movement.

"I have been amiss in not paying a call sooner," Nicholas was saying.

Anna answered with a charming laugh. "You are forgiven, dear boy. After all, you are a newlywed and have more important matters to attend to."

She slid a sly look at Helena, whose eyes dropped to the fringed edge of the seat pillow.

"We were blessed with Paul when I was about Helena's age and Percy not too long after," Anna continued in that same coy manner. "The nursery is the cornerstone to a happy marriage, I've always said."

At the image of a black-haired babe with his father's eyes, Helena's breath caught. A slow ache expanded in her chest. If only the barriers to her marriage could be surmounted ... how magical it would be to hold a part of Nicholas in her arms.

Beside her on the settee, Nicholas cleared his throat. "And Percy, how is she?"

"She is well, although lately she has gotten a bee in her bonnet about becoming a novelist. Can you believe it? A female writer, of all things." Anna gave a visible shudder, her hand stilling on the pug's head. "It is all those dreadful novels she reads. She visits the circulating library at least once a week."

"Percy has a good head on her shoulders," Nicholas said. "I am sure she will outgrow any foolish notions."

The door bell chimed, and the pug issued two high-pitched yelps. Moments later the two other Fineses appeared, their faces flushed from the outdoors.

"Nick!" With a wild cry, the younger Fines hurtled on coltish limbs toward Nicholas, who stood to receive her in a brotherly hug.

"Persephone Fines, where are your manners?" Anna chided. "Her ladyship is here."

"Oh." Percy stepped back, her heart-shaped face abashed. Helena thought she looked exactly as Anna might have as a young woman, with wayward blonde curls and lively blue eyes. Percy dipped into a pretty curtsy. "How do you do, my lady?"

"It is nice to see you again, Percy. And do let us forgo formalities—I am Helena."

"Delighted to be graced with your charming presence, Lady

Helena," Paul Fines drawled as he sauntered over. He swept over Helena's hand with practiced flourish. "The color of your gown is delectable. Like the ripest of peaches. It makes me quite ravenous, come to think of it."

"Thank you, Mr. Fines," Helena said, warmth tingling her cheeks.

"Paul. We are nearly family, after all, and need not stand on ceremony." His voice had a caressing quality to it.

"Fines," Nicholas growled.

"Yes, Morgan?" Paul asked innocently.

"Haven't you anything better to do but flirt with my wife?"

"Of course not," Paul said. "What could be better than flirtation?"

"Keeping all of one's teeth, perhaps?"

"Oh, stop it, you two." Rolling her eyes, Percy plopped herself down on a chair next to Helena. "They're even worse in the ring," she confided with sisterly derision.

Still aglow over Nicholas' rather husbandly reaction, Helena asked, "The ring?"

"You know, sparring." As if to demonstrate, Percy tapped a seat pillow with her fist. "Nick and Paul are mad over boxing. One time, they left Gentleman Jackson's with eyes big as coal lumps, the both of them. Papa had a fit. He said they looked like two bloody—"

"Percy, haven't you anything better to talk about?" Nicholas asked with a frown.

"Not really," Percy said. "My life is utterly boring."

"Lord, so commences the melodrama." Paul yawned. "Someone call the Minerva Press."

Percy spared her brother a scathing glance. "I'm not being dramatic. It's true. Nothing of interest ever happens around here."

"Really, dearest, I do not know where this vulgar desire for excitement comes from," Anna said, her tone reproving. "You ought to show gratitude for the comforts Papa has provided for us. There are so many less fortunate than you."

Percy crossed her arms petulantly over her chest.

"Yes, Percy, show some gratitude," Paul said.

"As for you, young man," Anna continued, turning a steely eye upon her eldest, "you would do well to change your attitude. All that debauched living can lead to no good end."

"Mama, let us not revisit this topic *again*," Paul said, groaning.

"You cannot dispute that you have been nigh living at Boodle's these weeks past. I cannot know where you have developed this penchant for cards—Heaven knows your dear Papa never condoned gambling."

"Yes, well, Papa was a saint."

"I do not like your tone, young man." Beneath Anna's softly spoken words was a core of iron. "If attitude is a prelude to behavior, then you had best begin reforming your mind. You need something worthwhile with which to occupy your time. Perhaps you should ask Nicholas for a position at the company."

"Can we not discuss this later?" A pleading edge entered Paul's voice.

"As Nicholas is right here, I can imagine no better time," Anna said firmly. "Nicholas, what think you about Paul at the company?"

"There is always a place for Paul, should he wish it," Nicholas said.

"Excellent. It is settled then. Paul will start next week." Anna patted the pug, who turned belly-up in pleasure. "Now, Percy, perhaps you'd care to entertain our guests on the pianoforte."

As Percy rose to her feet with obvious reluctance, Paul's expression shifted from sulky to devious. "Please, not the pianoforte," he drawled in tones of abject horror.

Helena saw that Paul's comment scored a direct hit.

"That is not amusing!" Percy said, her hands on her hips. "I have been practicing very diligently on the Concerto. It's not my fault if the instrument is poorly tuned."

"'Tis your ear that's poorly tuned, not the instrument," Paul said, calmly helping himself to the collation.

A cushion sailed through the air, the fringes spreading like a sunburst. It fell several feet wide of the target, who smirked and bit into a slice of cheese.

"Your aim is no better than your ear," he said.

Another cushion whizzed by, knocking the plate of buns off the table.

With a joyful squeal, the pug leapt from Anna's lap.

"Fitzwell, no!" Anna exclaimed. "Paul, stop him! Buns will ruin his digestion."

Paul reached gingerly toward the feasting dog. "Come here, you insipid beast ..."

Fitzwell growled, the hairs rising on his neck. With a resigned sigh, Paul put down his plate and lunged. At the same time, Fitzwell flung his stubby legs upward in a desperate bid for freedom. Anna screamed. Before Helena's shocked eyes, man and dog collided into the sideboard, sending a shower of food into the air. A symphony of dishes and silverware crashed to the ground.

In the general pandemonium that ensued, Nicholas waded in and picked the squirming dog up by the scruff.

Fitzwell issued a series of indignant snorts.

"Stop," Nicholas ordered.

The pug stopped and was deposited back onto Anna's lap.

Helena had remained quiet throughout. Flustered, Anna kept one hand on the dog. The other went to her chest. "What you must think of us, my dear!"

"Oh, no ... I ..." Helena shook her head, her shoulders shaking.

"See how you have shocked this poor lady with your disgraceful behavior." Anna's reprimanding glare included both her children and Fitzwell, who blinked innocently back.

Helena felt her face turn red.

"Take a deep breath, Helena," Nicholas said.

"I'll fetch the smelling salts," Percy volunteered.

"Get some for me, will you?" Wincing, Paul removed a bit of ham from his once spotless waistcoat.

"What you must think of us!" Anna repeated, wringing her hands.

It was too much, really.

"I think," Helena gasped, "you are all ... wonderful!"

She dissolved into laughter.

Chapter Twenty

What the bloody hell was Helena up to?

Anna had sent them to inspect her garden, so Nicholas found himself outside and alone with his wife. He didn't give a damn about the romantic vista of flower beds and well-trimmed hedges; what he wanted to know was Helena's intentions. Bending to sniff a yellow bud, she was acting as if she hadn't a care in the world. As if she hadn't spent the last hour enchanting the Fineses. As if she hadn't charmingly milked them for stories about his past—details that Anna, Percy, and Paul had offered up with great hilarity.

There was the time Nicholas had tried to help Percy glue her broken doll and ended up with his thumbs stuck together instead. Or when, as a lark, he and Paul had replaced Jeremiah's whiskey, filling the decanter with tinted barley water. Or the time they'd gotten into an overly vigorous sparring match and tried to hide the evidence by covering Paul's black eye with Anna's face powder.

Nicholas had sat there, listening to the fond reminiscing. Inwardly, he'd thanked God that Anna, Paul, and Percy didn't know the ugly truths, the tales that couldn't be shared over tea.

The time before he'd met them. His crimes, his brutality and cowardice—the past that had made him who he was.

As Helena straightened, the sunlight fell upon her chestnut hair, gilding the thick locks and the exposed skin above her neckline. Far too much skin, he thought with a scowl. Heat rose in his loins at the same time that guilt assailed him: what kind of a randy bastard was he, that the night with the whore had not even touched his desire for Helena?

"You're nearly falling out of that dress," he said before he could help himself.

Her lashes lifted in his direction. The corners of her lush mouth tipped upward. "Thank you for noticing, my lord."

"I am not the only one who noticed," he said curtly. "Fines couldn't keep his eyes off you the entire bloody tea."

"Mr. Fines was merely being polite." Her head tilted. "You're not jealous, are you?"

"Of course not," he said through clenched teeth. "What you do is your business. Which brings me to my point—what are you doing, meddling in mine?"

To his shock, she linked her arm through his. Gave him a smile that was like a battering ram to his defenses. Even his bones quivered with longing. "Come walk with me, Harteford. There are private matters I wish to discuss with you. About our marriage."

"I thought I made myself clear the last time," he managed to say as he fell in step beside her on the pebbled path. "We are going to get an annulment. It is the best thing for both of us."

"I disagree. I have decided I want to stay married to you. And I will not support an annulment—if it comes to that, I will make the case for one extremely difficult."

"What?" he roared, before he remembered where they were.

"You heard me," she said.

He dropped her arm. Stared at her. "Why are you doing this?"

She matched him look for look. With her hazel eyes spitting fire at him, her cheek rosier than all the surrounding blooms, she was more beautiful than any woman had the right to be. Damn her.

Her chin lifted. "Because I love you, you idiot. Why else?"

Her words fell like a hammer upon his heart. Blows of pleasure-pain that made it difficult to catch his breath. "What?" he choked out.

"Oh, Nicholas," she said, with a sad smile. "There's nothing wrong with your hearing, is there? Perhaps you don't want to know it, but that is the truth. I love you, and I shan't give you up without a fight."

There it was: everything he'd ever wanted to hear from her.

Don't give into temptation, you selfish bastard. You have no right. You have to protect her.

Seized with panic, he shook his head. "You don't know what you're saying. You don't even *know* me—"

"Don't I?" She began to walk ahead, determined little strides that forced him to lengthen his own. "I know more than you think, Nicholas. I know your mother was an opera singer, for instance, and that your legitimacy was not declared until quite recently. I can only surmise that you lived as a bastard in the time intervening and that that could not have been easy."

Not easy? There was an understatement. His head was spinning—too many emotions crowding in. "You have no bloody idea what my life was like. You couldn't begin to understand," he bit out.

"Try me." She shot him a challenging glance. "Instead of hiding or running away, just share something with me, this once."

Don't do it. Don't give in—

"Or perhaps you're the one who is afraid?"

His temper snapped. "You want to hear a story? Fine. But let me warn you, this one is nothing like the ones you heard over tea." When she continued to regard him with complete equanimity, he said tersely, "It was the day I met Jeremiah at the docks."

"Go on," she said.

"It's a charming tale. Late one night, Jeremiah was headed home when I approached him."

"Asking for work?" she prompted, as he knew she would.

"Wielding a bludger." Seeing the furrow between her delicate brows, he smiled with grim satisfaction. "Don't know what that is, do you? Let me explain. 'Tis a common enough weapon in the stews. You take a piece of cloth, you see, and wrap it around whatever can do a man injury—rocks, wood. Discarded horse shoes, now, they work especially well. Whatever you can get your hands on, you tie it up and to a stick. So it can be swung like this, see?"

Her eyes followed the menacing motion of his hands. Her fragile throat flexed. "Y-yes. I believe I understand now."

"I came at Jeremiah that night, figuring him for another soft pig on the docks. An easy mark. I thought to nab myself a fine pocket-watch or a purse full of mint. Didn't matter much how I got it—with blood or without," he said matter-of-factly.

"What happened?"

Nicholas smiled wryly. "Blood *was* shed that night—only it wasn't Jeremiah's. Tough old dog. Had me down on the dock, didn't he, the wicked end of his walking stick pointed at my throat." He could still feel the cold steel, the numbness that had come over him as he'd faced his demise. After the weeks spent running from his crime, dodging the street gangs and other criminals, death had seemed like deliverance.

"Did he hurt you?" she gasped.

"No."

"What happened then? What did Jeremiah do?"

Nicholas exhaled. "He just ... spoke to me. He said, *A man is what he makes of himself, boy. I don't know you from Adam, but I sure as hell know you can do better than this.*"

Unexpected heat prickled his eyelids; all these years, and the gratitude, nay *love*, he felt for his mentor had not faded a whit. Instead of death that night, he'd found a miracle: a new beginning.

"Jeremiah told me to find him at his warehouse when I was

ready to live better. I had little to lose, so I went to him the next day. He found me a place to stay, saw to it that I had clean clothes and decent meals. He also gave me a position with his dock crew working long hours, hard hours, but they were honest ones. It took me five years to work my way up out of the water and into the office. After several promotions, I eventually spent two years overseeing our operations in the West Indies. I returned when Jeremiah fell ill, and that was when he proposed the partnership."

"How I admire you." His wife's soft voice stirred him out of his reverie. He was startled to realize how much he'd revealed and even more startled by Helena's response. Her gloved hand rested gently upon his arm. "You have come from adversity and made something of yourself. You have garnered great success on your own merit. That is a claim few men can make."

"You astonish me," he was forced to say.

"I do?"

"You do realize that my *success* as you describe it is that I have a profession. I work for a living." He enunciated each word as if she did not understand its meaning. "In the view of the *ton*, that is regarded as a disgrace rather than an accomplishment."

His wife regarded him with inscrutable eyes. "And you think I care what the *ton* thinks?"

"You are a lady," he said. "Of course you do."

"Then perhaps *you* don't know *me* as well as you think," she said.

This is working. Helena had to hide a giddy smile at her lord's befuddled expression. *I am finally getting to know him—the real him. Yet if trust and honesty are to grow between us, he has to know a thing or two about me, as well.*

Drawing a breath for courage, she said, "It might surprise you to know that I, myself, have done things that would shock the *ton*," she said.

This drew a rare smile from her husband. His white teeth flashed against his swarthy skin. "Have you now?"

Helena nodded, a trifle light-headed at his nearness. He was standing very close to her, so close that she could make out the subtle striping on his grey waistcoat. She could smell his unique scent, sandalwood and lemon soap and ... potent male. She breathed him in before continuing.

"My parents despaired of my ever becoming a proper lady," she said, deciding it best to let him down gently. "When I was a girl, they used to send me to bed without supper for all the scrapes I got into."

"Their tactics worked. You are, after all, a paragon of ladylike virtue."

"That is *not* me!" At Nicholas' lifted brow, Helena flushed. What would it take for him to see her as she was? Not perfect. Far from. Recalling what Marianne had said about men not wishing to bed paragons, she said anxiously, "What I mean to say is there is more to me than decorum. *Much* more."

"Indeed."

Bristling at Nicholas' indulgent tone, Helena said, "When I went riding with my brother Thomas, I would ride astride once we got out of view of the main house."

When Nicholas looked unimpressed, she added, "With breeches on, I could beat Thomas up a tree."

Still no response.

"I once knocked the baker's son to the ground for making fun of my freckles," she said out of desperation. "His nose was bloodied. I may have given him a bruise or two as well."

"I do not see any evidence of freckles," her husband commented.

"They faded after my mother added a milk-and-vinegar wash to my daily ablutions." Glumly, Helena tugged at a spring bloom.

The petals drifted into her palm. Obviously, Nicholas preferred to view her in a certain fashion, and nothing she said was going to deter him. If he could not assimilate her childish antics with his vision of her, what would he do when she revealed her more recent, and certainly more serious, transgressions?

By the by, my love, I also dressed like a harlot and seduced you at a bawdy house.

Or perhaps a more roundabout approach: *Do you know I speak fluent French, Nicholas? "J'adore le cock", for instance—might that ring a bell?*

Thinking of the possible ramifications to such confessions, she shivered. Trust was a tricky business, after all. Best to proceed with caution and take small steps.

Very small steps.

"Are you cold?"

Warm fingers lifted her chin. Nicholas was studying her, his grey eyes tender with concern.

"No," she whispered.

Afraid to lose his touch, she closed her eyes and dared to lean her cheek against his hand. She felt him hesitate. Then his knuckles trailed along her cheek.

"Do you ... do you still think me a paragon?" she asked, her breath hitching.

There was a stilted silence. When he spoke, his voice was deep and husky. Ragged at the edges. "Ah, Helena, God help me, but I think you very sweet."

Her eyelashes quivered as he continued to stroke her softly, bringing a flush of heat to her skin. She looked at his lips, remembering the heat and texture of them upon her breasts. The way they had whispered delightfully wicked desires only three nights ago—fantasies that had rendered her hot and damp with longing. Her gaze traveled upward, and she found herself dissolving in pools of passionate darkness.

"Nicholas." Her head tipped back in invitation.

At the sound of his name, Nicholas made a noise deep in his throat and covered her mouth with his own. The kiss began softly, gently, like the whisper of dragonfly wings. She absorbed his warmth like a sun-starved flower. Yet even as his touch dazzled her senses, she was aware that he was holding back. Restraining himself ... because of his past? Because of some misguided notion that he was not good enough for her? Didn't he know that he was everything she wanted? If words would not convince him of her passionate love, then perhaps actions would.

Whispering his name, she parted her lips, and the flavor of the kiss changed completely. She heard a guttural sound and then she was invaded, filled with the masculine essence of him. His tongue thrust against hers and delved—demanding, claiming, leaving no doubt that he belonged there. Not that she had any doubt to begin with. Moaning, she twined her tongue with his. She threaded her fingers into his hair, yearning to feel him closer. Needing to feel the hard length of him pressed against her, deep inside her ...

"Nick, Mama wants to know if you will stay for supper—"

The cheerful voice fell like a guillotine in the spring garden. Helena was thrust aside so quickly that her head spun. She steadied herself upon a hedge. When her senses recovered sufficiently, she saw Percy standing there, with eyes big as dinner plates. Those blue orbs blinked back and forth between her and Nicholas, who looked far more composed than she felt.

"Thank you, Percy," Nicholas said, his tone polite, "but no, we won't be staying."

At least there was an edge of unevenness to his breath.

"I didn't mean to interrupt ... I'm so ... oh, bloody hell." Percy's face was redder than the roses. Kicking at a pebble with her slipper, she muttered, "I'll, er, let Mama know." She dashed off.

Helena turned to Nicholas. The joking rejoinder dissolved on her tongue when she saw the strain lining his rugged features. Heaving a sigh, she crossed her arms beneath her bosom. "For heaven's sake, must we do this again? I know what you're thinking, and the answer is no."

"Do what again?" His brows came together. "And what do you mean, *no*?"

"You were about to try to order me out of your life again, weren't you?" When he answered with a speaking look, she said in dulcet tones, "Your jaw gives you away. It looks hard as rocks when you're about to say something disagreeable. Well, whatever solution you are about to propose this time—living separate lives, getting an annulment or a dashed divorce—the answer is *no*."

He just stared at her. Good. Let him know that she was serious. She lifted her chin and returned him look for look.

After a moment, his lips quirked. "I suppose you do know me better than I realize."

Seizing the moment, she said steadily, "I love you, Nicholas. And you cannot deny that you feel at least something for me after the last ti—I mean, after the kiss we just shared." Dear heavens, she'd barely caught the slip! She rushed on in shaky tones, "Can you not trust me enough to tell me what is going on?"

The yearning she saw in his eyes raised goose-pimples on her skin.

"I—I do want you, Helena. It has been hell pretending otherwise." The admission sounded rusty, as if it was being pulled from a deep and seldom accessed place within. "Yet there are things in my past that threaten your safety, and I cannot allow that to happen." He cleared his throat. "And, by the way, the answer is no."

"No to what?" she asked, mystified.

"You were about to ask me about my past, and, no, I will not tell you about it." At her stymied frown, Nicholas' mouth took a faint curve. "Husbands are not as dull-witted as you may think. You, my lady, get an adorable little wrinkle between your brows before *you* bring up a difficult topic."

His confession that he wanted her and his affectionate banter made her heart thrum with hope. There had to be a way around this. "Whatever it is, I don't care," she said eagerly. "I would willingly take any risk to be with you. Besides, life is full of potential dangers, is it not? Why," she continued as inspiration struck, "just a few days ago I was being followed by a pair of criminals—"

"You were *what*?" Nicholas' face drained of color.

"Oh, do not concern yourself, my lord," she said quickly. "Nothing happened. It was just that I noticed two men in dark coats following me when I was shopping on Bond Street. I visited Lady Draven, and she, er, helped me to switch carriages and thus elude the pair."

"What did they look like, these two men?"

Helena wrinkled her nose. "I didn't get a very close look at them. When I tried to, they turned away, or disappeared into the crowd. But I did catch glimpses of their reflections whilst I was pretending to peruse the shop windows."

Rather clever of her, she thought.

"And?" Nicholas demanded.

"Hmm. They looked rather well-kept for criminals, actually. Clean-shaven, proper hats. Their coats were not by any means stylish, but not shabby either." Helena frowned, puzzling upon the point. "Come to think of it, their appearance reminds me a little of someone I can't quite pinpoint ..."

"Mr. Kent, perhaps?"

She looked at her husband in surprise. "Why, yes! How did you know?"

"Because, my dear intrepid wife, I hired those bloody Runners myself."

"To follow me?" she said, aghast.

"To keep you safe," he corrected.

Her hands fluttered to her chest. "What kind of danger am I in, exactly? What on earth is going on? Does this have to do with you being shot?"

"I don't know any of that for certain, Helena. All I know is that there is a villain out there, who wishes me and those nearest to me harm. Listen," he said firmly before she could interrupt. "When it comes to your safety, I will not take any chances. You are too important to me. I want you out of London, the sooner the better."

Delight and fear mingled at his words. "And you are important to me. Who is watching over *you*, Nicholas, keeping you safe?"

He continued as if she had not spoken. "If your parents won't have you, I'll find someplace else to send you—"

Her heart pounded in denial. Not now. Not when they were finally beginning to make progress. "I don't want to leave you. I won't. Not unless you tell me why."

"God's blood, woman, haven't you been listening? Your life may be in peril, and that is all you need to know!"

"Nothing's happened, has it?" Helena was rather proud of how reasonable she sounded. "I mean, as it turns out, the men I thought were villains were actually investigators hired to protect me. So, in truth, not only was I *not* in danger—I was safer than I realized."

Nicholas opened his mouth. Closed it. Raking a hand through his hair, he scowled at her. "Where the hell did you learn to argue like that?"

"The debates at the literary salon," she said. "At any rate, I want to propose a solution to our dilemma. A compromise of sorts."

"Compromise?" He snorted. "What makes you think I'm not going to throw you in the next carriage bound for destination unknown?"

"What makes you think I will not find my way back?" At his thunderous expression, she tried a placating smile. "Would I really be safer alone and in some strange place?" He frowned, and knowing she had scored a hit, she pressed her advantage further. "Wouldn't it be better for me to remain in London, under the protection of the detectives and yourself? If it is my well-being you are concerned about, I will vouch to take the greatest care. I will limit my activities and not go anywhere unaccompanied."

He crossed his arms, his eyes narrowing. "And in return?"

"First, if you have not done so already, you will ask Mr. Kent to safeguard your well-being. If I am to have protection, then so must you."

He grunted in what passed for agreement.

"And secondly, you let me stay here ... and agree to drop this ridiculous annulment scheme." Closing the gap between them, Helena placed her gloved hand against his taut jaw. "You agree to give our marriage another chance, Nicholas, the way Jeremiah gave you."

He quivered beneath her touch, a wild stallion ready to bolt at any minute. She feared she had pressed too hard. Her trepidation intensified when he captured her hand and returned it to her side.

"You will provide a schedule of your daily activities for my approval. If you must leave the house, it will be under protection. In a nutshell, you will stay out of trouble or, so help me God, you'll find yourself under lock and key. In the Outer Hebrides," he said evenly.

Relief made her smile tremulous. "Of course. You have my word, my lord."

"As for our marriage, I will think about what to do next. You will allow me to do so, madam, without interference."

"But—"

"That is the bargain. Take it or leave it," he said.

She bit back a retort. A wise woman knew when to retreat. "Yes, alright." Unable to help herself, she muttered, "You drive a hard bargain, my lord."

"In this one instance, it pays to be a merchant," he replied sardonically.

Chapter Twenty-One

"B*lackmailed?* Why in blazes did you not tell me this sooner?"

From across the stacks of ledgers and documents, Nicholas looked the incensed investigator straight in the eye. "Because I was not certain I could trust you, Kent. I'm still not. But I've decided to take the risk because I must see this thing ended."

Ambrose Kent rose from his chair and began to pace furious steps before the desk. "This changes *everything*, my lord. We will have to come up with a new list of suspects. Who are your enemies? What information do they hold against you?"

"I need to ask you something first." Nicholas kept his voice calm. Beneath the desk, his fingernails bit into his palms. "Say a man has had ... troubles in the past. Skeletons that he wished to remain in the proverbial closet. Would you respect that wish in your investigation?"

Kent arched his brows. "Hypothetically speaking?"

"Of course."

"I can't guarantee anything. In order to find the truth, I must look under every rock." Kent shrugged. "Sometimes I unearth evidence that my client would rather remain buried."

"And what would you do, if facts were to emerge that might potentially harm your client's reputation ... or worse?"

Kent looked at him steadily. "What sort of trouble are we talking about here, my lord?"

Proceed carefully. Give him only enough to assist his inquiries. You must do this, for Helena's sake ... and the sake of your marriage.

Hope sparked within Nicholas, pushing back some of his shadows. Since the talk with Helena two days ago, he'd ached with a ravenous hunger—she'd said she *loved* him. She wanted him as a husband. She'd fight for him. How could he resist her; how could he not give the same in return, when he loved her with all his benighted soul?

His fight would begin here and now.

Feeling like he was stepping off a cliff, Nicholas exhaled and answered the policeman. "For several years, I worked as a climbing boy for a man named Ben Grimes. He called himself a sweep, but he was a thief mostly. He ran a flash house. It burned down one night, taking him in the flames." As Nicholas glossed over the details—of murder, of the even more heinous act he had committed that night—panic burned in his lungs. But he managed to continue in composed tones, "Whoever is behind the blackmail notes has linked me to Grimes. He is threatening to make public this aspect of my past."

Kent had stopped pacing. His expression did not reveal much —a useful talent for an investigator and especially laudable given that the Marquess of Harteford had admitted he'd once been nothing more than a chumney working for a member of the criminal underclass.

"What does he want in exchange for silence?" Kent's voice was surprisingly mild.

"He didn't say. That night in St. Giles, when he shot me, he told me to await his demands."

"Await my bloody arse," Kent muttered. He started stalking again, his greatcoat flapping around his long legs. "We have lost enough time as it is. I must begin interviewing my contacts straightaway to see if anyone has heard of a criminal with a connection to this Grimes."

Though his heart skipped a beat, Nicholas jerked his chin in assent.

"In the meantime, my lord, I urge you once again to take one of my men for protection. There are too many coincidences—the warehouse ransacking, the shooting, and now this." Within his narrow face, Kent's eyes blazed with the intensity of night lamps. "My instinct tells me this is all connected. But how?"

Nicholas had no answer. He only knew that until the truth was uncovered, he would refrain from making any decisions about his marriage. He could not in all conscience go to Helena until he was free of his demons. Though he would wait, he at least had company now: hope. And that was a finer companion than he deserved.

Later on that week, Helena entered Hatchard's Bookstore on Piccadilly. It was a visit scheduled on the list she'd provided to Nicholas—or to his messenger, rather, who came to the house daily to pick up the document. As she wandered through the bookshelves, all too aware of the Runners who'd discreetly positioned themselves (one at the entrance and one by the fireplace just up ahead), she simmered with frustration.

Almost a sennight had come and gone, and she hadn't seen so much as her husband's shadow.

At first, she'd contented herself with the fact that he'd let her stay in London. Their exchange at the Fineses had seemed to signal a turning point in their relationship. With each hour that passed alone in the townhouse, however, she felt her optimism begin to fade. Restlessness plagued her, exacerbated by the omnipresence of the detectives and her own worries.

Why was Nicholas continuing to keep a distance between them? Had nothing, in reality, changed? Sweet heavens, what of the mysterious dangers that threatened him? Could something have befallen him?

But, no, each morning, he sent a polite note along with his envoy. A few lines inquiring about her health and activities, followed by a single sentence referencing how busy he was at work. That was all.

The impulsive part of her wanted to seek him out; the wiser part forestalled such an action. She had promised to let him come to a decision about their marriage in his own time, so she must not go barging in on him like some termagant after a mere week. Sighing, she turned into one of the stacks. Best she make use of this visit to Hatchard's rather than spinning her wheels. She inhaled the smells of parchment and dried ink, which soothed her ruffled senses. Winding her way through the well-ordered store, she browsed for a volume recommended by the Havershams.

She was skimming through a book when she heard her name called.

"Lady Harteford, fancy seeing you here!"

She turned and smiled in surprised recognition. "Miss Fines, what a pleasure to see you again."

Percy grinned, her curls sunny beneath a sky blue bonnet. "The pleasure is mine. Do you frequent Hatchard's often, my lady?"

"Hatchard's is one of my favorite spots in all of London," Helena replied.

"Mine as well," Percy said approvingly. She angled her head to get a better view of the volume in Helena's hands. "*Hypatia of Alexandria*. Never heard of it. It is a good read?"

"I have only glanced at a few pages," Helena said. "I chose it on the recommendation of some friends who are exceptionally informed in the realm of Philosophy. May I ask what brings you here, Miss Fines?"

"This," Percy said, waving a small, leather-bound book. "The latest from Regina Maria Roche. You have read her, Lady Harteford?" When Helena shook her head, Percy looked quite aghast. "You have not read *Clermont*? Or *The Children of the Abbey*?"

"My mother was most particular about my reading materials," Helena explained. "Horrid novels were not amongst the permitted selection."

"I am sure my own mother wishes she had been stricter." Percy's blue eyes held an incorrigible sparkle. "Alas, it is much too late for that. I have already been ruined by the excess of sentimentality. I daresay I have read every publication put forth by the Minerva Press."

"There are certain strengths to be associated with a strong sensibility," Helena said, recalling her recent readings on the matter. "For example, a natural empathy for the suffering of others."

Percy grinned again. "Yes, I do so empathize with the plight of the heroines. Why, in one novel, the lady is in pursuit of her own true love, a handsome stable boy wrongly accused of murder who also happens to be a long-lost Count in disguise. At the same time, she is being haunted by the roving, tortured ghost of the moors—who may or may not be the hero's half-brother. If only real life was half as exciting!"

Helena could not help but smile at the younger girl's spirited charm. At the same time, she noticed a few censorious glances aimed in their direction from the gentlemen seated around the fireplace, newspapers in hand.

"I wonder, Miss Fines," Helena said on impulse, "if you would care to join me for an ice? I had planned on a visit to Gunter's after this."

"I would be delighted," Percy said at once. "Let me fetch my maid."

The ride to Berkeley Square was short, and the driver found a cool spot to park under the boughs of a maple tree. It was a warm day, so there were many other carriages parked in the square. Helena sent Will, the groom, into the sweets shop, and he soon returned with a strawberry ice for Percy and a muscadine ice for herself. They remained sitting in the open-air carriage eating and chatting, the combination so delightful that Helena almost forgot the subtly lurking Runners.

"I am so glad I ran into you today." Swallowing the last spoonful of her ice, Percy made a swooning sound. "We were all so taken with you after your visit, and I despaired at having to wait until Friday to see you again. Have you decided what you will be wearing? You have the most gorgeous clothes, and I am sorely in need of some womanly advice."

Helena blinked, torn between confusion and amusement at the girl's plea for fashion advice. "I beg your pardon? Is there an event this Friday?"

"Oh no, do tell me Nick has not forgotten to inform you!" Percy wailed.

"Inform me of what, exactly?"

"I will murder him," Percy said darkly to her herself. Her eyes flew suddenly to Helena's. "No offense meant, Lady Harteford."

"Since you are to make a widow out of me, we might as well be on more intimate terms," Helena remarked dryly. "We shall be Helena and Percy, if that suits you. Now, what is this about Friday?"

"It is only *the* most important event of my entire life," Percy declared.

Helena hid a smile. The girl's flair for the dramatic was wasted on anything short of Drury Lane.

"I have been planning for *ages*. You and Nick left so, er, precipitously after tea last week that I didn't get a chance to remind you both. So I told Paul to do so when he went to have lunch with Nick yesterday. But he must have forgotten, or perhaps Nick never conveyed the message to you. Either way, it shall be cold-blooded murder for both of them."

Helena's head was spinning. "Percy, you still have not told me what event you are speaking about."

"My birthday, of course. Seventeen years of hum-drum existence culminating at long last in a celebration to end all celebrations. The party is to be at Vauxhall, Helena, *Vauxhall*, can you imagine it ...?" The girl's long lashes fluttered dreamily. "I have always longed to go, and now I shall. Paul has arranged everything. He rented two supper boxes for the occasion, and he has issued invitations to my friends from Mrs. Southbridge's Finishing School. And you and Nick, of course. My mother and her friends will be chaperoning, and there will be games and food and ... oh, I simply cannot wait!"

Helena forced a smile. Inside, her frustration boiled over. Even if Nicholas was trying to protect her, this was a dashed poor way of doing it. To bar her from an event hosted by the closest people he had to family ... how insufferable! *He* was going, wasn't he? If he could take the risk, why shouldn't she be given at least the option? Or, a malicious voice whispered in her head, perhaps he had other reasons for wanting to be free of a wife that evening?

Her hands balled in her lap. He might have at least discussed the situation with her. Of course, discussion would have been nigh impossible, given that he had chosen to absent himself from her life completely in the past week.

"You will come in spite of the mix-up, won't you, Helena?" Percy looked at her with pleading, anxious eyes. "I simply cannot enjoy myself if you are not there. My birthday will be utterly ruined."

Nicholas might be an ass, but Percy was a dear. Helena made up her mind. She would not hurt the girl's feelings just because her lord had seen fit to make a unilateral decision without her knowledge.

"Of course, I will be there," she said brightly. "I would not miss your birthday for the world. Now, do tell me about the ensemble you are planning to wear ..."

Chapter Twenty-Two

Helena sensed his presence the moment he arrived. She was sitting near the end of the long table in the supper alcove, chatting with a friend of Paul Fines. Her back was turned to the entrance of the supper box. One moment, the air was filled with lively chatter and the strains of the nearby orchestra—the next, a throbbing stillness filled her ears, as if they had been suddenly stuffed full of cotton. A tingling sensation swept down her nape, and it was all she could do to keep her attention on her dinner escort.

She could feel the intensity of Nicholas' gaze upon her back and knew he had recognized her instantly. Her heart fluttered like a captive sparrow in her chest. But she would not turn around and greet her husband as might a besotted bride. Let him come to her, if he wished to. Instead, she laughed gaily at Mr. Henderson Reed's witticism—or, more accurately, she assumed his comments were witty, for she'd quite lost track of the conversation.

Thankfully, he did not seem to notice. "I say, Lady Harteford, you look most becoming under the lights," Mr. Reed said. "Like some fairyland princess beneath a rainbow of stars."

"How very poetic of you, Mr. Reed," Helena said. "You rival Lord Byron in your romantic sensibility."

"Kind of you to say so," Mr. Reed replied with obvious gratification. "He is a hero of mine."

Helena thought that rather obvious, given the young man's artfully windswept brown locks and disheveled style. When Mr. Reed proceeded to bestow one of his smoldering looks upon her, she hid a smile. He had practiced this look on her on several occasions throughout the evening, and this attempt ranked among his best. Mr. Reed was near to her age, three-and-twenty at the most, and possessed all the burning intensity of a puppy. His good-natured brown eyes did not so much smolder as emit a hopeful spark. He reminded her a bit of Thomas, actually.

"I was wondering, Lady Harteford, if you would care to join me on a stroll after supper?" Mr. Reed asked as he broke a piece of bread. "Vauxhall is renowned for its ambling paths. The Grand Walk is particularly delightful and close to it is the Rotunda where many entertainments are shown."

"That sounds most genial," Helena agreed. She speared up a bit of thinly sliced ham. The savory meat was a trademark Vauxhall delicacy, but it might have been sawdust for all she noticed or cared. She had still not looked directly at Nicholas, but she could feel him advancing in her direction. She could hear the chairs scraping as guests moved to let him by. Picking up her wineglass, she took a fortifying sip of the arrack punch. And another.

"Good evening, my lady."

At the sound of her husband's deep tones, the sparrow in her chest broke into full flight. She counted to ten before turning around to face him. Sweet heavens, if any eyes could smolder, it was Nicholas'. His gaze fairly burned into hers. The strings of colored lights highlighted the harsh lines of his face and shadowed the rest, making him look more austere than ever. His jaw might have been hewn from stone.

She managed to keep her expression cool and polite as she rose to greet him. She dipped a shallow curtsy, her skirts brushing against the Grecian-style columns which separated the narrow supper boxes. "My lord, what a surprise."

"For me or for you?" Nicholas said.

She put on a puzzled smile. "Why would you be surprised to see me when you knew I was to be invited?"

"I do not recall this event on your list of today's activities," he shot back.

Then he looked her up and down, and his expression darkened further. He leaned closer to her, his subtle, expensive cologne drifting into her nostrils. For some reason, his scent fueled her irritation—why did he have to smell like the very essence of virility? Did he plan to seduce women tonight, was *that* why he had purposefully uninvited his own wife?

"What about your promise not to get into any trouble?"

"I'm certain I don't know what you mean," she said.

She lifted her shoulders in a show of innocence, knowing full well how that action jiggled her breasts and accentuated the crevice between them. She had practiced in front of the looking glass. Her diligence had paid off, too, as Nicholas' eyes narrowed.

"That dress is indecent," he said in the same low voice.

"I know. Is it not splendid?" Helena gave a light laugh and an impudent twirl to show off the garment. Not that there was much to see. Constructed of ivory-colored lace, the gown possessed tiny draped sleeves and a deep neckline which bared the swell of her breasts. The delicate material molded to her curves, parting beneath her bosom to reveal a simple silk under-skirt. Madame Rousseau had cleverly matched the silk to her skin tone; from afar, the gown gave the illusion that she was draped in sensuous lace and little else.

To accompany the dress, Bessie had coaxed Helena's hair into curls and piled them high, leaving a few tendrils to frame her face. Diamond-studded pins in the shape of bumble bees winked from amidst her dark tresses, and a golden ostrich feather dipped saucily forward. The style drew attention to Helena's eyes; for this occasion, she had allowed Bessie to darken her lashes and brush glittering gold powder on her eyelids. As a result, she knew her eyes looked luminous, almost as brilliant as the diamond-and-pearl choker circling her neck. The matching bracelet hung from her gloved wrist.

She knew she had never looked better. She had been waiting all night for her husband's reaction. She did not have long to wait.

Nicholas appeared to be gritting his teeth, likely against words unfit for present company. After a moment of tense silence, he spied the shawl hanging on the back of her chair. He reached for it and tossed it around her shoulders. She raised an eyebrow and smiled, knowing that the shawl would not offer much in the way of coverage—the golden gauze was entirely translucent.

With thinned lips, Nicholas began to unbutton his jacket.

"That will not be necessary," she said.

"You will catch cold dressed in this manner," he said, shrugging off the sleeves.

"It is an unusually balmy night," she said lightly, "and a stroll will keep the blood flowing. As a matter of fact, I believe I am engaged for a walk—is that not so, Mr. Reed?"

She directed the latter part of the sentence to her supper companion, who apparently had been listening with keen ears. In his eagerness to get to his feet, he nearly toppled his chair. The two men sized up one another. Helena could not help but notice the contrast between the two. Mr. Reed, with his gangly limbs and easy smiles, possessed the temperament of a good-natured spaniel. Nicholas, on the other hand, looked as churlish and unapproachable as a jungle cat.

"This is a friend of Mr. Fines," she said by way of introduction. "Mr. Reed, this is my husband, Lord Harteford."

The younger man extended his hand. "Fines has raved about your prowess in the ring, my lord, and claims you land a mean facer. I should love to spar with you sometime. But I must warn you: I've got a bit of a reputation as a neck-or-nothing myself. I have been training with the great Gentleman Jackson himself, perfecting a left jab to knock the wind out of anyone's sails."

Nicholas' expression was bland as he took the other man's hand. Mr. Reed's eyes widened, and his cheerful smile faded. A ruddy color rose upward from the starched tips of his collar. He tugged at his hand like a small animal caught in a trap.

"I look forward to meeting you in the ring," Nicholas said, releasing him.

"Yes, well, we will set a date sometime," Mr. Reed muttered, rubbing his hand. "Lady Harteford, if you are ready?"

"Of course," Helena said. She took Mr. Reed's offered arm and smiled sweetly at her husband. "Enjoy your evening, Harteford."

She attempted to glide forward on Mr. Reed's arm. Unfortunately, the space between the table and the wall of columns was quite narrow, and Nicholas made no move to let them pass. She had to follow Mr. Reed's lead and tilt herself sideways to squeeze by her husband, who stood, arms crossed, imposing as a statue of an Olympic god. Her leg accidentally brushed against his thigh; it was harder than marble and hotter than a thunderbolt. She half expected him to halt her progress—and to her shame she felt a quiver of anticipation. But he did not stop her. She made it past, and it took all her willpower to keep her gaze trained forward on her companion. She would not humiliate herself with a pathetic glance backward.

Breathing more rapidly than usual, Helena somehow navigated around the half-dozen or so chairs. She exchanged pleasantries with Anna Fines and her matronly cronies as she passed and stopped at the head of the table to chat with Percy. The birthday girl looked remarkably pretty in a white muslin gown trimmed with coquelicot ribbon. A matching hibiscus bloomed exotically in her blonde ringlets, which bounced with merriment as she moved her head to and fro between the gentlemen admirers seated on either side of her.

Looking up, Percy asked in a gay voice, "Where are you two off to?"

"I thought I would show Lady Harteford the grounds near the Rotunda," Mr. Reed answered.

"How delightful!" Percy exclaimed. "May I come? I have heard there is to be a rope dancer performing there this evening."

"Of course," Helena said.

"We would not want to interrupt your supper," Mr. Reed said at the same time.

There was an awkward moment.

"I am finished eating," Percy said, "so it would be no interruption at all."

The young bucks on either side of her rose as she did, each offering her his escort. Percy bit her lip, looking indecisively between the two men.

"Well, Percy, it seems you have a dilemma." This came from Paul Fines, seated a few chairs down. "To save Sands and Bellinger from disappointment, you must allow me to escort you. This way, you will show no favoritism, except toward your favorite brother of course."

"You are my only brother," Percy retorted.

"Then the odds are clearly in my favor, are they not?" Getting languidly to his feet, Paul bowed over the hand of the young miss seated next to him. Helena noticed the moonstruck expression on the girl's face. Percy had introduced her as Miss Sparkler, a dear school chum from Miss Southbridge's Finishing School. Mousy haired, slight, and with an unfortunate bout of spots, Miss Sparkler appeared to have a rather serious case of infatuation with her best friend's older brother. When Paul kissed her hand, the girl lit up like the famed Vauxhall fireworks.

Paul came over to his sister and offered his arm.

"I am come to do my good deed for the day," he said.

"Do not try to ingratiate your way into my favor," Percy said, though her eyes glowed with good humor. "I have not yet forgiven you for the comment you made about my skills at the pianoforte."

"It is not you for whom I am being a Good Samaritan." Paul gave a subtle nod toward the back of the supper alcove, where Nicholas stood glowering.

"Ah," Percy said.

Helena flushed. Splendid. Apparently, their marital discord was hung out like dirty laundry for all to see. Perhaps she ought not to have come after all. Or more to the point, perhaps Nicholas should have thought to invite his own wife.

Her chin lifted. "I merely wished to see the sights, and Mr. Reed offered to accompany me."

"Lady Harteford must have the escort of a gentleman," Mr. Reed said gallantly and rather pointedly. "Vauxhall is not a safe place for ladies of superior breeding. The gardens are filled with all manner of riff raff, especially after dark."

Given that the Runners were likely hovering nearby, Helena did not have much concern. At least the pair of investigators had gotten better at blending into the crowd these days.

"It is always a good idea to watch our step, Reed, no matter the company," Paul said. "But come, lead the way, and we shall endeavor to protect our lovely helpless charges."

"Who are you calling helpless?" Percy demanded.

Her brother rolled his eyes and led her out of the colonnade.

The four walked in pairs along the busy graveled walk. The gardens were brimming this evening with people of all classes. Anyone who could afford the two shilling entrance fee was permitted entrance into the magical playground. Thousands of lights twinkled overhead in the giant elm trees, and the breeze carried music and the scent of jasmine.

Pointing out the sights with his walking stick, Mr. Reed played guide most graciously. Helena willed herself to relax. She would not let the exchange with Nicholas ruin her evening. She would show him that, though patient, his marchioness had her limits; she would not spend the rest of her life waiting for him to make up his blasted mind. Smiling at her companion, she took in the triumphal arches along the South Walk and an excellent replica of Grecian ruins. She even laughed when Percy insisted upon touching a vista in order to be convinced that it truly was a painting and not the real thing.

They arrived at the Rotunda, and like many in the crowd Helena could not help but gawk at the grand two-story structure. Constructed of white marble and decorated with Oriental motifs, the building glistened like a giant, exotic cake in the middle of the dark clearing. Hundreds of globe lamps glowed from the edges of the dome-shaped roof, illuminating the orchestra playing on the second floor balcony. The light, lively tones floated over the audience below. Well-dressed ladies and gentlemen were entering the rotunda through a roped entrance guarded by footmen; many more stood in line on the red carpet for the privilege of entry. Beyond the line, guests of the middling sort and working class milled, eager to catch glimpses of the noble patrons.

Impervious to the jostling around her, Helena absorbed the magic of the night. Mr. Handel's composition washed over her and buoyed her spirits over vibrant waves. She found herself moving clockwise with the crowd and experienced its excitement herself as other views of the Rotunda unfolded before her. It seemed balconies sprung all around the structure, with different entertainments visible on each. On the next platform, she saw a theatrical duo performing an act of Shakespeare. Next there was a man juggling teacups whilst riding a one-wheeled machine. She caught herself gasping at the following act, the rope dancer, executing flawless jumps and pirouettes way up above the cheering crowd.

Helena turned to exclaim something to Percy and realized with a sudden shock that her companions were nowhere to be seen. A sea of strange faces surrounded her. She felt herself being pushed forward as people thronged to get a better view of the rope dancer.

The volume of excited voices swelled. A feeling of alarm rose simultaneously in her chest.

"Lady Harteford, over here!"

She saw Mr. Reed pressing toward her. He had lost his hat, and his face looked slick with the effort to reach her. He was struggling against the tide of movement, like a fish battling upstream. Stretching out his arm, he held his walking stick toward her. She reached for it, her gloved fingers closing around the polished mahogany.

"Follow me this way!" His shouted words could barely be heard over the din.

She hung onto the walking stick and squeezed herself through the tight path Mr. Reed carved through the field of bodies. The fumes of liquor and unwashed flesh rose all around her. The accents in her ear were harsh, unfamiliar. She felt a tug on her reticule, and she clung fiercely to it, looking wildly about. No one seemed to be looking at her, yet there was something menacing about the facelessness of the crowd and the roaring laughter. A hand landed on her posterior and squeezed. She screamed. At the same time, her grasp on the walking stick slackened. She felt herself being sucked backward into the mob.

Raw panic clawed her insides as she struggled desperately to get free. A sharp pressure burned briefly at her wrist; she knew without looking that someone had torn loose her bracelet. She felt fingers grasp at her coiffure, the charming bumble bees now dangerous attractions to avarice. She cared not; they could have it all, if only she could get *out*. She felt the increasing suffocation of the mob. The heated bodies and deafening voices depleted the air. An arm wrapped around her waist. She could not draw breath enough to scream again.

"I've got you. Hold on."

She felt herself being hauled against a strong form. Powerful arms lifted her from the ground, and she was too weak with relief to protest at being hefted over the muscular shoulder like a sack of grain. The next moments passed in a blur as her rescuer forged relentlessly through the crowd. There were shouts on either side as he scythed a path with his fists and elbows, but apparently no one dared retaliate. She lifted her head to see the sea of faces passing behind her, but mostly she concentrated on holding on for dear life.

When she saw the clearing disappearing into the distance, Helena mustered enough courage to say, "You can put me down now."

"Not on your life," came the growled reply.

"Milord!" One of the Runners came huffing up. "Is Lady Harteford alright?"

"I'm fine," Helena squeaked with as much dignity as she could muster.

"I was a step behind her, my lord. I had to stop to pummel a brute to get back her bracelet. My partner is just retrieving her reticule—"

"Keep watch over the entrance to that alcove ahead. Let no one pass. I wish to speak to my wife there privately."

"Yes, milord."

Helena gulped as she was carried onto a narrow path off the main walk. To judge from the lack of lighting, this was one of the many secret lovers' niches that made Vauxhall infamous. Not that her rescuer was acting remotely lover-like. He set her—or, more accurately, he *dumped* her—onto a wooden bench surrounded by dense hedges.

"Now," her husband said, looming over her, his eyes darker than the night, "you have yourself some explaining to do."

Chapter Twenty-Three

Nicholas waited for the beast to calm. At the sight of Helena helpless in the mob, the animal inside him had bared its fangs and roared with fury. He had never felt such primitive rage in his life. They were mauling *his woman*. He had leapt in, intent upon blood. If anything happened to her ... Swearing, he leaned over her for closer inspection. By the faint glow of the moon, he saw she had not escaped entirely unscathed. Shallow scratches marred the perfection of one cheek. Her disordered curls tumbled around her shoulders. Her bodice was torn, revealing a great deal of vulnerable flesh.

He ripped off his jacket and threw it over her shoulders. He was breathing too raggedly to speak. Anger and fear made him inarticulate.

"What in bloody hell do you think you were doing?" he said at last.

Helena glowered up at him as she drew the velvet lapels closer together. *She* actually had the temerity to glower at *him*. "What everyone else was doing, my lord. Enjoying the sights. It was not my fault the crowd erupted into madness."

"It was *not* your fault? You, madam, go traipsing alone in the dark dressed like ... like *that*"—here Nicholas closed in and waved a furious hand up and down her person—"and you expect not to encounter trouble?"

For some reason, this perfectly sound argument seemed to infuriate Helena. She pushed on his shoulders with both her hands. He did not budge.

"I was *not* alone, for one," she said, her eyes spitting sparks at him. "I was accompanied by three others. Not to mention the Runners. And even you, sir, would be hard-pressed to explain how my perfectly fashionable attire had anything to do with what transpired back there."

He snarled at her logic. "Your dress is indecent. It invites indecent behavior. That bounder Reed—who, incidentally, I am going to kill—was drooling down your neckline."

"It seems we have been down this road before, my lord," his wife said in a sweet voice that instantly raised his hackles. "What I wear is no business of yours. Nor is anyone I choose to consort with."

"*Consort with*?" Nicholas felt momentarily dumbfounded by the rush of blood to his head. He could barely hear himself over the roaring in his ears.

"In a manner of speaking," Helena said hastily. "There is no need to shout. It is just the two of us here."

"I am not shouting, I am merely trying to get you to speak some sense!"

He pushed himself away from the bench and began to pace in front of it. *Be calm*, he repeated to himself. *I will be calm.*

"I am speaking perfect sense," Helena said. "You have never cared whose company I've kept. In fact, I doubt that you have ever noticed. How could you, when you never deign to show your face at home?"

That stopped him in his tracks. "I have been busy," he snapped. "I told you that in the notes I sent you—every day, I might add!"

"Yes, about those notes." She crossed her arms, and her damned chin tilted upward. "I have been waiting to see you for days, Nicholas—and what do I get instead? Three wretched sentences. Poor substitute for a husband, I should say. Can you blame me for wanting a little distraction?"

Yes, I bloody can when you nearly get yourself killed!

He wanted to shout. But he did not, because he was not one for shouting. At least, he had never been until his wife decided to act like a candidate for Bedlam. He tried for calm again. He attempted to think of a reasonable refutation to her argument, one he could utter without the use of profanity or an unduly raised volume. After a minute, he abandoned the impossible endeavor.

"What do you want from me, Helena? A sodding sonnet?" he bit out.

His wife studied him. He wished her eyes did not appear so bloody large and luminescent in the moonlight—it was distracting to his anger, and he planned to remain angry for a good long while. Had he truly believed that Helena was a demure little thing? He shook his head in disbelief. This woman could drive a man to distraction. As if to prove his point, the minx had the nerve to smile. Her lips curved, and she actually dimpled. The smile dissolved into a gale of giggles.

"Oh, a sonnet ... from *you* ... man of many ... many words," she gasped between fits of laughter.

He should have been outraged at her levity, or at the very least offended by her lack of wifely respect. Instead, the sound of her unexpected laughter had a strange effect upon him: it soothed the beast. It diluted the bloodlust still pumping in his veins. Bloody hell, it was good to hear Helena laugh, to see her alive and well and bewitching under the star-filled sky. Despite the seriousness of the situation, Nicholas felt his own lips soften.

He firmed them immediately. "You married a merchant not a poet," he reminded her.

"Oh, Nicholas," Helena said, wiping her eyes. "I don't want a sonnet or an ode to my eyes or some such silly nonsense. Don't you know that?"

As a matter of fact, he didn't. Besides, if he were to compose a poem to his wife's body parts, it damn well wouldn't be about her eyes. Best keep *that* thought to himself.

"What do you want, Helena?" he said.

"You. Just you, my stubborn, foolish husband." Potent as the sun's rays, her words reached and thawed all the chilled parts inside him. "Come, have a seat beside me before you fall down. You look like you defeated Bonaparte singlehandedly."

He sat and flinched when Helena touched a handkerchief to his brow.

"Hold still," she said. "You are bleeding."

He had not realized it. In the heat of battle, all that had mattered was keeping her safe. Now, as he looked down at his hands, he saw that some of the knuckles were torn and swelling. He was not concerned. He had been in far worse condition before.

But Helena inhaled sharply. "Your hands."

At once, he saw his hands as his wife must be seeing them: work-hardened and welted with violence. His were a brute's hands, unfit for a lady's eyes. A sickening feeling churned in his gut and seemed to prickle the scars on his back. Reminders of who he was. He started to turn his hands over, to hide these deformities at least, but Helena grabbed hold of them. He watched her slim fingers trace gently over the broken skin.

"Pay it no mind. I heal quickly," he said, still unable to meet her gaze.

"But it is my f-fault."

"I trust you will remember that the next time." At the sound of his own words, he frowned. Had he just implied that there was the possibility of a next time? That he would permit her to engage in another such escapade? The idea seemed ludicrous, but one could never be certain with his wife's hare-brained logic. He opened his mouth to clarify his edict.

But before he could say anything, something warm splattered on the back of his hand. Another drop followed, landing between his knuckles and trickling down between his fingers. A succession of warm, wet drops plinked against his skin.

Bewildered, he looked up to see his wife's tear-drenched eyes.

"You are not ... crying?" he said.

She shook her head, the tears rolling down her cheeks now.

"'Tis the stress," he said, a little desperately. "Your sensibilities are overwhelmed."

"Yes, the stress, that must be it," she said, her smile wobbly.

Then she began to weep in earnest.

He searched for a handkerchief. Then he remembered he had one in the pocket of his jacket—the jacket that she was currently wearing, that dwarfed her as her entire body shook with sobs. God, she was crying like a child might, gulping for breath as her eyes and nose dripped. There was nothing for it. With a groan, he scooped her into his arms. He cuddled her against him, whispered Lord only knew what nonsense against her curls as she cried her heart out.

He did not know when her arms came to wind around his neck. Or how her face came to be tilted under his. Or whose lips moved first to find the other's. But hers tasted as sweet as he remembered, felt just as soft as they parted beneath his. He could taste her tears now, too, licks of salt between their clinging mouths. He had never kissed her or anyone in this fashion before—with the intent not to possess or pleasure but merely to comfort.

He held her for a long time, under the dark canopy of trees.

And then something changed. His lips had been undemanding at first, seeking only to soothe, to calm. She sighed, seeming to melt into his embrace. It was the kind of softness a man could drown in, and he lost himself in the succor of her honeyed mouth, the gentle caress of her fingers along his nape. He drank of her sweetness until she made a sound, a little moan, and her hands moved restlessly to his shoulders. She molded herself against him at the same time that her mouth burst into flame.

God, the *heat* of her. Her tongue twined with his in a molten dance. He knew without words what she felt, what her breathy sighs and unconscious movements conveyed. He knew it was the aftermath of fear shaking her body with desire, leading it to press pleadingly against his for relief from the tensions coursing within. He himself had felt the after-effects of violence many a time before. But his sheltered Helena had never experienced such a shock before, and it grieved him that she should do so now. On the morrow, he was going to tear Reed's head off. But, for now, he understood all too well the need to affirm life after death brushed by. He knew precisely what she needed.

By God, just this once, he wanted to be the one to give it to her.

He let his mouth wander from her mouth to her neck, licking and nibbling his way down her throat. She squirmed in his lap, and he groaned as the curve of her buttocks moved snugly against his cock. It would take every ounce of his self-control to survive this night, for he meant this loving to be about her. For her. If he could, he wanted to give her the mindlessness of release. Leaning her back against his arm, he parted the velvet lapels of the jacket. Her skin glowed pearl-like in the shadows. As he eased down her torn bodice, her head rested against his upper arm. He saw that her eyes were closed, her lips parted.

He cupped her breasts, molding the luxurious weight in his palms. She shuddered as his fingers found her nipples and played with them. He rolled the hardened points between thumb and forefinger, tugging gently. When he bent down to draw one of the ripe berries into his mouth, she let out a keening cry. He suckled her, circled his tongue round the puckered fruit. Aye, delicious. He felt her hand clench the linen of his shirtsleeve. He pulled her more deeply into his mouth even as he reached beneath her skirts.

His breath came harshly as his hand caressed the silk-encased length of her leg. Even here, she was all feminine curves, and he had to ward off the image of himself between her legs. Of his thighs pressing down into hers, his rod long and thick and poised to plunge into her heat. No, this was to be about satisfying her and her alone. Not that he had complaint. It made him drunk with pleasure to touch her thus, under her chemise, past the ruffle of her garter. He skimmed the trembling insides of her thighs, pausing at the brush of silky curls against his knuckles.

"Don't be afraid, my darling," he whispered, looking into her eyes. "I won't hurt you. You know that, don't you?"

She nodded, her eyes heavy-lidded and trusting.

"Let me then," he said, his fingers finding her. "Let me."

Helena made a choked sound as he lightly petted her pussy. His nostrils flared to encounter the slick moisture that had not been there on their wedding night. If her breathy whimpers were any indication, she wanted this, wanted *him*. His chest expanded with that knowledge even as he used her wetness to create a silky rhythm, gliding up and down her feminine folds. She was panting now, her head thrown back and eyes closed. He found the heart of her sensations and rubbed there gently with his thumb.

Helena let out a scream which he quickly smothered with his mouth. He swallowed her cries as he continued to stroke her pearl, pressing harder, alternating up and down movements with ones that spiraled. Perspiration formed on his brow as he felt her juices rain upon his hand. His palm moistened with her essence. Excitement raged within him. By God, she had a passionate streak in her. She was lusciously wet, so very eager, and she did not yet know the ecstasy that awaited her. That *he* would give her.

His tongue delved into her mouth at the same moment that his middle finger eased into her channel. Her thighs quivered.

"Stay open for me, darling," he coaxed against her lips. "I promise there will be no pain this time. Your body wants what I can give it."

He slid his finger in deeper, and she shuddered.

"Can you feel how your body wants this?" he asked. "I can. I can feel every throb, every pull of your delectable self on my finger. Feel how you pull me in deeper, how ready you are for my touch. Can you feel it, my love?"

"Yes." Pleasure slurred her voice. Her thighs slackened.

"And this?" He pushed deeper still, until her nest feathered against his knuckles.

"Oh my God, *Nicholas—*"

He withdrew his finger and plunged all the way in. Helena's moans filled his ears as he continued to finger her. His cock pulsed in unison with the thrusts of his hand, experiencing vicariously the tightness, the voracious heat of his wife's cunny. He groaned as she began to gyrate upon his lap, her pelvis tilting to meet his strokes. She had no idea what she was doing to him. If this continued much longer, he would come in his smalls.

He could imagine a worse fate.

He increased his tempo to match the quickness of her breath. Her breasts tempted him with each bouncing movement; he could not keep himself from licking along one plump underside. He worked his way upward, sighing at the decadence of orange blossoms and soft flesh against his cheeks. He could have stayed there, pillowed between her tits, forever. But he could tell from the slickness of his fingers, from the way she was biting her bottom lip to keep her cries in, that she was close. So very close. He wanted her release to be perfect.

He nuzzled her ear.

"Open your eyes, my love," he said.

Her eyelids quivered open, revealing hazy, unfocused depths.

"Yes," he said. "Stay with me. Let me watch you fly apart."

He plunged into the core of her, thrumming her little knot at the same time. It did not take long. Her inner muscles clutched at his finger and then he was surrounded by a flutter of convulsions that stiffened her body.

"Yes, love, come for me now," he urged.

In the next instant, Helena cried out, her hand gripping his shirtsleeve, her back arching over his arm. The sound of infinite pleasure, of her *first* climax, inflated his chest. The satisfaction he experienced could barely be contained within his skin. Likewise, the agonizing desire threatening to burst from his cock, but he didn't care. He'd made his lady come, and that was all that mattered.

Gently, he extricated his hand from beneath her skirts and cradled her close. He smoothed back her hair as he waited for both their passions to subside.

"Beautiful," he said. There was wonder in his voice as he stroked her cheek. His fingers glistened, and he could smell the musky sweet scent of her release. "Every inch of you, so unbelievably beautiful."

"Mmm." Her eyes had drifted closed again.

Nicholas heard familiar voices echoing down the walk. He made attempts to rearrange their clothing, securing his wife's bodice as best he could and buttoning his jacket over top. Helena made no move to help; from her rhythmic breathing, he thought she might have fallen asleep. Brushing away a damp tendril of hair, he pressed his lips to her forehead.

"This wasn't a dream, was it?" Her voice was cloudy with sleep.

He rather thought it was. A wondrous dream he would give his life for.

"Sleep, my love," he said. "We will talk in the morning."

Chapter Twenty-Four

Helena opened her eyes. In the dim light, she blinked at the brocaded bed hangings for several moments before she recognized her own bed chamber. She had no idea what time of day it was. Her slumber must have been deep, all consuming, because her mind seemed to be having a difficult time adjusting to wakefulness. She rubbed her eyes and yawned. Oh, the dreams she had had—such vivid, aching dreams ... She turned her head on the pillow.

A single red rose lay on the table next to her bed. Beneath it was a letter, addressed to her in her husband's untidy scrawl. Heart thudding, she sat up and reached for it. Her hands trembled as she broke the seal. Six lines instead of three this time. The first sentence began, "*An Ode to My Wife's—*"

Helena's eyes widened at the bawdy verse; she felt her cheeks flame, even as warmth seeped elsewhere. She gave a choked laugh. The man wasn't going to win any literary accolades, that much was certain. But, Lud, he did have a wicked sense of humor and the most amazing hands ... Flopping backward onto the pillows, she gazed dreamily up again at the canopy of swirling golden flowers.

Last night at Vauxhall, Nicholas' loving had been selfless,

tender beyond words. He had coaxed pleasure from her every nook and cranny and asked for nothing in exchange. She had been so caught up in the maelstrom of sensations that she had not given thought to how she might return the favor in kind. Truth be told, she had experienced no thoughts at all—just a rapture that melted her bones like butter on fresh baked bread.

Their lovemaking had been rather one-sided, but she would be sure to see that oversight remedied as soon as possible. As a matter of fact, she wondered where Nicholas might be at this moment. She yawned. What time was it, anyway? Sitting up again, she reached for the bell pull.

The chamber maid appeared straightaway, as if she had been waiting for the summons. Bobbing a curtsy, she set a tray down by the bed. "Good afternoon, milady."

"Afternoon?" Helena asked. "What time is it, Mary?"

"'Tis 'alf-past two, milady. You slept yourself a sound one last night." Mary drew open the curtains, and a colorless afternoon light filled the room. "'Is lordship says you was not to be disturbed."

"Where is my husband?"

"'E left at the crack o' dawn this mornin'. Business, 'e said. I o'erheard Mr. Crikstaff remind 'im o' the ball this evenin'. 'Is lordship said 'e'd meet you there."

Lord and Lady Hayfield's ball, Helena remembered. She had not been enthused at the prospect, but with Nicholas as an escort the event suddenly sounded divine. A perfect start to the rest of her marriage. Smiling, she sipped on the cup of chocolate and nibbled on a pastry as Mary lit the grate. Bessie entered carrying linens and clothing.

"Good afternoon, my lady," Bessie said. "Ready for your bath?"

Helena soon found herself relaxing in hot vanilla and citrus scented suds. As Bessie massaged soap into her hair, Helena rested her head against the towel draped over the edge of the tub. Cooling slices of cucumber covered her eyes, and water lapped against her shoulders in a lulling tide. She drifted into another world. A world full of colorful dancers, whirling round and round. She was standing on the edge of the dance floor looking on. When the music stopped, the dancers parted into two lines, one on either side of her.

Nicholas stood at the opposite end.

Impeccable, gorgeous, his presence dwarfed the dance floor. He strode between the lines of dancers toward her, the soles of his polished Hessians slapping against the floor. When he stopped in front of her, she could hardly breathe, so fierce was the possessiveness in his gaze.

"May I have this dance?"

It was not really a question. The moment she went into his arms the room faded. She did not know how long they danced, five minutes or an eternity, for she lost count of time. The only beating was that of her heart and his as they moved together in perfect unison. They did not speak, and such was the flawlessness of the moment that they did not need to. For once, she could read his thoughts and he hers.

They danced through an open door. The room was a blur of red and gold as he spun her around. They came to a halt against a desk, her thighs backing into the wooden edge. With fearless joy, she pulled his head down and kissed him. Open mouthed, her tongue mating with his. She could feel his desire for her, and it fanned her own. Tugging free the hem of his shirt, she ran her palms beneath the linen, along the contoured planes of his chest and the jutting ridges of his abdomen. How strong he was, how she savored the contrast between the iron muscles and wiry hair.

He encouraged her explorations with harsh breathing and guttural sounds torn from the back of his throat. Emboldened, she went to her knees so that she was eye level with the top of his trousers. One by one, she freed the buttons along the hidden placket, watching his face as she did so. His eyes were half-lidded, and his mouth was taut with anticipation as she exposed his manly flesh. He was built like the statue of the satyr, long, thick, and hard as marble.

Groaning, he pushed himself into her hands. She began to pump him, the delicious friction heating her palms. His hips moved faster and faster, and beneath her skirts her pussy dampened and clenched in shared excitement. She loved him this way, when he abandoned himself to savage pleasure. When he surged heavily, shouting out, she was saturated with infinite satisfaction.

She stood, words of love trembling upon her lips.

His face was relaxed, his gaze searching. He reached out a finger to touch her cheek. To her shock, she felt not the warmth of his touch but the press of velvet against her skin.

He was looking at her but seeing the mask.

"Who are you, *mademoiselle*?"

Helena came to with a start, her heart pounding. Water sloshed around her in the tub. Steam clouded the bathing room. Bessie was humming a low melody as she arranged a dressing gown on a hanger. She turned when she heard Helena sitting up.

"You fell asleep, my lady," Bessie said. "It must have been quite an event last night."

The maid clucked her tongue as she brought over a towel.

"And a grand ball in but a few hours. You had best keep your strength up, my lady. Who knows what excitement tonight will bring?"

Nicholas was no stranger to death. One could not come up in the rookery without witnessing the mortal end. Yet, in all the times he had encountered death, it had been an oddly vital thing. Dying had been fresh, drawn with blooms of scarlet and newly stilled flesh. Its horrors paled in comparison to this, the death of decay. This death was old, cased in bloated blue skin and crusted in violet-black. The once familiar face was now shreds of rotted skin and gutted eye sockets, the refuse of rats come and gone. Buzzing over the straw pallet, the flies provided the only shroud.

The room in the bowels of the flash house was ill-ventilated and the size of a linen closet. Upon receiving Kent's missive this morning, Nicholas had come immediately to the decrepit wood structure deep in the heart of the rookery. Kent's man Caster had led him inside and down the narrow, twisting passageway below the main floor. Here, the ceiling hung low, and the walls were cracked and blotched with yellow. The smell was that of a butcher's shop several days past cleaning. Nicholas bit back a surge of nausea.

Kent looked up from his crouching position next to the body. "Are you certain you wish to be present, my lord? Perhaps you would care to wait outside in the carriage."

"How long has he been this way?" Nicholas said.

"Two days, mayhap three," Kent said. "The body has passed the initial stage of stiffness."

"And the cause of death?"

"Different for each of the victims, if they can be called that. Bragg, here, appears to have bled out from the knife wound in the gut. There is no excessive blood spill in the room, so I would guess he received the injury in a pub brawl or some other dispute and dragged himself here to die. My men are searching above stairs for signs of an altercation."

"That will be like searching for flies in a rubbish heap," Nicholas said dryly. He gestured to the second body at the back of the room. "And this one?"

"Ah, yes, our second victim." Kent rose and took the few steps over. The corpse lay on its back, the lone object on the dirt floor. It was difficult to see anything aside from the blackened flesh. The face had been entirely burned, its features obliterated by fire. The only spot of color were the tufts of hair, singed at the roots but blooming into ginger-colored tips.

"Now this one was definitely done here," the policeman said. With his boot, he nudged the side of the body. Nicholas could see the large dark stain soaked into the earth. "Given how charred the corpse was, I had Dr. Farraday take a look. In the good doctor's opinion, this man was dead several days before Bragg and killed prior to being burned. Notice the laceration along the neck? Made by the blade we found in Bragg's boot."

Nicholas felt a sickening pity. "Gordon?"

"Likely so, given the hair color and the fact that he had gone missing around the same time. Poor fellow had his throat cut before being set aflame. Not a pleasant way to die, I would imagine. A brutal end to a brutal life."

"But why burn a body after he's dead?"

"Why do some murderers kill with poison, others with a blade, and yet others with a pistol?" Kent shrugged. "There is meaning in the act of killing that we cannot understand. Passion or hatred can render a man's actions inexplicable."

"And the motive?" Nicholas asked quietly.

"Love or money, usually. In this case, given there was no love lost between the stepbrothers, I would wager money was the culprit. But you need not take my word upon it, my lord. Come this way, if you please."

Nicholas followed Kent, taking cue from the taller man to duck his head under the low beam as he exited. He felt relief at leaving the cramped space, though the hallway was narrow and smelled of vomit. Kent turned right and stopped in front of a door sealed with a padlock and chains. He withdrew a heavy key from his pocket.

"Found it on Bragg," he said by way of explanation.

After the chain clanked to the ground, Kent pushed open the door.

"Ah," Nicholas said.

This room was more spacious than the previous, though just as cramped. Crates and sacks piled upon each other floor to ceiling.

Nicholas examined the nearest barrel; he ran a finger over the familiar black stamp of Fines and Company.

"A fine rum, that one," he said.

"Spirits, tobacco, sugar, tea—there's a veritable trove inside this room. Of course, 'tis but a fraction of what has been pilfered, but it will serve as evidence. From what I have gathered of the inventory, Bragg was an equal opportunity thief. Yours is not the only company represented—there's Milligan, Hottswald, Pendergrast to name a few."

"So you believe Bragg masterminded this whole scheme?" Nicholas still found the notion difficult to believe, although the proof loomed in incontrovertible stacks before him.

"He had help. We found on his person a ledger containing names of men to whom he paid weekly wages. My men are investigating those names as we speak. Apparently, Bragg had his employees infiltrate all the companies along the docks. Once they were in, the rest was easy enough."

"All it required was one good idea on Bragg's part," Nicholas murmured. "Yes, I suppose that is possible, even of him. But what of Gordon? Why did Bragg kill him?"

"Gordon is listed on the ledger. Bragg sent him to work for you. I believe all went well for awhile, and then Gordon lost nerve. I questioned his mistress at the brothel again. She claims that prior to the night your warehouse was ransacked, Gordon had been rambling on about having enough and wanting out."

"So he went to his stepbrother and asked to be released from his duties," Nicholas said slowly.

"Yes, but he was relieved of much more." Kent's lips twisted. "He paid for that moment of conscience with his life."

They stood silently for a moment.

"I have something else, my lord." His light eyes darting around to ensure they had privacy, Kent withdrew a slip of crinkled parchment. "I found this on Bragg. I suppose he was preparing to exact his payment."

Nicholas looked down at the familiar looped ink. *Five thousand pounds or your secret is out.* He crumpled the note in his fist.

"The night you were shot, the only man you saw was Bragg. Perhaps he altered his voice. Perhaps your injury distorted your senses," Kent said. "We found a pistol in the other room. It appears to have been recently discharged."

Nicholas blew out a breath. "So it was Bragg all along. But how did he discover my connection to Grimes?"

"If you wish, I can continue my investigation of the matter. I had just begun to interview my contacts before my men found Bragg here. I can resume—"

"No, that will not be necessary." Nicholas was not fool enough to look a gift horse in the mouth. The evidence was all here before him: the stolen goods, the blackmail note, and a dead man who'd held a grudge. Although he had no satisfactory answer to how Bragg had come by the knowledge of Grimes' murder, Nicholas told himself to let it go. It was dangerous to poke a sleeping beast; he had no wish to awaken the snapping monsters of the past.

Kent nodded in understanding. "Well, I suppose that is that. The mysteries of the thefts solved and your would-be blackmailer dead. A sad business, but in the end justice has prevailed."

Nicholas wanted to believe him. For an instant, he could see a young man with red hair and shy eyes. A boy, really, with two left feet and a life ahead. But not any longer. A future snuffed out as easily as a candle. Was that justice? He was not at all certain, but Kent's earlier words resonated in his mind.

A brutal end to a brutal life.

By God, life was short and not to be wasted. The past had imprisoned him all these years; now, at last, he had a chance at freedom. And a future.

Nicholas took Kent's hand in a firm grasp. "Thank you, Mr. Kent, for all your efforts. The Thames River Police can expect an expression of gratitude from Fines and Company come Monday morning."

"Thank you, my lord." Kent jerked his head toward the merchandise. "Would you like my men to load up your goods?"

"Not at the moment," Nicholas said. A sudden truth reverberated in his bones. His chest lightened. "Right now, I have more urgent matters to take care of."

"Oh? Anything I can be of assistance with?"

Nicholas was already headed up the stairs. He stopped and turned, grinning. "Not unless you waltz, Kent. And even then, I would not let you within ten paces of her."

"Ah." For the first time in their acquaintance, Nicholas saw Kent wear a genuine smile. The expression made the policeman's thin, worn face appear unaccountably wistful. "Have a good evening, then, my lord. And please give my regards to Lady Harteford."

Chapter Twenty-Five

On the ride to the Hayfield ball, it seemed to Nicholas that his newly acquired horses moved at the pace of snails. He had purchased the matched greys at Tattersall's last month; the auctioneer had claimed the animals could outrun the wind. A half-hearted breeze, more the like. Nicholas rapped on the carriage ceiling to hasten the driver. He heard a whistle and the snap of the reins. His booted feet tapped an impatient beat against the floor as he looked out into the shifting shadows of St. Giles.

As a boy, he had once carved a boat from driftwood and set it down the river. He had watched it sail downstream until it became a speck, finally disappearing altogether. Now, watching the slums flow by, he experienced that same sense of freedom and finality. The mysterious blackmailer was dead, the thieving ended. The voice he had heard that night had been Bragg's, not some ghost he had conjured from the past. Aye, he could hear the resemblance now.

He told himself his past was laid to rest. Dead and buried and no longer capable of hurting him. It was time to move on.

When he arrived at the grand Palladian residence, the place was already ablaze with the brightest lights of the *ton*. Nicholas handed his hat and coat to one of the liveried footmen. He paused at the top of the wide marble dais. Scanning the throng below, he realized that this was his future. He was no longer a scared boy running the streets or a porter with dirt under his fingernails.

He was a man, a peer of the realm, with a wife he desired beyond the consciousness of words. A wife who had trembled with ecstasy in his arms but a few hours past. If all went according to plan, she would be moaning his name before the night was out. Now if only he could get past the bloody receiving line, he could find her and show her that which lay in his heart.

He chafed at the butler's droning voice. One by one, the guests ahead of him were announced as they descended the steps to the ballroom. Nicholas looked below onto the packed dance floor. The glittering morass of color momentarily disoriented him. Then he saw her, and the world righted. Standing under a bower of blossoms, Helena held court like an exotic princess. Her rich sable locks gleamed in ringlets around her laughing face, and the green material of her gown kissed the lush curves of her body. Her breasts beckoned from a poor excuse for a bodice: two sweetly rounded scoops of flesh designed to incite a man's hunger. Nicholas frowned, noticing that he was not the only one to admire her bosom. The admirers hovering all around her were stealing clandestine eyefuls.

They were lusting over *his wife*'s breasts.

Pushing by several guests and the startled butler, he strode down the stairwell. He heard his title being hastily announced and felt the heat of curious glances as he cut a straight path to his quarry. He did not give a damn and did not stop until he reached Helena's side. He slid a proprietary arm around her waist, leveling a warning stare at the randy young bucks. Casually, he turned Helena to him and brought her hand to his lips.

"I trust I have not kept you waiting, my lady," he said, allowing a slight emphasis to the possessive pronoun.

Helena's eyes glimmered like a sunlit pond, warmth illuminating the clear depths of green and brown. She smiled, and unmistakable in her expression was the gladness, the rightness that calmed his very soul. The other men must have seen it too, for one by one they buzzed off to more promising territory. Wordlessly, Nicholas offered his wife his arm and claimed her for a stroll around the dance floor.

"Good evening, my lord," Helena said, her voice sounding as if she had recently been engaged in vigorous activity.

Strange, he seemed to be having difficulty catching his own breath. "You look very fine this evening," he managed.

"Thank you." She cast her eyes demurely downward as they rounded the bend. "For the compliment ... and for the lovely poem."

Before he could reply, they were stopped by a gaggle of ladies. He had to suffer through dithering nonsense about reticules and slippers before he and his wife were free to walk again.

"Liked my ode, did you?" he began in a low, intimate voice, but then he heard someone call his name. He had to paste on a smile and nod to some bloody viscount whose name he could never recall. Why couldn't these buggers mind their own business and let him flirt with his wife in peace? Leaning closer, he said, "I found myself quite inspired by your—"

"La, there you are Lady Harteford! Splendid night, isn't it?"

Nicholas scowled as Helena gave a charming reply.

"Perhaps we could continue this discussion another time," his wife whispered to him, her cheeks a charming pink as they picked up the stroll again. "Others are watching."

"The *ton* can go to hell for all I care. I want to talk now," he said. "I have many things to say to you, my love, and, after that, many more things I want to do with you. All night long."

With her color high and her eyes aglow, she resembled a demure, complacent marchioness not a whit. Not one bloody whit, praise God. He had not realized how much he had wanted it so—to have a passionate wife waiting for him beneath the ladylike exterior. Perhaps he had always suspected her ardent nature, even throughout the months of dry as crumbs courtship. Something about those eyes of hers, the naughty fullness of her bottom lip ...

"You seem different, Nicholas," she murmured. "What has changed?"

He wanted to tell her everything. That he was free and that he loved her. He needed to beg her forgiveness and ask for another chance to be the kind of husband she deserved. But at that moment, the orchestra issued a readying note, and he saw another opportunity. Before Helena could utter another word, Nicholas drew her onto the dance floor. Other couples followed suit around them. The beginning notes sounded ... a waltz. Could life be any more perfect? Grinning down at his wife's bemused expression, he pulled her closer at the waist and led her into the first steps.

Nicholas did not dance often; having learned the skill only after his succession to the title, he considered himself a passable partner at best. Yet, as the sweet lush melody wrapped itself around him, he forgot to be concerned about the proper steps and positions. He had his wife in his arms, and nothing else mattered. He spun her, drawing her closer as he did so, so close that her skirts slapped against his thighs and her bodice brushed against his jacket.

They moved in flawless unison. Against his palm, her back was soft, yielding. His hand slid lower, onto the curve of her spine. Provocative, elegant, the indentation beckoned him to the lush hills just below. He had to focus to remember the steps. As the music rose in crescendo, he twirled her with dizzying speed. She clung to him. When her eyes met his, he could see the laughter there, the shared exhilaration of being alive, together ...

In love.

He caught her in another spin, this time bringing her against the burgeoned heat of him. For a moment, pressing her against his turgid, endless desire for her.

His lips found her ear.

"I want you, my love," he whispered. "Always."

Her eyes were wide as they separated. The other couples, the music, the ball itself all faded away from his awareness. All that remained for him was the woman in his arms. The woman he craved more than his next breath.

"Harteford," she said.

"Yes?" He felt an insane urge to kiss her right then and there.

"The music has stopped."

Belatedly, Nicholas came to a halt. He saw the other men bowing and the ladies curtsying in return. Heat tinged his cheekbones, though it did not compare to the conflagration farther south. Flicking a glance downward, he knew that he needed to calm himself or risk public embarrassment.

"My dear, allow me to procure some ratafia for you," he murmured. "Shall we meet outside on the terrace? I should like to continue our discussion, if it would suit you."

"Yes, my lord." His wife's eyes were glowing. "Thank you for the waltz. Apparently, you dance as well as you write."

He was going to explode then and there if she did not stop smiling at him like that. "Outside, in ten minutes," he muttered, ushering her off the dance floor.

It took Nicholas several minutes in the cool night air to collect himself. That, and several subtle adjustments of his trousers. When he once again gained self-control, he went in search of refreshments. He did not even mind the snubs and tittering voices; his thoughts centered fully on his wife.

During the dance, she had moved with him in perfect accord, joined with him beyond mere physical passion. Exultation quickened his breath. With his past behind him where it belonged, they had a chance to start afresh. First, he would have to make amends to her—for his treatment of her, for his ... he swallowed as the familiar guilt twisted his gut. Could she forgive his acts of infidelity? How could he have been so bloody stupid, seeking out a whore when the only woman he'd ever wanted was his own wife?

The thought crossed his mind to keep his indiscretion to himself. But the idea of omission struck him as yet another betrayal, and he wanted honesty in their marriage from this moment forth. Somehow, he'd have to find a way to explain himself to Helena. To beg her forgiveness and to vow that he would never betray her again. That, in truth, in his heart, he never had.

His faith in their love was such that all this seemed possible.

Nicholas returned to the terrace with warm punch in hand. It was past two o'clock in the morning, and the crowd had begun to thin. He scanned the wide stone veranda but did not see Helena. He noticed that the west side of the balustrade was obscured by dense hedges, designed no doubt to provide privacy for amorous pursuits. A smile touched his lips as he considered finding his wife behind such conveniently placed greenery.

This time, unlike their wedding night, he would not paw at her like some sex-crazed beast. No, this time he would take her small gloved hand in his and whisper an endearment. He would watch her eyes, wait for that welcoming rush of gold before slowly unbuttoning her glove. He would coax the satin down her tender skin, exposing her delicate wrist. He would bring her hand to his lips and press a kiss on the down-soft underside. A gentle brushing of his lips against her fluttering pulse, nothing more. A prelude to wooing his wife.

Heart hammering with anticipation, he strode over to the leafy barrier.

Slightly out of breath, Helena hurried back toward the ballroom. The wait for the privy had been excruciating. She hoped Nicholas had not been waiting long. Something had altered in him tonight, she could feel it. His behavior spoke less of restraint and entirely of desire. During their dance, the intensity of his focus on her, like a pirate laying claim to bounty, had made everything else fade; there'd been nothing but the feel of his body moving with hers.

As she neared the double-doors leading to the terrace, she collided with a flash of turquoise moving in the opposition direction.

"*Oof.*" She righted herself. "I beg your par—oh, Marianne, 'tis you. I did not know you were in attendance tonight ..."

She trailed off, taking in the paleness of her friend's face and the haunted look in the normally vibrant green eyes. "Marianne, what is it?"

"Nothing. I am fine." Marianne's smile was clearly forced. "I am afraid that I have developed a megrim and need to leave."

"A megrim? Should you like Harteford and me to accompany you back?" Helena asked, concerned.

"No, no. I need to rest, that is all."

"Really, Marianne, you ought to—"

But it was too late. Marianne had slipped away without another word.

Baffled, Helena watched her friend disappear into the crowd. What was going on with Marianne? She would have to call on her tomorrow. But for now, she had her own matters to attend to. Once outside, she felt a rush of relief to spot Nicholas' broad back. He stood away from the others, on the farthest side of the veranda next to a series of hedges. Helena hastened over to him, words of greeting on her lips. The words died when she heard the voices rising from the other side of an enormous leafy divide.

"Brazen bastard, isn't he? Thinks just because he married Northgate's girl he can trample about in Society." The man's voice boomed, inebriated and indignant. "Well, I still say blood shows—his mother was a whore, after all, and his fortune is from *trade*. He positively trails the scent of shop."

"And that, dear Sir Jacoby, is why he is our own dear *Merchant* Marquess," responded a woman with a tinkling laugh.

"I'll be damned if the bastard isn't eyeing my stables, too, what remains of them," the male voice continued viciously. "Circling like a hawk, he is. Last month, he snatched up my finest greys at Tattersall's—and he didn't pay half what they're worth, the bloody skinflint. I wager he heard about my misfortune at the tables through those merchant friends of his. Mark my words, he's no better than those tradesmen knocking on the door. It is a sorry state indeed, my dear, when the lower classes don't mind their place."

Helena heard the sharp snapping sound at the same time that Nicholas whirled around. She had never seen such raw anger, from the molten obsidian of his eyes to the raised fists that looked ready, nay *eager*, for a brawl. Punch dripped, blood red, from one of his hands, as shards of delicate crystal cascaded to the ground. His large, powerful figure quivered like a hound with prey in sight. At first, he did not seem to recognize her. When he did, his face flamed.

"Nicholas ..." she said, reaching out her hand.

"Eh, who's there?" A moment later, a portly middle-aged man stumbled from the other side of the bushes. His ruddy, thickly veined jowls grew even redder when he saw Nicholas.

"Come back, Jacoby. I am sure it is nobody ..." A stick-thin woman emerged, tugging at her sagging bodice. Her small eyes protruded almost comically from her narrow face.

In the awful silence that followed, Helena's heartbeat grew louder and louder in her ears. In the periphery of her vision, she saw other guests circling, drawn to the hunt and the scent of blood. Murmurs, mocking laughter surrounded them.

"I say, what are you about, Harteford? Skulking like a common thief," Jacoby said.

The woman, cueing in on her lover's strategy, chimed to the

offensive. "An invasion of privacy, that is what I would call it. Most ungentlemanly behavior!"

Nicholas' gaze swung to Jacoby. His face was expressionless, yet Helena could see the strain of rigid control. Nicholas' fists bulged at his sides. Despite his well-tailored evening clothes, he emanated a savage physicality that only a fool would overlook. Jacoby instinctively inched backward, his throat bobbing. Nicholas' knuckles expanded and whitened. The quiet seemed to crackle with tension.

Then slowly, oh so slowly, Nicholas unclenched his fists.

Nicholas turned to face the woman, who clutched her hands to her shallow chest. An ostrich feather drooped limply over her eye. He swept her a mocking bow. His colorless voice chilled Helena to the core. "Pray do not concern yourself, madam. As you have said, I am nobody to worry about."

As he turned to leave, the crowd's jeering whispers grew in volume. *Coward. Bastard. What do you expect of the lower classes?* His eyes did not meet his wife's as he walked past.

Rage, brilliant and pure, washed over Helena. Red clouded her vision as she regarded Jacoby and his tittering consort. Without another thought, she crossed over to them.

"Yes, well, what is it?" Jacoby demanded uncomfortably. "It's not polite to stare, young lady. That's what comes of rubbing with the inferior classes. Would have thought Northgate brought you up to be ..."

He never had a chance to finish. With a resounding *crack*, Helena's reticule connected with his jaw. Yelping, Jacoby stumbled backward. Helena dimly heard the collective gasps of the gathering crowd, but she did not care. *How dare he malign Nicholas in such a manner? The pompous prig.* She swung her reticule again. As the beaded silk collided with flesh and bone, she realized she felt alive: every inch of her astride-riding, tree-climbing, baker's son-pummeling self burst into song.

The feeling was so satisfying, so very rewarding, that her arm drew back again of its own accord. Only to be restrained by an iron grip.

"Enough, Helena," Nicholas said quietly.

Helena leveled a withering stare at Jacoby and his lover. Both backed away from her, their faces immobile with shock. In a voice that shook with anger, she managed, "Shame on you. Shame on you both."

She turned to Nicholas and slipped her hand in his. Without a word, he led her away.

Chapter Twenty-Six

Nicholas handed Helena up into the carriage. Instead of following, however, he shut the door behind her and said to the driver, "Take Lady Harteford home. Do not stop, no matter what she says. I'll be along shortly."

The driver gave his cap a pull and the reins a snap.

As the horses started off, the window opened, and Helena's head poked out. "Nicholas?" she called out anxiously. "Where are you going? Why aren't you coming—"

He blocked her out. Couldn't bear to face her or the pity in her eyes. The equipage rounded the corner and disappeared from sight. He began to walk with no direction in mind. Given that his other option was to return to the ball and beat the living hell out of Jacoby, it seemed the better course of action. A gentleman would probably call the bugger out—but he was no gentleman, was he? He'd killed before, and he had no desire to murder another man, for any reason, no matter how justifiable. His honor—whatever there was of it—was certainly not cause enough.

Bloody fool, how could you have believed you were good enough for her?

With a savage stride, he trudged on. Humiliation ripened

within his chest as he thought of Helena having to defend him in such a way. By the morrow, she'd be a laughingstock and shunned by the world she came from. They'd be tittering about her over breakfast, at every fashionable tea and club in town. All because of him. Because every word Jacoby had said was true: Nicholas was a bastard, a coward ... and a fool who'd deluded himself into believing that his past could be left behind. At times he wished his bleeding sire had never acknowledged him at all. Better to live a bastard's life than to have a tantalizing dream dangling forever out of his reach.

He didn't know how long he walked. It seemed he'd been wandering the streets all his life—St. Giles, Mayfair, the docks, what did it matter? Peace eluded him everywhere. By the time he climbed the steps to the townhouse several hours later, he'd at least worn himself out physically. He wanted nothing more than to fall into his bed and into oblivion. Before he could ring the bell, however, the door opened. Helena stood there, still in her evening finery.

"Where have you been?" In a frantic motion, she grabbed his sleeve, and he let himself be pulled inside. "Don't you know how worried I've been? Sweet heavens, you didn't even get your coat or hat—you must be freezing!"

He hadn't felt cold. Hadn't felt much of anything until he'd laid eyes upon her and all his earlier hopes sliced through him like one of Farraday's scalpels. Fine, delicate cuts that left no mark and yet could bleed a man to the bone.

"Let's go to your study," she said decisively. "I'll pour you a brandy and we'll have Crikstaff bring some warm blankets—"

"I don't want to do this." His words resonated in the antechamber. They sounded as flat, as empty as he felt.

"The drawing room, then—"

He shook his head. "I mean I can't do this. With you. Not tonight." He hadn't the energy, the wherewithal to sort out the best course of action. Right now he needed to get to his bedchamber and bar the door. "Tomorrow, perhaps."

"*Dash it all*, we are going to talk now."

Helena's fierce tone took him aback. Her eyes were spitting fire at him. Had the night's events sunk in then? Had she finally realized the price of being married to the *ton*'s outcast?

A responding flare of anger lit his insides. He'd tried to warn her, hadn't he? Tried to tell her this was all a mistake—but she wouldn't listen.

"You want to talk? Fine," he said and headed to the study. He held the door open, gave her a mocking bow.

Head held high, looking more like a marchioness than he'd ever seen her, Helena marched by him. Crikstaff had left the lamps burning low, and the curling flame of the fireplace and lingering traces of tobacco added to the study's cozy ambiance. Helena strolled around Nicholas' private domain as if she belonged there. She inspected the wall of books spanning from floor to ceiling, running her finger along the spines.

Nicholas headed in the opposite direction, straight for the tray of spirits. He poured himself a glass from a crystal decanter before pausing and turning to look at her.

"Forgive my manners," he said shortly. "I do not keep sherry in here. Shall I ring for tea or hot milk?"

"I am not a child, Nicholas, who needs milk before bedtime. I shall have whatever you are drinking," Helena said.

He frowned. "I am drinking whiskey."

"Fine."

Helena seated herself in one of the wingchairs facing the fireplace. He could not help but note how the masculine furniture dwarfed her, how small and feminine she looked against the studded burgundy leather. As he handed her the glass, their fingers brushed, and he felt the jolt all the way to his toes. Damn her for having that effect on him. He sprawled into the adjacent armchair.

Keeping his gaze fixed upon leaping flames, he silently drank his whiskey.

He heard a slight sputter. "Is everything alright?" he said.

"Y-yes." She coughed again, then muttered, "How on earth can you drink this stuff?"

If she'd had the occasion to sample blue ruin, the milk of the stews, she wouldn't have to ask. The mellow tingle of whiskey was nothing compared to the gut-melting burn of gin. "An acquired taste," he said and tossed back the rest of the spirits. "But it's not my preference in beverages that we're here to discuss, is it? You're the one who insisted on talking. So talk."

She put down her glass. Her hands clasped amidst the folds of her emerald skirts. "I had hoped we would have a discussion, my lord. About what happened tonight. I understand that you are upset—"

"I am not upset," he said curtly. "You forget being issued a cut direct is hardly a novel occurrence. I deal with this most every day, my lady, and I can assure you I do not give a damn."

"Then why did you walk alone for hours? Why are you trying to shut me out?" For some reason, her soft, reasonable tones irked him further. He had to look away from the pleading shimmer in her big eyes. "Earlier this evening, you seemed different. You—you told me you wanted me. Always."

"I was mistaken." He could not keep the bitterness out of his voice. "Surely you can see such a relationship is not possible between us."

"I *cannot* see that, don't you understand? I cannot see *anything* when you keep me in the dark. I cannot read your mind, which is blasted mercurial by the by, and I am tired of trying!"

He stared at her. That was his first mistake. Her cheeks had blossomed with roses, and her plump bottom lip was quivering. With her decadent breasts straining with each agitated breath, she embodied temptation itself. She also looked hurt and angry, and if he hadn't thought it possible to hate himself more, he now realized his error. He cursed himself a hundred times over for causing her distress. He'd thought to spare her the truths that no lady should know—but had he just been rationalizing his own fear? Who was he truly protecting—her or himself?

Seeing her bewildered pain, he knew he could not run any longer.

"Of course you cannot read my mind—I lost it from the moment we met," he said in a weak attempt at humor. When she only continued to look at him, he sighed. "I have not been the husband you deserve, Helena. For that, I do apologize."

Her next words tore at him. "Is it because of me? Have I done something or not done—"

"*No.* This is not, and never has been, about you. I told you before—the problem lies with me. With who I am." His throat felt scratchy, abrading his words. "And what I have done."

"Tell me, Nicholas. For God's sake, just talk to me." Her eyes glimmered. "*Please.*"

He felt himself weakening. His second mistake. "You are asking me to speak of things I've never spoken of before. Not with anyone—not the Fineses, not even Jeremiah." He struggled to make her understand. "My past, Helena ... it is not fit for a lady's ears."

"I am not just a lady." Her chin lifted. As he was learning, an ominous sign. "I am your *wife*. And I love you, and nothing you say could possibly change that."

He swallowed. "I ... I want to believe you."

"Then take the chance. Let me know you, my husband," she whispered. "About your childhood, how you grew up to be a man ... everything."

The sincerity he saw in her beautiful eyes twisted a knife deep in his gut. The shame of the evening's earlier events did not compare with the torture of the present. He would have to witness Helena's love turn to disgust once she knew him for what he was. Rising, he returned to the beverage tray to buy himself time. And courage. When he splashed more whiskey into his glass, he was surprised to find his hands trembling. Liquid sloshed onto the silver.

"You have no idea, do you, what you are asking me to share," he said. "The ugliness of it, Helena—you will wish you had not asked."

"Let me be the judge of that."

"As you wish." Gulping down another shot, he let the burn ease the way into the past. "I was not born a bastard, but I lived as one for all the years up until the last. There is little about my sire's sordid affair with my mother, a beautiful opera singer half his age, which has not been bandied about. How he competed fiercely for her affections with two of his cronies, how daily wagers were placed in the betting ledger at White's on who would triumph in claiming Sylvie—that was my mother's name—under his protection. In the end, it was the marquess who won."

"That he set her up in a cozy cottage was known to all. What the *ton* did not know was that in a reckless fit of passion, he married Sylvie. In secret, by special license. For the first few months, he visited her regularly. It was no surprise, then, that Sylvie found herself increasing within a short time. She thought this would cement her position in the marquess' life, but she was mistaken. When she lost her shape, she also lost his interest. Weeks before she was to give birth, she found out that the marquess had a new mistress, younger and more beautiful than she. In a rage, she confronted him. He responded by throwing her out."

"He abandoned his pregnant wife?" Helena said in disbelief.

Nicholas shrugged. "My mother had no proof of the marriage, and my father was a powerful man. He threatened to have her thrown into Newgate if she so much as breathed a word of their relationship. She had no choice but to leave with the clothes on her back."

"What did she do then?" Helena asked faintly.

"She bore the child, a boy, and left him in her sister's charge.

So great was her fear of her husband that she never spoke a word of the boy's true parentage. For a while, she found employment as a singer again." Nicholas let his shoulders rise and fall again. "I believe she may have sought the protection of other wealthy patrons—she did send money now and again, mostly in the form of jewelry."

"Did you ever see her again?"

"No. She died when I was nine, from consumption I was told." Nicholas remembered well his aunt's red face as she had imparted the news.

Sylvie's dead, with nary a shilling to her name. We've got six mouths to feed as it is, so don't go thinking you can live on our charity. The workhouse is where you're headed, my boy. The place where all the bastard brats go.

"What happened ... after?"

He curled his hand reflexively around his glass. "My aunt could no longer bear the responsibility for my upbringing. I was sent to a workhouse." As he had learned, even orphans possessed a social hierarchy. Those who occupied the top rung had respectable parents—shop owners and tradesmen, even the occasional penniless squire—who had expired in some unfortunate circumstance. Bastards, in particular those born to whores, clung to the very bottom tier, a lesson he had learned through bloodied noses and torn fists. "Eventually, I ran away and found my way back to my aunt's house."

"She took you back in," Helena said, clearly relieved.

"No." Nicholas wondered how he could have been so naive, so stupid as to think that his aunt would welcome him back once she knew of the workhouse conditions. He'd thought if he could just explain that he was willing to work his share, to contribute to the household ... what a fool he had been. "No, she did not take me back."

"Then ... then what happened?" His wife looked at him, wide-eyed.

He expelled a breath. "She sold me."

The words popped like a cork into the silence. Finally, Helena appeared shocked, bereft of words. But he had gone too far already; as the ignominious tale poured forth, he found he could not stem the flow of words. His lips seemed to move of their own accord.

"It happened that a sweep named Ben Grimes was looking for apprentices. He wanted young boys, no older than the age of seven. Do you know why, Helena?"

She shook her head, a barely perceptible movement.

"Because the stacks are narrow. Tight so that only a small child can pass. At places no wider than three hands across."

He advanced toward her, using his hands to illustrate the girth of the airless tunnel. Panic gripped his throat, reflexive, ineffaceable. Even if he lived to be a hundred, he'd never forget the times he'd gotten stuck in the soot-choked darkness, certain he'd be left to die. For the chumney was a disposable commodity—children being so cheap and easy to come by that a master sweep would sooner find a new child than try to save a useless one.

"You ... you worked as a chimney boy, then?"

He blinked. Dropped his hands. Helena was looking steadily at him, and he had to swallow down the tide of revulsion before he could speak again.

"I was ten at the time, but puny enough to pass for younger. Grimes took me on. The three years I worked as a climbing boy were a hell you cannot imagine. I lived in soot so thick that it fills your lungs, every crevice of your skin." As he spoke, the scorched stench filled his nostrils, the filth permeating every cell of his being. "And somehow you get used to it. From dawn to dusk, I climbed the stacks, up passages so narrow that a mistaken breath could jam you into a grave within the brick walls."

"How did you manage not to get trapped?" she asked in a trembling voice.

He gripped the back of a chair. "I didn't always. When it

happened, Grimes had powerful incentives to get a boy loose. Lit straw, for one."

"He *burned* you?" Helena gasped.

"It got me loose."

Before he realized her intent, Helena came to him. He shuddered when her arms wrapped around his waist, her cheek pressing against the rigid muscles of his back. Her voice sounded muffled, choked. "No boy, no *human*, should ever experience such horror. How strong you are to survive it, my darling."

He gave a mirthless laugh. He moved out of her embrace and turned to face her. "The days in the stacks, that was the respite. Most days I took extra care, polishing the flue until it was spotless to avoid being hauled up again."

"But ... why?"

"Because of the nightly entertainments. Because after a hard day's work, Master Grimes expected 'is boys to help 'im unwind."

Helena stared at him. He noticed how tightly she was clasping her hands; he imagined her fingernails would leave marks on her smooth perfect skin. He looked past her, thankful for the numbness spreading over his insides. The truth tumbled from his lips with a force of its own.

"Some nights, 'e wanted one o' us to ... to service 'im while the res' o' the lot watched. Other times, 'e made us to play wif each other. I ne' er stopped 'im. I was one o' the good boys, did whatever 'e asked ..."

The small, hollowed faces flashed in his mind. As if from the outside, he saw himself amongst the tattered bunch. All of them with eyes flat and dead, past caring. Past most anything save the instinct to stay alive.

"You did what you needed to survive." Helena's urgent words returned him to the present. "You must see that."

Self-revulsion churned in his gut. "I was 'ungry. Like a bloody mongrel on the street, weren't nothin' I wouldn't do fer a scrap."

"Nicholas ..."

"Ev'ry time, I tol' myself it would be the last. I swore I'd kill 'im if 'e touched me again." Feral satisfaction pulled his lips back. "An' then one day, I did."

"Did what?" Helena whispered.

"I killed him. Stuck 'im in 'is bleedin' black 'eart and left 'im to die."

Chapter Twenty-Seven

For a moment, the sides of Helena's vision wavered, compressed. *Nicholas had killed a man.* Even though she knew intellectually that death came quick and ugly for many in the streets of London, it was another thing altogether to comprehend that her husband had taken a life. As she watched, Nicholas stared at his hands and flexed his fingers. A look of revulsion crossed his features as he studied stains that only he could see.

If there were stains, they contained the blood of a man who deserved to die. How many children besides Nicholas had been fouled by the villain? The thought of such cruelty, such predation on the weak and vulnerable, tightened Helena's throat. She was not so innocent that she did not see the justice in Grimes' end. She bled for the pain Nicholas had suffered as a boy ... and for the self-hatred and guilt he carried as a man. He still stood there, held captive by his invisible sins.

"Nicholas! Stop it. Come back, now!" Helena grabbed her husband's forearms and gave him a shake. When he did not respond, she shook him again. Firmly.

Nicholas blinked. She saw the moment he returned to the present, when anguished shame replaced the blank sheen in his eyes. She never thought to feel relief in his pain, but she did. Pain meant he was with her, alive, and not drowning blindly in the quicksand of his past.

After a pause, he continued woodenly, "There is more. After I stabbed Grimes, I panicked. There ... there was another boy in the room. I don't even remember his name." His voice catching, Nicholas knuckled his eyes. "He was a new boy, younger than me. He witnessed what I'd done. I went over to him, with the knife still in my hand and blood dripping everywhere, and I ... I ..."

Despite the fear clutching her heart, Helena said, "What did you do, my love?"

He raised his tormented gaze. "I threatened him. Told him that if he ever breathed a word about that night, I would slit his throat. And all he did was look at me, his face whiter than a ghost's and he said ..."

Breath held, Helena waited.

"*Take me with you. Don't leave me here.*" Nicholas' eyes shut against the memory. "He kept begging me, grabbing my arm. By God, he was no older than seven or eight; he must have been frightened out of his wits. But I was frantic to get out, and when he wouldn't let go, I struck him. I still remember the sound of him crying as I escaped through one of the windows." His voice throbbed with self-hatred. "Not only am I a murderer, I am a cursed coward."

She couldn't stop the tears from falling—for the unknown boy, for Nicholas, for the suffering that neither of them had deserved. "You are not to blame, do you hear me, Nicholas? Not for any of it." Reaching up, she took his jaw in her hands. Forced him to look at her. "You were *thirteen years old*, Nicholas. A child and a brave one to fight back. But you could hardly protect yourself, let alone another boy. I cannot imagine how terrified you must have been after ..." He trembled within her touch. "You must forgive yourself—Grimes is the one responsible for all this suffering. At least you freed that boy and the other children from his clutches."

"Did I? Or did send him and the other boys to a worse end?" Nicholas' grip on her arms bordered on painful as he looked upon her with a ravaged expression. "Later I learned that the flash house went down in flames that night. I do not know what caused the fire, and at first, I was relieved, for it was named the cause of Grimes' death. His remains were found in the wreckage, you see. Then I heard that several children had perished in the inferno as well and"—his voice cracked—"I have always wondered ... if that boy ... if I had only. . ."

Helena could think of no appropriate response. So instead she circled her arms around her husband's waist and held him as tightly as she could. She felt shudders travel through his large frame as he held onto her like a drowning man to a piece of driftwood. She could feel his hot, unsteady breathing above her ear.

"For years, I heard the boy's voice in my dreams. And I could feel the breath of the magistrate down my neck, smell the foul stench of the waiting prison hulks. In my bones, I always knew justice would find me sooner or later."

She tipped her head back to look at him. "Any magistrate would see you had just cause," she said firmly. "That you acted in defense of your well-being. Grimes was the criminal, not you!"

"I killed a man, Helena. Indirectly, I may have caused the death of an innocent child." He shook his head in bleak resignation. "I am a murderer, and nothing can change that."

"The offenses Grimes committed were far greater than yours. In the end, justice was served. Please tell me you see that." The expression on his face shredded her heart. For so many years, he had hoarded his pain, let it fester inside him. She did not need to ask why. The guilt, the self-loathing—he was still paying penance for what he had done. "You have suffered enough. All you have done is survive, and you must forgive yourself so you can go on. So *we* can have a life together."

Nicholas let go of her and stepped back. Beneath his swarthy skin, he was pale, his gaze haunted. "You cannot mean that. After all I have said—Helena, you must see I am not deserving of you."

"I see that you are more of a man than I ever knew," she said fiercely. "One I am proud to call husband."

And still it seemed he could not allow himself to believe her. Raking his hands through his hair, he went to the fire and began to pace before it. "There is more, you know. Before I met Jeremiah, I spent a year running with one of the dock gangs. I was a thief, a ruffian, a good-for-naught—"

"Who turned his life around," she finished. "Who, despite the greatest odds, made something of himself."

Nicholas stopped. Turned to look at her again. "Odd," he said hoarsely, "those were almost his exact words. My sire's, I mean."

"You met your father? I thought you learned of your inheritance after his passing."

"You are correct. My father's solicitor approached me, a month after his death. When he realized he was dying, my father had had a Runner track my whereabouts. His second marriage had produced no offspring, you see. Apparently, he found my progress in life to his satisfaction—in his will, he named me the legal heir to his land and entitlements. There was a copy of a marriage certificate to confirm my legitimate status. He left me a note—two lines actually. *Against odds, you have surprised me and made something of yourself. I trust you will attend to your duty with similar diligence.*"

So that was where Nicholas had inherited his penchant for laconic missives. Really, could his sire not have summoned a single iota of fatherly affection? "It must have been a shock finding out the truth about your birth," she said gently.

"Aye, to put it mildly. At first, I wanted nothing to do with my father. Not his estate, not his bloody title—I would have had it all buried to rot with the rest of him."

"What changed your mind in the end?"

"Jeremiah." Nicholas' jaw tautened. "He, too, was dying. He

told me I was a fool for throwing away my birthright, for refusing a gift that he himself could only dream of. You see, rich as he was, Jeremiah could never escape his origins. He made his fortune as a merchant, so the doors of Society would forever be closed to his wife and his children. Do you know what his fondest dream was?"

Helena shook her head.

"To have Percy presented at court. So trivial a matter, is it not? Yet so utterly impossible, this crossing of two worlds." The bleakness in his eyes caused her throat to constrict. "Tonight's fiasco was just another reminder of the irreconcilable disparities between us. You, my love, are everything good and pure and innocent. Whereas I ..." His shoulders moved, a movement as heavy as if he carried the world there. "I am what life has made me."

She went over to him, made him face her. "What has happened to you is not who you are. *You,*" she said, placing a hand over his furiously thudding heart, "are the finest man I have ever known. The only man I could ever love."

"How could you mean that?" Nicholas released a serrated breath. "After all that I have done—"

"You were a blameless child, for God's sake!" Helena cried.

"I could have left sooner. I could have found someplace else to go, rather than endure Grimes' brand of hell."

"Where would you have gone? Back to the workhouse, or perhaps one of the rookeries which swallow up young children and spit out hardened criminals?" Desperately, Helena gripped his arm and waited for him to look at her.

"What do you know of rookeries?" Nicholas finally asked.

"The Misses Berry invite political conversation at their parties. I know children die every day, of disease and starvation. And I know many more live on, in filthy conditions and unspeakable terror." The rawness of her husband's gaze drew tears down her cheeks. "Oh Nicholas, do not blame yourself for the wrongs that were inflicted upon you!"

"Don't cry," he whispered. "I'm not worth it."

"I'll cry if I want to," Helena said fiercely. "And you would be worth every tear. Haven't you been listening? *I love you.*"

Nicholas closed his eyes. "How could you?"

The words hung in the air which suddenly felt as thick as the fog over the Thames. For the first time, however, she could see clearly through the miasma that separated them. His shame and self-doubt swirled in the ghostly, brutal images from his past. A far cry from her own sheltered upbringing, for certain. And yet ... were he and she all that different? For did she not also harbor shame and self-doubt and secrets that she feared to reveal?

Trust in a marriage had to be earned, by husband ... and by wife.

"Wait here one moment," she said. "I'll be back."

The trip took her less than five minutes, yet when she returned to the study and her husband, she realized she had been taking this journey all her life. Nicholas was sitting in one of the wingchairs, his head held in his hands. At her approach, he got to his feet. His gaze honed in on the reticule in her hands.

"What is this about, Helena?"

She wet her dry lips. "I ... I have a secret of my own to confess, Nicholas. Something rather shocking."

Nicholas' smile was sad. "Compared to my sins, what unworthy thing could you have possibly done?"

It was his certainty, his absolute faith that she existed in a moral realm above him that pushed her over the edge.

She held up the reticule. Embroidered with orange blossoms and clusters of seed pearls, the bulging satin bag looked innocuous enough. Which only lent credence to the adage that one should not judge a book by its cover. Nor a wife by her demure disposition. She hesitated under Nicholas' intent regard. Her hands trembled on the strings.

"What is it then?" Nicholas asked, his brows drawing together.

"I have acted in an unworthy manner, as you call it. Indeed, it was a most wanton action which I committed. And, unlike you, my behavior was not performed under duress. I"—Helena paused to fortify herself with a deep breath—"*chose* to act in this fashion."

"Wanton manner? What is it that you have done?" Amused wariness crept into Nicholas' tone. "Did you filch a slice of Chef's cake before supper, Helena? Take a morning ride with your bonnet askew?"

Every fiber of her being pulsed with dread and anticipation. "No, my lord," she managed to say calmly. "I went to a bawdy house and enticed a stranger to bed me."

It took a moment for Nicholas to react.

"You did *what*?"

Relieved to see the spark of life returning to his eyes yet wise enough to fear the rapidly rising flames, Helena loosened the strings and tipped open her reticule. Curls of brassy red spilled out. At the sight of them, Nicholas froze.

"*Oui, monsieur.*" The breathy quality of the accent emerged naturally, given the way her throat constricted with love and fear. "It was me those two nights at the Nunnery."

"You were ... were at the Nunnery?" If circumstances had not been so dire, Helena might have laughed at the comical look of incomprehension on her husband's face. He looked like someone who had bitten into an apple and discovered it to be a lemon. She could see him struggling to assimilate her revelation with his own vision of her—it was a long fall, she supposed, off so high a pedestal.

"Yes, I was there." Helena bit her lip when he said nothing. "At the masquerade. And a fortnight ago."

"It was you. Both times. You were the nymph." Nicholas looked dazed. "But I ... you ... *we* ..."

"I know. I was a harlot." Truly, it felt relieving to confess herself, to no longer hide her nature. Still, Helena squeezed her eyes shut to confess the last, most secret part of her deception. "And, my lord, I found the experience quite exhilarating. In truth, I can profess no regret for my behavior."

Silence followed her words. Unable to bear the tension, Helena peeked through one eye. Nicholas was staring at her as if he had never seen her before.

"Well, say something," she begged, her tone rising with desperation. "Lecture me or berate me or …"—she swallowed, fearing the worst— "tell me how disappointed you are in me for failing to be the virtuous wife you wanted."

"You pretended to be a nymph." Perhaps Nicholas thought that repetition might allow him to absorb this fact. "A *French* nymph. And you seduced me."

To her mind, the seduction had been rather mutual, but she thought it prudent to allow his assertion to pass. She nodded.

Her husband continued to look as if he had been struck by a bolt from above.

"Forgive my slow wittedness," he said at last, "but I still fail to comprehend what you were doing at a brothel in the first place."

"The first time I went to find you." Suddenly embarrassed for chasing after him like a jealous fishwife, Helena looked down at her reticule. The red wig did not look so alluring and seductive now. In the light of the lamp, the wiry curls appeared tawdry and false. "By happenstance, I saw you possessed a ticket to the Nunnery masquerade, and it was not difficult to surmise your purpose in attending. If you recall, you were avoiding me at the time, so I did not have the opportunity to discuss with you my feelings on the matter."

"So you followed me there." Nicholas fixed her with an astounded look. "To discuss your *feelings*?"

"That was my initial plan, yes. But things got rather … out of hand," Helena mumbled. A wild blush stained her cheeks. "I did not plan that part, my lord. It just sort of happened."

Nicholas quirked a brow. "Did it, *mademoiselle*?"

"Oh. The accent," Helena said in a small voice. "Truly, 'twas not a planned deception, my lord. It was more of … of an extemporaneous measure."

"But why the ruse?"

"I was afraid," Helena admitted. "My behavior being so wanton, I feared you would react with disgust to discover that I was not the wife you believed me to be. You see, I know how much you value my virtue and strength of moral character."

"And the second time? Why did you invite me back?" he asked evenly.

She bit her lip. No one had ever said honesty was easy. "I was angry and hurt by your rejection. I thought to teach you a lesson, to seduce you in the doxy's disguise, then reveal myself as the wife you had professed not to want."

"Then why did you not follow through with your plan and divulge your identity that night? It was because of my behavior, wasn't it? Bloody hell, I must have shocked you out of your wits." Ruddy color spread over his cheekbones, and his eyes slid from hers to focus on the ground. "Helena, the things I did ... said ... Had I known it was you, I would never have—"

"Oh no, it wasn't that," she assured him, her face aflame. "I, um, liked that part very much. It was that you shared some of your past with me, and I realized that what I wanted was not revenge. What I truly desired was honesty and trust between us—and I couldn't bring myself to reveal my deception. But at that moment, I vowed to myself that I would never lie to you again. That I would try to win your affection through honest means."

When he did not respond, her chin lowered. "Have I disgusted you, Nicholas, with my wanton and immoral behavior? Are you disappointed that I am not the virtuous wife you expected?"

A finger tilted her chin up. The look of fierce tenderness in Nicholas' dark eyes robbed her of breath. "You are far more than I could have ever expected. More than I deserve. The woman I love with everything that I am."

Tears welled in her eyes.

"Helena, do you think you could ever ... ever forgive me?" Now it was his turn to falter, an aching uncertainty in his tone. "I can make no excuses for my infidelity. I can only say that it was my foolish intention to spare you from my needs. After our wedding night, I could not bear the thought of hurting you again. The truth is that in my fantasies, I was making love to you." Taking her hand, Nicholas placed it upon his chest. His heart thudded strong and steadfast beneath her palm. "Could you believe me? Forgive me? Here, in my heart, no other has ever existed but you."

Remembering the way he had uttered her name in the depths of his desire, she nodded and said, "And you could love me, knowing that I am a ... a harlot?"

In answer, Nicholas caught her in his arms. She reveled in the familiar warmth of his embrace and the whispered words against her hair. "Helena, don't you know it is *you*, I love? Every part of you—my proper marchioness, brave, sweet wife, seductress of my body and soul."

Joy blossomed within her. "I do love you so, Nicholas. I—"

But the time for talk was clearly over, for his lips claimed hers in a kiss more passionate, more ravenous than she'd ever imagined. She responded with all her heart. With all the loving desire she no longer had to hide.

Chapter Twenty-Eight

Nicholas set his wife on the carpet before the fire. Threading his fingers through her silky ringlets, he feasted on the sight of her beloved face. No masks between them. No ghosts. Her eyes glistened with tears. Edging away the beads of moisture with his thumbs, he thought to say something, to express in some eloquent fashion the soul-deep bliss he was feeling, but his throat constricted, and no words came.

So, being a man of action, he showed her. He worshiped the outer corner of her mouth with his lips, loving the way it seemed to naturally tilt up, even in kissing. He kissed the dip on her top lip, the luscious ledge of the lower, exploring the landscape with reverence before seeking the sweetness within. He ran his tongue coaxingly along the seam of her lips.

With a small sigh, Helena acquiesced, and Nicholas entered like a starved man, needing the sustenance of her taste, her honeyed flavor. When her tongue met his, his hands clenched in her hair. He went deeper, thrusting inside her mouth. He heard her excited purr, and he growled her name in answer. He plundered her mouth, giving her no purchase, no means of escape. *She was his.* He possessed her mouth with violent urgency and shuddered when her hands clutched at his shoulders, drawing him closer still.

Soon, the kissing wasn't enough. He had to have more of her. Looking down with wonderment at her kiss-plumped lips, the sultry swirl of gold in her eyes, he brought reverent fingers to her cheek.

"Helena, my love," he said unsteadily, "I want you to know from now on that things will be different between us. I would not hurt you for the world."

"Hurt me?" Helena's gaze appeared unfocused, her eyes soft and blurry with passion.

"I know our wedding night was not a pleasurable experience for you. And at the Nunnery—I did not make love as a gentleman ought." Nicholas ran a callused fingertip over her delicate skin, riveted by the contrast of bronze against white, hard against soft. "Not that it is any excuse, but I had not made love to a lady before you."

His wife blinked at him. "*You* were a virgin too?"

At that, he roared with laughter. He could not stop, even when his wife said in a none-too-pleased tone, "What is so amusing?"

When she began pushing on his shoulders, Nicholas caged her arms beneath his and looked tenderly into her flushed, annoyed face.

"I have been called many things, Helena, but never that," he said with a grin. He pressed a kiss onto her forehead. "I meant I had never had relations with a well-bred lady before. Of the other sort, I am acquainted."

"Oh."

Her nose wrinkled, and her small huff of feminine jealousy made him feel ridiculously proud. "That displeases you, madam wife?"

"Would *you* enjoy hearing about my dalliances with other men?"

"I would kill anyone who touched you." The words came out

fiercely, from a dark primitive place inside him. "You are mine now, Helena, as I am yours. I will never give you cause to doubt me again."

He lowered his mouth to hers to seal the vow. Tonight, he was determined to properly pleasure a lady. *His* lady. As he continued to explore the sweetness of his wife's kiss, Nicholas ran light fingers over her shoulders and along the clothed side of her breasts. Feeling her tremble, he carefully cupped one of the full mounds, his groin tightening as the supple flesh overflowed his palm. He squeezed gently, and when he was rewarded by a sprouted bud beneath the thin cloth, he lowered his head, capturing the engorged nipple between his lips. He flicked his tongue back and forth, dampening the material until her nipple stood proudly visible.

Helena's moans grew louder and more insistent. Taking that as a positive sign, he drew down her bodice. Her breasts sprang free, so gorgeously full, the peaks so deliciously pink that he wasted no time in tasting the offered bounty. He trailed a hot, glistening trail from one nipple to the other. He felt a surge of delight when Helena panted his name, and her fingers speared into his hair, pulling his mouth closer, demanding more. He obliged her, her sounds of pleasure making his cock twitch inside his smalls.

Easing her onto her side, he rained kisses down her neck as his fingers worked on the column of buttons down her back. Damn, but there was an army of infernally small pearls, each one guarding the path to ecstasy. With a muffled curse, Nicholas yanked the last ones free, ignoring the dull scatter of beads across the carpet. He would buy her a new dress—a wardrobe of new dresses—just to get her out of this one. When he finally managed to divest her of her gown and undergarments, he lost all power of speech. He stared at his blushing wife as she laid there, her lush white curves juxtaposed against the dark green carpet, a pagan dance of firelight over her skin.

"By God, you take my breath away." Running a possessive hand over her hip, he let his eyes follow the creamy line of her legs all the way to the delicate curls at the top. "I shall never tire of seeing you thus, my love."

He watched in fascination as the blush moved all over her body. His wife ducked her head into the crook of his shoulder, and for a moment he wondered if he had offended her sensibilities with his ardent words.

Instead, she whispered against his ear, "Nicholas, I should like to see you, too. I didn't get the chance, not really, those other times."

Her request sent a quiver through his body. Rising, he stripped off his clothes. Not wanting to hide himself from her any longer, he stood there naked, his hands at his sides. He saw her eyes widen as they took in his arousal. It was so fierce that his cock curved upward, the bulging crown brushing his abdomen. His sac throbbed with a heartbeat of its own. With held breath, he awaited her response.

"Oh, Nicholas," she breathed, "you are so beautiful."

With a groan, he came to her, marveling at the perfect counterpoint between her velvety lushness and his own rigid strength. As he kissed her, he learned the delicate curve of her legs, the delightful dimples of her knees. His hands wandered upward, glorying in the lack of impediment and the feel of skin upon skin. God's blood, how long he had hungered to be with her thus, with nothing between them.

Heady with triumph, he combed through the silky curls of her mound. He coated his fingers in the dew, rubbing it in small glistening circles over her swollen flesh. His wife's hands grabbed at his shoulders as her hips arched in pleading surrender. Obliging her silent demand, he carefully parted her and slipped a finger halfway into her hole.

"Oh!" Helena gasped.

Nicholas gritted his teeth as her muscles tugged at his finger, drawing him in deeper. He wanted to go slow, but her fiery throbbing was beginning to rob him of control. When her pussy pulled at him again, he fed a little more of his finger into her and then more until he was buried knuckle-deep in her wet heat. Watching her flushed face, her half-lidded gaze, he felt near delirious with lust. He began to move his finger.

Helena's reaction was immediate. "Oh, my," she sighed. Her eyes closed as her hips lunged helplessly against his touch. "That feels so very *good ...*"

The edges of his vision darkening, Nicholas watched his oh-so proper wife impale herself on his hand, her juices flowing into his palm. He answered the tight, desperate glide of her pussy by inserting another finger to join the first; her whimpered cries expanded him with satisfaction. Delving into her luscious folds, he found the little nub and circled it with his thumb. Helena stiffened, her eyes rolling back as she let out a squeak. It was almost too much to bear. The lust pounding through his veins fueled his head downward.

Her initial inhalation melted into a long moan as he tenderly tongued her. The salty sweet taste of her filled his senses as he fulfilled his long-held fantasy of feasting upon her. Overcome with ravenous hunger, he licked and sucked her sex, his breathing going raspy as she cried out his name. He could not get enough of the womanly cream coating his lips and tongue. Exposing the center of her pleasure, he lapped at the vulnerable bud, drawing circles that drew sounds of delight from his wife. Egged on by the sudden tautness of her legs, he suckled her, pulling with gentle suction.

Helena's climax rocked him with unutterable joy and voracious lust. When she shuddered, moaning as the spasms shook her body, he positioned himself over her and entered in a thick, breathless glide. He held himself in rigid check, wanting to allow her time to accustom to his invading thickness. The tight rim of her stretched over his erection, and he closed his eyes, trying to ignore the siren's call of silken muscles, the aftermath of her climax rippling around his shaft.

He felt something flutter against the bunched muscle of his

forearm. His lids opened halfway to the sight of Helena looking languidly at him. He almost blew his seed at the erotic sight of her tongue moistening her kiss-swollen lips.

"It is considered impolite to keep a lady waiting," his wife informed him in a sultry tone.

Nicholas made a sound, half laugh, half groan.

"I shall endeavor to please the rules of etiquette, of course," he said and began the torturous pleasure of withdrawing from her tight passage. He was determined to go slow, be gentle, and see to her pleasure before his own.

When he pressed in again, Helena arched to meet him, her eyes squeezing shut. Her cry of delight ripped at his self-control. "Oh my. Nicholas, you make me feel so ... *oh* ..."

"Yes, my sweet?" Sweat glazed his forehead as he slowly repeated the motion. Clenching his jaw, he drew in and out of her intoxicating cunny with ruthless self-mastery. "Do you like this?"

Her lashes lifted, and the lustful, loving gleam in her eyes destroyed him. "I love the feel of your big cock, *monsieur*," she whispered. "I've dreamt of you taking me, not holding back, giving me everything you've got—"

For him, the world went mad. With an inhuman roar, he drove himself home. All the way, nothing held back. He encountered no resistance—only sweet, snug heat. Bliss pulsed along his shaft, bubbling to the base of his spine.

"Like my cock, do you wench?" he growled.

She smiled at him, so radiantly that his heart skipped a beat. "*Je t'aime*. Your cock and all the rest of you, my husband. Now will you please make love to me?"

With a groaning laugh, he gave into her. Into himself. The sure, strong strokes made her sigh and him shudder with animal delight. Nothing had ever felt like this, had even come *close*. Restraint shed from him, and in this new skin he experienced a startling new vibrancy. He felt drunk with pleasure. Bathed in it, joy overflowing every cell of his being. With each plunge, he sank deeper into her loving heat, and still he needed to be closer. Could not get enough. Grasping her knees, he pushed them forward, angling her pussy so that it surrendered further to him, so that each pounding movement of his shaft grazed her sensitive peak.

By now, she was panting his name, her eyes dazed with ecstasy.

He ground his hips, penetrating her so fully that his stones slapped the lips of her sex. "Feel my cock." His head whirled at the sight of her pretty tits bouncing with each thrust. At the perfect squeeze of her creamy cunt. Shutting his eyes, he hissed, "Feel me inside you, loving you, a part of you."

"Love me," she gasped. "Please don't ever stop ..."

"Again." Another plunge and drag, and he was shaking with the effort to hold on. "Come again, love, and take me with you."

As if on command, her pussy began to flicker around him. The contractions grew stronger and stronger, milking him, wrenching a shout from his throat. With her cries of completion echoing in his ears, he slammed into her again and again. Fire sizzled up his spine. Melted the last vestiges of his control. He exploded with unending pleasure, his seed, his very being splintering inside her.

Chapter Twenty-Nine

Helena burrowed into the sheets, resisting the initial tugs of wakefulness. She wanted to stay in her dream forever. She wanted Nicholas to continue kissing her, murmuring sweet words in her ear as he moved within her. Oh, how lovely that felt, the pressure of his thick cock gliding in and out. She nuzzled the sheets. They smelled of Nicholas, a musky male fragrance that aroused her senses. Come to think of it, they felt like him too, all warm and solid and scratchy with hair ...

Her eyes popped open. She blinked once in the pale morning light, but her vision did not change. A low fire burned in the grate. Her line of sight was partially obscured by a hairy chest. Last night returned to her in a flash, and joy flamed so brightly within her that she did not dare to move. She wanted to bask in the glory of waking in her husband's arms—literally, for she was sprawled atop his very muscular, very naked body. Sometime during the night he must have wrapped his jacket around her, for the velvet was the only cover to her nakedness.

"Good morning, my love." Nicholas' voice rumbled under her ear.

Startled, she raised her head to look at him. His hair was

tousled with sleep like a boy's. The lines on his face had eased, and his eyes were smiling. He had never looked more handsome. All at once, desire stirred again, syrupy warmth trickling over her insides. Color rose in her cheeks. She hadn't been awake more than a few minutes and already she ached for her husband's lovemaking. What a wanton she was.

"You're up?" She blurted.

"Most definitely." The smile spread to Nicholas' lips as he shifted his hip. Iron-hard flesh pressed into her thigh. "I've been up for quite a while watching you sleep."

"You were watching me sleep?"

Nodding, he reached to tuck away a lock that had fallen over her forehead. "When you sleep, you look like an angel." His fingers danced along the sensitive shell of her ear. She shivered when his fingers drifted over her eyelids and cheeks. "Your eyelashes flutter like wings. Your skin is as smooth as Devonshire cream." His voice deepened as he mixed his metaphors. "It makes me want to eat you up."

Her heart beat madly at his words, at the way he devoured her with his eyes.

"I confess I am rather hungry too," she dared to say.

His husky laugh rolled over her at the same time that he did. Pinned beneath him, she could not help but marvel at his virile strength. She ran her fingers over his shoulders and down his arms. He had made love to her three times during the night, and each time he had aroused her to the point of madness with his skillful fingers and devilish mouth. How she longed to return the favor.

"Nicholas," she murmured, "would you teach me how to please you?"

"You already please me, Helena," he said, his breath hot upon her neck. She sighed when he licked his way down. "You cannot imagine how much."

"You would find me an apt pupil," she managed. "One who practices her lessons most diligently."

At that, he raised his head. She loved the gleam in his normally somber eyes.

"Eager for a lesson, are you?" he intoned as sternly as any schoolmaster.

Helena swallowed a giggle.

"Yes, sir," she said, meek as a schoolgirl.

"Very well," he said. She could tell he was trying hard not to smile. He rolled onto his back. "Your first lesson, then, is to touch me."

Helena got to her knees, the jacket sliding to the carpet. She looked at the expanse of sinewy male flesh before her. Her hands twitched in her lap. There were so many places to touch, so many intriguing contrasts—the smooth, hard slope of his shoulders, the soft yet coarse hair on his chest. Her eyes moved downward, widened slightly as she appreciated his manhood in the morning light.

Oh my. He did have the satyr beat, didn't he?

By several inches at least.

"Perhaps this lesson is too advanced, hmm?" Nicholas had been watching her all the while, a half-smile on his face. Now he moved to sit up, his voice apologetic.

She placed both palms on his chest and pushed.

Flat on his back, he looked up at her with startled eyes.

She ran her fingers across his chest, noting his quick intake of breath when she brushed his flat nipples. She did it again, smiling now, as she saw that despite the differences between their bodies, there were similarities too. His flesh hardened under her touch.

"How is that, sir?" she inquired.

"You're doing very well," he allowed.

She liked the hitched quality in his voice, as if he was having difficulty catching his breath. It made her feel powerful, bold. She explored the flat ridges of his abdomen, running fingers lightly over muscles which jumped at her touch. Navigating around the mighty pole for the moment, she stroked downward over his powerful thighs and calves, all the way down to his large masculine feet. There was a sprinkling of hair, she observed, even on his toes.

"You're hairy," she said.

"You're a tease," he said hoarsely.

She laughed, liking the sound of that.

Slowly, she traced her way back up his thighs and paused, admiring the view of his male flesh. It was so *forward*, this part of his body. The turgid length could not hide its primal nature. Under her gaze, it swelled even larger. She touched a tentative finger to the base of the purple-veined shaft. Instinctively, her other fingers joined the first, curling around the thick rod. She could barely contain him within her fist. She marveled at the contrast of textures, like an iron poker wrapped in satin. At the bulging tip, she discovered a slit. She watched, fascinated, as a bead of moisture oozed out.

She dabbed her fingertip in the dew and smeared it around.

Nicholas, who had been breathing heavily all the while, let out a groan. His cock spurted again. That had to mean she was doing something right. She rubbed the rosy head a little harder.

"Like this," Nicholas rasped, grasping her hand and wrapping her fingers around him. His eyes closed as he moved his hand with hers, teaching her to stroke his cock. She learned how much pressure he liked, what rhythm tore sounds from the back of his throat. Her own breathing escalated with the thrill of watching her fingers and his, intertwined, sliding in unison over his glistening flesh. Dreamily, she reached with her other hand to cup the plum-shaped sac below, finding it heavy and surprisingly supple.

His hand stilled on hers.

"Enough." He had her beneath him in a second, not an inch of air between them. The head of his sex dipped into her passage.

"Did I pass the first lesson, sir?" Her tone was a bit smug. She could not help herself. It was not every day that she drove her husband insane with passion.

"With flying colors," he assured her.

He pushed a little deeper. She gasped at the hot, thick stretch.

"And now for the second lesson," he said.

"Wh-what second lesson?" She could hardly think with the liquid heat bubbling between her legs. He impelled himself deeper, and she gasped again.

"The lesson," he murmured in her ear, "in which naughty schoolgirls receive their just deserts."

The conversation quite halted after that.

The time for serious conversation came afterward, when Helena and Nicholas retired to her bedchamber. After sharing a breakfast tray brought in by a beaming Bessie, Helena snuggled into her husband's embrace and absorbed the rest of his tale. In halting tones, he told her about the mysterious blackmail notes. The threats of the man who'd shot at him in St. Giles. The discovery that a dock worker named Isaac Bragg had been behind all of it and now Bragg was dead.

"A part of me still cannot believe that Bragg was the mastermind behind these crimes," Nicholas said. "He had the brawn for certain, but the brains? The man seemed a bit simple, if you ask me. Yet the evidence was all there in the flash house."

Frowning, Helena asked, "But how did Bragg learn about your past? From what you have said, Grimes died over sixteen years ago. Surely your secret must have died with him."

"I have asked myself the same thing," Nicholas admitted. "In truth, I can think of no answer save one. Besides me and Grimes, only one person witnessed what transpired that night."

Realization dawned. "The boy," she breathed. "He's still alive."

Nicholas expelled a breath. "We do not know that. He might have survived that night, living only long enough to tell someone what he saw. It might have become a rumor, a piece of gossip that somehow reached Bragg's ears years later. As for the boy ...

anything could have happened to him. The odds are not favorable for an orphan alone in the stews," he finished grimly.

"But if he *is* still living, what would you do?" Helena asked.

She felt his muscles bunch beneath his dressing gown. "I would find him," Nicholas said quietly. "I would do whatever it took to make amends for what I did."

She wanted to tell him again that he was not at fault, but she knew words could do little to dissolve the guilt of a lifetime. Perhaps taking action would help. "Then why not begin investigations to find him or at least discover his fate?"

"I have thought about it." Nicholas' charcoal eyes were troubled. "For so long, I have been driven by fear, striving to outrun the past. Never once did I look back. To stop now and go in the other direction ... the risks are great, Helena. I don't know who I'd trust to look into the matter."

"Mr. Kent, perhaps? He seems a decent man," Helena said thoughtfully. "And you wouldn't have to tell him everything, would you? Just that you are looking for a boy you once knew in Grimes' employ. You could say the business with Bragg made you wonder what had happened to him, which is no more than the truth."

"I will think on it." His arms tightened around her, and after a pause, he said gruffly, "And you would support me, no matter the outcome?"

"I will love and support you no matter what," she vowed and leaned up to kiss him.

The next few days passed in a blur of happiness the likes of which Helena had never known. By night, Nicholas continued to instruct her in the art of passion. He proved a most dedicated tutor, teaching her about her body as well as his own. She had not known that such variety existed with lovemaking. It was as if Nicholas presented her with a buffet of delights, and she could not prefer one above another.

Some nights he loved her tenderly, slowly, prolonging pleasure until her body exploded at the gentlest touch. Other nights, he showed her a rougher sort of loving. The rawness of his needs elicited a corresponding wildness in her. At first, she tried to hide her passion, but he saw through her blushes and punished her with such sublime wickedness that she gave up all pretense of being anything but a complete wanton in his arms. He showed her that when he'd said she was perfect just as she was, he'd meant it.

If the nights were spent unraveling the mysteries of lovemaking, the days yielded further revelations. Helena had not expected much to change in their daily routines, given the demands of Nicholas' profession. Knowing what she now did about his past, she felt immense pride watching him go off to the warehouse, to the empire he had created through sheer force of determination and a will to succeed. She told herself she would be content to spend their evenings together, lingering over supper and talking into the wee hours of the morning. As it was, they would be in each other's company more than most fashionable couples, who might encounter each other once a week at a social affair.

Once again, Nicholas surprised her. He returned home earlier than expected most days, and on several occasions, eschewed work entirely to spend the day showing her sights around Town. He took her on drives through Hyde Park, where they picnicked on the banks of the Serpentine. They visited the British Museum and the Royal Academy, admiring exotic artifacts and exhibits by talented young painters. She reveled in Nicholas' attentions, absorbing his presence as a light-starved flower might the sun.

What was more, she was discovering hidden facets in her husband: the sly humor beneath his reserved countenance, the raw passion beneath his controlled façade. She loved that he seemed to laugh more in her presence. She loved that the powerful man who ran the docks by day shuddered in her arms at night, growled her name as he poured himself into her ...

Much as she craved his company, however, she could not allow her love to become an unwelcome distraction. She did not wish Nicholas to neglect his duties out of marital obligation. One morning, she ventured into his bedchamber to tell him so.

"So, you see," she said, perching on the bed as the valet put the finishing touch on Nicholas' cravat, "you need not fear I will be bored without your company. I have plenty of things with which to occupy my time."

Nicholas nodded, and the valet bowed and departed.

Her husband walked over to the bed. Her heart flipped at his handsomeness. Freshly shaved, smelling of sandalwood and soap, he was the most delicious man in the entire world.

And he is mine.

She could scarce believe it at times.

"Are you saying I interfere with your busy schedule, my dear?"

Mesmerized by the warm, teasing look in his eyes, she struggled to keep her mind on the purpose.

"No. That is, yes, I do have household matters to attend to, but more to the point, you are a busy man, Nicholas. You really need not feel obligated to escort me on errands and such. I can carry on well enough on my own."

"Ah. But perhaps I do not carry on half as well on *my* own."

He stood between her knees now, his thighs wedging her legs apart. Her palms dampened on the coverlet.

"You are teasing," she said. She attempted to scoot backward onto the bed, only to find he had trapped her by her skirts. "Nicholas, I am attempting to be serious. I know how much the company means to you. I would not have your life's work suffer out of a sense of misplaced duty."

"Duty, hmm?"

He was not listening to her, she was quite sure of it. He was too preoccupied nuzzling a spot beneath her right ear.

"Y-yes," she managed.

He licked her earlobe.

Sighing, she tilted her head to offer him more access and was instantly lost in the spell he cast over her senses. His hand captured hers, brought it to his arousal. She inhaled at the fierceness of him.

"Do you think this is duty, my love?" He pushed into her hand, and she felt a corresponding throbbing between her thighs. "Is this obligation? A misplaced sense, perhaps, of husbandly responsibility?"

"That is not what I meant," she said in a desperate bid to reason with him before her wits abandoned her entirely. "It is just that I know you must have many appointments, many people counting upon you ..."

"Mmm," he said.

He had unbuttoned his trousers; the satin-steel length of him burned against her fingers and evaporated the last iota of reason. Greed, pure and unadulterated, surged in its place. She made to sink backward into the mattress, but he stopped her. He kept her sitting on the edge of the bed as he tossed up her skirts and chemise. Instead of mounting atop, he cupped her hips and brought her closer. Her legs dangled, not quite touching the floor. She sat thus, splayed by his knees, open and vulnerable. Her pussy quivered and moistened.

As she watched, he ran a long finger up the crevice of her sex. He parted her curls, and his eyes darkened as he took in her womanly secrets. She whimpered at the decadence of his touch, groaning as he slowly, deliberately, slicked a path to her bud.

"Do you think," he said, his voice raspy and low, "there is anything of greater importance to me than you?"

She could not speak. Her hips arched upward, a silent plea. His eyes smoldered with smoke and flame as he obliged her, notching the head of his rod to her eager opening. In one swift thrust, he vanquished the emptiness. Her legs clenched around his thighs.

Her head fell back. There was no room for thought, for words, for anything save the devastating pleasure churning between them.

"Do you actually believe that anything could matter as much as you?" He withdrew and thrust again, to the rhythm of her cries. "As my desire for you, as my need to be with you, inside you, every waking moment?"

Still, she could not speak, so filled was she with his loving.

He lifted her hips and brought her down against him at the same time that he drove upward. Their bodies collided; the sound of panting, of skin meeting skin filled the room. Over and over, he penetrated her to the depths of her being. She was impaled fully upon his cock, suspended between bed and floor, with no purchase save the thickness of him holding her aloft. He was her fulcrum, the center of all sensation. Hands fisted in the bedclothes, she ground against him, every fiber straining with need of him. She began sobbing, the feelings too intense, too exquisite to be contained.

"Yes, my love." His tones were gravelly, harsh with his own need as he urged her on. "Reach for it. Take it, Helena. It is yours."

"I love you," she cried the moment before she shattered.

He followed, his shout of satisfaction mingling with hers.

A while later, she blinked drowsily. She lay on the bed, Nicholas beside her. He was still fully dressed, but his eyes were closed. He looked to be asleep. A good thing, as the man rested too little. Perhaps time away from work might prove good for him after all.

With a tender smile, she reached to brush back a wayward tuft of black hair.

His lips twitched. "Still fretting about my important appointments?"

Whatever am I do with this husband of mine?

"Oh, do be quiet and kiss me," she said.

He laughed and, rolling over, did just that.

Chapter Thirty

The following afternoon, Marianne came to call. Helena greeted her with an impulsive hug. She was much relieved to see her friend in usual spirits, looking ravishing in a walking dress styled *à la militaire*.

"Well, I suppose that answers my question about the state of your affairs," Marianne said dryly as she rearranged her epaulettes. "To think, I came to check in on you after hearing the latest *on-dit*."

Helena lifted her chin. "I do not care what they are saying." It was true—after a week spent in a dreamy cocoon of love and passion, she couldn't give a fig what the world thought. She had everything she wanted. "Jacoby deserved every wallop he received."

"I know he did, my dear." For once, the smile reached Marianne's eyes. "And so does the rest of the *ton*. The gossips have made you a heroine."

"Me? A heroine?" Helena asked, dumbstruck.

"Of the most romantic sort," Marianne confirmed as she seated herself and removed her gloves. "The innocent young wife who defends her lord with the dark past, *et cetera, et cetera*. They are calling Harteford a hero, too, for the brooding dignity he has shown while curs like Jacoby yapped at his heels. Mrs. Radcliffe may yet write a novel about the two of you."

Helena dropped onto the chair opposite. "I cannot believe it."

"It is the way of the *ton*," Marianne said with a philosophic shrug. "Once you care not what they think, they welcome you into the fold with adoring arms. Harteford is the Makeshift Marquess no longer. But tell me, dearest, you are happy, are you not?"

"I have never been better." Helena smiled and shook her head. "Nay, I never thought to be so happy."

"I take it matters with Harteford have been reconciled?"

"Yes."

"And you have told him everything?"

"Everything," Helena said with pride. "And you were right—he does not care that I am not a paragon. He loves me as I am."

Marianne smiled slowly. "Your husband is a wise man, my dear."

"A lucky one, at the very least."

At the sound of the deep, male voice, Helena spun around in her seat. Nicholas must have recently arrived home for his dark hair bore the mark of his hat and his cravat appeared ruffled by the wind. To someone who did not know him, he appeared somber, austere even. But she did know him, and the silver warmth in his eyes nigh stopped her breath.

"You are home early," Helena said.

Crossing the room, he bent to kiss her cheek. His lips lingered for the briefest instant. "Am I interrupting anything?"

"Not at all." Suppressing the urge to give him a proper welcome, one that would be decidedly *im*proper given the company, Helena murmured, "Marianne and I were just enjoying a bit of a chat."

"How nice to see you again, Lord Harteford," Marianne said.

Nicholas bowed over her extended hand. "The pleasure is all mine, Lady Draven." He slid his wife a devilish look. "And I understand you had something to do with that. Please accept my most sincere gratitude."

"None necessary, my lord," Marianne said approvingly, "for my friend's happiness is reward enough. And speaking of rewards, Helena, I saw Madame Rousseau this morning, and she wanted me to tell you your new gowns are ready. I had a glimpse of them—they are divine."

"I suppose I could go see Madame after tea." Helena tipped her head at her husband. "That is, if you don't mind?"

"Not at all. In fact, I will accompany you," Nicholas said.

"You are sure this is not a waste of your time?" Helena asked as the modiste led her to the mirrored platform.

"Not in the slightest," Nicholas replied. He took her hand and kissed it before settling into a chair. "In fact, I could not imagine a better use of my time."

Helena smiled at his chivalry.

She was not smiling several minutes later when the agenda behind her husband's visit became evident. Nicholas was voicing yet another suggestion regarding her new silk toile gown.

"*Six inches?*" Using her hand, she raised the imaginary neckline up to her throat. "You might as well dress me in a ... a nun's habit! It would ruin this gorgeous gown completely. Tell him so, Madame."

Madame Rousseau looked skeptically at Helena's reflection. "It would be a trifle, how do you say, *dow-dee*? I am certain my lord would not wish his lovely wife to be dressed in the manner of the country cousin."

"I wish to see my wish dressed. Period," Nicholas said.

"Ah." Madame Rousseau sent a placating look to Helena. "This is the prerogative of the husband, no?"

Helena clenched her teeth. Clearly, the modiste thought it

prudent not to cross swords with he who footed the bills. She, herself, had no such qualms.

"'Tis *my* prerogative not to resemble the veriest bumpkin," she said. "You shall leave the gown as it is, if you please, Madame."

"For God's sake, your breasts are falling out of the neckline," Nicholas snapped.

She spun to face him. "You did not complain of that in the drawing room last week!"

"I will not have you sharing your charms with the world." Nicholas' brows lowered, a portent of storms ahead.

Madame Rousseau intervened with a subtle cough. "*Alors*, I believe I comprehend the problem. My lady, she wishes to display her beauty to an advantage. My lord, he appreciates his wife's beauty but perhaps wishes more of it might be kept to his own private enjoyment. This is true, yes?"

"That about captures it," Nicholas said. "I will not have my wife, the Marchioness of Harteford, dressed like a common—"

"Yes, yes, my lord, I do believe I understand," Madame Rousseau interjected, but Nicholas' gaze remained steady on Helena's.

"You are mine, and I will not allow what is mine to be bandied about like cheap inventory."

Helena's jaw dropped. For a moment, red spots danced before her eyes.

"Of all the arrogant, high-handed, *insulting* ..."

"Call me what you will, but you belong to me," her husband said. "Do not forget that."

"I am *not* a piece of ... of inventory, yours or otherwise!"

"Please, my lady, my lord, if I may suggest a compromise?"

Helena's rapid breaths strained her bodice as she focused on the modiste. She had nearly forgotten the woman's presence. She forced herself to count to ten. "Yes, well, what is it?"

"Perhaps a small, how do you say, *negotiation* might be in order?"

A tense silence greeted the dressmaker's suggestion. Nicholas sat brooding in the chair. Helena raised her brows, and Madame Rousseau sighed, her eyes darting between her clients. She turned Helena to face the mirror again.

"The gown, it would be a small matter to elevate the neckline, say three inches?"

"It is not nearly enough," Nicholas said.

"It is too much," Helena said at the same time.

Madame Rousseau sighed again. "The integrity of the gown, it will be maintained. Lady Harteford, you will be *très fashionable*. This you have on the highest authority—my own. Look again, if you please."

Helena looked into the glass. The modiste's fingers drifted a fraction upward. Although reluctant, she was forced to admit that Madame Rousseau had a point. The alteration was not so great. Truth be told, her breasts *were* a trifle exposed; having those inches of added protection would allay her worries about potential malfunctions of the bodice. More to the point, it would not damage her principles overly to agree to such a change. Perhaps it might even teach her bull-headed husband a thing or two about compromise.

She gave a stiff nod.

"It is not enough," Nicholas repeated.

Helena crossed her arms.

"Ah, but my lord, the gown will now display your lady's charms most modestly," Madame said in tones as smooth as morning chocolate. "Especially when compared to what she will wear for your private *tête- à-têtes*."

"I beg your pardon?" Helena said, frowning.

Madame Rousseau crossed over to a work table piled high with bolts of cloth. She returned with a roll of black material. With obvious care, she unrolled a length and held it up for Nicholas' inspection.

Helena blinked. The material was not cloth at all but lace.

Black lace so diaphanous she could see the considering expression crossing her husband's face.

"This is the finest lace from Belgium, my lord," Madame Rousseau murmured. "A clever needle it takes to create magic with it, but of that I am possessed. I envision a negligee. Something simple, you understand, unfettered, for your wife to wear during quiet evenings at home. And stockings to match, of course."

Nicholas cleared his throat. "Stockings, you say?"

"Of the sheerest black silk," Madame responded. "And, if I may suggest, satin garters, also black, ornamented with, shall we say, bows of scarlet ribbon?"

"This is outrageous," Helena muttered.

Nicholas shifted his gaze to her. The silver gleam set her stomach aflutter.

"By all means, then, let us negotiate," he said.

Nodding to an acquaintance, Nicholas circulated the crowded room in search of his wife. He smiled with satisfaction when he spotted her standing in a small circle. She wore one of her new gowns, an elegant burgundy garment with a demure ruffle along the neckline. He still thought her breasts enticed too much; when she spoke, he noticed the gentlemen around her paid more attention to her bosom than her words. Yet compared to the other ladies present, he had to admit she cut a modest figure. At least, on the surface.

He alone knew what she wore beneath.

Those delightful undergarments, compliments of Madame Rousseau, had delayed their arrival to the salon by over an hour.

Negotiation, he was discovering, had its benefits.

"Lord Harteford, well met. How's the head?"

He turned at the sound of the thick Scottish brogue.

"Dr. Farraday." He shook hands with the physician. "I did not expect to see you here."

"I might say the same for you. Thought you weren't much for society affairs."

"I'm not, usually. My wife favors this particular salon," Nicholas said.

"Say no more, lad. 'Tis a wise man who knows when to retreat." Dr. Farraday bestowed upon him a sympathetic look. "Now, myself, I come from time to time to hear the lectures. The Misses Berry always invite the cream of the crop of learned minds. Such a wide variety of topics are presented, and most of them quite scintillating. What made you of tonight's discussion concerning the habits of native birds?"

"We missed it, I'm afraid."

The doctor's grey brows drew together. "I am sorry for you, lad. 'Tis a pity to miss so fascinating a subject."

To be honest, Nicholas did not feel so sorry for himself. He'd wager the bank that he'd enjoyed himself better than the poor sods stuck here listening to the mating calls of pheasants. After all, he'd been occupied with mating behavior of his own. Heat flared at the memory of a certain corset, red as cherries, the way it had framed his wife's ...

"Though I am but an amateur naturalist," Dr. Farraday said, "you must allow me to elucidate some facts for you."

Nicholas made a noncommittal sound, but it was too late; Dr. Farraday had launched into a recitation of the lecture. Nodding politely, Nicholas let his mind wander over the past weeks with Helena. For the first time in memory, he was experiencing a buoyant lightness of being. As if the stones he had hefted all his life had dropped magically from his shoulders. Aye, joy. Not just from the lovemaking, either. The talking, the laughter, the companionship of body and mind—he had not thought such closeness with another human being possible. At times, he fancied he and Helena shared the fabric of a single soul.

"... to be distinguished from the brown grouse, which has

flecks rather than stripes of white ..."

At other times, fear would creep up on him. He could not stop the irrational worries that would suddenly cloud his mind. What if something were to happen to Helena? What if she should change her mind, see him for what he was? Never before had he felt a need for another the way he did for her—as if his happiness, his very life, depended upon her love and affection. He felt consumed by possessiveness and a primal need to bind her to him in every manner possible. As a consequence, he found himself acting the role of the overbearing husband, scrutinizing her dress and her companions, hovering over her like a hawk. Sighing, he could only imagine what she thought of his behavior.

"I can see your sympathy for the hatchlings," Dr. Farraday continued. "Yet one must also consider the design of nature, for an offspring to one is sustenance for another ..."

Overall, Nicholas thought, Helena had tolerated him with admirable patience. He best not press his luck concerning her décolletage this evening.

"Harteford, there you are." Helena came up beside him. Her fingers brushed his upper arm. Beneath the jacket, his muscles leapt in response. Her touch stirred him as no other's had or ever would.

"My love," he said. "You remember Dr. Farraday."

"Yes, of course. Good evening, sir."

"A pleasure, my lady." The physician bowed, a stiff, military movement.

"How kind of you to say so," Helena said. "I am afraid I was rather overwrought at our last meeting."

"No need to explain, my lady," Dr. Farraday said. "Circumstances being such as they were."

"Such as they were," Helena agreed. "Yet I do apologize for any unseemly behavior on my part. My husband could not have been in more capable hands."

Dr. Farraday's posture relaxed. "Thank you, my lady. I, too, am glad to see Lord Harteford's full recovery."

"And now you must allow me to introduce you both to my dear friends, the Misses Haversham," Helena said.

As his wife made the introductions, Nicholas' gaze returned subtly to her neckline. He felt his blood begin to simmer all over again. He had a mind to get his wife alone in the not-too- distant future. Alone and naked.

"Harteford, you must defend me. I am outnumbered."

The doctor's desperate voice dragged his focus back to the conversation. Standing between the Havershams, Dr. Farraday looked like a tiger cornered by kittens.

"There is no defense for your statement, sirrah," Miss Lavinia Haversham said. She rapped the physician on the knuckles with her fan. Her eyes blazed in her time-worn face. "A female ring-necked pheasant is as capable of protecting her chicks as the male is! More so, I daresay. Am I not right, Sister?"

The other Miss Haversham gave a vigorous nod.

"I meant only to assert that the male is larger in size and therefore ..."

"What has size got to do with anything?" Miss Lavinia demanded.

A choked sound escaped Dr. Farraday.

Nicholas stifled a laugh. *Out of the mouths of spinsters ...*

An elbow wedged against his ribs.

"You are absolutely right, Miss Haversham," Helena said, frowning at him. "'Tis the size of the intellect, not the brute, that matters."

"Exactly my point, Lady Harteford," Miss Lavinia said.

Nicholas thought that if Miss Haversham became any more indignant, the smoke rising from her steely curls might blast her lace cap clear and away. Farraday might have been of a similar mind, for the doctor wisely stepped beyond the range of her gesticulating fan.

"The mother pheasant uses her *sense* to defeat the predator,"

Miss Lavinia persevered. "Why, what could be cleverer, more effective, than faking a broken wing to detract from the brood nearby?"

The moment her words pierced Nicholas' consciousness, all traces of humor vanished.

Bloody hell.

The truth—had it been staring him in the face all along?

Three nights later, Nicholas rubbed the back of his neck and stood, stretching his cramped muscles. The window reflected pure darkness; not even the barges were visible, though he felt their omnipresence beneath the layers of night and fog. Removing the watch fob from his waistcoat, he traced his thumb over the filigreed cover. He was inordinately proud of this new ornament. A fine piece it was, made finer by the engraving inside.

To my husband, with love.

The tiny golden arms winked in the lamplight and indicated the time as half past seven. He had been so absorbed in his perusal of Kent's notes that he had not noticed the lateness of the hour. After he had shared his new theory concerning the warehouse thefts with Kent, the latter had made good on his reputation as a relentless pursuer of justice.

In the past two days, the inspector had personally interviewed all the merchants of the West India Dock and quite a few workers as well. He had taken copious notes, for a single detail might lead to the suspect. Nicholas himself had spent the bulk of the day reviewing Kent's organized files. Captured somewhere within the neat rows of ink was the key to a mystery—he could feel it in his bones.

A scuffling noise outside the office had Nicholas tensing. He jerked around as the door creaked open, his gaze flashing to the bottom desk drawer where he stored his pistol. His hand shot to the brass pull.

"Lord Harteford! Begging your pardon, I did not think you were still here."

Nicholas exhaled and straightened, his hand falling to the side. "Quite alright, Jibotts. You gave me a start that is all. Why are you not yet home?"

"Finishing up on the Rigby account, my lord," Jibotts said, mopping at his brow with the usual tattered handkerchief. Even in the golden glow, the steward's face appeared shiny. "The shipment is ready for delivering when Lord Rigby's man of business presents us with payment."

"Excellent work as usual, Jibotts."

"Thank you. Is there anything else I can do before I depart?"

"Just lock the doors behind you. I will see myself out."

"Very good, my lord. Good night."

After Jibotts departed, Nicholas gave a rueful shake of the head. He was abraded by unease and too edgy by far. He shuffled the papers on his desk, debating between locking the files in the cabinet and taking them home. Perhaps he could mull over the details of the case with Helena tonight. He'd shared with her his hunch that Bragg had not been the only villain involved. It was no doubt unusual to share so much with one's wife, but his marriage was not proving the usual sort. Unlike most men of his acquaintance, he enjoyed conversing with his spouse. Helena, he was learning, had a sharp mind—and a sharp tongue, too, if one crossed her.

Of course, he had ways of quelling that organ of hers, of putting it to a different use altogether. Heat unfurled in his belly. His wife had not been boasting when she professed herself an able student. In her nightly lessons, she was proving an exceptional protégée indeed. He crossed the room to the cabinet and locked the papers inside. Work would wait until the morrow.

Behind him, the door creaked again.

"Still here, Jibotts?"

The answering laugh ran down his spine like an icy hand.

Chapter Thirty-One

At the rumble of the man's voice, Helena's hands stilled on the ivory keys. Relief washed through her. For the past hour, she'd been fretting over Nicholas' unusually late return from the docks. It hadn't helped that last night she had been plagued by uncertain dreams, triggered undoubtedly by the discussion with Nicholas about mysterious villains and possible suspects. She'd begged him not to go to work today, but he'd chuckled and told her there was nothing to worry about. He and Mr. Kent were on the alert. Yet traces of tension had trailed her every movement, her every thought today.

It was just a dream. You see, Nicholas is home now. All is well.

"She's my gel, I tell you. I don't need an appointment!"

The door to the drawing room veered on its hinges, coming to a thunderous stop against the wall. The paintings trembled in their gilt frames. Startled, Helena found herself confronted by her sire's bristling countenance.

"Papa! Wh-what are you doing here?"

"Kindly inform your servant that the Earl of Northgate need not be announced to his own daughter!"

Helena gave a slight and apologetic nod to Crikstaff, who

stood guard in the doorway. The butler departed, but not without a suspicious glance backward.

"You need to keep your servants in better hand," Northgate muttered as Helena came to kiss him. "Nobody knows their place these days. The damned frogs caused this mess. Hell of a nuisance, this revolutionary business. Now the tenants are clamoring for this and that, calling it their *right*. Next thing you know, they'll be demanding we heat their homes and school their brats."

Wisely, Helena held her tongue.

"Come, Papa," she said instead. "Let me pour some tea while you share the purpose of your visit ..." A sudden realization struck her. Sweet heavens, he hadn't come to fetch her, had he? "Papa, you did receive my second letter, telling you I was no longer planning to come to Hampshire—"

"Course I got it." Snorting, the earl plopped down on the settee, straining the buttons on his crimson and maize checked waistcoat as he did so. "Damn good thing too. Your request came at a deuced inconvenient time, gel. In the middle of a hunting party, wasn't I?"

"Yes, well, I am glad it all worked out—"

"Not sure it has, my girl, and that's the truth." Northgate gulped his tea and winced. "Haven't you anything stronger?"

"Of course, Papa." Helena went to fetch a glass of whiskey. She sat beside her father, who downed the spirits immediately. He smacked his lips in appreciation.

"The whoreson keeps a good cellar, I'll give him that," he said.

"Please do not refer to Nicholas in that manner," Helena said, frowning.

"Why not? His mother was little more than a pretty piece. You are too good for him by far. I received the short end of the bargain, Helena, and don't think I haven't my regrets."

Helena felt the fraying edge of temper. "Papa, please, I cannot allow you to insult my husband in his own home. Nicholas is the kindest, most generous of husbands, and he is your son-in-law.

Cannot you find it in your heart to like him? If for no other reason than for my sake?"

"Generous, bah!" Northgate slammed his glass down on the rosewood coffee table. His face turned an apoplectic red, and his whiskers quivered with rage. "That bastard is as miserly as they come. Probably counting his gold as we speak, and me left out in the cold. Well, I won't have it, I tell you. No one cuts off the Earl of Northgate, no one!"

"Papa, what are you talking about? Are ... are you in some sort of trouble ...?"

"Dammit, gel, what kind of question is that? Deuced impudent, if you ask me." Scowling, Northgate reached for the biscuit box. The silver lid squeaked on its hinges as the earl rummaged through the contents and fished out the largest biscuit. "Should have never let you marry beneath you—his inferior breeding has tainted you already."

Helena closed her eyes and counted backward from ten.

"Papa," she said in a firm voice, "is this visit about money?"

"By Jove, Helena, where's your delicacy? Your mother would expire on the spot to hear you speak in so common a manner." As he spoke, crumbs scattered on his beard. His fingers drummed on his knee. Her father was not, Helena noticed, wearing his favorite signet ring. Nor did a jeweled stick pin reside in his cravat. Nor did the usual assorted jangle of gold fobs decorate his person.

Familiar tell-tale signs, all of them. Had she not been so taken aback by his sudden appearance, she would have noticed sooner.

"I should not bring this topic up myself, you understand, but since you have mentioned it ..."

"Yes, Papa?" But already she knew the answer.

"I have been short of the ready lately. Just a temporary setback, of course," her father added quickly. "The tenants have been deuced slow on paying the rents. And I've had a bit of a bad run on investments—speculations didn't come up as I expected. Nothing to do about it, of course."

"I see."

"Wouldn't want to have to cut back on the household expenses —keep your mother in her accustomed manner and all that."

"How much?" Helena asked quietly.

"Just a few hundred pounds—some blunt to float me over until the next ship comes in." Her father laughed, an awkward, braying sound. "Metaphorically speaking. Wouldn't have anything to do with trade myself, of course."

"A few hundred pounds?" Helena said, aghast. "Papa, I do not have such funds."

"Didn't I just hear you call Harteford the kindest, most *generous* of husbands? Ask him for it. The man's got more gold than Croesus."

"I expect Nicholas to be home at any moment. Perhaps we might discuss this situation together, the three of us," Helena said, even as her stomach flipped at the notion.

"Are you mad, gel? Haven't you been listening?" Northgate roared. "Your blasted husband is the cause of this whole mess. I can't ask him for the money!"

"What do you mean *Nicholas* is the cause ...?"

"The skinflint cut off my allowance! Not a shilling he said, if he caught me at the cards, and damned if the bastard didn't hold true to his word." Her father was breathing heavily now, so much so that despite her rising frustration, Helena placed a hand on his shoulder. He shook her off. "Now he's got word around that my vowels aren't worth ashes—no one will put me up, not even for a single bloody round."

"Papa, Nicholas is trying to help you," Helena said.

"Help me? The bastard has ruined me!"

"You have ruined yourself." The truth, when spoken, lifted a weight from her chest. "You cannot blame Nicholas for your own wrongdoing."

"*Wrongdoing*? How dare you!" Her father rose above her, his fist raised. For a moment, she thought he meant to strike her. He had not done so in the past, but never before had she the courage to oppose him.

She sat up very straight, her eyes holding his. "Nicholas has the right of it. I will not interfere with my husband's wishes."

Her father's fist came slapping down into his palm. Hazel eyes, so like her own, blazed at her. "By God, what kind of daughter are you? Thomas would have never allowed me to be treated this way. If your brother was alive, he would call out your bastard merchant and give you a beating for good measure. Thomas would—"

"Thomas is dead and has been these years past," Helena said. "There is no changing that, or the fact that you are a degenerate gambler."

"Why you insolent—"

"What is more, I am glad Thomas did not live to see what his father has become." A tear escaped, but Helena held her voice firm. "You need help, Papa, and I am glad to give it, but not in the form of money. Neither I, nor my husband, will give you so much as a farthing if it is to buy your passage to perdition."

Her father stared at her as if he had never seen her before.

Perhaps he never had.

"You are dead to me, do you hear? *Dead*!"

When he slammed the door, the walls vibrated with the finality of his words.

Helena remained sitting for a long time.

So deep in thought was she that she was startled by Crikstaff's voice. "Is everything alright, my lady? Anything I can bring you—warmed milk, perhaps?"

"No, thank you." She wiped away the last of her tears. "Have we heard from Lord Harteford?"

"No, my lady."

Disquiet flooded her. Something was not right. Nicholas ought to have been home almost two hours ago, and he always sent word when he was to arrive late. "Have the carriage readied," she said. "I wish to leave immediately."

"Of course. Shall I inform the groom of your destination?"

"I wish to go to the docks. To Lord Harteford's office."

"Now? At this hour? But my lady—"

"See that it is done, Crikstaff. That is all."

Gathering her things, she prayed her intuition was wrong.

As the carriage came to a stop, Helena pushed back the curtain. In the darkness, she could make out the outline of the warehouse. The building was plain-faced, with no ornament whatsoever. The door bordered the street and looked of solid wood, with no decoration save a slot for looking out. The rectangular structure stood three stories high, a slumbering beast resting on a street dotted with similar creatures marked for function rather than fashion.

The door to the carriage opened to reveal the groom's tense face.

"We're here, milady, and I can't but say again as 'ow I 'ave a bad feelin' about this. 'Is lordship's like as not to flay me alive for bringin' you 'ere."

"Never you mind, Will. It's my orders that are to be obeyed in this instance; I will take full responsibility for the outcome."

"Master'll still 'ave my 'ide," the groom predicted with dour certainty. "Dangerous place, the docks at night. Full o' cutthroats an' thieves. And it's too quiet by far—gives me the chills."

All the talk of criminals fed into her unease and resurrected the anxiety of her dream.

"You are, ahem, prepared, Will, for any eventuality?"

"O' course I am. What do you take me fer?" The groom patted the pocket of his caped greatcoat before letting down the steps. "I'm always prepared."

"Excellent. Though I am sure there will be no need for it."

But just in case, it occurred to Helena that it might be wise to secure her own instrument of protection. If only she had thought of it sooner. On impulse, she flipped up the cushions on the seat opposite, where her husband had once shown her a hidden compartment. She lifted the wooden door, hoping for a pistol or a blade. Nothing. With a sigh, she rearranged the cushions. As she did so, her fingers encountered a sharp edge.

The Wollstonecraft volume. She had meant to return it to Miss Lavinia at the salon this week but had forgotten it in the carriage. Nicholas' words suddenly floated into her head. *A bludger ... you take a piece of cloth ... wrap it around whatever can do a man injury.* She hefted the book in her hands; it was a solid weight. Stuffing it into her reticule, she alighted and followed the groom to the front door.

"Door's probably locked," Will said. "There's no light about the place."

He twisted the knob.

The door swung open.

"Can't say as 'ow I like this," the groom said again, this time in a whisper. "Best be following close behind, milady."

Helena did as the groom instructed, staying behind him as he scouted the seemingly infinite darkness. As her eyes adjusted, she began to discern mountainous shapes, like behemoths from a mystical land. Her pulse raced.

No need for a fit of the vapors. It is just the inventory. Just crates full of the tea and coffee you drink every day. Imagine it in the pretty yellow pot, the one with the cornflowers around the rim—

Was it her imagination, or was there movement in the shadows?

She felt Will's hand on her arm, urging her down toward the ground. She crouched beside him, her back against a wall of boxes.

"I think I see the stairs, milady, up to the first floor. Probably where we'll find the master, if 'e's 'ere." She could not see the expression on Will's face, but the grimness was evident in his hushed tones. "I would feel a sight better if you was to wait fer me 'ere. Master might be needin' help, and I can't be o' use with you hangin' on me coattails, beggin' your pardon."

At the thought of Nicholas in danger, her heart clenched.

"Yes, go. I will stay here," she whispered back.

"Don't move from this 'ere spot, milady, 'til I tells you it's safe to come out."

Helena watched as the groom crept stealthily forward, melting into the darkness. Alone, she huddled against the crates. Time passed in sluggish beats, minutes or hours she could not be certain. The stillness became deafening. Every rustle, every creak increased her vigilance until she feared bursting out of her very skin. Her eyes flicked everywhere, her muscles trembled with anticipation. Something scurried over her skirts, and she jumped, stuffing her fist in her mouth to stifle the scream.

It was then that she heard it.

At first, she thought she had imagined the faint sound. But, no, there it was again. A thumping noise, from somewhere above stairs.

A shot rang, shrill and piercing.

She did not know that she had moved until she found herself racing up the steps.

Chapter Thirty-Two

"Did you get him?"

"Aye. Bleedin' like a stuck pig, 'e is." The man nudged the fallen figure with a dirt-crusted boot. "You think there's more of 'em, sir?"

"Likely so, Bertie. I'd wager he's one of Kent's men, so the rest are not far behind. Best we finish up here quickly. Tie up the body and bring it downstairs. We'll toss him to the tides before we leave."

"Yes, sir."

With impotent rage, Nicholas watched as the man called Bertie trussed the fallen figure. William—for he was sure it was his groom William—moaned as his arms and legs were bound. Nicholas strained forward; ropes bit into his wrists and ankles, keeping him prisoner in the chair. He looked on helplessly as Bertie dragged the groom out of the room. A crimson trail marked his departure.

"No use struggling, Lord Harteford," James Gordon said, advancing upon him in an agile stride. His blue eyes danced with menacing mirth. "You can't move any more than that poor sod."

"Release him, Gordon. It's me you want, not him."

"True, but we can't have loose ends trailing about." Gordon

stopped a foot away, so close that Nicholas could see the freckles on the younger man's skin. But there was not a trace of youthful innocence on that smooth face now. No stammer in the confident drawl. Gordon's red hair gleamed in the lamp light, as did the pistol he held in his hands. "You have caused me quite a bit of trouble, my lord."

"I would cause you a great deal more," Nicholas growled.

Gordon laughed, a high boyish sound. "I don't think so. But before I put an end to your interfering ways, you must satisfy my curiosity: how did you know it was me who masterminded the thefts?"

Keep him talking. Buy yourself time. Kent will pick up the trail and come.

"I didn't, at first. I thought it was Bragg like everyone else." Nicholas saw the smugness enter Gordon's smile and added, "A clever ploy on your part."

"Yes," Gordon said, "it was clever. To think, I was afraid the device was too transparent. After all, *Isaac Bragg* a criminal genius? My step-brother hadn't the brains to organize a party at the tavern, let alone the systematic robbing of every merchant on the dock."

"So you used him. He was your stool pigeon."

"My insurance, yes, should my plans be uncovered. Isaac was very good at following orders. At stirring up trouble with the workers. At appearing a suspicious, trouble-making sort. The little act worked quite well at the other warehouses. I used other men, of course, not just Isaac."

"You used different aliases, different disguises," Nicholas said, "so no one would recognize you from one company to the next. Once you infiltrated a warehouse, you imported your own men, had them hired on your recommendation. And the stealing started, only so little at a time that it would take months to uncover the losses. By that time, you had moved on. Faked an illness or, in this case, your own death."

"I am impressed," Gordon said. "Tell me, how did you know it was me?"

"There was no crutch next to your supposed corpse. Why would a crippled man be without his walking stick?" Nicholas paused. He thought he saw a movement from the door, a flicker of a shadow. Or was it just a trick of the light? He needed to stall Gordon. "When I realized this, I had the body exhumed and re-examined by the doctor. Even with the decay, it was obvious the limbs were equally developed on both sides. There was no evidence whatsoever of a limp."

"Very good indeed." Gordon's white teeth gleamed in appreciation. "You alerted Kent to this fact, and he began to question all the merchants along the dock about an employee with an affliction of some kind."

"Exactly. And there emerged the pattern—always a young man, timid, self-effacing, with a physical disfigurement: a blinded eye, a lame arm, a limp. Someone you felt pity for, whom you would never suspect capable of nefarious deeds."

"So you have flushed me out," Gordon said. "But, to be fair, I know a bit about you, too. Remember my words to you that night in St. Giles?"

Nicholas felt an icy twist in his gut. "It was you who shot me that night."

"Isaac, the great fool, led you straight to my quarters. Another reason he deserved to die." Gordon's eyes narrowed. "I considered killing you that night, but you're worth more to me alive than dead. After all, it's not every nob who's born in the gutter and ends up a marquess, is it?" Gordon cocked his head. "How much are your secrets worth to you, my lord?"

Keep him distracted. Let him talk. "How did you find out about Grimes?"

"The fact that you stabbed him in the heart, you mean?" Gordon's teeth flashed again. "Let's just say I have it from a reliable source. But to be certain, I sent those little notes to gauge your reaction. To see if the Marquess of Harteford could be shaken up, if he truly had something to hide. And I must say, my lord, my test was quite effective: for anyone who knew to look, you wore your guilt as obviously as a priest wears his collar. I knew then that my information was true."

"What do you want, Gordon?" Nicholas demanded. "Money?"

The other man rolled his eyes. "But of course. It's always about money. The question is how much." He wagged his pistol. "How much would it be worth for a marquess to keep his ignoble past a secret?"

"I'd go to jail for murder before I'd hand a farthing over to you," Nicholas snarled.

For some reason, this made Gordon smile. "Ah, but there are things worse than murder, are there not, my lord? Let me illustrate with a little tale. We all had our heroes growing up, and Benjamin Grimes happened to be one of mine. He was a legend among the flash house crowd. Cleaned out half of London—and I don't mean their chimneys. A master thief he was, known for his love of violence, gin, and, ah yes, one unfortunate vice." Gordon shook his head with mock regret. "Well, even the great Achilles had his weakness. Who is to judge that for Grimes it was young boys?"

Nicholas felt his stomach give a greasy lunge.

Don't let him get to you. Stay focused. Calm.

"It was said Grimes enjoyed a game of bury the bone." Gordon peered into his face; Nicholas cursed the betraying trickle of sweat that slid down his forehead. "How many times did he play it with you, my lord? Or make you play it with the other boys?"

It's over. Grimes can't hurt you.

"Did you come to beg for it, like a dog that will do anything for a few scraps from the table?"

"Goddamn you!" With mindless rage, Nicholas flung himself at Gordon. He toppled to the floor, unbalanced by the chair he'd forgotten he was bound to. The side of his head slammed against the wooden boards. Before he could regain his senses, a boot crushed into his jaw, pinning him to the ground. He welcomed the pain, the rusty-sweet surge inside his mouth. It alerted him, brought him back to the present.

"Unwise, my lord." Gordon ground his boot, and black dots danced before Nicholas' eyes. "I caution you against further retaliation. It will get you nowhere."

Gordon was right. Nicholas needed to regroup. Think.

The boot lifted. "From this little show, I have obviously hit a nerve. Ergo, my silence on the matter of your relations with Grimes should fetch a pretty price. Unless you want it bandied about London that you were buggered by the man?"

You were a child, Nicholas. You are not to blame. Like a beacon, Helena's words flashed in his mind. *You are the finest man I have ever known.* He saw her sweet smile, the one that lit all the corners of his soul. He felt the darkness retreating, banished by the golden fire of her eyes. *The only man I could ever love.*

His breathing steadied. His strength returned.

Gordon's voice came from above him. "As time is of essence, we will dispense with the formalities. You have a choice before you, my lord, so listen carefully. You may live a hero ... or die a bastard who whored for his bread and murdered his master."

"The price?" Nicholas said evenly.

"Ten thousand pounds, my lord. A pittance against your estate, but I am not a greedy man. We will leave together this night, upon the barge I keep docked nearby. On the morrow, you will issue me a bank note. Once the funds are in my pocket, I will release you. You may tell one and all that you attempted to apprehend me but were overcome by villainous means. You will be made a hero for your brave efforts."

Not bloody likely. I'll be floating face-down in the Thames the moment you get your money.

"If I refuse?" Nicholas asked.

The boot descended out of nowhere, slamming Nicholas' head back to the ground. His vision splintered into bright shards.

"You will die tonight, slowly and with a great deal of pain. Tomorrow, a story will be printed in all the papers. It will fuel drawing room gossip for decades to come. Your lovely marchioness will not be able to show her face again. Why, the shame of it might kill her on the spot. That is, if something else doesn't get to her first."

Fury exploded, clearing Nicholas' head. He thrashed with renewed strength. "Leave her out of this, you bastard! She has nothing—"

He gagged as a pistol jammed into his windpipe. The metal barrel bored deeper; he could feel the edge of it cutting into his skin. Lungs burning, he struggled for air, wheezing when the pressure was suddenly released.

Gordon smiled down at him.

"So, my lord, which will it be? Life or a slow, painful death?"

Chapter Thirty-Three

Calmness settled over Helena as she watched the man called Gordon cut the ropes loose. Nicholas stood, wobbling a little as his hands remained bound behind his back. She saw the trickle of blood on her husband's temple, and her hands tightened around her weapon. Her heart beat in steadfast rhythm as she readied herself in the shadows beside the doorway. Strangely enough, her earlier fear had vanished the moment she'd witnessed Will being dragged through the hallway. Upon reaching the first floor, she'd hidden herself into one of the offices, flattening herself against the wall at the sound of voices. From her vantage point, she had seen a hulking brute of a man pass by, tugging a length of rope behind him and Will ...

She would not weaken now, for his sake. For Nicholas. For all of them. Gordon's man might return at any moment, and she had to act while there was yet an advantage. Footsteps sounded within the office; she pressed herself more tightly to the wall. Nicholas would emerge first, if Gordon meant to have a pistol pointed at him. The footfalls grew closer, the floor boards vibrating beneath her feet. She held her reticule-bludger over her head.

Nicholas stepped into the hallway. She had no time to see his [illegible] Gordon followed next. She swung her reticule with [illegible] There was a shout as her weapon connected, not [illegible]p of Gordon's head as she'd planned, but with his arm. [illegible]ol skidded onto the floor and into the shadows. Gordon appeared stunned but unharmed. For a moment, all seemed to be happening in slowed time. She tried to move but found her feet turned to stone. In the next instant, everything roared to life. Gordon fell upon her, his hands closing over her throat.

"You little bitch," he hissed.

She clawed at his hands, but he held firm, choking her of air. Her vision clouded, her arms weakening in their struggle. She felt herself falling into lightness ... but when she landed, it was with painful impact against the floor. Gasping for breath, she came to her knees in time to see Nicholas, arms still bound, charging into Gordon like an enraged bull. The two men bounced off the walls of the corridor and crashed through the doorway into the office. She tried to follow but tripped over something. The book—it must have escaped from her reticule. Hauling herself off the floor, she scooped it up and raced into the office.

She stopped short at the sight of overturned chairs and scattered papers. The men were in the center of the room, circling each other. Nicholas, she saw, had a cut above his right eye, which was beginning to swell purple as a grape. Though his arms were immobilized, his stance was aggressive, ferocious even. Gordon gestured at her husband with his fists, a cocky grin on his face.

She swallowed when she saw the glint of a blade in the villain's hand.

How dare he take such unscrupulous advantage!

She let the book fly from her hands. The heavy volume sailed through the air just as Gordon began to advance upon Nicholas. As if on instinct, Gordon turned his head. A look of surprise flashed across his face. But it was too late. The leather corner caught him in the forehead; with a grunt, he lost his balance, stumbling backward. Nicholas pounced upon him immediately, kicking out at the other man's arm. The knife arced through the air and clattered out of sight. Gordon cursed as he warded off Nicholas' barrage of kicks and body blows. Helena bit her lip; how long could Nicholas persist at such a disadvantage?

She must assist him to unleash his full power. What she needed was ... the knife.

She scanned the room with desperate eyes.

"The desk, Helena—bottom drawer!"

Nicholas' shouted words galvanized her into action.

She raced toward the desk, her hand wrenching open the drawer. There, nestled in a velvet-lined box, was not a knife, but a pistol. The weapon was shiny and black. Menacing. With trembling hands, she grasped it, the metal icy in her palms. She gripped the pistol more firmly and raised her arms. Inhaling deeply, she took aim.

"That will not be necessary, Lady Harteford."

The voice from the doorway stilled her finger, which twitched against the trigger.

"Step away from the suspect, if you please Lord Harteford."

Mr. Kent crossed the room, his pistol pointed at Gordon, who stood panting and cornered. The policeman whistled, and two of his men appeared. One withdrew a blade; in a swift motion, the ropes slithered loose from Nicholas' arms. Dropping the pistol, Helena stumbled toward her husband, his arms crushing her in a fierce embrace.

"My men have captured your vessel and rounded up your men, Gordon," Mr. Kent said as his other man placed Gordon in chains. "Your evil doings are at an end."

Gordon smiled even as the lock clicked and his fate was secured. "Oh, but evil does not end with me," he said. Though his youthful face was relaxed into good-natured lines, his blue eyes glowed with a sinister light. They narrowed upon Nicholas. "I'd watch my back if I was you, my lord. You never know when the past might come knocking at your door."

From the safety of her husband's arms, Helena shivered.

But Nicholas said quietly, "Let it come. I no longer have anything to fear."

The villain was marched away to meet his fate. A hangman's noose, no doubt. Helena could not bring herself to feel pity.

"It has been quite a night for the two of you," Mr. Kent said. "I am sorry I did not arrive sooner."

"I am glad you knew to come at all," Nicholas said.

"Gordon's whore gave it away. We were keeping an eye on her, on account of your hunch that Gordon might still be alive. She had her bags packed and ready for a long trip. We tailed her back to the docks, where she boarded a ship we could find no record of. Apparently Gordon had an official in his pocket; he floated his boat in and out of the docks as he pleased, carrying out stolen goods and returning for more."

"How is Will?" Helena asked, a quiver in her voice.

"Your groom is a bit worse for the wear, but he will survive. Dr. Farraday is attending to him as we speak."

Helena sagged with relief against her husband.

"I am sure my lady is exhausted," Mr. Kent said. "We can continue our explanations at a later time. Shall I have my men escort you home?"

"There are some things I wish to discuss first with my wife. Will you ensure our privacy and safety?"

"Of course." Mr. Kent paused, spotting something on the floor. He bent to retrieve it. As he examined the book, a smile rippled across his thin features. "Yours, my lady?"

"A loan from a friend," Helena replied. With a shudder, she saw the brown stain marring the edge of the pages. "Though I don't suppose I will be returning it now."

To her surprise, Mr. Kent bowed and kissed her hand. "You have married a most remarkable woman, Lord Harteford."

As he left, the investigator could be heard chuckling to himself, "A vindication, indeed!"

Then the door closed behind him, and it was just the two of them.

Helena looked at Nicholas. He was turning a chair back on its legs, his expression grim. Her heart throbbed to see the injuries he had sustained: his eye had swelled even larger, the size of an egg now, and patches of dried blood had crusted along his jaw and throat. He looked paler than usual, the spreading bruises a dark contrast against his skin.

"Dr. Farraday should examine your injuries," she said as she approached him. He continued to straighten the furniture. "Do not concern yourself with this now, my love. We must have you attended to first."

She placed a staying hand on his arm. To her surprise, he flinched at her touch and pulled away. He walked to the fireplace and stood there, his back to her.

"Is ... is your arm hurt?" she stammered.

"My arm is fine."

Taken aback by the venom darkening his words, she asked in an uncertain voice, "What is the matter then?"

"The matter? You have to ask me what the *matter* is?"

He turned to look at her. Glare, more the like. Restrained emotion glittered in his obsidian eyes.

"Nicholas, you are overwrought." She tried for a placating tone, though her head was beginning to spin. "The after-effects of this night's violence, no doubt. Why don't you sit, my love, and I will see about making us some tea. Do you have a kettle perchance, or—"

"I do not want any bloody tea." Nicholas came toward her, and she took an instinctive step backward at the aggression of his advance. He stopped close enough so that she could feel the power of him towering over her, a full six feet of furious, bridling male. He did not touch her. "What I want to know is what the hell you were thinking coming to the docks in the middle of the bloody night!"

"Really, Nicholas, there is no need to shout—"

"I will shout if I damned well please! When my wife decides to risk her neck, coming alone—"

"But I was not alone," Helena said hastily. "Will accompanied me."

"If the man was not injured at the moment, I would be beating him to a pulp." Nicholas ran his hands through his hair, further disarraying the wild ebony tufts. "He will still have to answer to me when all this is done."

"Well, in the end, it was a good thing I came, was it not? After all, had I not arrived when I did ..." Helena stopped, seeing the stark rage on her husband's face. "After all," she continued with more caution, "I was able to be of some assistance."

Her husband had his hands fisted on his hips.

"Not that you needed any help, of course," she added.

He said nothing, his lips tightening.

"Obviously, you had everything well in hand when I arrived. I could see you had everything perfectly well under control. I am sure you had a plan all along to defeat that nefarious man—"

"Goddamnit, Helena, I had no such plan!" His bellow echoed through the chamber and shook the walls. "Do you know the danger you put yourself in, you reckless fool? By God, seeing you run headlong into peril, seeing his hands wrapped around your neck, I almost—" He choked off, his chest heaving.

In the next moment, she reached him and threw her arms around his waist. His strong, lean frame was quivering from head to toe. Her voice emerged muffled against his chest. "I'm sorry I frightened you."

His arms wrapped with violent force around her. "Don't ever do it again." Burying his face in her hair, he rasped, "Tonight I discovered that the past no longer has power over me. It cannot hurt me. You showed me that. But if I lost you—I do not know what I would do," he said between serrated breaths. "You are everything to me, Helena. My heart and my soul."

"I love you, too," she sniffled.

They stayed that way for a long while, holding each other.

Then Nicholas's embrace eased. He tipped up her chin, and the hungry adoration she saw in his dark eyes made her pulse leap with excitement. A squeak startled from her lips when he quite literally swept her off her feet.

She retained sufficient wit to whisper, "What about Mr. Kent's men? They're just outside the door."

"Now she worries about propriety." He grinned at her blushing face. "Come, my prudish one, there's something I want to show you."

Nicholas carried her toward what appeared to be a door to a wardrobe. She cocked her head. Then he pushed open the door. To her amazement, Helena found herself looking into an anteroom, fashioned as an exercise salon of sorts. In the center of the chamber was a rectangular area demarcated by poles at the four corners and cordoned off by two lines of thick rope. The floor was lined with mats. A sparring ring. Percy had mentioned that Nicholas enjoyed the sport.

Her husband clearly had another sport in mind when he set her inside the ring and closed the door behind. Then he fell upon her like a man starved, unbuttoning, unfastening, his mouth consuming hers in a greedy kiss. As the layers fell away, she experienced a freedom she had never before known, had never known to be possible. For the rest of her life, she would not forget this moment when their love burned so brightly, so fiercely that it chased away all the shadows—of his past, of her insecurities.

Her chemise followed the rest, and soon she stood naked in front of her husband. She felt nothing but sheer feminine pride. She held her shoulders higher, giving her full breasts a generous wiggle, loving the way Nicholas' nostrils flared in response. Then she tugged at his shirt, eager to have nothing left between them, not even a scrap of clothing. She heard his wicked chuckle as he caught her in his arms. Her legs slid around his hips as he maneuvered her backward. After a few steps, she felt the bite of rope against her bare back. Sandwiched between her husband's iron strength and the rough cord, she trembled with arousal.

"Tell me, my lady," Nicholas murmured, his tongue doing magical things to her ear, "are you also my harlot?"

Helena sighed as he discovered a particularly sublime spot. "Mmm, yes."

"Then I want you to tell me what a harlot likes," her husband continued in the dark, seductive voice that she loved. "I want to hear those lovely, naughty lips of yours ask for what you desire."

He released her and took a step back. He stood shirtless before her, unabashed in his bold virility. Although he still wore his pantaloons, she could see the bulging wedge of his erection. His gaze roved over her nakedness, and the possessiveness of the look brought a tingle to her belly. Aroused, but shy, she mumbled, "I like it when you touch me. Here." Her hand fluttered near her breast.

Nicholas shook his head sternly. "Any self-respecting doxy knows that she must use specific and proper language in her requests. I seem to recall teaching you the correct words during our lessons. Apt student that you are, you cannot have forgotten so quickly. Again, where do you want me to touch you, Helena?"

"My tits," she whispered, excitement flaring at her own boldness. "Please touch my tits."

"Like this?" Nicholas cupped her full breasts firmly. As he played with her, his eyes remained on her face. He gently squeezed her nipple, and her lips parted on a whimper of delight. "I asked you a question, Helena. Is this what you want?"

"Your mouth," Helena gasped, leaning back against the ropes as he obliged her. "Oh sweet heavens, Nicholas, your mouth ..."

He took a nipple into his mouth, his tongue dancing playful patterns over the engorged bud. "How does it feel, sweet?"

"It feels so *good*," she panted. "Your tongue, oh Nicholas, it makes me feel so ... so ..."

"Yes? How does it make you feel?" Nicholas murmured against her other nipple.

"Tingly and hot ... between my legs," Helena confessed with a breathy sigh as he rewarded her with more licks, more nips against her swollen tits.

Giving her a playful swat on the buttocks, he stepped away. "Show me."

Helena blinked. "How do you mean?"

Nicholas' voice was rough velvet and dark as midnight. "Touch yourself, Helena. I want you to show me exactly where it aches, where you burn for me."

Helena's knees wobbled slightly at his request. Could she be as bold as he asked?

"Come now, you did say you were a harlot," Nicholas chided, his eyes gleaming with wicked laughter. "Or perhaps you are not quite as wanton as you would have me believe?"

The playful challenge emboldened her. Slowly, Helena ran her hands down the sides of her waist and over the curves of her hips. The subtle quiver of Nicholas' broad shoulders and rippled chest fanned her excitement. It appeared her husband enjoyed watching her explore herself. She moved her hands inward toward the curly thatch of hair. She ran a finger along the moist crevice.

At Nicholas' sharp inhale, her lips curved into a siren's smile.

"It aches here, my lord," she murmured, parting her curls to expose the delicate pink flesh to his rapacious gaze. Dew lubricated her fingers as she lightly stroked the swollen folds. She teased the opening of her pussy, before sliding her fingers up to the hard nub which magnified her pleasure. With a soft moan, she rubbed the knot of sensation. Sparks skipped along her legs. Her eyes joined his.

"Yes, that's it," Nicholas encouraged in a hoarse voice. "Rub your sweet pearl for me."

Helena sighed, leaning back against the ropes so she could spread her legs further apart. Her hair fell from its remaining pins, becoming fully undone. Silken strands spilled over her shoulders and tangled with the ropes.

"Tell me what you are thinking, love, when you are playing with your delectable pussy."

Helena's pussy grew wetter at his command.

"I am thinking of how good it feels when you do this," she admitted obediently. "When you touch my pussy."

"What else, love?" Passion made his voice deep and gravelly. "What else makes your cunny so wet and glistening for me?"

Helena's eyes closed as her breath puffed faster. The sparks were blending now into one blazing line of fire that traveled from limb to limb. The touching felt good, but she needed more. "I am thinking of when you kiss me here. When you ... use your tongue, taste my cunny ..."

His strong hands clamped on her thighs as he knelt before her. Relief mixed with lust as she watched his dark head nudge between her legs. He kept his gaze trained upward, drinking in her every reaction as he began to eat her. Slowly. Voraciously.

"Oh, yes, oh *please* ..." Wild with need, Helena felt herself sinking toward the floor.

"Hold onto the ropes, sweet," Nicholas ordered thickly. "I want to feast while you stand spread and open for me."

Wordlessly, Helena gripped the rope. The prickly texture of the hemp abraded her palms as Nicholas pleasured her. His tongue invaded her folds and slicked over her pearl repeatedly as his fingers pumped her with firm, upward thrusts. She could not get enough of the friction and ground herself against him. He groaned out endearments, hot words of lust and love that released her from earthly moorings. She flew free in an explosive, mind-blanking climax.

When she opened her eyes, she was lying on the mats. Nicholas lay on his side next to her. He grinned, pressing a soft kiss on her nose.

"You are lovely, wife," he said.

Helena sighed, soaked to the bones in bliss. She trailed her fingers idly along the hard contours of his chest. She smiled when the flat nipples hardened under her touch. Nicholas caught her hand and brought it to his lips for a kiss.

"Your turn," she said, wriggling provocatively against him.

He rolled on top of her, his weight bearing her down deliciously into the mats. His turgid sex brushed her damp curls, and a fresh wave of lust washed over her. "Are you sure you are ready so soon, my love?"

In answer, she wrapped her legs around his hips and impelled herself against his cock. She heard Nicholas' strangled groan as the tip of his rod stretched her as his fingers had, only more so. Thicker. Harder. Making her want more. She wiggled further, frustrated when the weight of his hips prevented her from deepening the penetration.

"Nicholas, please," she panted, nipping his neck. "I need more of you."

With a husky laugh, he rolled onto his back, bringing her on top of him. His sex throbbed heavily against the curve of her buttocks.

"It seems, impudent miss, that you wish to avail yourself of my rod." His obsidian eyes flashed, and his smile belonged on a pirate. "Have a go, then."

Helena tilted her head as she tried to construe his meaning. "How should I ... you mean I get to ...?"

"For as long as I can take it, my love."

As understanding dawned, Helena experienced a most unladylike excitement. Her husband uttered an oath as she grasped him in her hand and placed him exactly where she wanted him to be. Unused to this position, she squirmed in her efforts to take him inside. The wiggling served to heighten her desire, and she hummed with pleasure when his cock slipped against her pearl. Their contact slickened; she could hear the wet sounds of luscious rubbing.

"I can't take much more of this." Nicholas' eyes were heavy-lidded, and his jaw was tight. "Sweet, let me—oh, God, *yes* ..."

His hiss of pleasure melded with hers as she sank onto his pulsing shaft. Her eyes closed as she filled herself with his masculine power. With her hands splayed on his chest, she slid sensually upon him, slowly, a queen dictating her passion. Her subject did not seem to mind. He took in her delight with desire-slit eyes, issuing earthy words of encouragement all the while.

"How hot you are." He shaped a breast in his palm, pinched the nipple gently between his fingers. "Do you like riding astride, my wanton one?"

"I love it," she breathed as she bounced upon his prick. "You are so huge. You fill me completely ..."

He liked that, she saw. His nostrils quivered. With a twitch of his hips, he thrust upward at the same time she bore down. The intensity of the penetration elicited a helpless cry from her. He repeated the motion, groaning as he did so. He was so deep inside her, brushing up against her womb, her soul. She began to shake. Tremors of pleasure emanated from her core and rippled down her legs. She plunged upon him, harder and harder, desperate for the relief only he could provide.

His hands cupped her hips. At first, she thought he meant to dismount her, and she clamped her knees firmly at his hips. He could not mean her to stop. She was so close ...

He chuckled darkly. "No need to panic, sweet. Lean forward a little. Yes, like that."

When she moved again, lightning pierced her insides. She moaned her approval of the subtle adjustment, shimmying herself along this delicious new angle. Each stroke rubbed her pearl and sparked bursts of pleasure. She moved with increasing speed until the little bursts began to blur together. Then, suddenly, it swept over her: a single white wave of blinding joy. At the same instant, Nicholas shouted out, and she had the perfect ecstasy of his fulfillment within her own.

When it was all over, Nicholas settled her to his side and collapsed heavily onto the mats. His breathing was still ragged. "You have unmanned me."

Thoroughly sated and pleased with herself, Helena asked, "Do you regret having a wife who has uses for your manhood, my lord?"

"Never. I shall endeavor to keep it up." With a sigh of pure contentment, Nicholas pulled her into his arms. "You are the wife of my dreams, sweetheart, in and out of bed."

"We are not in a bed," his wife reminded him coyly.

"God help me," he said, so fervently that she giggled.

Epilogue

"I have a present for you," Helena said, her voice barely audible above the clattering of the carriage wheels.

Nicholas looked down at the elegantly coiffed head snuggled against his shoulder. He had thought his wife asleep by the way her body swayed with the movement of the carriage. They were returning from their first social outing since the birth of the twins two months ago. The childbirth had not been an easy one—his forehead prickled with sweat at the recollection—and he had insisted that she take a full recuperation at the country estate. Last week, however, Helena had declared herself fit for traveling. Unable to deny her anything, he had made the necessary preparations, and they descended upon their London townhouse with wet nurses and nannies in tow, just in time to catch the start of the Season.

He had taken her to the Opera tonight, and he smiled, recalling her exuberance. She had looked every inch the proper young marchioness in her sapphire gown, pearls glowing at her neck and ears. The jewels had been outshone by the joy on her face as she listened to the music with unfashionable absorption.

"How can you possibly give me more than you already have,

my love?" he murmured against her sweet-smelling curls. "Scant sleep, endless feedings, slobbering on every surface ... and that is only one of the scamps. What man could want for more?"

His wife giggled. "I do hope Thomas and Jeremiah behaved for Nurse this evening. We have not been apart from them for so many hours before."

"I have no doubt we will be greeted with remonstrations when we arrive home." Nicholas' lips curved at the thought of chubby fists grasping determinedly at his lapels and hair.

How his life had changed.

The day after the arrest of James Gordon, he had approached Kent with Helena at his side. She had insisted upon accompanying him, upon being present as he lay open his past. Truthfully, he might not have been able to do so without her hand in his, her courage sustaining him as surely as her love. Kent had listened to the tale with the impassive expression of an officer. He had said nothing as Nicholas spoke of stabbing Grimes, of the nameless boy who'd witnessed it all and disappeared since.

At the end of it, Kent had looked thoughtfully at him. The policeman's clear eyes seemed to probe the depths of his soul, yet this time Nicholas had not felt afraid. He might always bear the scars of his past, but the demons had been vanquished. They could hurt him no more.

"It seems to me, my lord, that justice has been carried out by an authority far greater than my own," Kent had said. "Flames can kill a man as well as a blade; who are we to know what truly happened that night?" Relief had flooded Nicholas as the investigator continued, "As to the boy, I will make inquiries. I cannot promise to find him, however, for so many years have passed, and we have less than a name to go on."

"Thank you, Mr. Kent."

This had been Helena speaking, for Nicholas had not been able to find the words. He could only shake the policeman's hand with a grip firmer than usual; Mr. Kent had responded with a slight inclination of his head. And that had been that.

Aye, Nicholas had not thought it possible to have all that was now his. Freedom from his earlier life. A home filled with children and laughter. A wife who, even now, was watching him with loving eyes.

He ran his knuckles along her cheek.

"Did you enjoy yourself tonight, love?" he asked.

"Yes, it was nice to have a change of scenery. And to escape our country house guests," Helena added with a rueful smile. "You have borne my parents' presence with remarkable grace, Nicholas."

"Who would have thought Northgate a doting grandfather?" Nicholas mused.

Helena sat up, her eyes large and luminous in the dim carriage. "You have been all that is generous with Papa, and he is finally recognizing it. But, really, dearest, we have more pressing matters to attend to. I am most looking forward to giving you your present. It is our anniversary, you know."

"Sweet, you are mistaken. We were wedded a year ago last month." Nicholas wagged his brows. "Do not tell me you have forgotten our festivities already. If so, I am losing my touch."

"That is not the anniversary to which I am referring."

"What other is there?" Nicholas asked, bemused.

In answer, his wife began unbuttoning his greatcoat. Instantly, desire leapt to life, and just as instantly, concern kept it at bay.

"Darling," he said, capturing her hands in his own. "Are you sure this is a good idea? The doctor did say ..."

"Nicholas," his wife responded in exasperation, "do stop fretting. I am fine, I assure you." She tugged her hands free from his one by one, and the familiar glint in her eyes sent his pulse galloping. "However, I cannot guarantee I will remain fine if I am deprived of my wifely rights much longer."

"Your wifely rights?" Nicholas could not help but chuckle. The chuckle became a strangled groan as his dexterous spouse pushed aside his thick woolen outer garment and started working on the buttons of his waistcoat.

He closed his eyes, feeling his cock swell. "Are you complaining about my recent lovemaking then?"

With alarming ease, she sank onto the floor of the carriage. She tossed aside her wrapper, baring the pale, rounded tops of her breasts to his greedy gaze. Settling onto her knees, she set to work on his trouser buttons.

"Of course I am not complaining. You are always most gentle and adept, my lord."

He clenched his teeth, feeling himself grow harder and longer from the pressure of her industrious fingers. His floundering self-control received a serious blow from her next words.

"You know how I love it when you eat my pussy. The feel of your tongue when it slips inside me—I come for you every time, Nicholas."

Nicholas growled in desperation. "When we arrive home, I shall pleasure you all night, all morning, if it comes to that."

But Helena shook her head, her eyes sultry as she tugged open another button. He grunted when her fingers brushed the bulbous head of his sex. The traitorous organ nudged back with interest.

"Tonight, I want more than your mouth, my darling," she whispered. She popped another button free. Her breath caressed the length of his rigid pole. "I need to have this beautiful, colossal cock deep inside me."

Nicholas' head fell back on the cushion as his last vestige of self-discipline flew to the winds. He had never *felt* more colossal. "Helena, I do not want to hurt you. It is too soon ..."

"I want ... you ... *now*." Helena punctuated each word by releasing another button, and then another, until finally he fell huge and hard and throbbing into her soft hands. He watched, mesmerized by the sight of his wife kneeling between his legs, studying his exposed rod with a distinctly lustful gleam in her eyes. Bending forward, she licked the stretched dome, swirling fire over his senses. Desire seeped instantly from the tip, and she tasted it, giving an approving hum before planting kisses along the thick shaft. Light, teasing kisses that made him burn for more.

"Minx." He slid his hands into her perfect coiffure, dislodging feathers and sending pearls clattering onto the floor of the carriage. He pulled her head firmly toward his turgid prick. "If you wish to suck my cock, then do it properly as I have taught you."

"Yes, sir," his wife said, her tone meek, her eyes laughing. "Your wish is my command."

Nicholas growled in pleasure as she obeyed his direction, taking him deep into the blazing recesses of her mouth. Her head bobbed up and down, fallen strands of hair brushing against his thighs as she tasted him. Savored him. Licked him from swollen tip to throbbing sac, before sucking him deeply inside again. The carriage jolted suddenly, bumping the sensitive crown upward against her throat.

He let out a feverish groan. "Yes, like that. Take me all the way into that sweet mouth of yours ..."

"Mmm mmm," his wife responded, her mouth clamped like wet fire around him. She softened the suction of her mouth, and he slid deeper inside again, nudging against the silken barrier. She squeaked in excitement, the sound muffled by the massive truncheon she was swallowing with unbearable enthusiasm.

His hands tightened in her hair. "Helena, my love, my God ... oh *fuck*," he gasped.

He felt himself spurt a little, the pleasure raging over him too early, too fast. Tonight he did not want to spend himself in this fashion, not when a surfeit of delights awaited him. Panting harshly, he pulled her head away. She released him with a moist popping sound. Her lips glistened with the essence she drew so easily from him.

"You are delicious," his wife pouted. "I want more."

Nicholas was so consumed by lust he could barely speak. Instead, he hoisted her upward and turned her around, bending her over so that her upper arms rested on the squabs of the opposite seat. With a rough hand, he threw up her satin skirts and petticoats.

"Christ," he uttered, amazed by the soft, lush, and, most remarkable of all, *naked* curves exposed to him. He palmed her ass. Her flesh quivered, filling him with infinite satisfaction. "Have you been like this all evening?"

"Without my unmentionables, you mean?" Turning her head on the cushions, Helena sent him a flirtatious smile. "Of course, my lord. I did not want any impediments to our romantic explorations. And I was just so that night at ..."

"The Nunnery," Nicholas finished hoarsely. It was unbearably erotic, the image of his proper marchioness conversing politely with visitors to their Opera Box while underneath her demure exterior ... damn, underneath ... He reverently caressed the swell of her bottom before fingering her lower. Hot, drenched with longing for him, she was all a man could ever want. All *he* would ever need. "The anniversary you spoke of. How could I have forgotten our first night of passion?"

"Yes, my lord," his wife purred, as she worked herself against his hand. "The night you mistook me for a harlot."

"Not just any harlot. *My* harlot." Bending on one knee, Nicholas grasped her thighs firmly in his hands and drove his tongue into the hot core of her. Helena's cries swelled his chest with the pleasure that had somehow grown stronger, even more intense, with time. He could not get enough of her. Their love had washed away shame and insecurity so nothing separated them now—it was as if their two hearts, two bodies, lived as one. He licked higher, tracing the crevice of her ass until he reached her perfectly puckered hole. He paused before circling it slowly, deliberately, with his tongue.

"Nicholas, what are you ...?" Helena began, but her words lost their shape, became a high keening cry, as he continued to tenderly explore her ass. He spread her luxuriant cheeks further apart and loved her, her cunny, her bottom, until every inch of her quaked and glistened with longing. Dipping his fingers into the thicket of curls, he spread her honey upward, slicking her with her own desire.

"Nicholas, *please*," Helena begged, her hands clenching the seat cushions.

He could not deny her, or himself, any longer. Standing, he positioned himself at the entrance of her pussy. The carriage bumped, nudging his cock against her swollen flesh. Helena gave a helpless moan. Balancing himself with the wall strap, Nicholas drove his hips forward, and his nostrils flared at the sight of his sex sliding into her. He moved gently at first, afraid to hurt her. It had been months since he entered her thus, and she felt so snug, so damned hot and tight. Her channel gripped him like a wet, velvet fist. He gritted his teeth, forcing himself to go slow. Inch by inch, he eased himself in and out of her luscious slit.

"Darling," his wife said, with an impish glance backward, "if you wish to fuck me, then do it properly, will you?"

With a strangled laugh, he obeyed her. When he saw that she writhed in pure pleasure, without any sign of pain or discomfort, he began to pump her more vigorously. He found a pace to match the jostle of the carriage, his balls slapping rhythmically against his wife's soaking cunt. He took her fiercely, utterly absorbed in the possession of her. In this moment, there was nothing but Helena: the softness of her hips in his hands, the plush pull of her pussy bringing him home. He drove into her, giving her what she needed, even as he took and took of her. Her cries soaked into the squabs, muffled words, sounds eclipsed by feeling. By just being. But he understood anyway, for the same sentiments ballooned in his chest, summoning his ecstasy.

"I love you, Helena. Every part of you."

Reaching under, he rolled her knot between his fingers, loving the way it made her gasp and plead for more. He played with her until he felt her begin to tighten around him. As he pumped steadily inside her, driving her higher and higher, his dew-slickened finger found her ass. He breached her virgin hole with his fingertip. Instantly, Helena stiffened.

"*Nicholas ...*"

He pushed his finger in deeper. Her unused muscles clamped around his digit, at the same time that her pussy began to convulse around his cock. He flexed his hips powerfully, plunging so deep that his sex brushed her womb. His wife screamed as a shattering climax racked her body.

"You are mine," he groaned as wild pleasure swept through him. "Mine, as I am yours. Take me, my love ..."

He exploded in an endless release that fused his very being with hers. With his last ounce of energy, he managed to scoop her up and sprawl her atop him onto the seat. For several moments, the only sounds were their panted breaths and the clip-clop of the horses.

"Why is the carriage still moving?" Nicholas mumbled with sudden awareness. He was too sated to truly care, but they should have arrived at home more than a quarter hour ago.

"I told the driver to take the scenic route home," his wife answered, nuzzling her cheek contentedly against his chest. "So I might surprise you with my anniversary gift. But it seems, my lord, it is you who showed me something new this evening."

Nicholas grinned roguishly as he drew his greatcoat more snugly around her shoulders. "There is plenty more where that came from, my dear. I should not want you to bore of my husbandly affections."

Helena snorted. "That hardly seems possible." A few heart-beats later, she tilted her head and smiled drowsily up at him. "Happy anniversary, my darling. I hope you enjoyed your gift."

"You are all that I have ever wanted." Nicholas' eyes were free of ghosts as he looked at his beloved. "Harlot of my fantasies and wife of my dreams."

From Grace's Desk

Dear Reader,

Thank you for reading *Her Husband's Harlot*! I hope you enjoyed Nicholas and Helena's passionate married lovers romance. This debut novel holds a special place in my heart; when I wrote it, I had no idea about the journey that it would take me on. I just wanted to write the story in my heart and the characters in my head...and I feel blessed to still be doing that :-) It wouldn't be possible without my amazing reader family. Your support, reviews, and word of mouth mean so very much. Thank you, thank you!

If you loved Nicholas and Helena, you will see more of them in the Mayfair in Mayhem series. I also recently wrote a book starring their son Thomas as the hero (*Fiona and the Enigmatic Earl)*... how time flies! But I am getting ahead of myself. Next up in this series is *Her Wanton Wager*, in which Plucky Persephone Fines meets her match in the devilish gaming hell owner Gavin Hunt!

A game of seduction. An epic battle of wits. In this steamy enemies to lovers romance, the winner takes all...

"Naughty and romantic, this is not your cookie cutter romance." - Goodreads

To what lengths will a feisty miss go to save her family from ruin? Miss Persephone Fines takes on a wager of seduction with notorious gaming hell owner Gavin Hunt and discovers that love is the most dangerous gamble of all.

Until the next time…hugs and happy reading,

Grace Callaway

Acknowledgments

This book was made possible by a community of amazing people. With appreciation and love, I dedicate this book to them.

To my critique partners, Virna De Paul and Tina Folsom. Virna, your talent and generosity inspire me so much. Thank you for your support and those walks on the beach. Tina, I don't know what twist of fate led us to finding each other on that list-serv, but I thank the universe that it did! We've come a long way since our first manuscripts, haven't we? You are a true friend, a fabulous travel companion, and a writer whose talent, courage, and zeal motivate me to get to my keyboard every day.

To my mentor, Diane Pershing. Without your keen reading and insightful feedback, my work would be at most a gem in the rough. Thank you for your generosity and for being one of the first to tell me I could write.

To the community of bright, warm, and gifted romance writers I have had the privilege to meet over the past few years. Members of my local San Francisco Bay Area Chapter of RWA—you rock! And fall just isn't the same without a visit to the Low Country RWA Beach Retreat and all you lovely ladies there.

To my family. Mom and Dad, you have always taught me to reach for my dreams—and look, I have! Thank you for a lifetime of love and support; you're my inspiration. Candace, you are the sister I would have chosen for myself. Thanks, sib, for sharing the laughter and the tears along this journey. And to Stu and Renko, the parents I was lucky enough to gain: thank you for being the loving, open, creative, wonderful people that you are!

Finally, to the two men in my life. Brendan, you may be small, but I don't know anyone who has your courage and resilience. Your smiles light my way. Love you, buddy, beyond words. And to my husband, Brian. I'll always be grateful that life led me to you, my true partner and soul mate. You are every hero I've ever written. I love you.

About the Author

USA Today & International Bestselling Author Grace Callaway writes hot and heart-melting historical romance filled with mystery and adventure. Her debut novel was a Romance Writers of America® Golden Heart® Finalist and a #1 National Regency Bestseller, and her subsequent novels have topped national and international bestselling lists. She is the winner of the Daphne du Maurier Award for Excellence in Mystery and Suspense, the Maggie Award for Excellence in Historical Romance, the Golden Leaf, and the Passionate Plume Award. She holds a doctorate in clinical psychology from the University of Michigan and lives with her family in a valley close to the ocean. When she's not writing, she enjoys dancing, dining in hole-in-the-wall restaurants, and going on adapted adventures with her special son.

Keep up with Grace's latest news!

Newsletter: gracecallaway.com/newsletter

facebook.com/GraceCallawayBooks
bookbub.com/authors/grace-callaway
instagram.com/gracecallawaybooks
amazon.com/author/gracecallaway

Made in the USA
Las Vegas, NV
28 March 2024